# Dove With Yellow Socks

by:

Naomi Fenstra

MAPLE
PUBLISHERS

Dove With Yellow Socks

Author: Naomi Fenstra

Copyright © 2024 Naomi Fenstra

The right of Naomi Fenstra to be identified as author of this work has been asserted by the author in accordance with section 77 and 78 of the Copyright, Designs and Patents Act 1988.

First Published in 2024

ISBN 978-1-83538-073-4 (Paperback)

Front Cover by Naomi Fenstra

Book Cover Design and Book Layout by:
White Magic Studios
www.whitemagicstudios.co.uk

Published by:
Maple Publishers
Fairbourne Drive, Atterbury,
Milton Keynes,
MK10 9RG, UK
www.maplepublishers.com

A CIP catalogue record for this title is available from the British Library.

*"The Moving Finger writes; and, having writ,*
*Moves on: but what is writ cannot be changed ,*
*or imagined to be gone."*

*—after Omar Khayyám*

*"Yet the deepest truths are best read between the*
*lines, and, for the most part, refuse to be written."*

*—Amos Bronson Alcott*

*"Everything, however finely spun, finally comes*
*to the sun"*
*"Nederlandsee spreekwoorden"*

*—Peter Breughel the Elder*
*1559 – no 74*

*"Ignoring the Elephant in the*
*Room doesn't make it disappear."*

# RECIPE

**INGREDIENTS**

- One Dove- Dressed
- Pair Yellow Socks
- 1.5 Tablespoons AC
- 2.5 Tablespoons LD
- 1.5 Tablespoons PJ
- 10 Tablespoons PE

**PREPARATION**

- Set Tablespoon contents to one side separately
- Mix as required at frequent short intervals
- Leave to stand between intervals
- Examine and taste mixture frequently
- Add/remove mixture until satisfied with size and texture

**PREPARATION TIME**

- Approximately 4 Years

# CONTENTS

# 1

# Tuesday, May 10th, 2016

Hanging by thin steel wires from the ceiling, the lobby of the Median Hotel at Gatwick Airport featured a large model replica of "Jason," the biplane in which Amy Johnson made the first solo flight by a woman from England to Australia. If you were exceptionally tall, passing underneath "Jason" on your way across the lobby to the revolving exit door required a little awareness, careful negotiation, and attention to the notice that advised you to "Mind Your Head" in several assorted languages.

Statisticians tell us that Dutch males are the tallest in the world. If that were the case, then Piet Kuppers wasn't among them. In his late fifties, he was of medium height, and of a somewhat overweight, "chunky" build, he had nonetheless retained some of the clean-cut, handsome features of his earlier years.

This facial appearance was marked, but not marred, by a narrow, slightly raised, pinkish scar, running vertically straight upwards, or downwards, whichever way you looked at it, from his right eyebrow up to his hairline -if he still had any hair, that is. He had the habit of running the inner tip of the second finger of his right hand up and down the scar tissue- the original injury resulting from a boyhood accident.

Casually, but smartly dressed, with a beige short-sleeved shirt under a lightweight, tan jacket, cream-coloured trousers, and brown suede shoes, Kuppers tucked his reading glasses into an inside jacket pocket and walked briskly and purposefully across the lobby, through the revolving doors, and out into the air. Jason remained undisturbed.

It was one of those occasional early May days in England that was almost perfect. The clear morning blue sky presaged the sunny day to come. At that time of day, just after 8 am, the air was still, cool, and sharp, with none of the cloying humidity of the heat of the later English summer months.

Kuppers had just arrived on a very early flight from Amsterdam, made himself known to Reception, left his only piece of luggage, a bulky briefcase, in an anteroom, and had decided to take the air before breakfast.

He stopped after a few paces and breathed the coolness deeply into his lungs, and then walked briskly on, away from the hotel. As he did on almost every working day, he considered the tasks that had to be done on the day to come. He only had that one day and was returning to Amsterdam later that evening after his meetings, and detailed review of the hotel facilities, with Leila Zafiri, the Hotel Conference and Events Manager, and more briefly with Matthew Collison, the Hotel Manager.

It was the twentieth anniversary of the founding of the Duifs- the English translation of the Dutch word being "Doves"- who were the members of the Doventenar Motorcycle Club- hence the name. Doventenar was somewhere between a large village and a small town, located about ten miles northeast of Amsterdam, it had easy access to the windmills of Zaanse Schans and the peace of Monnikedam. It was a popular choice for affluent retirees from Amsterdam to which classification most of the Doves belonged.

To mark the anniversary occasion, a three-day meeting had been decided upon some time ago. Dirk Van Heemskerk, the President of the Doves, had proposed holding the meeting in England, and Gatwick had been selected as convenient for travelling, and close enough to the locations of the special events that had been lined up. Van had worked in England for a few years and knew Gatwick—and The Median in particular.

The meeting itself was to begin on the morning of Wednesday, 18th May. Of the ten attendees, most were flying from Amsterdam and arriving on Tuesday afternoon, but a couple were travelling together by motorcycle from Holland, and also scheduled to arrive later on Tuesday.

Willem Vonk was in Switzerland on business and was planning to catch a late flight into Gatwick on Monday evening to attend another business appointment on Tuesday.

"Van," Dirk Van Heemskerk- everyone called him "Van"- wasn't arriving until Wednesday morning, as he had business commitments the previous day. Kuppers himself was scheduled to check in to the Median on Monday, to give himself adequate pre-event preparation and set-up time.

Kuppers was one of the newer Doves, but Van Heemskerk had still put him in charge of the Meeting planning and arrangements. Good job, he thought, Van must know that the others, as the English might say, "couldn't organize a piss up in a brewery," and, besides which, he had worked with Van on overseas assignments in the past, so Van knew he was efficient.

He went over the schedule in his mind. Tuesday, arrivals, then informal dinners, the members making their arrangements depending on arrival times, and the times they wished to eat. Wednesday morning a relaxed 11.30 am start for the meeting, followed by presentations. Van was the morning speaker, his subject matter was entitled "The Doves- 1996 to 2016". A buffet lunch, and in the afternoon, technical presentations, and discussions, and finally a formal dinner in the hotel restaurant for all. Thursday morning a visit to Heskey Motorcycles in Cobham, then in the afternoon to Brooklands, and finally back for another formal dinner. Friday morning was to be spent at the London Motorcycle Museum at Greenford. A free afternoon, then an evening meal followed by an after-dinner speech by Jeff King, the legendary six-time winner of various Isle of Man TT races, and subsequently a successful businessman. He made a mental note not to forget to double-check all the coach timings when he met Leila.

Saturday morning after breakfast was return home time.

Having satisfied himself that he had everything properly planned, his thoughts turned elsewhere.

He cast his mind back. How long was it since he had been in England? It must be twenty-five years or more. As a youngish aircraft engineer, it was potentially a very good assignment. It was intended to last for three years, working on the Industrial Estate at Maxton House in Crawley for Fokland Aircraft Company, who were providing additional aircraft to Eurair, the rapidly growing, UK-based, travel business.

It all went wrong when Eurair went spectacularly bust overnight in early 1991 and he had to return to Amsterdam. Then there was that unfortunate business with the older woman, of course. 'I had everything she would need- sex, money, travel, a large house at home base in Holland, servants-and there was the ring. I never did get it back' he thought. 'If she's still living at the same address I should call and collect it. What did she have instead? A sexless marriage to a dull, boring husband.' Kuppers mouthed a silent expletive.

Still, his current arrangements were far from perfect. 'Lucky I never married', he thought.

His present relationship, with a lady called Angelique Durand, although now two years old, had soured after a while, and had anyway started primarily as one of convenience. The sexual attraction had diminished, then disappeared altogether some time ago. Angelique was well educated, intelligent, and strikingly attractive, certainly to other men. Not that it concerned him. Nowadays they lead increasingly separate lives. He had little interest in her art, and she none in his passion for motorcycles. They slept in separate bedrooms in his large house in Holland, and when they travelled, they always tried to arrange separate rooms.

Through Van, he had managed to get one of the Median's adjoining rooms, with the interconnecting door, on the second floor, so that was good. There were no children to complicate matters. She didn't want children, and he never had any interest in that either.

He pondered for a minute. 'Maybe that co-habitation agreement I signed last month wasn't such a good idea. She had pushed so hard for her Dutch nationality, though. Never mind, I'll call my Accountant next week and see what can be done. If there's a legal, or on the face of it legal, way around things, then Geert's your man.'

'Well, enough of that.' he thought, turning back to return to the hotel. 'Let's have some breakfast, and then keep the appointment with Leila.'

Kuppers went back through the revolving doors and across the concourse towards the breakfast room, which was on a lower floor, with access down a short flight of stairs after passing the Reception Desk.

As he went past the desk, he noticed a man and woman checking out. The woman was engaged in conversation at the Desk with Sally, a lively, attractive lady in her thirties, one of the Senior Receptionists. The man was taking no part in this discussion and was looking out towards the exit.

As Kuppers approached the man looked up, and their eyes met for a few moments. They stared at each other for a little longer than would be considered normal, and made as if to speak, but neither did, and Kuppers went on his way.

The man's companion turned to leave. The man spoke to her.

'You go to the car, dear, I'll join you in a minute, I just want a quick word with Sally.'

'Alright, Robin, I'll see you at the car, then' she replied.

'Goodbye, Sally' she said, turning back briefly towards the receptionist.

'Goodbye, Mrs Mason. We'll see you again, soon I hope,' said Sally.

✳

Kuppers settled back in his seat on his flight back to Schiphol that evening and gestured to the Air Hostess for another Amstel.

The day had all gone rather well. The Events Manager, Leila Zafiri was an intelligent, efficient, and very attractive, dark-skinned Eurasian lady in her early thirties. They had agreed on all the minutiae, the "behind the scenes "work that made such events successful. Attendees' names, addresses, contact numbers, their expected arrival times for the Reception Desk, the details of the visits to Heskey and Brooklands, Conference Room seating, the sound, screen, and other equipment, and so on.

Leila had reminded him about the special gifts, and he was annoyed that it had almost slipped his mind. These were the welcome presents of a bottle of Bols Genever for each attendee, in lovely brown, stone bottles, courtesy of

Willem Vonk. They were to be placed in each of the guest rooms by Leila, prior to their arrival. Leila was liaising with Vonk on that arrangement on the Tuesday morning before the meeting, so there was no direct involvement for him.

He wondered if Vonk would include him in the "surprise" gift list. He had been sworn to silence as to its happening, to which he had agreed. Maybe he would include him, maybe not. Anyway, if he did, he would certainly drink it. Genever was one of his favourite tipples. On reflection, perhaps he should make sure by asking Leila to slip one of the bottles into his room. There must be a spare around somewhere.

It was a pity she had turned down his suggestion of lunch or a meeting before his flight. Never mind, there was always next week when the Conference proper would provide more opportunity.

The lunch reference reminded him he had made all the Kamada arrangements, including the money.

Kuppers' thoughts then turned back again to Willem Vonk.

A little younger than Kuppers, Vonk was the wealthiest of all the Doves, and Kuppers knew that Vonk had insisted on bankrolling all the costs of this meeting. He had even paid for everything in advance.

Vonk and Kuppers had both worked for Fokland in the UK at the same time, but during that period they weren't particularly close, either during working hours or outside of them.

Vonk was immediately made redundant by Fokland because of the Eurair collapse, and his marriage followed swiftly, collapsing shortly afterward. After his divorce, over the years he built up a motorcycle sales business, "Motovonk," now the largest distributor in Holland, and other Benelux countries, which had made his fortune.

Vonk had never remarried but occupied a large property in the countryside outside of Doventenar, which included a personal gymnasium, swimming pool, classic motorcycle collection, and purpose-built art gallery.

Most of the paintings in the gallery had been personally purchased by Kuppers' partner Angelique Durand. She had been brought up in the art dealing world and had inherited her father's art dealership after his death.

Kuppers sipped at his Amstel and then finished it. 'It was good thinking on my part' he mused, 'that I made sure I distanced myself from the circumstances surrounding the redundancy notice that Vonk received from Fokland that screwed up himself and his marriage so much.'

He wondered how much Vonk really knew of his, Kuppers, role in the redundancy. He had been a Dove for three years or so, and Vonk had joined the Doves a couple of years before him. In all that time, whether together or not, Kuppers had never heard Vonk, or any other Dove, mentioning the Eurair situation or the involvement of either of them in it.

'Well, it was every man for himself then, wasn't it? All's fair in love, war, and business, as the British say, and he hasn't done so badly for himself after all, has he?'

Kuppers congratulated himself mentally, and idly thought, with a self-satisfied smile, of how many British people would know how to paraphrase any Dutch proverbs, or even know any Dutch. He tucked his empty beer can and plastic glass into the netting compartment on the back of the seat in front of him, closed the retractable tray, and shut his eyes for a short rest.

2

# Tuesday, May 17th, 2016

Willem Vonk had arrived at the Median on a delayed, late flight from Zurich the previous evening and had gone immediately to his bed.

Vonk was a big man. A very big man. He cut an imposing figure, around six feet six inches tall, and sixteen stones of solid humanity. Despite his advancing years, regular use of his private gym and swimming pool had kept his body in very good shape.

His appearance was more akin to an international rugby union lock forward than a collector of seventeenth-century maritime art, although there is no reason that the two should not go together.

His hair was closely cropped, and the careless look of his designer stubble was actually the product of careful cultivation.

He stood in front of the mirror in his room and brushed his hands downwards over the lapels of his suit jacket. The suit was dark blue, clearly expensive, and exquisitely tailored, but not obtrusive.

A white silk shirt was open at the neck. Pristine, polished black shoes completed his appearance.

It was as if he had dressed for an appointment with his Bank Manager. In fact, he did have such an appointment that he was scheduled to attend, in London, later that day.

However, before that visit, he had arranged to meet the Median Hotel Conference and Events Manager, Leila Zafiri, at 7:30 am in the ground floor Conference Room. Although they had never met in person, they had exchanged emails, texts, and occasional telephone calls over the past couple of months.

The reason was a surprise gift that Vonk had been organizing for the Doves attending the Conference.

He was providing a bottle of Genever-Dutch gin-for each of the Doves, together with a welcome message printed on a cleverly designed bottle tag which looped over the neck, and then rested on the shoulders of the bottle.

A gift bag would hold the bottles with a neck tag attached.

Vonk had the bottles custom-made in Amsterdam to his precise specifications. They were replicas of the original antique Dutch brown stoneware, ceramic, glazed, gin bottles with the lettering "Erven Lucas Bols Het Lootsje Amsterdam "etched deliberately indistinctly into the bottles, towards the top. He had even insisted on the three-quarter litre bottles having the letter "A" stamped on them, near the base. The cork stopper completed the authenticity of their appearance.

He had arranged for them to be shipped over to Leila from Holland, in a compartmentalised case, of 12 bottles, a couple of weeks earlier.

Leila had organised the purchase and printing of the bottle neck hang tags and the acquisition of tall gift bags to hold the bottles. The design, and payment, of those items had been down to Vonk. He had chosen the radiant orange colour of the Netherlands Football team shirts for the bags. The tags were of a paler orange hue featuring a short text in Dutch printed in cursive handwriting black script.

*"Hier is een klein cadeautje om u welkom te*

*heten op de bijeenkomst van Motorclub Doventenar*

*Median Hotel Gatwick, Mei 2016"*

They were to be put into each of the Doves' hotel rooms, to be there on the bedside tables as they each arrived on Tuesday afternoon Special arrangements had to be made for Kuppers, who was already installed in the Hotel, and Van Heemskerk, who was arriving on Wednesday morning

Under instruction from Vonk, Leila had moved the case of bottles from her office to the Conference Room the previous evening and put the bottle tags and orange gift bags alongside them on the floor.

Vonk was about ten minutes early but was able to let himself into the room with the keypad code that Leila had emailed to him prior to his arrival. He had brought with him a large "airline pilot style" carry case, presumably to aid a swift exit for his London meeting.

He lifted a long, fold-up table from its resting place against one of the side walls, brought it into the centre of the room, and erected it. He took the bottles, one by one, from the compartmentalised case and placed them on the table.

He stopped and contemplated them for a few moments, then opened his carry case, rummaged around in it, and then brought out a seemingly identical bottle. As he held the bottle in his hand there was the noise of the door behind him closing. He hadn't heard it open. It seemed to give him a start.

He turned to see a petite, dark-haired, dark-skinned, strikingly attractive, and immaculately uniformed young lady, a tan-coloured, leather wallet holder tucked under one arm. Vonk hastily put the bottle he was holding onto the table with the others, then spoke.

"Ah, you must be Leila Zafiri" he said.

"I am Willem Vonk. Please call me Willem. I hope you don't mind if I call you Leila," he said, proffering a meaty hand in her direction.

He looked at his watch. "Aren't you a little early?" he said.

Vonk's spoken English, though grammatically excellent, was delivered with a heavily accented, somewhat nasal inflexion.

Leila transferred her wallet holder from under her right arm to under her left to release her right hand and shook Vonk's hand gingerly.

"Yes, I'm sorry. My timing's been thrown out somewhat. I'm expecting an urgent call from the organiser of our visit to Brooklands which hasn't yet come through. Please forgive me if I have to leave the room for a few minutes."

"….and, of course, you may call me Leila. It is nice to meet face to face."

Vonk, oddly, seemed pleasantly surprised by the fact she might have to leave the room, and they exchanged further trivial pleasantries.

Side by side they made an odd couple-the huge frame of Vonk accentuating the more than head and shoulders height difference between them.

"Well, let us get down to business," said Vonk. "I have an important meeting in London, to which I must go straight from here, so I haven't much time. I expect to be back later this evening."

Leila's mobile interrupted with its shrill ring. "Leila Zafiri," she answered, listened, and then addressed Vonk.

"I'm sorry Mr Vonk. I mean Willem. It's my Brooklands call. I'll be as quick as I can," she said and left the room.

Vonk looked at the table full of bottles, studying it carefully, scratching his head as he did so.

Then there was a noise outside. Vonk hurriedly selected one of the bottles, and quickly put it inside his carry case, closing it in almost the same movement, like a conjurer performing the handkerchief trick.

Leila came in through the door just as he was closing the case.

"Sorry again, Willem," she said. "One of those days. I'm going to have to pick up the Brooklands thing later this afternoon, so I was much quicker than I thought I would be."

"No problem," said Vonk.

"Now, where were we?" he said, speaking more to himself than Leila.

He took one of the bottles from the table and turned it, with unexpected delicacy, carefully between his fingers. He held it up to his eye level.

"Just look at that Leila," he said, "isn't that beautiful?" He stared at it appreciatively for a few seconds.

Leila had taken a quick look at the bottles after they had arrived, but Vonk's aesthetic appreciation had passed her by. With her busy schedule, she was more concerned with ensuring the quantity of the bottles delivered was correct rather than their appearance.

"These old-fashioned cork stoppers are coming back into vogue, you know," he said. Then his voice took on a lower, more serious tone.

"OK, Leila, have you brought your list of Doves and room numbers?" Vonk asked.

Leila nodded in the affirmative. She knew that this was a surprise welcome gift, and so great care had to be taken to have the gift on their bedside table without their knowledge, but before their arrival.

Leila opened her tan document wallet and read out the list of Doves with their Room Numbers, Vonk checked them off as she did so.

Piet Kuppers in 205, with Angelique Durand in 206, the interconnecting room. Angelique wasn't receiving a gift, as she wasn't part of the Conference.

Arjen Arends in 105, Bruno Englesman in 106, Klaas Hartog in 107, Bert Koenes in 108, Willem de Bakker in 109, Marko Staal in 110 and Johann Rep in 111. Vonk himself was in 504, and Dirk Van Heemskerk – from Wednesday – in 312. There were also two spares.

"So that agrees the numbers," Vonk said to Leila. "Twelve bottles."

Vonk looked towards the bottles for a moment before speaking further, then continued.

"Leila, do you remember when I made the original order, we had allowed for eleven Doves and two spares as a contingency? However, that made thirteen bottles, so I reduced the order by one spare, to make a total of twelve. You see, I know the English regard thirteen as an unlucky number."

He looked at Leila as if expecting a round of applause, but nothing was forthcoming, so he carried on.

"Marco Koeman dropped out just last week, so we now have two spares, and are back to the original twelve: seven "bikers," Kuppers, Van, me, and the spares."

"I am giving myself a surprise bottle, so keep very quiet and don't tell me."

"The real surprise is that he has a sense of humour," thought Leila appreciatively.

"So that makes ten Doves and two spares."

Vonk then began to group the bottles, a little uncertainly, explaining to Leila as he went along.

"The bottles, tags and bags aren't named, they are identical. I suggest you pencil a room number, in very small lettering, on the top back of the gift bag, so you make sure they are correctly distributed."

"We have the seven Doves on the first floor," and he pushed seven bottles into a group at the top of the table.

"Then Kuppers in 205 on the second floor."

He separated Kuppers' bottle from the first group.

"As I have mentioned, there's no bottle needed for Angelique Durand. She's spending most of the time in London with a girlfriend of hers and won't be arriving until much later tonight."

He continued. "I will keep Van's gift, which I will present to him formally tomorrow, at the start of proceedings."

He separated the Van Heemskerk bottle.

"And there is my own bottle. I won't need the gift bag."

He stood that bottle by itself.

"So, there will be two spares left over. I won't be going back to my room; I don't have time now. Could you put the spares in the container they came in, and drop that into my room, together with Van's bottle and my own?"

"Thanks."

"I'll leave it to you to make up all the gift bags and put them in the correct rooms All the first-floor Doves are arriving this afternoon, but Kuppers is already here, so be careful to watch his movements, and put his bag in his room when he's not around."

"That Piet's gift is a surprise is very important. He doesn't know if he is receiving one or not, but I want to thank him personally as he has done so much to make this Conference a success."

Whether or not there was a touch of sarcasm in his tone Leila couldn't say one way or the other.

He took the bottle that he had designated for Kuppers from the table. He took a gift bag, and bottle tag, slipped the tag over the neck of the bottle and put it inside the bright orange gift bag.

He picked up a pencil.

"Look," he said to Leila, "I will mark Piet's bottle bag, so it is clear which is his," in addition to the already pencilled room number, he drew an asterisk of reasonable size carefully onto the back of the gift bag.

Leila thought for a moment.

"I have a meeting arranged with Mr Kuppers for four o'clock this afternoon. He mentioned to me that he was skipping breakfast and going to Crawley for a few hours this morning, but I will check if he has gone."

"That would be very useful, as I can then put his gift into his room before the first-floor people."

"Ok. But make sure you go to Piet's room first," he said.

With that, Vonk looked at his watch. His huge hands gripped the handles of the briefcase with a movement akin to the operation of a demolition crane grab and hurried from the room.

3

# Wednesday, May 18th, 2016

Although a start time of 11.30 am had been set for the first session of the Conference to allow for any unforeseen problems with Van's travel arrangements, and to allow him set up time, most of the Doves were already taking breakfast in the downstairs dining room.

It was 8.20 am. Leila looked around the busy room, then scanned it again more carefully. The person she was looking for wasn't there.

She looked at her watch again.

After about twenty minutes of their four o'clock meeting the previous afternoon Kuppers had told her that he was feeling a little unwell and would have a rest in his room, then an early night, but would see her outside the Restaurant at eight o'clock the next morning, as there were several last minute checks for them to complete just before the start of the meeting- the seating, the set-up of the computer equipment and screen, times of refreshment breaks, mealtimes, and more.

Besides, she was expecting Van's arrival on the flight from Amsterdam between nine o'clock and nine-thirty.

She had rung Kuppers' room number, at five past eight, and then a few minutes ago on his mobile, but had received no reply on either occasion. She had heard a faint, dull ringing tone from the room phone, but no response at all from the mobile.

She looked around again, and noticed, in the far corner, at a table for two, Willem Vonk, with his red leather zipped document holder on the table in front of him.

He was accompanied by a very striking, younger woman, with short, stylishly cut, blonde hair, probably in her early forties. She wore very little make-up, just subtle touches of nude eye shadow and pale pink lipstick.

A rather over-wide mouth seemed to add to, rather than diminish, her attractiveness.

She was casually, but elegantly dressed, in a white roll-neck cable stitch sweater with large front pockets, black trousers, and Barbour ankle boots. Leila assumed this to be Angelique Durand, Kuppers' partner, or girlfriend, who she knew was not arriving until late last night, and who was booked into the connecting suite with Kuppers.

She walked over to the table. "Good morning, Mr Vonk…er…Willem," she said, then turned to the woman and extended her hand.

"May I assume you are Ms Angelique Durand, the companion of Mr Kuppers?" "Oui, c'est moi," the woman answered, taking the hand.

Leila continued, "Bonjour, je m'apelle Leila Zafiri. Je suis le Directeur de la Conference pour d'hôtel. Je cherche Monsieur Kuppers. Il est dans sa chambre?"

Angelique looked up and smiled. "I will henceforth speak in English. I have six languages, you know," she said, pronouncing the phrase as if expecting an Oscar. "You may call me Angelique, and I will call you Leila." It was a statement to which there was no answer.

As she raised her hand, Leila couldn't help but notice Angelique's very distinctive nails. On each fingernail, a cascade of tiny silver stars of reducing size made their way from the pink top of the nail down to a deep mauve semi-circular cuticle.

Angelique saw her looking and smiled. "I had them done yesterday. You like?" she questioned.

"Yes, very much," replied Leila.

Although Leila herself possessed a degree in Hospitality Management, her elder sister had undertaken an apprenticeship with the Goldsmiths Company in Hatton Garden, and their closeness meant that Leila was well versed in jewellery and design, so she had also noticed the Jean Schlumberger Tiffany ring on the second finger of Angelique's right hand, with its intertwined rose gold and diamonds, and the Omega Constellation Gold Diamond Watch on her wrist.

She didn't need to ask for their retail price.

Leila's reverie was broken by Angelique's answer to her question as to Kuppers' whereabouts.

"I am sorry, I do not know. As you may be aware I arrived late last night, I looked into Piet's bedroom very briefly, and he seemed to be fast asleep. I had some urgent business to conclude with Willem here, and we had to work through the night in his room, so I have not seen Piet this morning, but I assume he is in his room."

Leila let this pass, without the slightest facial movement. She looked down at the table.

"I see you have almost finished your breakfast. Could I ask a favour? I have tried calling the room a couple of times without success, and reception hasn't noticed him down here. You have an interconnecting room. Could we go up together and check to see if everything is all right? I'll wait in the corridor, whilst you go into the room. That will be a great help."

"Of course. As you may know, I'm not involved with the meeting itself, that is left to Piet, Willem, and the others. Later on, I catch a train to Brighton to see the Royal Pavilion, and tomorrow I will arrange a taxi to take me to Petworth to view the Turners, which I have not seen before, and bring me back here. I am dining in the evening with the motorcycle people." She pronounced the last phrase with undisguised disdain, almost contempt.

"The train to Brighton had better have a first-class compartment," thought Leila to herself.

"That will be alright, will it not Willem?" she said, getting to her feet, and looking down at Vonk.

"Yes, of course, I will wait here," Vonk replied.

"Oh, by the way, Leila," Vonk said. "Thank you for all your help with the gifts yesterday, everyone is very pleased. They are still trying to guess whether it is Kuppers or Van who has given them." He smiled.

Leila and Angelique made their way to the lift, exchanging snippets of small talk. Angelique asked how long she had worked at the Median, and if she liked art, and Leila told her she would like the Turners.

They exited the lift and walked down the red-carpeted corridor to Angelique's room, number 206. Angelique operated the key card and went through into her room. Leila stayed outside in the corridor.

There were a few moments of silence, then a high-pitched, hysterical scream, followed by the urgent, frantic speech.

"Leila, Leila, come here quickly.... quickly," she repeated, stressing and almost shouting the repetition. "Something awful has happened."

Leila rushed through Angelique's door, then turned right through the connecting door. Angelique was standing to one side of the double bed, her face drained of colour, and one hand, with its brightly painted nails, over her mouth as if she were about to be sick.

She was stock still, transfixed, staring down at the man on the bed. He was lying face down, his head to one side, partly buried into a pillow. At one point he must have been covered by the duvet, but it had slipped, not quite completely off the bed, but sufficiently to reveal one side of his face and body. An exposed left arm hung over one side of the bed, almost touching the floor. The heels and remainder of his yellow socks could be seen, each of his dark brown suede shoes partially on the fronts of his feet, and the laces undone, as if he had been trying to put his shoes on. He was fully clothed.

Leila breathed in deeply and went over quickly to the body and bent down to look more closely at his face. The body seemed stiff, there were no signs of breathing, no rise and fall of the chest or back. She felt carefully for a pulse, disturbing as little as possible, but there was none. As she felt for the pulse, she noticed the distinctive gold-coloured ring around the black face of his TW Steel watch. She glanced at the time on his watch. It was 8.30 am.

She could only see one half of the face, but the eye she could see was dilated. He was still wearing his reading glasses, but they were set at an odd angle, above the bridge of his nose and his eyes, level with the base of his forehead, as if he had pushed them upwards whilst lying on the bed.

The face was a pallid, greyish white, contorted but not extensively so, but, curiously, the scar on his forehead had retained its pinkish hue. His face couldn't have been seen from the door, as the body was facing the other way, towards the window, but trailing down from the pillow to form a congealed pool on the carpet was an artist's palette of red blood, vomit of an ochre colour and assorted lumps of unidentifiable, regurgitated food. A sickeningly sweet odour of diarrhoea came from the lower part of his body.

Piet Kuppers was dead.

Leila turned to Angelique, who was still staring down with a glazed expression, unable to speak. Leila placed one arm around her shoulders and guided her towards, and through, the connecting door and into one of the armchairs at the back of the room near the window.

"Just sit here for a few minutes," she said, organising a glass of water. "Here, drink this, whilst I see to everything. Don't move. As you will appreciate, I must make a couple of phone calls. I'll only be next door, just call if you need me. I will be as quick as possible."

She closed the interconnecting door and went through to Kuppers' room. She took a glance around. He was still in the same position.

Leila somehow felt strangely ice calm. Perfectly in control of herself and her actions, as if in an altered state, but anchored to present events. 'In the zone', as a sportsperson might say.

She shut out the image of the motionless body on the bed, walked across the room towards the window, took out her mobile, and dialled the number of Matthew Collison, the Hotel Manager.

After a short pause, he answered. "Collison," he said.

"Matthew, it's Leila. I'll be as brief as I can. We have a very urgent and serious situation on our hands. I am in Room 205, which is that of Mr Piet Kuppers, who as you know is the main organiser of the three-day Conference that the Doves, the Dutch motorcycle group from Holland are holding, starting in the Johnson Conference Room at 11.30 am today."

"I'm afraid to tell you that Mr Kuppers is dead. I am sure of that. Ms Angelique Durand, his partner, girlfriend or whatever, is here also, but in the interconnecting room, 206, and can't hear me. She discovered the body a few minutes ago. I was with her. I was concerned Mr Kuppers hadn't shown up to meet me at breakfast as planned, and Ms Durand and I went up to his room together. I saw the body immediately after her. I felt for the pulse. There was nothing."

Leila then briefly, but accurately, described the symptoms and positioning of the body.

"There is no sign of forced entry, and at a quick look no sign of external injury. The room is very tidy. I'm not expert enough to even hazard a guess as to the reasons for his death. Could you come up as quickly as you can? I need to organise someone to look after Ms Durand, who appears to be still in shock, and the room needs to be secured."

There was a pause, then Collison replied.

"Thank you, Leila. Of course, this must all be attended to quickly and efficiently, for the people involved and the good name of the Hotel."

'Yes, of course, we mustn't forget the good name of the hotel, must we?' thought Leila.

"However, I have a slight problem. I am about to attend to the departure of a couple of our very important VIP guests. That will only take about twenty minutes or so, but it's something I can't get out of, and as you are aware, Derek, our Assistant Manager, is on compassionate leave in Australia for a couple of weeks with his father's funeral."

"So, could you step in for the moment, which makes sense anyway? You have the facts and are on-site, so you are best equipped to deal with the emergency services."

"Please call 999 straight away and ask for both an Ambulance and Police. It is critical that is the cause of death must be established as quickly as possible, at least on a reasonably well-grounded preliminary basis. We may need a paramedic as well as the police."

"I will also call Hargreaves immediately."

Doctor Hargreaves was a retired local GP, who formerly had a practice in Stone Hill, where he still lived. Since retiring, in addition to a wealthy private elderly clientele, he had discovered a lucrative side-line as an "on call" medical consultant to several of the Airport Hotels, of which the Median was one.

"I will tell him to check in at Reception when he arrives, ask for you, and follow your instructions. He should be over quickly. Get him to work immediately on examining the body and giving his preliminary opinion on the cause of death. I should be there, but go ahead if I'm not."

"Just off the cuff, there are many other things to consider when I've finished with this VIP." He spoke quickly. "Here are a few of them."

"Make sure you ask Reception if they have any other reports of guest sickness. That's very important."

"We will need Kuppers' health records and so forth from Holland, and there are all the meeting arrangements for today and the next few days, which may have to be completely reorganised. Everything will all have to be done as fast as we can."

"Now, make sure no one comes into the room, keep it exactly as it is. Call Kevin MacAllister, the Security Manager, and tell him to get up to the room quickly, and he can take over, or add to guard duties."

Leila interjected.

"Don't forget Mr Van Heemskerk, the Doves president. He is flying over from Amsterdam this morning to open the Meeting at 11.30. He is due to land at South Terminal at around 9.15. He should be informed."

"Quite right, Leila. I'll check the flight arrivals as soon as I'm clear. Assuming his flight is on schedule I'll call Mr Van Heemskerk at about 9.25. He should have cleared customs by then and be on his way. Text me his mobile number. I assume you have it."

"Yes, I do. Leave that with me."

"See you in twenty minutes or so. You sound very calm. Good work."

"Oh, by the way, Leila, from the information you have given me so far, it would appear to me that the death is unexpected. So, it's either accidental, suicide, or —" he paused but didn't finish the sentence, leaving the word hanging in the air, and continued.

"... let's leave that to the medical people and the police, shall we..."

"... And in my hotel, too," he muttered as he rang off.

Leila could almost see the head shaking slowly from side to side and hear the deep sighs at the other end of the phone.

✳

Leila rang 999. She answered all the questions from the call handler quickly and efficiently. 'Is the person breathing? What is the address you are calling from? What number are you calling from?' and so on.

She stressed the urgency and importance of the situation, that there appeared to be no necessity for any attempt at resuscitation, and that the death was almost certain to be unexplained. She was assured that an ambulance would be dispatched immediately and that the police would be similarly immediately advised. It was likely that a local police officer would be the first to arrive.

The call handler's parting words were in Leila's mind. "If it's clear the person is dead, don't touch anything," and "Don't disturb the surrounding area." Before leaving Kuppers' room she took a long, hard look around, trying to memorise the scene as accurately as possible.

Looking from the connecting door into Kuppers' room there was a long, slim table to the left. It looked as though Kuppers had been working at that table, and there were three neatly stacked columns of paper, and beside them a single sheet, as if he were about to start another stack. All very organised. A Dell laptop computer was on the right of the tabletop. Its screen had been pushed back into the typing position, and it was still plugged into a nearby wall socket.

There was also the gift of the bottle of Bols Genever, its accompanying bottle neck welcome card put to one side, and a drinking glass. The gift bag had presumably been discarded.

Propped up inside the desk keyhole was a large, black leather zipped case, possibly to hold papers, or a tablet computer, or both. To one side of the desk was a large, cylindrical, faux leather waste bin. She spied the orange bag poking from the top of the bin but couldn't make out any other of its contents clearly.

She was about to go back through the interconnecting door to see Angelique when she heard a knock on Angelique's door. She assumed it would be Matthew Collison.

She took a last look around. 'That's strange' she thought.

His key card was in the switch holder on the wall near the door, and all the room lights were still on, which she hadn't really noticed before. The deadbolt on the inside of the door was secured, and so was the additional safety lock.

'Mr K certainly didn't want any unexpected visitors' she contemplated.

Before she could carry that train of thought any further, she put that to one side, and returned to the urgency of the present situation.

She went through the interconnecting door. There was another person with Angelique, but it wasn't Collison. It was the burly figure of Willem Vonk.

He looked around as Leila came in, and then back to Angelique. She had let Vonk into the room, and had returned to the chair near the window, her face pale, and the glass of water untouched on the small, round table in front of her.

"What has happened?" asked Vonk, looking at Angelique with concern in his voice. "I thought you had been a long time, so I came up to see if you were all right."

He put his document case that he had with him at breakfast on the same type of long, low wooden unit that was in Kuppers' room, and went over to Angelique and held her hand. She didn't speak or react.

"Well, Mr Vonk," said Leila, trying to think quickly.

"I'm afraid that Mr Kuppers has been taken very ill during the night. We have called an ambulance, which should be here very soon. The Hotel Manager will also be here shortly, and he will arrange to make a general announcement to your party as soon as that is possible. In the meanwhile, no one is to enter that room, and nothing anywhere is to be touched. I have to make sure Ms Durand is taken care of. You should return to the rest of your group. Please do not mention anything of this situation to any of them until you are advised otherwise."

Vonk nodded in concurrence.

She paused for a moment.

"Wait a minute, since you are here Mr Vonk," she stressed the 'are', "Perhaps you could help me? I am going to find our senior Chambermaid- the room is further down this corridor- and she will be there at this time. She can accompany Ms Durand to my office on the ground floor, and they can stay there until Ms Durand is needed further. I should be no more than two or three minutes."

"Of course," said Vonk, "I will take good care of Angelique in the meanwhile."

Leila hurried down the corridor to the chambermaids' room, and located Jane Wheeler, the senior chambermaid, a short, stout older lady, with a frizzy, blueish-grey rinse, gold-rimmed glasses, and a pronounced limp. She was wearing the chambermaid's uniform- a light blue tunic blouse and sensible, flat black shoes. As they made their way back down the corridor, at a limping pace, Leila explained the general situation and told her the key code to her office.

The door to Angelique's room was closed, and Leila knocked to gain entry. Vonk opened the door.

"Angelique is beginning to feel a little better," he said. 'She certainly has more colour,' thought Leila, 'and appears more composed.'

Vonk picked up his red document case from the unit. "I will leave now," he pronounced, "as you say, to join the others. Also, I will say nothing at all of this until it is right to do so."

He went over to Angelique and kissed her on the cheek, more in a business-like than loving manner. Before Vonk departed they exchanged some words with each other, not in English. 'Probably Dutch,' thought Leila, 'but unfortunately, I only have two languages.'

She joked with herself. 'I must learn four more in my spare time,' she said to herself.

Lelia addressed Angelique.

"I'm glad you are feeling a little better."

She gestured towards the chambermaid.

"This is Mrs Wheeler – Jane – who will be looking after your welfare for a short while. She will take you to my office on the ground floor. There are some comfortable chairs there, and Jane will get you coffee, or whatever else you would like. If you feel you need the First Aid Room, that is just a couple of doors down from my office. Then, when things have been sorted out a little more with the emergency services, someone will come to see you."

"Do you have your mobile with you, Jane?" Leila asked.

Jane nodded.

"Please look after Ms Durand, we will make sure your duties are covered. If you need it, get the key to the First Aid Room from Reception. Explain I have asked you to look after one of our guests who is not feeling well."

If you need coffee or any food, please call room service, on my authority, but do not go to get them yourself. You can order for yourself as well, though. Call me if Ms Durand appears unduly upset, or if there is anything you feel unable to handle."

"Angelique, you must stay with Jane until someone arrives. It may take a little time, so please be patient."

Angelique nodded, then stood up for the first time for a while, but seemed back to her former, assured self. She was very aware of how attractive she was.

She spoke.

"I wish to go outside for some air, and to have a cigarette."

It wasn't a question.

A whitish cream-coloured, expensive-looking Dorothy bag was propped up against the side of the bed. She delved into the bag and brought out a slim box of cocktail cigarettes.

She put the cigarettes into one of the large front pockets on her sweater and rummaged around further in the bag and finally produced a small, gold, ladies' lighter, which followed its way into the same large pocket.

"Come, Mrs Wheeler, let us proceed," she said. 'Strange,' thought Leila, 'she has said nothing at all about Kuppers, in my presence at least. Very strange.'

"OK," said Leila. "Jane will wait in the lobby whilst you go outside. You are a very important witness. You must not move out of her sight."

'Although you might fancy your chances of doing a runner once you know about her limp,' she thought, mischievously.

As they went out of the door Leila suddenly realised, she hadn't phoned MacAllister, the Security man. She did so, took a deep breath and sat down.

She was alone for the first time in this hectic course of events.

Alone, that is, apart from the dead man in his yellow socks in the room next door.

❋

Leila's opportunity to collect her thoughts in her own space was short-lived. "It's the old London Bus syndrome," she muttered to herself, as Collison, followed by Doctor Hargreaves, whom she had met once or twice in the past, and then MacAllister, entered Angelique's room in short order.

Collison had bumped into Hargreaves at reception, and as Hargreaves's entry and Collison's VIP farewell had coincided, they had accompanied each other to the second floor.

Hargreaves was a bald man, wearing glasses with lenses the thickness of the window glass in the US President's Limousine. To call him portly would be a considerable understatement. He was smartly dressed in a tailored grey suit, white shirt, and plain crimson tie, and someone had spent a long time polishing his shoes to a mirror-like sheen. He may have told his patients to eat healthily and keep fit, but his own expansive waistline and several chins demonstrated that he spent very little, if any, time taking notice of that advice.

He had with him a large medical bag, presumably full of the required medical paraphernalia. He took off his jacket, revealing crimson braces, the colour of which was an exact match to his tie, and delved into his bag. He brought out a pair of vinyl medical gloves and slip-on shoe coverings, and put them on, the slip-on shoes providing some degree of difficulty caused by his girth.

On the way up to the room, Collison had provided him with a few brief facts, such as he knew. Kuppers' nationality, sex, approximate age, build and general appearance, and apparent health.

"The body is through here, I assume," he said to Leila gesturing toward the interconnecting door.

"As I told Mr Collison on the way up, I am very hard-pressed for time. I have a patient of mine that needs my urgent attention in her home."

Leila's opinion of Dr Hargreaves, even after a few short previous encounters, was not a favourable one. "I expect he has to get there in time to make sure he's mentioned in the will," she thought to herself.

"Mr Collison has provided me with some information on the deceased, but I understand that you were dealing with Mr Kuppers on a regular basis with respect to the Conference, and also discovered the body."

"Yes, and not quite correct, are the answers to your observations Doctor Hargreaves."

"I had been working quite closely with Mr Kuppers, particularly at times over the last two weeks, but the initial discovery of the body was made by Ms Angelique Durand, the occupant of the interconnecting room where we are standing now."

"I entered Mr Kuppers' room immediately afterwards, as she had cried out for my assistance. Ms Durand was in trauma, in which state she remained for some time. She is now being looked after in my office."

"I just looked over the body and searched for a pulse. It was clear to me he was dead. I looked briefly around the room, but nothing more. I left everything untouched. I think Angelique- Ms Durand-was too shocked to do anything."

"The body was discovered at 8.30 am. I noticed the time on his watch, which agreed with mine."

"If it helps, I had arranged a final "wrap-up" meeting with Mr Kuppers yesterday at 4.00 pm after he returned from his lunch. After about five or ten minutes he said he was feeling a little unwell, that we had finished our joint preparations anyway, so, therefore, he would go back to his room, work there finalising his own preparations, and have an early night."

"'See you in the morning' were his last words to me."

"Thank you," said Hargreaves. "Now let's get on with it," he said.

"I will go through now. Wait here until I have finished, which won't be long. I will disturb nothing. That will be for the police and medical people to decide when they arrive."

"I am anxious to have some opinion very quickly, however preliminary," said Collison.

'For the good name of the hotel,' thought Leila, wryly.

Leila waited with Collison. MacAllister had called his assistant to begin setting up the CCTV requirements and moved to guard duty outside the door.

After a very short interval, Hargreaves emerged. He wasted no time, removing his gloves and overshoes as he spoke. He addressed Collison and Leila in a rapid, rather pompous tone.

"The first thing to say is, as Ms Zafiri has already observed, Mr Kuppers is clearly dead."

"The body shows no signs of physical assault that might contribute to death. No wounds from any weapon. No lacerations, abrasions, or contusions. No defence wounds."

"Nothing in the surroundings of the room suggests any break-in, or disturbance whatever."

"Assuming Mr Kuppers had no health issues, which, of course, is purely an assumption until his medical records can be accessed, the death can be regarded as unexplained."

"The symptoms, such as I can observe externally, in my opinion, indicate Mr Kuppers' death was a result of poisoning. Possibly food poisoning. The symptoms are similar to e coli."

"What!" spluttered Collison, "E coli. Here at the Median!" Leila and MacAllister exchanged glances.

"Let's not jump to conclusions, Mr Collison," responded Hargreaves.

"I said, 'Similar to'. That is just to give you some idea, and you have not advised me of any other reported cases."

"Finally, no obvious suicide note in sight, which occurs frequently in such cases."

"I will complete some notes for the investigating authorities later today," he announced, "which I will email to Mr Collison."

"I think it best if you all remain here and await the emergency services and the police. My statements to you are to be regarded as initial and preliminary."

Hargreaves clearly had no intention of obeying his own advice by remaining at the Median for any longer than he could help. He checked his apparatus quickly and hurried off in pursuit of his aged, and no doubt very wealthy, patient.

Collison had been so consumed with the possibility of adverse blanket media coverage of an e-coli outbreak at the hotel that he only remembered afterwards about Barrowclough's instruction for him to ensure Hargreaves remained until the Forensic Scientist, Mrs Parkinson, arrived. By the time he did remember, Hargreaves was probably trying to disentangle the will documentation from his stethoscope.

4

It was just after 7 am, and Detective Inspector Ian Scott was already at his desk in the Guildford Headquarters of the Surrey and Sussex Police. Scott had worked with the Surrey and Sussex force in Guildford for some four years as a Detective Sergeant, but this would only be his third day as a Detective Inspector, and he was determined to prove his worth.

Scott cut a tall, spare, athletic-looking figure. He had an interesting, varied, and cosmopolitan background.

Born to a Jamaican mother and English father, his skin was of a permanent light tan tone, English summer or winter notwithstanding. His Jamaican grandparents had arrived in Tilbury on the "Empire Windrush," in 1948. They were initially housed, along with about 200 others, in a deep air raid shelter in Clapham Common, and they subsequently settled in Brixton.

His mother moved from Brixton to Crawley, where she was a nurse at Crawley Hospital. Whilst there she met Ian's father, Malcolm Scott, an English doctor, and they made their home in Crawley, where Ian was born, in 1983.

He went to university, in Norwich, studying law, but, after graduation, decided to pursue what was previously a personal preoccupation and spent eighteen months at the Auteur Studio in Brighton obtaining a Diploma in film studies. His speciality was the films of the 1940s and 1950s. Then, another career change. He joined the Police Force in 2004, as a Constable in Crawley, spending four years there. He became a Sergeant, based in Brighton for three years, then a Detective Sergeant in Guildford, and now a Detective Inspector. His star was on the rise.

In the meanwhile, he had married and was father to two girls, now aged seven and five. He was living in Shalford, a village two miles to the south of Guildford.

Scott flipped through his intray and laptop, examining the case file data to scope and organise his day, and the longer-term tasks in hand. He was familiar with several of the cases, the interviews to be continued, the crime scene unit to be contacted, and follow-up with the forensic analysts.

'All this always takes much longer in real life than in detective novels', he mused, wryly. He would now oversee those cases, managing the detective sergeants, and acting as Senior Investigating Officer where the case warranted it.

The last few weeks had seen significant changes in the Guildford HQ organization. The former Detective Chief Inspector had already moved to Leeds, to take up a promotion to Superintendent. His replacement was to be a lady, from the Thames Valley Force, apparently coming into post with a very high reputation. She would be Scott's immediate boss. In fact, according to his diary, she was due to arrive in the Office that very day.

Scott himself had been promoted to Detective Inspector because of the sudden death a few weeks ago, from a heart attack, of his D.I, Ray Kinninmonth. A hard-drinking Scotsman, Kinninmonth was a tough "old school" career copper, totally dedicated to the job, who the more cerebral Scott had respected for his drive, effectiveness, and work ethic.

He went over to the automated drinks machine, pressed the requisite buttons for a latte, returned to his desk and absorbed himself in the casework. Time passed quickly. His reverie was interrupted by the two people who came into the office. He looked at his watch. It was just after 8.45 am.

A portly man of medium height was followed by a slightly built, small woman, with closely cropped dark hair, little or no make-up, and gold, horn-rimmed glasses. She wore a smart, nondescript outfit, mainly blue and black, with flat-heeled black shoes.

The portly man was the Superintendent, Bob Barrowclough, a blunt, straightforward Yorkshireman. A couple of years away from retirement, he had spent most of his initial police service in Northumbria, then on to the Met and latterly, the South of England. His diction had a curious mixture of the local dialect of his Hunslet roots, sprinkled with what might be called "cockneyisms," acquired at the Met, and more recently acquired "Americanisms," the origins of which were unknown.

As they passed Scott's desk they stopped briefly. Greetings were exchanged. Barrowclough did the introduction, wasting little time with formalities.

"Scott, this is DCI Harriet Graham. As you know, she will be your immediate superior. We are just going through to my Office. I'll give you a shout when we're finished, and then you two can get to know each other better."

Ian knew a little already. He had looked up a broad outline of her career when he knew she had been appointed to the position in Guildford. He ran quickly over her details in his mind, recalling them in an abbreviated manner, as if in a checklist.

Graham was 37 years old, unmarried, with no children. She was born in Morecambe in Lancashire, where her architect father was working on an assignment for the development of the iconic Midland Hotel, but she was brought up in Hove and educated at Roedean School, then to Somerville, Oxford. Worked for a year in the UK Department of Justice. Joined the Met, then the City of

London police, on to Thames Valley CID, then to Surrey and Sussex. Worked her way through the ranks on a fast-track programme to her current position of DCI.

'Altogether a smart cookie,' thought Ian, 'or was that too American a phrase?'

Barrowclough and Graham went through to Barrowclough's Office and Ian re-absorbed himself in his work, pausing only to acknowledge the other staff members who were coming into work.

After about an hour of assiduous concentration, Ian had made some inroads into the pile of papers. He took a mental break, breathed deeply and adopted the "considered thinkers" position, leaning back in his chair and interlocking his fingers, cradling his head at its base. He looked through the glass-paned walls of Barrowclough's office which was almost in front of him.

Harriet Graham was about to get up from her position to one side of Barrowclough's desk and was halfway up from her chair when a call must have come through, as Barrowclough picked up the phone. He listened for a few moments, then motioned for Graham to sit down. He picked up a pen and began making notes, writing quickly and extensively for several minutes, then replaced the receiver, and picked it up immediately, presumably to make another call. It all seemed very intense, and Ian was intrigued. He made a pretence of attending to his desk work but kept looking and trying to second guess the topic of conversation.

Barrowclough finished the second call and then made a third. After that call had finished, he got up from his chair, leaving Graham seated, and popped his head around his office door. He beckoned in Ian's direction.

"Come in, Scott," he said, "Something urgent has come up."

Ian pulled up a spare chair and sat alongside Harriet Graham.

"OK, listen on, both. There's a group of Dutch bikers, motor bikers, that is, about ten of them, call themselves the Doves. 'D-U-I-F' is the Dutch spelling, but it's pronounced almost exactly the same, so as far as I'm concerned, and you as well, 'Doves' it is from now on."

"Well, these Doves are holding a conference at the Median Hotel, which is adjacent to the North Terminal at Gatwick Airport. Very easy to find. The Conference was due to start today and finish Saturday morning. Older guys, motorbike enthusiasts. No Hells Angels or rockers, as far as I'm aware, that is." He smiled.

"Well, one of them, a guy called Kuppers, has been found dead in his room about three-quarters of an hour ago. There is a hotel doctor, his name is Hargreaves, who has examined the body briefly. He is almost certain the guy died from poisoning." Ian wondered why he said "guy" so much. 'All those American crime programmes, I suppose. I'd better watch out, or I'll go the same way.'

Barrowclough continued, "It's certainly unexplained, most probably suspicious. The good thing is the scene is self-contained, primarily his room and the hotel, I guess. The scene has been sealed. There's a young PC who just arrived on the scene from the Gatwick station who is the First Attending Officer, and there's Hotel security as well, so very little contamination likely."

"I've got the nod from the Chief Super to go ahead, and just to keep him appraised as necessary."

"We must work very fast. We probably have about three days at the most to interview people and to try and get to the bottom of it. We may be able to use the hotel as a temporary incident room during that time, then switch to the Gatwick Station."

"Graham, you will be the Senior Investigating Officer for the investigation. Scott, you will be the assistant SIO. I don't think we need a large team. I don't think it will need HOLMES, the Home Office Large Major Enquiry System, but I suggest you get a team over there pronto, and I think you will need a Forensic Scientist lined up as well."

"Scott, do you remember that little eccentric old Welsh forensic pathologist lady? Sian Parkinson?"

"Quite glamorous, always immaculately turned out. Toxicology specialist. She was on that messy case at Horley a few years ago. That middle-aged woman who murdered her much younger lover and his fiancée. The "Toy Boy" murders. The woman put some obscure poisonous Indian plant in their curry that this lady had a hunch about. Saved us weeks of work."

"She was freelance and semi-retired then, so might be available at short notice."

"Very clever lady. Set up her own home Lab. Converted a spare room into an office, packed it with hi-tech equipment."

"She can work from the post-mortem exam room of the Surrey and Sussex Hospital at Redhill, which is close to Gatwick. She lives in Milford, if I remember correctly her home address is the same. Her home lab might be useful as a backup."

"Get in touch with her immediately. Her number will be on file. Make sure she's still registered with the Home Office. If she's not available, or not registered, work through the list of approved forensics people."

"You will need a Scene of Crimes Officer there as well. Call Mike Selby, I'll give you his number if you haven't got it. He can pick up the van and his box of tricks from here. Tell him approximately what time you want him at Gatwick."

"As it's a police matter now, I will contact Priscilla Stansfield, the Coroner for the Surrey area to report the death. She will request the police to investigate the death on her behalf, and agree to the assignment of a Pathologist, then confirm the Pathologist's name. So don't forget to let me know who is appointed in the end, Sian Parkinson or whoever."

"I will get moving on the Dutch end as quickly as I can. I have a possible contact there who I met when I was on an anti-terrorism course a couple of years ago. He may be able to pull some strings for me. I understand he's in a very senior position in Amsterdam. Very smart. Good guy."

'There he goes again', thought Ian, 'any minute now he'll start calling me 'bro', and using words like 'mug shot' and 'pled'.'

For the moment Barrowclough refrained from any such phraseology and continued.

"I'll ask him to get the facts up to the right people in Holland as a matter of urgency, and for them to come back to me immediately. As soon as I have anything I'll pass the information on to you."

"I have spoken to the Hotel Manager, a Mr Collison, and to a very efficient and composed young lady, a Ms Leila Zafiri. She is the Conference and Meetings Manager at the Median. Discovered the body. She has been closely involved with the Dutch people for some time, so she is the "go-to girl," but keep Collison advised."

"I suggest you use your car, Scott, and you can work out your approach to the case together while you are making your way down to Gatwick."

"I will fix up the main Dutch contact in Holland. Once I have done that, I will contact Zafiri and ask her to provide Holland with the names and any other information on all the Dutch attendees and ask Holland to check to see if there is any "previous" for any of them, and to get Kuppers' health records over to you. All a.s.a.p."

"I've told Collison to make sure Hargreaves stays put until the Forensics person arrives."

"Now, in addition to the main biker group, there is a guy called Dirk Van Heemskerk, who is the Bikers Club President. He is coming over from Amsterdam this morning, to open the meeting, so wasn't in the Median yesterday."

"Zafiri advises me there is also a lady called Angelique Durand involved. She is, or was now, I suppose, Kuppers' partner, companion or whatever. Apparently, she arrived at the Median late last night, but discovered Kuppers' body at the same time as Zafiri this morning. I will ask Zafiri to include both in the "previous" request to Holland."

"I have also arranged with Collison and Zafiri for us to use the Conference room that had been booked for the bikers meeting as our Police Ops Room until Sunday. It was booked until Friday anyway, and fortunately, it had been allocated only for an internal training meeting at the weekend, and they were able to move that without undue difficulty."

"We will then move the Ops Room to the Gatwick Station on Monday morning if the investigation isn't all finished."

"You will also need to stay in the hotel. We don't want you wasting all that valuable time going backwards and forwards to your homes, do we? So, I've asked Collison to provide you both with hotel rooms for the four nights. Make arrangements for someone to get a change of clothes to the hotel for you."

The corners of Barrowclough's mouth turned upwards very, very slightly. It was the nearest he could get to a smile.

"Get in touch with Zafiri and Collison, get your team together, then off you go. You'll have to get to know each other on the job, so to speak."

"Good luck. I'll be in touch concerning the Dutch liaison."

"Always keep me abreast of events but use your initiative. Don't ask me to wipe your bottoms for you."

"Remember, three days. Every minute counts. Remember as well, if it becomes a murder case, everyone is suspected. Even the delightful Leila Zafiri."

He shut the door.

5

Harriet and Ian left Barrowclough's Office and sat together at Ian's desk.

Ian had been impressed with his summary of events, and action plans. No messing around. He hoped Harriet felt the same, but had no chance to ask, as she got down immediately to the business in hand.

"One thing before we start the investigation proper," said Harriet, looking straight at Ian.

"When we are with others, call me 'ma'am' – not 'madam' – but 'ma'am'." She smiled.

"I will call you D.I. Scott, or Scott when we are with others. When we are working together, I am Harriet, and you are Ian. We are a team. OK?"

"Yes, ma'am ...I mean Harriet," he responded.

He had a good feeling about their future working relationship. The "call me madam" comment made it clear that Harriet had read his CV very thoroughly.

Harriet continued.

"You call Selby and Parkinson now. I'll speak to Collison and Zafiri and obtain some quick, summary information from them."

"That will give us some indication of the resources that we might need, apart from the SOCO and Forensics. We'll assemble the team and can always supplement or reduce it as necessary as things go along. I'm sure we won't be far wrong. I'll brief them with whatever we have before we all make our way to the Median."

"In view of the location, one of the sergeants can double up as Exhibits Officer, which will save time and resources. So, whilst I make the calls to Collison and Zafiri get in touch immediately with Mrs Parkinson to find out her availability. That is crucial. Then call Selby and get him on the move. If Mrs P isn't available, we'll have to trawl the Home Office directory."

"I'll then call Collison and Zafiri from the car for more detailed info while you're driving to Gatwick. That's the best utilization of the limited time available. It's about forty minutes or so journey time. That should allow sufficient time for my calls to them, and, after that, to brief you on what has been said to me."

Barrowclough had given Collison and Zafiri's mobile numbers to Harriet. She called Collison first, introduced herself and Ian briefly, but spoke only for a short time. She rung off and turned to Ian.

"I told Collison about the CCTV. He's going to get a Kevin MacAllister, the hotel security manager, to work on that immediately. I told him, for a start, that we want all available CCTV of Kuppers' movements since he checked in to the Median, and activity around his and Ms Durand's rooms, entries and departures from them, and from the second-floor corridor in which his room is situated."

"Anything else we want at this stage we should speak with Leila Zafiri. He has given us "carte blanche" in that respect. No need to check with him unless absolutely necessary. As Barrowclough said, she is the "go to" lady, and has most of the available facts at this stage."

She then called Leila Zafiri. They spoke for about five minutes, with Harriet doing most of the listening.

"I have more questions, Leila."

"You don't mind if I call you Leila, do you?"

Leila answered in the affirmative.

"...but I must wrap up now," Harriet said. "I'll call you again in about 20 minutes. Please make sure you're available."

With that, Harriet rang off, turned to Ian and recounted the main points of her call with Leila. Ian did most of the listening.

Ian had been in luck with both of his earlier calls.

Sian Parkinson was at her Surrey home, and remembered the "Toy Boy" case, Barrowclough and, somewhat more vaguely, himself. He provided her with as much information as he could, based on Barrowclough's briefing. She was immediately interested, and available, as, since her husband's death, she took only a selected few of the cases she was offered.

She wasn't sure what time she could be at the Gatwick Median, maybe early afternoon, but she would let him know. Ian didn't like that much, but he agreed anyway.

He relayed that good, or almost good, news to Harriet.

Sian Parkinson was born Sian Davies, in 1950, in Tre'r Ddol, a small Welsh village where the A487 wound its way through the countryside between Aberystwyth and Machynlleth. A road straightening and widening scheme in the 1970s had bypassed her birthplace, leaving it in an isolated, and somewhat neglected loop off the main road.

An only child, she was educated in the small, Welsh-speaking Eglwys Fach village school, progressing to Ardwyn School in Aberystwyth and then to Aberystwyth University to study sciences. In each of the University vacations, she worked in Mr Roberts Chemist's shop, just at the back of Great Darkgate Street in Aberystwyth. She developed an interest in, and in-depth knowledge of medicines, particularly of the many plants, poisonous and otherwise, that grew in the extensive surrounding countryside.

After graduation, with an eye on a career in the Police, she moved away from Wales to London to study for a Crime and Forensic Science MSc at the University College of London. There she met a much older, divorced, Detective Inspector from the Midlands, Patrick Parkinson.

They subsequently married, and moved to Stourbridge, where she became a Forensic Scientist attached to the West Midlands Police Force.

There she built a significant reputation, and was recognizable, not only for her small stature and striking dark looks, but particularly for her expertise.

Using her knowledge of plant biology she assisted in the solving of several high-profile investigations, including the murder of gangland associate Brian Kinnear, whose partly decomposed body was found under a hedge. Her knowledge of crop husbandry enabled the precise time and location of his killing to be pinpointed.

Following her husband's retirement they moved to Milford, in Surrey. Unfortunately, he died very shortly after they arrived. Afterwards, she became a freelance Forensic Scientist, forming her own company, and it was in that capacity she met Barrowclough, and worked on the "Toy Boy" case.

Mike Selby was the SOCO. Which is the acronym for a Scenes of Crime Officer.

A Scenes of Crime Officer is not a police officer but employed by constabularies across the country as police civilian staff, a member of the police family.

Selby was an experienced officer, at the top end of the salary band for the role. He had worked with the Surrey and Sussex Force on several occasions in the past, although not directly with Ian. In relation to this particular investigation, he had the useful attribute of his entry qualification in forensic science.

In his early thirties, Selby appeared older than his age. Bespectacled, he was stocky, with Brylcreem-ed, carefully parted black hair. He was dressed as if his outfit had come out of the shop window of the Fifty Shilling Tailors in 1951-all sober greys and blacks. He looked altogether like the reliable, meticulous individual that he was. He had an excellent reputation for his thorough and knowledgeable approach. If there were any hidden clues in Kuppers' room, then Selby wasn't going to miss them.

Ian had briefly explained the circumstances of the case to him, and he was very keen to be involved. The poison factor seemed to attract him like a dog with a bone.

He seemed delighted with the assignment and ready to collect his equipment from the Guildford HQ and make his way promptly to the Median. His only problem was shortage of time, as he had another job that day which he could defer, but not postpone, but Ian grabbed the chance to utilize him, and instructed him to get himself and his equipment to the Median a.s.a.p.

*

Harriet had scribbled a rather hurried note and proceeded to read it out in a terse manner, abbreviated for the purposes of speed.

"OK Ian, as now- and it may change- these are the resources I think we need."

"SIO, myself. Assistant SIO, yourself."

"Roughly 10 people to interview, to begin with. Shortage of time. So, three sergeants, and two constables. That may reduce after the first couple of days. One Office Manager, who can also act as Receiver. One typist. One Exhibits Officer, and we'll use one of the sergeants for that role. One SOCO - Selby, and, of course, our Forensic pathologist, the famed Sian Parkinson, who you have got on board. I am looking forward to meeting her."

"You know the other people. If there is a choice, you choose them. Collect them now. If they're working on anything urgent already, then they aren't now. This is the A1 priority. Explain that this case is likely to be quick, but exciting and interesting. Anyone missing, leave them a message."

"I'll be briefing them in five minutes."

Ian gathered the team together. All were available, apart from the intended typist, who had the morning off. Ian drafted in another available replacement.

Apart from the Forensic Pathologist, Sian Parkinson, and the Scene of Crimes Officer Selby, both of whom would be going straight to the Median Hotel, the team was complete and ready to head for Gatwick.

Harriet stood up to deliver the briefing, the team sitting scattered around in a loose semi-circle in front of her. She introduced herself, but made little reference to her career, as she knew a memo and e-mail had been circulated to them following her appointment.

She asked each of them to name themselves in turn and welcomed them all to her team. She gave a rapid summary of the known facts of the investigation, emphasized the need for speed and accuracy, and told them to make their way to the Gatwick Median as soon as possible, car sharing "de rigeur" and report to herself and Ian on arrival at the hotel.

6

As Ian and Harriet walked together through the station and across the car park. Harriet spoke.

"One good thing is that the crime scene, or the scene of unexplained death, is at a hotel where everyone we might need to see immediately is, or should be, on hand."

"The other good thing is CCTV. Hopefully, the hotel will have an up-to-date system. I've told Collison already to obtain as much CCTV footage of the Doves as he can, particularly that around Kuppers' room."

They located the car, a rather battered Vauxhall Astra. Harriet, having not seen it before, looked at it somewhat askance. "No James Bond car chases, just routine usage," Ian smiled.

He got into the driver's seat and wrestled with the seat belt.

"I want to be at the Median Hotel as soon as you can get there," said Harriet.

"Then I suggest we take the scenic southern route," said Ian, before starting the car. "The A25 through Shere and Gomshall, then just before Dorking turn off down to Beare Green and from there cross-country through Newdigate and Charlwood to the airport. That section is all country lanes. I used to have a girlfriend in Horsham, and I know the area like the back of my hand. We spent a lot of time admiring the scenery around there."

"Theoretically, it's a bit slower than going north first, but it keeps us off the dreaded M25, where you're never sure of anything. The road to hell may have made Chris Rea a fortune, but it's never been a friend to me. The longest car park in the world."

"The scenic route doesn't usually have much traffic on it, either, and if I really put my foot down, which I will, I reckon I can make it in forty-five minutes or so."

"Ok, off we go, down the road less travelled, then. Watch out for frost, though," said Harriet.

"No frost at this time of year," replied Ian, with a puzzled look.

"Don't worry about it," she remarked. "I'll explain later."

Ian turned the key in the ignition. The engine started somewhat hesitantly, and the battered Astra headed off along Margaret Road.

Harriet got through to Leila Zafiri very quickly, and they spoke together for about ten minutes, Harriet taking notes as she went along, before she rang off. She looked down at her notes.

"I wish I could write as fast as you," Ian observed, turning onto the A25.

"Greggs," replied Harriet.

"Greggs?" queried Ian, "You mean the sandwich place? What's that got to do with anything?"

"No," smiled Harriet, "Gregg's shorthand. Fastest shorthand method in the world. Some people can do 250 words per minute. Taught myself. I find it a big help in these sorts of circumstances. Only teasing you."

"Here's the information we have now, which includes the latest good word from Ms Zafiri, just told to me."

"Barrowclough has already given us the background-Doves, Van Heemskerk, Durand and so on, so I won't repeat all that."

"The plans were for most of them to be at the Median for four nights. Tuesday until Friday. Leaving on Saturday morning. Most arriving sometime Tuesday afternoon. They have talks, AGM, and all that stuff in the hotel Conference facilities, but trips out on three days. Meet up in the evenings for group dinners together."

'So she almost speaks in shorthand as well,' thought Ian as Harriet continued. 'It's Greggspeak I suppose', recalling the film of Orwell's 1984, and making the analogy.

"The dead man - Kuppers - was the chief organizer. The advance stuff was done mainly from Holland, but he had visited for a day the week before, and arrived this Monday afternoon, the day before most of the others, both visits to check on things 'on the ground'."

"He worked very closely with Leila Zafiri who, as Barrowclough told us, is the Conference and Meetings Manager for the hotel. She reports to the Hotel Manager, Collison."

"The Durand woman and then Leila were the first to find Kuppers body this morning, so they are key witnesses, and priority for the first interviews."

Before Ian could comment, Vivaldi's "Four Seasons," the classical music ringtone that Harriet had chosen for her mobile, sounded.

Barrowclough came through on the phone.

"Graham. It's Bob Barrowclough."

"I have a couple of things from my contact in Amsterdam. He is a guy called Jordi Haan. I mentioned I was on the anti-terrorism course with him a few years ago."

"He will ensure that the Dutch will contact you as a priority, as soon as they have any information as to "previous" with any of the Doves, Kuppers' health records and any other important information. I would expect that to be reasonably fast."

"Information on the Durand woman will probably be later. You will have to form your opinions on her when you interview her as to how much data on her you might need."

"Secondly, Jordi has given me some info on the Van Heemskerk guy which may help you."

Harriet picked up her pencil and notebook, listening intently, although having to strain at times with the noise created by the Astra's tyres and suspension as they engaged with the typically uneven patchwork surfaces of a British road, then utilizing her rapid Gregg's again.

Barrowclough finished, wished her good luck, asked her to keep him posted, and then ended the call.

Harriet relayed to Ian the latest information that Barrowclough had passed on to her, then moved on to Van Heemskerk.

"Now, this Dirk Van Heemskerk, the Doves President," Harriet paused. "Let's call him Van from now on ...but not to his face just yet."

Ian interrupted, "He'll be a White Van Man, then," he remarked, giving Harriet an amused sideways glance, as he went round a couple of sharp bends almost on two wheels, with the tyres squealing in protest.

She smiled and carried on.

"As I was saying, this Van is also known to the Dutch police."

"What did he do then, poison his boss?"

"Now, now," said Harriet, "That's two jokes in two minutes. That's your daily allowance gone."

"I'll put in for a raise."

"Back to the matter in hand," said Harriet, her tone becoming more serious.

"Barrowclough has just told me that Van's relationship with the Dutch police is in fact very positive. His record is clean. Not the slightest blemish, in fact just the opposite, and here's the reason."

"You may possibly recall that, a few years ago, a Keruva Airlines MV20 light aircraft went down shortly after takeoff on a flight from Bali to Jakarta, killing everyone on board. One of the passengers was one of the cousins of the Dutch Royal family. Van was at the time the Head of Engineering for Fokland in Indonesia, and Fokland were the manufacturers of the plane. The Dutch police suspected foul play, but Van was on the spot, went out to the site and very quickly identified the cause as contaminated fuel, which was proved correct. Saved the Amsterdam force money, time, and manpower utilization, and enhanced their standing with some very grateful royals."

"Ever since then, Van has been the "blue-eyed boy" as far as the Dutch police are concerned."

"So, Barrowclough and I agree. We think this Van could be an extremely useful asset in this investigation. Assuming the death is a deliberate act, and that's my inclination at present, and isn't a "Murder on The Orient Express" solution number two job, then Van is very unlikely indeed to be implicated."

"In view of his position, he is likely to have been a member of the Doves for some years, he would know all the members who are at the Median. He may know Kuppers and Vonk well. Speaks Dutch, of course, which may come in handy at some point."

"We should buttonhole him, Collison and Zafiri immediately, then we can properly scope the investigation, brief our team more fully, and get on with things."

"Get the SOCO and Sian Parkinson together on the scene immediately. It isn't normal practice to have the forensic pathologist straight at the scene, but in this instance, I think it will be time well spent. We already have Hargreaves' opinion, and he will be on hand, and so we can cover a lot of ground before she arrives."

7

Dirk Van Heemskerk had just cleared customs after landing at Gatwick South Terminal on the KLM early Wednesday morning flight from Amsterdam. Van cut a dapper, patrician figure, tall and angular, with a trim grey whisper of a moustache, and a full head of carefully barbered grey hair. He was wearing a light grey suit, open collared white shirt, and tan-coloured brogues. Well-respected and popular, he was the President of "The Doves".

The Doves were a good bunch, he thought, although Vonk was a bit of an odd one, a loner. He couldn't quite figure him out. His "Motovonk" business consumed a good deal of his time, and so he was often away, attended fewer of the meetings than the others, and consequently had less interaction with the other Doves.

With Kuppers, too, it could be hard to penetrate his ostensibly charming exterior.

Van admired the gleaming chromium of the Hell's Angels Harley "Road Kings "and "Road Glide "models with their personalised longer fork ends and louder exhausts, and their attention to their vehicles, but the Doves were different.

Apart from Vonk, they were retired, or semi-retired businessmen, most between 50 and 70. The majority had been employed as engineers or in engineering. Their speciality was the restoration of classic motorcycles, amongst them a couple of Ducati 250s, a Norton 16H, a Kawasaki Hi Mach III, and the iconic Husqvarna Viking

360cc, the model made famous by the 1960s actor Steve McQueen.

They were real experts. Precise people with encyclopedic knowledge of the component parts of classic motorcycles. People who had spent a great deal of time immersed in the world of coil valve springs, clutch chain wheels, Amac carburettors, Ewart's fuel taps and gearbox sprockets.

Whilst Vonk was extremely knowledgeable in the field of classic motorcycles and had several very valuable machines garaged on his Doventenar property, none of these were self-built. They had all been commissioned, at significant expense, from the renowned Heuveland Brothers business in Amstelveen.

Van had finished his business on Tuesday and was looking forward to the Conference, particularly the visits to Heskey and Brooklands. All his PowerPoint presentations were prepared. They, and the videos of the past years' events, were all on a memory stick in his briefcase.

He knew that everything would run like clockwork with Piet Kuppers in charge of the arrangements. Kuppers wasn't best-liked amongst the Doves, but he was certainly the most efficient.

Van Heemskerk probably knew him better than the other Doves. They had worked together in Indonesia and Japan – they were both career employees on the engineering side of the Fokland Aircraft Company. Van Heemskerk was the more senior, ultimately reaching the position of Head of Engineering for the Far East.

However, they hadn't worked together in England. Van Heemskerk had been instrumental as a consultant when Eurair leased several Fokland aircraft in the late 1980s but had returned to the Far East just before Kuppers commenced his assignment to the UK as one of the engineers responsible for the fleet of newly acquired Fokland F30A Aircraft to be based at Gatwick Airport.

He thought about Kuppers for a moment. Not a straightforward character. Excellent worker, of course. Charming on first meeting, but not quite so charming on further acquaintance. A ladies' man. Yes, ladies seemed to like him more, or at least be attracted to him more, than men, and then there were those Indonesia rumours, although I neither knew nor bothered to investigate any further details about that situation.

He glanced at his watch as he made his way towards the inter-terminal shuttle that ran between the Gatwick South and North terminals. It was about 9.15 am, just about right for the 11.30 am start of the Conference, he thought. Time to settle in, check the Meeting Room and equipment set up with Leila Zafiri and run through my introductory presentation.

As he stepped onto the shuttle, the shrill ring of his mobile phone made him start a little. He took the nearest available seat. "Hello," he said, lifting the phone to his ear. "Mr Van Heemskerk?" queried the voice at the other end of the line.

"Yes, who is speaking, please?"

"This is Matthew Collison. I'm the Hotel Manager at the Median Hotel. I believe you knew my predecessor Bill Worthington."

"Yes, yes, we knew each other from many years ago."

"I'm afraid I have some bad news for you, Mr Van Heemskerk. There has been a fatality at the hotel. One of your party, a Mr Piet Kuppers, the group organiser, has been found dead in his room a short time ago. The circumstances of the death are unexplained, and the UK ambulance and police services have been called."

"I assume you are almost at the Hotel, as we checked the arrival time of your flight. When you arrive at the hotel, come to reception. They will direct you to my office, and we will speak more fully then."

"Good heavens," Van exclaimed. "That is shocking news. Terrible news. I have just boarded the shuttle at the South Terminal. I'll be with you very shortly and will come to your office immediately. I will, of course, be at your disposal for any assistance you may require."

8

Ian had made the turn down towards Horsham and branched off into the country at Beare Green. He took the narrow roads through Newdigate, then Parkgate and into Blanks Lane, progressing to Charlwood.

"Nice scenery," remarked Harriet, looking out of the window.

"Yes, the upholstery of the back seat of an MGB GT is very attractive," Ian remarked.

"Quite," said Harriet, "but the good word has it that you are a very happily married man, these days."

"Absolutely true," said Ian, "couldn't be happier."

They were just proceeding along the Horley Road, skirting the perimeter of the Gatwick North Terminal. They had made the airport comfortably under Ian's forecasted time, and would arrive about fifteen to twenty minutes before the others.

It was then that Harriet's phone rang. She answered.

"Graham. It's Barrowclough here again," Harriet could sense the urgency of his tone. "Where are you?" He asked.

Harriet told him their position.

"Is there somewhere you can pull off the road?"

"Give us a minute," replied Harriet. "Ian, pull off the road as soon as you can… look, just up there, about twenty yards, it's a turn-off to the industrial estate. We can park up somewhere unobtrusive."

Ian took the turning and found a quiet spot in front of a disused garage.

Barrowclough continued. "The Kuppers investigation. It's just got very messy, political, very political. There's no one else with you apart from Scott, is there?"

"No sir, just us. Can I switch the speaker on in order that Scott can hear as well?"

"Go ahead. No problems."

"Let me fill you in quickly. While you've been enjoying your nice little jaunt through the West Sussex sticks, I've had the Chief Super bending my ear, and his orders come from the very top."

"As you know, I spoke with Jordi, my Dutch contact earlier, explaining the situation, and he gave me some immediate info that I passed on to you."

"He also presumably fed up the facts of the Kuppers saga that I had told him to his superiors."

"It may have passed you by, and it certainly did me, but about a month ago, the Dutch General Election produced a surprise win for the very Right Wing "Friends of Holland" party. Their leader, and now Prime Minister, being a Mr Wopke Weibes, or however you pronounce it."

"Two weeks ago, his newly appointed Minister of Justice, a guy called Arnold de Boer, was killed in a car accident."

"Now it transpires that friend Kuppers is, or rather was, a university buddy of Weibes. They continued to keep in touch occasionally after university. Meals together, Birthday and Christmas Cards and all that. Since Kuppers' retirement, he has been seeing a lot more of Weibes. Apparently, they were meeting every month. What was discussed I have no idea."

"Anyway, Kuppers was on the contact list kept by the Police and IAVD - Dutch Intelligence. They contacted Weibes immediately. First, his Justice Minister and now his mysterious drinking buddy are both dead within a short space of time. Co-incidence? Misfortune? Possibly."

"Anyway, the events have spooked Weibes and the "Friends," and he has spoken with the PM. The upshot is that they both want this case wrapped up very quickly, but they also want it very low-key, which is why you are going to continue to handle the case. Just a normal local force investigation but take care. Don't mention the Kuppers/Weibes connection to anyone unless anything is proffered to you in an interview or conversation."

"Handle any press interest very cautiously. If there are any reporters who can connect Kuppers to Weibes, and there shouldn't be, tell them you can't release any information until the next of kin can be contacted, and that may take some time."

"In the meanwhile, the UK Government are getting a DSMA -the Defence and Security Media Advisory Notice -out pronto. As far as any Hotel guests or curious members of the public are concerned it's a heart attack. The same goes for hotel staff, apart from those like Zafiri who are closer to events. We will deal separately with them. I'll convey that to Collison."

"The line with the Doves is that it is an unexplained death that we, the UK police, have a duty to investigate, and we will provide them with more information as and when."

"There may, of course, be a perfectly innocent explanation, but somehow, I don't think so."

"The Dutch appear to be worried enough to have suddenly doubled Weibe's personal bodyguard count."

"And there's also another complication. A character named Vonk."

"Vonk?" Queried Harriet.

"Yes, Vonk. V-O-N-K. Willem Vonk. He's one of the Doves at the conference, and the founder and owner of a chain of Motorcycle dealerships, Motovonk. Very big deal in Holland and Belgium. Very wealthy, big art collector."

"It so happens that Mr Vonk has a lucrative sideline, in which the Dutch police have been interested for some time, and they knew Vonk was going to be at this shindig well before it started. According to them, he is the mastermind behind a major drug smuggling operation using the baggage handlers at Schiphol Airport, and has used his business, and art collecting, to launder the drug money proceeds for several years."

"The Dutch police have accumulated a lot of watertight, incriminating evidence and now have an IAW -International Arrest Warrant- out for his arrest. They were going to grab him on his return to Schiphol on Saturday, but with all this occurring they are afraid he might hightail it for the hills before then, so you are to keep him under close observation. Don't let him leave the hotel. Make his interview a priority."

"If you suspect he is involved in any way in Kuppers' death, then, as you know, we can only legally hold him, without charge, for 24 hours, and maybe a further 12 hours, which I can authorize as holding the rank of Superintendent. Anything further would need the involvement of a Magistrate and is too time-consuming, and I think, unnecessary. So, in any event, time is of the essence."

"If he is innocent, or even if we have insufficient proof, then I have arranged to call the Dutch police, who will come over immediately to escort him back to Holland. In either of those eventualities, we should provide him with daytime and overnight accommodation in the comfort of a police cell at the Gatwick Station, with an officer to guard him at all times."

"If and when the Dutch police come over there will be two of them. They will be very discreet. Plain clothes, visitors to London and all that. I will give you their names later if that approach is necessary."

"He may be mixed up in this Kuppers business, or not, but remember this is our case. We take precedence if any conflicts of interest arise unless our superiors tell us otherwise."

"Finally, I want to be informed of any developments of importance as they occur."

"Is that clear? Good luck."

There was a very short pause.

"Oh, by the way, just a reminder. As I told you earlier since time is critical in this investigation I've arranged for you both to have single rooms at the hotel for the next few nights, adjacent to each other."

"We don't want you spending all that money travelling backwards and forwards from your homes, do we, and think of all the overtime pay or time in lieu coming to you from all those available extra hours after midnight."

"Don't forget to tell your nearest and dearest not to expect you until this is all cleared up."

Barrowclough sighed audibly.

"Who would have thought that a bunch of ageing foreign geezers on a little jolly could cause an international incident?"

He rang off.

Harriet looked at her watch, then at Ian.

"We're still well ahead of the team. Let's stay here for a while longer, digest what we've heard, and form an outline plan before we go into the Median."

She paused, then spoke.

"Whatever we do, we must do it quickly, but still proceed carefully, and keep it as low profile as possible. A difficult balancing act."

"There are a lot of difficulties to overcome, but, as we mentioned before, there's also a lot going for us, location, early preservation of the scene, certainty of the dead person's identity, and so on."

Time is against us, and we have next to no facts or background information to work on right now. We need at a minimum a good idea of time and cause of death, so forensics is key.

We want Mrs Parkinson here sooner rather than later. I'll call her in a minute. We also need to deploy the SOCO immediately after he arrives. I also want to get a look at the scene without delay, and I want Mrs Parkinson to do the same as soon as she arrives.

Harriet paused. "Just had an afterthought," she said. "As I just said, this has now all got to be low profile. I guess that Mike Selby, the SOCO, will be on his way -just. He'll be coming in a liveried van, with all the gear, cameras, PPE, packaging materials, fingerprinting equipment and so on. Call him and tell him to park his Van around the back of the hotel, as discreetly as possible, and to cart all his stuff up the back stairs if necessary. Speak to Collison and get that arranged. He should also have more than one set of PPE with him, but just check on that for me."

"Now, the other van man. Mr Van Heemskerk."

"On the facts we have about him, I think we have to trust him, so we should involve him quickly. We need him to help carry out my plan, which I'll outline shortly. I'm also confident that the Dutch police will give us whatever information they have promptly."

"So, this is the action plan, as I see it."

"Get ourselves "in situ" asap. Collison said he had it all set up for us."

"This opening meeting, which gathers all the Dutch attendees together, is due to take place at 11.30 am in the Conference Room, and Van Heemskerk was due to address the assembled multitude first off, right?"

Ian nodded, more out of politeness than understanding.

"This gives us the opportunity to keep the Doves all together in the conference room, while our team searches their rooms, then after the searches are completed, they can be taken back to their rooms, one or two at a time for interviews. I will ensure we have master key access to all the rooms of the relevant Doves."

"Fingerprinting of the Doves shouldn't be needed on any significant scale. I want the CCTV available ASAP, and I've already asked Collison to set this up with the Security Manager. I'll get hold of Collison to ask him to add this Vonk character to the priority CCTV footage."

"I think it would be a good idea to look at the CCTV before the key people are interviewed, but not the other Doves."

"The sergeants will take note of the Doves' detailed movements over the time since they arrived at the Median, and we can compare their interview notes with the CCTV findings later."

"Obviously, there will be no CCTV in the rooms, but Collison has confirmed to me that there will be recordings both from the public areas and the corridors. This footage should tell us who had entered or approached Kuppers or Ms Durand's rooms along the corridors since Monday. This may include the Doves, and we may need Van Heemskerk to identify any Doves involved. Collison, or Leila Zafiri can help with the rest at a later stage."

"We will commandeer the Conference Room as our main ops room, as it will have been booked through to Saturday for the Doves anyway. I'll ask Collison for a smaller room for us, close to the main Conference room. I'm sure one will be available."

"The SOCO and Mrs Parkinson can do their business at the scene, and we can interview Leila Zafiri, Angelique Durand, and Vonk."

Harriet thought for a minute or so.

"On reflection, I think it would be better to talk to Van Heemskerk before any of the interviews to see if he has any insights or opinions on the Doves and Kuppers and his death He probably knows them all quite well as they are a small group."

"With the political pressure from the Dutch, I'm sure that Van Heemskerk's cooperation won't be a problem."

"As well as Van Heemskerk we also need Collison, and Zafiri in particular, to give their time, approval, and assistance. So, we will need an immediate meeting with the three of them together to get the whole process moving forward. I'll call Collison to get that set up."

"Comments?"

Ian looked at Harriet.

"I know I've been quiet," he said, "but I've been thinking about the case, not worrying if Brighton are still going to persist with a back four, good idea though that might be."

"A few quick, random observations," he said.

"I think your plan is the right thing to implement at the beginning, and I think you will get the cooperation you want from the main players."

"My hunch is that this is not an accidental death or suicide, so I would just be careful with the glamorous and efficient Ms Zafiri. She is right in the mix. Conference organizer, lots of contact with Kuppers over a period of time, discovered the body, or as good as. No lack of opportunity knocking that's for sure."

"Secondly, poisoning can be difficult. It's hard to determine when any poison might have been administered, what the poison is, how long it takes to kill, and the precise time of death. So, although it may have been alright for the Rolling Stones, time is not on our side. Forensics will have to get a move on. If it requires an autopsy and results from it, that often doesn't happen too speedily. Let's hope Sian Parkinson is not only clever, but faster than the average bear."

"Finally, your plan, as it stands, seems to be predicated on the basis of an inside job, which it probably is, and has to be the first presumption, but I've just got a funny feeling that, whatever the politicians want, this assignment isn't going to be either quick or easy, or both."

"Thanks. Very helpful," said Harriet, "and I thought it was going to be a nice, easy open-and-shut investigation."

"I'll just get on the phone to see if I can find out Mrs Parkinson's ETA. I'll see if I can give her the hurry up. The afternoon is far too late," and she picked up her mobile.

As the phone waited for connection at the other end, she gave Ian a sideways glance.

"By the way, I always prefer two holding midfielders, and to wait for the opposition to make mistakes, then catch them on the counter with our speed merchants."

Ian allowed himself a small, inward smile, appreciative of both the verbal jousting and the knowledgeable nature of the remark.

# 9

I an parked the car and they both entered the Median Hotel. They knew of the hotel, but neither had been through its doors before.

Although built in the 1970s, the façade of the Gatwick Median Hotel was in quasi-art deco style. Each floor was demarcated by plate glass windows set into steel framings arranged in continuous horizontal bands with curved ends. This maintained a streamlined appearance, reinforced by the plain white stucco walls beneath the glass.

This opulent art deco style didn't extend to its much less expensive, and more practical interior. Perfectly adequate, but clearly constructed and furnished with one or more eyes on the profit and loss account and its clientele of business and holiday travellers and conferences and meetings.

One or two nice touches of aircraft memorabilia were scattered around on the lower floors. A Sopwith Camel propellor was screwed tightly to the wall of the restaurant, and a Smith and Sons Motor Aneroid Altimeter and Boeing 747 Cockpit Gauge were securely encased behind toughened glass on the walls of the Conference Rooms.

And there was, of course, "Jason," at which Ian was glancing tentatively upwards. At a lanky six feet four he just avoided the landing wheels.

"Hope it's not an omen," remarked Harriet, "the mystery of her death hasn't been solved to this day."

"Her?" queried Ian. "Amy Johnson," answered Harriet.

"First woman to fly solo from London to Australia. "Jason" was the name of her plane on that flight. Fantastic pilot, but in 1941 she went down over the Thames Estuary during a routine flight. Lots of conspiracy theories."

"Let's hope we have a routine flight and a safe landing, but I've got a funny feeling about this one, for some reason."

They went over to reception and checked into their rooms that Barrowclough had arranged for them but remained in reception, with whom they confirmed the number of Kuppers' room.

Harriet spoke to Ian.

"As we know, the meeting with Leila Zafiri, Matthew Collison and Dirk Van Heemskerk has been set up already. We must find out which room we have been allocated for that meeting, which will also be the room we will be working in together."

"Ask reception to give Collison and the others a bell and assemble them in our designated room."

"I want to quickly familiarise myself with the hotel layout, conference rooms, restaurant, guest rooms, lifts and staircase positionings and so on."

"After that, I want to take a look at the scene of death. Selby should be there, so can provide me with the proper gear, and the FAO, and maybe hotel security will be safeguarding the room. I also want Mrs Parkinson to have a nose around Kuppers' room as soon as she arrives. I know all that is a bit unusual, but I have my reasons."

"Give me a call to tell me the room you will be using. I won't be long, and I'll see you there soon."

With that, Harriet walked down the short flight of stairs in the direction of the restaurant.

Her quick recce completed Harriet headed up the stairs to the second floor then along the corridor to the interconnecting rooms 205, and 206.

A young PC was stood outside the door of 206. Red and yellow striped barrier tape was affixed across the front of the door at waist height. The door to Kuppers' room, 205 was locked. Entry to it was only via 206, the room of Angelique Durand, and then through the interconnecting door.

Harriet introduced herself to the young PC.

"Your SOCO is here ma'am," said Daniel Ryan, the young PC. "He's waiting for you in the room, and he left some gloves and overshoes for you," he said, handing the articles over to Harriet.

"Apart from him only Dr Hargreaves, who is the hotel doctor, has been inside, ma'am, and he had protective clothing, gloves and all that, so the scene will be untouched."

"Mr MacAllister, the hotel Chief Security Officer was here earlier, but he said he had some urgent CCTV work to attend to, and that he thought the room was safely secured, so he left."

"Good work... er... Constable...er...," queried Harriet, donning the gloves and overshoes. "Constable Ryan, Daniel Ryan," he said, providing the answer, and at the same time unhooking one end of the barrier tape to allow Harriet access.

"Let's take a look at the deceased dove, Mr Kuppers," said Harriet, moving towards the door.

The PC held his arm out, in front of Harriet, to halt her progress.

"Excuse me, ma'am. Did you say Kuppers?" he asked. "No one told me his name."

"Yes, Kuppers," Harriet repeated. "Why do you ask?"

"Well ma'am, that seems to me an odd coincidence."

"I was on the duty desk at the Gatwick Station all day yesterday, when a call came in from the Median Hotel, just after I came on duty at about ten o'clock in the morning. One of their guests had either lost their wallet, or it had been stolen.

Apparently, the person wasn't too bothered, so the Median lady said. He told them that the wallet contained a reasonable amount of cash - he gave no exact details of the amount- an Amex Gold Card, and a couple of business cards, but no other personal information.

I thought it was a bit odd. I know I would have wanted to get a wallet with a shedload of money in it back to me as quickly as possible.

The Hotel had sorted the immediate things out, paid for a taxi back for him and so on. They wanted us to keep an eye open in case anyone had handed it in, or phoned in, or whatever, and tell them immediately. They seemed more concerned about it than he did.

The thing was, the gentleman's name was Mr Kuppers, it must be the same Kuppers who is the dead man on the bed. It was an odd name, to me anyway. I remembered it straight away."

"Whereabouts was Mr Kuppers when the wallet was lost?"

"Well, the lady at the Median told me the call was made from "Artimesias," the restaurant at the top of King Street, at the start of the pedestrianised section, so I assume Mr Kuppers was there.

No luck with the return of the wallet, though, unless it's at the station this morning. When I went off duty at six in the evening there was no news at all on the wallet."

"Thank you, PC Ryan. Good job. Well done."

"I would like you to prepare a report for me as soon as possible, describing exactly what you have told me, with your personal impressions and everything, and get it over here. Mark it "urgent," for D.C.I Graham or D.I. Scott. Thanks."

"I want you to stay here until the body is moved, then you are free to go. No one gets in here without my say-so, ok? Here is my mobile number if you have any problems."

Harriet gave him her number, and then went through to view the corpse and its surroundings.

The solid figure of Mike Selby was standing in front of the bed encased in an all-white outfit. Jumpsuit with hood, mask, paper shoes, and latex gloves. He was accompanied by a professional-looking array of photographic and other equipment.

Selby had on display a Nikon SLR camera with wide-angled and close-up lenses; filters to assist in identifying blood, semen, and, in this instance, regurgitated food; flash with radio trigger; a lightweight tripod; memory cards, and photo log and notebook.

On the floor was a pile of assorted police evidence bags in a range of different sizes.

"Good morning, ma'am," he said, lowering the mask. "I've not been here all that long, but I've not been wasting my time."

"Good morning, Mike," responded Harriet. "Glad to hear it. Carry on."

"Well, ma'am, I haven't touched anything in here. I thought I would wait for you before starting on this room."

"What I have done is complete my work in Room 206, the adjoining room we have just come from before moving all my kit in here."

"From the articles there it looks like it would have been occupied, or intended to be occupied, by a lady, possibly Mr Kuppers' partner."

"I have completed the photography, fingerprinting, and examination of the articles in the room."

"No personal articles in any of the drawers, wardrobes, or on the tables, or in the bathroom. Nothing in any of the waste bins. The table had a full jug of water and drinking glass on it."

"On the floor were the following," he took a notebook from his pocket and read from it.

"A locked Gucci Gran Turismo travelling case, re-enforced bright red metal with the gold monogrammed initials "A.D" on the front, apparently unopened; a large shopping bag marked "Chloe of Bond Street," containing a new dress, a large box of 'Abaira' cigarettes with cellophane covering, and a small empty bag, plain white, but of good quality."

"Very few fingerprints anywhere."

"All showing signs of a very brief visit, at some time yesterday or very early this morning."

"You can examine all of this in detail when you wish."

"Excellent work, Mike," said Harriet. "I'm not going to waste any of your time either."

"I just want to take a quick look around, then you can get on. In view of the location and circumstances I expect you to be finished in a further hour to an hour and a half. If they are available and you need them, you could commandeer a couple of the sergeants to help you with the exhibits' side."

Selby nodded, and Harriet walked around the room, carefully examining the body, and all the surroundings without touching or disturbing them.

She went back to stand next to Selby.

"You have probably picked some of these up already, but here are the things I've noticed.

As regards the body, I see that his watch is still showing the correct time, which means that it doesn't provide a specific clue to the time of death and would also support the fact there is no evidence of a physical altercation involving a third party.

The presence of his glasses on his person tends to make suicide less likely. Suicides often take off their glasses, fold them neatly and put them to one side before their final act. There is also no visible suicide note.

There's also the angle of the glasses. Their raised position on the bridge of his nose seems unnatural, even if he were writhing in pain. Just a thought.

Now for the table. Basil Fawlty would have called it the 'bleeding obvious'. On the table is an old-fashioned bottle of 'Bols' and next to it a half-empty glass of clear liquid, presumably also 'Bols'. That would be the first port of call, if you pardon the unintentional pun, for anyone looking for an explanation of a case seeming to involve poison.

By the way, I do know that 'Bols' is Genever, a Dutch gin.

So why, I ask myself, has no one mentioned this to me so far? I can name several people who would or might have known. I don't like it at all.

Finally, making up the set with the bottle and glass, there is this clever little card alongside them. It would appear to have sat over the neck of the bottle and Kuppers had removed it and put it to one side. There is some wording in black script, that I would guess is Dutch.

Clever deduction, eh?"

If Selby had appreciated the jest, he didn't show it.

"...and there was the room number, of Kuppers' room, written in pencil, clearly and distinctly, together with a large pencil asterisk alongside."

"I know you will be all over these items," Harriet said to Selby, "but I will take a picture on my mobile of the bottle and card and obtain a proper translation shortly from Mr Van Heemskerk. He is the Dutch president of the bikers."

"What do you think about my observations, Mike?" Harriet asked.

"Right on the ball," said Selby, "Couldn't have put it better myself at this stage."

He picked up a large aluminium case with a black handle and black reinforced corners and bent over to delve into the contents.

"If you give me your mobile number, I'll give you a call immediately after I have finished, ma'am," he said. Selby was anxious to get moving. Harriet gave him the number and departed. She was "en route" to see Angelique Durand.

Selby had just finished his examination of the room and contents when there was a soft knocking on the door. Selby went across and opened it. Standing there was the petite, beautifully groomed figure of Sian Parkinson. The two already knew each other, so no formal introductions were necessary.

"Hello, Sian. Good to see you. Perfect timing as well."

"Hello, Mike. All looks fairly straightforward, doesn't it?" said Sian. "Which is lucky, since Barrowclough wants it wrapped up in double-quick time, apparently."

"A famous last word is 'straightforward'," retorted Selby. Sian grinned at him.

"If you've finished, I'll take a quick look around then take the rectal temperature of the deceased, since it wasn't done earlier, as it should have been, by Doctor Hargreaves."

She donned a pair of protective gloves and shoe coverings, then spent a few minutes taking in the rooms and the body. Selby knew that, despite the brevity, her mind was working very quickly indeed, absorbing every little detail.

They exchanged a few words on body positioning, facial colouring and expression, and Sian remarked on all of the other matters raised by Harriet earlier.

"Now for the rectal temperature," she said.

"Since he's lying face down that makes the rectal bit relatively easy," she said, fishing a thermometer and small tube of lubricant out of a black instrument bag that she had with her, and checking that her gloves were fitting snugly. The rectal thermometer had a similar bulb-like shape as an oral thermometer but with a shorter and stubbier tip.

She performed the necessary and announced the reading, "80.6 degrees Fahrenheit."

She gave a little smile. "Would you now like to tell me the estimated time of death, Mike? Using the body temperature method."

Selby smiled back. "OK," he said.

"As you well know," he said, "this is only an estimate, based on assumptions, and is a guideline, but here goes."

"The ambient temperature of the room is normal. The usual body temperature of the corpse when alive is 98.6 degrees Fahrenheit. Deduct your body temperature rectal reading from the deceased, of 80.6 degrees Fahrenheit. The result is 18. A dead body cools by 1.50 degrees for each hour from the time of death. So, 18 divided by 1.5 equals 12. Therefore, death occurred twelve hours ago. Time now 11.05 am. So, the time of death 11.05 pm on Tuesday. Approximately," he said with a smile.

"Well done, Mike. Bang on," said Sian, "and not a calculator in sight."

"I will feed this through to Detective Chief Inspector Graham as soon as possible and get the necessary permissions to activate my arrangements for the transfer of the dead body for the postmortem."

Selby nodded. He picked up a separate evidence bag that he had put down on the floor whilst he completed his GCSE mathematics calculations.

"I'm on my way to see the D.C.I as well. With this," he said, indicating the evidence bag. "Let's go along together." They both left the room, acknowledged the young PC guarding the rooms, and went on their way.

Harriet's first call was to visit Kupper's partner, Ms Angelique Durand. She called Leila Zafiri, who advised her that she, Leila, had arranged for Angelique to be taken to the First Aid room, accompanied by Jane Wheeler, the cleaning staff supervisor.

Harriet also contacted Ian and also Collison, to make their way to join her in the First Aid Room.

# 10

A ngelique was there with Mrs Wheeler when they
arrived.

"Mademoiselle Durand?" queried Harriet. Angelique
nodded. "I am Chief Inspector Graham, this is Detective
Inspector Scott and this is Mr Collison, the Hotel Manager."

"How are you feeling?" asked Harriet.

"A little better, thank you," Angelique replied,
"However, I wish for a cigarette. I will go outside with the
cleaner woman." Mrs Wheeler gave Angelique a sharp
glance but refrained from demonstrating to her the effect
of a cleaning woman's fist making contact with a nose of
perfect facial symmetry.

"All right," said Harriet, "but there is in fact no need
for Mrs Wheeler to be with you any further. An officer will
accompany you outside and return with you to this room
and be stationed outside. As I am sure you will appreciate,
we need to speak with you concerning the events of this
morning. I will contact you later to arrange the time and
place for an interview."

"Your room is required for police investigations.
Therefore, Mr Collison has arranged for another bedroom
to be organized for you, and your effects will be transferred
there in due course, and you will be supplied with a key. As
with all the other Doves, your room - the adjoining room
to that of Mr Kuppers - will be searched, which we have
permission from the hotel management to so do."

"There will be no necessity for the officer to be with
you when you are in your new room. You may either order

room service, or dine in the hotel restaurant but you must not leave the hotel unless accompanied by an officer."

"You will no longer be needed further, Mrs Wheeler. You are free to return to your duties. I will wait with Ms Durand until the officer arrives. Thank you for your help," said Harriet.

Angelique said nothing. Mrs Wheeler gave Angelique a farewell stare worthy of the basilisk of Cyrene, both in the manner and the hoped-for outcome of instant death, but when that didn't occur, she limped away at an accelerated pace, muttering to herself.

"I trust the room will be of appropriate standard, comfort, and location?" queried Angelique.

"I'm sure Mr Collison is aware of the requirements of his most valued clientele," said Harriet, disdainfully. "Isn't that so, Mr Collison?"

"Yes, of course," said Collison, "we are a completely guest-focused establishment here." The phrase ran rapidly and automatically off his tongue like a newspaper rolling off the production line.

'Dead bodies assured a complete rest at the Median,' thought Harriet, turning to Angelique.

"You will be called for an interview when appropriate. You may now go with the officer if you still wish to smoke."

# 11

The Dutch authorities had acted speedily. Within half an hour copies of Kuppers' Medical Records, several head and shoulder photographs, and his Government Record Card were on Harriet's laptop.

The text was in Dutch, but the sender had added some helpful notes in English to the email attachments. Harriet ran her eyes over them, then spoke to Ian.

"Here is the gist of it, Ian," she said.

"Health very good. Took a couple of blood pressure tablets each day, Dutch equivalent of amlodipine, ramipril. Common stuff. Non-smoker. Used to play squash, run in his earlier years. No heart problems Moderate drinker of fine wines."

"Photographs with and without beard. Bald, generally clean-shaven. Minor but distinguishing scar on forehead above right eye."

She read over the third part, the record card, again, and then looked up.

She pushed her laptop towards him, "You read it."

"CONFIDENTIAL" had been written across the top in large capital letters.

Ian was able to make out the gist of the document.

Name, age, address, family, education, health, career, a list of financial assets, property interest, hobbies*, which included the membership of the "Doves".

He noted, as Harriet had done, with similar curiosity, his lengthy real name, "Pieter Marius Franciscus Kuppers."

As they had read on the separate Medical Report, his health was given as 'Very Good'.

'One Company' employee, with Fokland Aircraft Company, Amsterdam. His career CV, particularly in his younger years, featured frequent overseas postings. USA: Tulsa (1982) ; Hawaii (1983) ; Thailand(1986-7) ; UK (1989-91) ; Indonesia (1991-92); Japan(1993-4) South Africa (1995).

Notes: a) 2 minor speeding offences Tulsa 1982, Hawaii 1983.

b) 1990 (12.5) Traffic Accident Crawley. No fault involvement. Uninjured. Company car written off.

Retired 2007 (Age 50)

Harriet waited for Ian to finish reading.

"Notice anything?" she asked.

"Yes," replied Ian, "I wish I had one-half of one per cent of his assets."

"Apart from that."

"Yes," said Ian, "Why is there an asterisk against 'hobbies'? And where's page two?"

Harriet smiled, "Would you like to do my job?" she remarked.

"Yes again," said Ian, "and in the not-too-distant future."

Harriet smiled again, but she knew he was serious.

They were both correct. The asterisk couldn't be explained immediately, but at the very bottom of the page were the figures "1 of 2". But page two wasn't there.

Harriet picked up her mobile, and dialled Barrowclough's number.

"I've just received an email from the Dutch authorities, sir, a Cornelius Anholts. I think from their equivalent of our Home Office. I didn't see you on copy, and I think it should have come through you first, but I'll just give you the details, and I have a few requests, but I'll give you a quick update on general progress first."

She went through a summary of the overall situation, and then came on to the Kuppers data and his record card. Before she could commence relaying the information on the card, Barrowclough interrupted.

"Too damn right it should have come through me first. What the hell do they think they're playing at," he spluttered. Harriet tried to envisage the apoplectic fit occurring at the other end of the line.

"I'll sort that out right away. Now what were the things you wanted to ask me about?"

"Two things, sir, but I'd appreciate it if you ask the questions - and get the answers - before you rip their heads off."

"One. I know Kuppers' record card info should have been two pages, but only one seems to have been sent. When you speak to the Dutch sender, ask why we haven't got page two, and get a copy to me straight away."

"Two. They haven't sent a similar record card for Vonk. If nothing comes through for him we will have to interview him without it and rely on what we have gleaned from Van and Leila Zafiri. Too short of time otherwise."

They ended the conversation.

"Let's get hold of Mister Security, MacAllister," she said to Ian. Call Collison and get him to tell MacAllister to come to see us without delay. I want as much information from CCTV as possible, and as quickly as possible, and I want to brief MacAllister as to his priorities.

# 12

Kevin MacAllister was a squat, very wide man, with muscle and fat stretching his shiny grey suit into bulbous, balloon-shaped pockets in various bodily locations. His neck, ears, and lips were all thick, and his head was topped with a closely cropped crew cut. Each hand protruding from his shiny sleeves resembled a bunch of concrete-coated South American Fairtrade bananas.

Despite his white shirt, blue tie, and black shoes as shiny as his suit, he gave off a rather menacing, pugilistic appearance, akin to a night club bouncer, in which position he had in fact once been employed previously, keeping the shady, violent East End denizens of the Double D Club in order.

Imagining him in vest and tights, he reminded Harriet of a Rowlandson sketch of the famous bare-knuckle boxer of the early 19th Century, Bristolian Tom Cribb.

Harriet and Ian both eyed him up and down.

"Now then, Ian," Harriet whispered the aside. "You'd better not let him see you taking those extra apples out of the Breakfast Room tomorrow."

She addressed MacAllister and performed the introductions.

"Detective Inspector Scott and I are leading the investigation of the, so far, unexplained death of a hotel guest, a member of a Dutch Motorcycle group who are meeting here over the next few days.

You will be aware of these facts already, and will have commenced your retrieval work, but I prefer to cover the ground thoroughly.

We need to resolve this matter with the utmost urgency, and we have a very limited amount of time available. The hotel CCTV footage will be a key element of this investigation.

From your footage we need to know as much as possible about the recorded movements of the dead man, Mr Piet Kuppers, who was occupying Room 205; Ms Angelique Durand, the occupant of the connecting Room, 206; and the other members of the group, whose names and room numbers will be given to you by Ms Zafiri. Of that group, we are particularly interested in a Mr Willem Vonk, Room 504.

We will take those three people as a priority now. Anything else we will pick up later.

Mr Kuppers was visiting, but not staying at the Hotel on Tuesday, May 10th. He then returned this past Monday, May 16th. Ms Durand was due to check in late last night.

Vonk was arriving Monday night. The other members of the Doves were also arriving yesterday afternoon, at varying intervals.

We need to see as much internal footage as you have from the corridors, entrance lobby and other communal areas, and anything outside, car parks etc. As it is all recent, I assume you will be able to retrieve all this information quickly and without difficulty."

Mac Allister moved his thick chin down towards his thick neck in a nodding motion.

"Good," said Harriet.

"We will be interviewing all those people over the remainder of the day, and also searching their rooms My officers will do that, and our Scenes of Crime officer is already at work in Kuppers and the connecting room of Ms Durand.

I guess you will already have some of this work in hand. How long will it take you to produce the rest of that information we need?"

MacAllister pondered for a moment. "About an hour and a half to go through everything and get it organized."

"That's fine. Go ahead. Detective Inspector Scott and I have an important meeting at 11.30, and some of our time may also be needed immediately following that meeting." "As we have, said your information is very important to us, so complete your work and keep yourself on standby." "Don't go anywhere. One of us will give you a call as soon as possible to arrange to meet up with you in your CCTV room."

13

It was as Ian had said. Van had checked in quickly, leaving his overnight case with reception, but carrying his briefcase. They all met in the small office allocated to Harriet and Ian.

It was Harriet and Ian's first face-to-face meeting with Leila Zafiri and Dirk Van Heemskerk, and they agreed that both protagonists were a rather uncanny fit, in appearance, and subsequent manner, to their imagined profiles.

Leila Zafiri was a strikingly beautiful, slim, Eurasian young woman in her mid-thirties, with jet black hair, large eyes of a very deep brown and open, trustworthy, face and dressed in the Median uniform of a tailored mid-blue jacket, black skirt and sensible black shoes.

The "Van Man" was very much the tall, authoritative and smartly dressed figure that had emerged on his arrival at the airport. If a hair on his head had been displaced it would have made headlines on the "DutchNews.nl" website.

A guess at his age would have been in his early seventies, although later actuality proved him to be older than his appearance. He gave off a friendly, but calmly authoritative air, and he spoke grammatically perfect English, delivered with impeccable intonation.

He looked as though he had just walked out of a Savile Row tailor, or the de Oost shop in the Amsterdam Valeriusstraat, and not someone who had a short time ago hurried from a busy early morning short-haul aircraft and through a crowded airport to be told that a long-standing colleague had just died suddenly and surprisingly.

Collison continued to present the same appearance and manner as they had seen in their brief visit to Angelique in the First Aid Room.

He was a tall, thin man in his late thirties, with a very white face, and long jaw. Large, black-framed glasses were perched on an aquiline nose. He looked smart, wearing a grey suit, white shirt, and blue tie. His demeanour seemed somewhat dour for a customer relations business, but he dealt with everything quickly and very efficiently.

Harriet took Van to one side, whilst Ian engaged the others in small talk. She took out her mobile and showed Van the pictures of the genever bottle and the card.

"Could you provide me with a translation of the words on the card, please, Mr Van Heemskerk?" Harriet asked.

Van Heemskerk peered at the screen of the mobile.

"The message on the card reads as follows," he said, in a very precise manner.

"*Here is a small gift to welcome you to the meeting of Motorclub Doventenar. Median Hotel Gatwick, May 2016*"

"Thank you, Mr Van Heemskerk," said Harriet. "Were you aware that this gift was to be given to Mr Kuppers, and have you any idea by whom?"

"It is a complete surprise to me, but Willem Vonk may be involved in some way. I am aware that he is financing almost all of the costs of this conference from his own resources, but this is to hazard a guess only."

"Thank you," said Harriet, and they rejoined the group.

Harriet outlined her plan, and all three were keen to support the investigation and agreed with the plan. Zafiri and Van Heemskerk for altruistic reasons, Collison's were reputational. His own, and that of the hotel, in that order. His eyes were clearly on a future promotion as quickly as it could be achieved.

They agreed to gather in the Conference room at 11.10 am, to be there before the Doves, organize the seating for themselves and the Doves, and raise any last-minute thoughts or concerns that anyone might have had.

Harriet told them all, and particularly Leila, to be available at any time after the 11.30 am meeting for further discussions with herself, Ian or either of the sergeants.

She looked up at Ian. "OK, Detective Inspector Scott," said Harriet "Let's go and watch some TV, shall we? They might even be showing 'Lonesome Dove'."

14

Tucked unobtrusively around a corner at the end of a long 8th-floor corridor to which guest entrance was barred, an unmarked door led to the hotel CCTV Control Room.

Mac Allister operated the combination lock on the wall, and the heavy metal door swung open.

He led the way inside and pushed down a circular light switch on the wall with a stubby finger. The room was filled with a harsh white light.

The set-up was far more professional than Harriet had feared.

Neat banks of smaller screens were arranged around a much larger one. There was a row of computer chairs and several grey steel filing cabinets along the far wall, with small white cards on their fronts carefully labelled in black lettering. Alongside those was a large desk with a brown leather top. By this time Harriet wasn't surprised to see that the papers on the desk were in neat stacks. MacAllister was continuing to disprove her expectations.

"There we are," pronounced MacAllister proudly.

"First thing I did after I took the job three years ago. Converted this from an old storeroom. You won't find better in any similar size hotel in the UK."

He adjusted the circular control until the room was dimmed.

The screens which each showed different areas of the hotel were constantly flickering in arrhythmic motion, and gave the room an eerie feel.

'Just like the fairground ghost train on Brighton's Palace Pier,' thought Harriet. It was almost as if the body of Fred Hale was about to appear at any moment.

Instead, a swivel Ergo Mesh computer chair with arms was spun around from its position facing the large screen. Doing the spinning was a thin, pasty-faced young lad, casually dressed in blue jeans and trainers. A black T-shirt emblazoned with the words "Simon is A" in white letters, and underneath the name was a large white capital "W" and white anchor leaning against it.

"This is Simon," said MacAllister.

"I've almost worked that out," said Ian, "nearly, but not quite. Hello, Simon."

"Simon has been working on your requests, so I'll let him show his findings to you. I'll only comment if necessary."

"Bring up a few chairs," said Simon, "so you can all see the big screen."

He typed some instructions into a keyboard alongside him. The screen flashed, and up came the name "Kuppers. Tuesday 10th May 2016."

The quality of the CCTV pictures was excellent. They watched the chunky figure come through the revolving door at the entrance and approach the reception desk. The time was 7.30 am. He was carrying only a large black business briefcase.

The remainder of the film for that day showed him meeting Leila and Collison, entering and exiting the large Conference room, leaving and returning to the Median briefly in the afternoon, and finally leaving the hotel at around 5.30 pm.

"Nothing particularly out of the ordinary, there," said Simon, "so let's proceed to this week, starting with Monday." The screen flashed up "Monday 16th May".

Simon went quickly through Kuppers' movements as picked up by the CCTV cameras.

"So, Monday 2.00 pm he checks in, with a suitcase, at reception and goes straight to his room. 3.00 pm he met with Leila Zafiri, the Conference Manager. Spends some time in the main Conference Room. Retires to his room at 4.15 pm. 7.15 pm Room Service comes along and delivers a meal, and he doesn't appear again until the next morning."

Harriet had rapidly revised her initial impressions as Simon continued to disprove the message on his self-deprecating T-shirt with his organized and efficient presentation.

The screen moved on to Tuesday 17th.

"Kuppers was seen leaving the hotel just before 8.20 am to take a taxi from the hotel forecourt, and then returning at 10.00 am, again by taxi, then proceeding to reception, where he was in conversation with the receptionist for several minutes. He went to the coffee lounge on the ground floor, drank a couple of cups of coffee, and made notes on a piece of paper, I think provided by reception, returning to his room at 10.35 am.

He wasn't seen again until 12.50 pm, when he left the hotel. This time no taxi. He turned right and walked away from the hotel.

He returned to the hotel at 2.45 pm and went to his room.

He left his room at 3.55 pm, went to the Conference room, and met Leila Zafiri there at 4.00 pm, emerging at 4.20 pm. He returned to his room at 4.25 pm, and that was the last time, probably, that he was seen alive, or certainly the last time he was seen on the hotel CCTV."

"Hold it there, Simon," said Harriet. "I just want to make a quick phone call."

She picked up her mobile and dialled.

"Leila Zafiri," the voice answered.

"This is Detective Chief Inspector Harriet Graham. Could I ask you a quick question?"

"Go ahead," replied Leila.

"We know you met Mr Kuppers at around 4 pm yesterday, in your office."

"Do you know what he was doing in the few hours before that, say from 1 pm until the time he met you?"

"Not for all of that time, but I know what he was supposed to have been doing between 1 pm until 2.30 pm or so. He was to be lunching at the Kamada Japanese restaurant, just a short walk from the hotel."

"Very swish. It's always booked well in advance."

"He told me he had made arrangements some time ago for that specific date, and that he had been to Japan on several occasions, business and pleasure, and was a connoisseur of Japanese cuisine, but he had never eaten at the Kamada, and was looking forward to the experience."

"In fact, he had asked me a couple of times, on his previous visit, if I would join him for that lunch date, but, charming though he was, I pleaded pressure of work, and opted out."

"May I ask you if you ever felt that invitation was intended to be an offer of more than a business discussion?"

Leila didn't seem fazed or upset by that question. "Possibly," she responded, "but I showed no interest, nor did I have any, but he was very persistent and flattering."

"It was rather odd, though, that by his arrival on Monday, he had changed his mind. We bumped into each other in the hotel, and he said he still wanted me to dine with him at the Kamada, but it would be better at a later date. It was almost as if he wanted to be alone yesterday lunchtime, or at least not with me. Maybe he had someone else lined up. Jane Wheeler, perhaps?"

Harriet let the sarcasm go.

"My last question. We know he felt ill, and cut short your meeting, but did he mention the Kamada? If he had appreciated the food and the ambience, whether it lived up to its reputation, and how you would enjoy it together at some time in the near future? That sort of thing."

"No. He said nothing of the meal at all, or meeting me outside of my working hours. Just Conference business."

"Thank you, Leila. We will need to talk to you later and will be in touch about that. Keep yourself available."

With that, Harriet rang off.

"Carry on Simon," she said, "Keep up the good work."

Simon continued.

"The only other entrant to his room during this time was Ms Zafiri, who entered the room at 11.10 am, with what looked like a bottle and card."

Simon zoomed the screen to better show these articles.

"She left the room no more than a couple of minutes later, without them.

..and now, let's turn to the delightful Ms Durand. Room 206.

We shouldn't forget that rooms 205 and 206 have an interconnecting internal door, with just a door handle, without any lock, so any entrant to either room could also gain easy access to the other.

She arrived at reception at 11.35 pm, wearing a lightweight coat, black trousers, and black boots. She was holding two carrier bags, a big one with a large letter "C" on the side and another, slightly smaller, black, with a funny-looking crest on it. She checked in and took the lift to her room.

Earlier in the day, just after 1.00 pm, her room had been entered by one of the hotel porters, carrying a Louis Vuitton monogrammed, pink-coloured travel suitcase, and a smaller St Lauren, cream vanity bag.

He left and re-locked the room at 1.05 pm.

She entered room 206 at 11.40 pm, and then left it, very soon afterwards, at 11.45 pm, carrying the vanity bag, the large carrier bag and the briefcase.

Now, what different feature do you notice about her appearance when she left the room?"

He looked at Harriet and Ian. He deliberately didn't zoom in on the elegant figure.

"You mean the gloves?" asked Ian.

"Very good," said Simon.

"Not wearing them from reception to entering the room, but on the way out she is featuring a nice pair of cream leather gloves."

He gave Harriet a knowing stare, then turned back to operate the computer controls. A picture of Angelique exiting the room, with gloves on, appeared. She was carrying one of the shopping bags and the vanity case.

"Thanks, Simon," said MacAllister. "I'll take over for a few minutes."

"Any guesses where she is headed now?" he questioned.

Blank looks all around.

They watched as she went down the corridor at a leisurely pace and summoned the lift. The screen went blank for a second, then showed her leaving the lift.

"Fifth floor," MacAllister informed them, as she emerged, with accoutrements.

She walked unhurriedly down the deserted corridor, not concerned that anyone might be following her, paused to check the room number on the door, and then knocked twice. The occupant answered quickly, and she went in.

MacAllister looked at them and spoke slowly and deliberately.

"Room 504."

"Occupant, our friend Mr Willem Vonk."

Harriet and Ian exchanged glances.

"Carry on Simon," said MacAllister, and Simon returned to performing the commentary.

"She is next seen leaving room 504, together with Mr Vonk at 7.45 am, making their way to the breakfast room. At 8.25 am she leaves the breakfast room, together with Ms Zafiri, and they go to Ms Durand's room, using the entry key to her door.

Just before 8.40 am Mr Vonk leaves the breakfast room and makes his way to Ms Durand's room, knocks at the door, and she lets him in. He is carrying a distinctive red leather document holder. Shortly afterwards, Ms Zafiri leaves Ms Durand's room and goes down the corridor to the cleaner's room."

Harriet interjected, "Leaving Mr Vonk alone with Ms Durand?"

"Yes, that would appear so," replied Simon.

"A few minutes later Ms Zafiri comes back from the cleaner's room with... erm... some old lady with a limp... " Simon hesitated, leaning forward to get closer to the screen, and screwing up his eyes.

"That's Mrs Wheeler, the cleaning ladies' supervisor," MacAllister provided the name.

"I know who Mrs Wheeler is Kev, but just couldn't make her out clearly."

'Probably couldn't see the owl' thought Harriet.

"Then there's the other Dove people," said Simon.

"During the Tuesday morning, before any of them had arrived, all of those people's rooms were entered by Ms Zafiri. She had a large bag, which she left just outside each room, in the corridor, took out a bottle and card at each room stop, and let herself into the room. I guess they were similar to those she took into Mr Kuppers' room."

"Nothing out of the ordinary after that."

"OK," said Harriet, "let's stop it there. I don't need to see all of that footage but keep it in your records."

"Have as much further footage of today in good order, ready for us to look at immediately. Concentrate on the same people, plus Ms Zafiri."

"We'll call you if we need you."

She turned to MacAllister. "Good job, Mr MacAllister, and you, Simon," she said.

MacAllister's muscular chest seemed to puff out even further with pride.

"Cool," said Simon.

15

It was 10.55 am. The police team were all in the Ops room listening to Harriet outlining their search and interview roles that would follow the conclusion of the 11.30 am meeting in the main Conference Room.

The Detective Sergeants, Sandra Coppell, Brinda Tulsi and Dermot Power, and Detective Constable Zoe Alderton who were undertaking the immediate search and interview roles were told the particular doves to whom they had been assigned.

After about five minutes the briefing was interrupted by Mike Selby, who knocked, then entered the room, carrying an evidence bag.

"Excuse me, ma'am. Sorry to interrupt, but I've finished my examination of Mr Kupper's and Ms Durand's rooms, and I have to leave now, I have something that might interest you."

"If it's that urgent, you'd better carry on then, Mike," said Harriet.

Mike was going to carry on anyway, but he appreciated the go-ahead.

"As you know, but I can confirm, there is nothing much in Ms Durand's room to bother you with. Some shopping items and a travelling case with clothes."

"But these items," he said, holding up the evidence bag, "have come from Mr Kuppers' room. They were in a portable safe in the wardrobe. Had to force it open I'm afraid. Lack of time. I've logged them in and photographed and fingerprinted them. His fingerprints only, but I think you might be interested in them, and they are for you to examine more closely. I'm going on to my other job now, but I'll write my report and email it to you tonight. You have my authority to release the body for the postmortem from now. And don't forget to inform the coroner," he added.

"If you have any more questions, give me a bell," and so saying, he departed.

Harriet opened the bag and looked quickly at the items. There was a considerable quantity of cash, in notes of large denominations- Euros, sterling and US Dollars, held together by a black metal spring clip. There was also an American Express Gold Card and his passport.

In addition to that group of items, which were those you would expect from a standard traveller, were some more personal effects, a small notebook, about three inches square, with a plain red cover, and a very small, unobtrusive, black mobile phone.

In a separate, small yellow document wallet were what appeared to be airline tickets and associated documentation.

It was clear that this was going to take more than a cursory glance.

Harriet had to think quickly. She now had multiple tasks to handle, with virtually no time available, each requiring an immediate decision in order to progress.

She had to liaise with Barrowclough and Sian on the postmortem, wrap up the search and interview roles of the police team, and then go along, with Ian, to the meeting with Van, Collison, and Leila Zafiri. All had to be concluded before the 11.30 am gathering.

She spoke quickly to Ian, "Give Collison a ring. Van and Zafiri will be going to his Office, so one call will be enough. Just tell him we will be a few minutes late, that's all you need to say."

"We need to split the tasks between us. I'll take the postmortem part. You can take the team briefing. We'll link up again together at the Collison/Van/Zafiri meeting at about 11.20. Take someone out of the search team to go over the items from Kuppers' room. I'll leave who and how up to you. Good for your organizational skills development."

She then turned to the police team.

"There are a few little tweaks to our schedule. Detective Inspector Scott will fill you in, as I have urgent business elsewhere," said Harriet, leaving the room.

Ian addressed the team.

"Slight change of plan. As D.C.I. Graham said. I'm taking one of you out of the search team to examine these items from Kuppers' room that I have just received. That officer will be you, Detective Constable Coppell." Scott looked at his mobile, then over to Coppell, and spoke.

"I'm not going to be available until around about quarter to one, so that gives you plenty of time to look in detail at these articles from Kuppers' room. I'll come to meet you here, together with Detective Chief Inspector Graham. I've then got a window until half past one, for us to progress anything that might come from these items If it's obviously a 'no-no' from the start, give me a call on my mobile and we'll forget the quarter-to-one meeting."

You should have time to write a draft report for D.C.I Graham and myself to study later, if necessary."

He signed off his instructions to Coppell with a brief 'good luck', and turned to the rest of the team, confirming the doves to whom each had been allocated, splitting Coppell's original allocation between them.

"Remember, before you do anything else, find the genever bottle and photograph and bag it and label the bag with the room number and occupant name. Bags, labels, and gloves are on the table over there." He pointed to the table.

"Don't worry about taking fingerprints but handle everything with gloves on."

"I expect all of the bottles to be in the rooms, unfinished, but look in the waste bins if not. Bring the bagged and labelled bottles back here to the conference room immediately. There will be a courier who will collect them and take them for forensic analysis in London."

"Get yourselves equipped, then wait outside the conference room."

"Detective Sergeant Steve Blishe here –" he indicated Blishe, "will be performing an 'on guard' role in the conference room, keeping eyes on the doves whilst you are undertaking the room searches.

We don't want any of them flying out of the cage before we are ready to release them, do we, D.S Blishe?"

Blishe gave a little smile.

"Everybody got all that?" asked Scott, looking around the room.

"Any questions?"

There were none.

"Well, let's get on with it, then."

"Start immediately the Doves meeting breaks up. Be quick but be thorough."

Scott took Detective Sergeant Power to one side before he could exit and spoke to him. He was the officer who had been deputed to search Willem Vonk's room.

"One of your assigned doves, Mr Vonk, is different. He is a key player in this case. Search his room first and make it as thorough as you can.

Report back to me immediately after you have finished his room and before you begin anyone else's. If anything is slightly suspicious, note and photograph it. Take fingerprints."

"You won't be needed to interview him. D.C.I Graham and I will conduct any such interview later, when we consider it appropriate. You can interview the other doves to whom you have been assigned."

# 16

As soon as Selby had left, Harriet had called Barrowclough, to update him and obtain his consent to proceed with the postmortem and the associated administration. The call took a little longer than she had imagined, but as soon as it concluded she made her way hurriedly to the Ops Room and went over to Sian Parkinson.

She was sitting at a desk reading a battered Penguin paperback. It was entitled "The Poisoner's Handbook: Murder and the Birth of Forensic Medicine in Jazz Age New York". She invariably carried a forensically related book along with her when assigned to a case.

Harriet gave it a glance. "Found it in Kupper's room, then, did you?... and didn't tell anyone? Was it signed "Best Wishes, W.V.? In Dutch, of course."

Harriet raised her eyebrows and Sian gave a smile.

Harriet's tone became more serious.

"Mike Selby has now given the 'all clear' for the body to be taken for the postmortem, and the coroner to be advised," she said. "What were your plans for moving the body and conducting the postmortem?" Harriet asked.

"You mean what are my plans," said Sian, stressing the 'are', and continuing quickly.

"I made a provisional arrangement with the Surrey and Sussex at Redhill for them to send over an ambulance at 12.00 pm to collect the two bodies. Kuppers, the dead one, and myself, the - hopefully - breathing one. I would then perform the postmortem at Redhill ASAP and get any conclusions over to you."

"Also, one hour later, at 1 pm, Surrey and Sussex would send over a vehicle for the genever bottles recovered from the Doves' rooms, which wouldn't be ready for shipping over for testing until 1 pm. I would analyse the contents as speedily as possible after they arrived at Redhill."

"Redhill are just waiting for my 'o.k.'"

Harriet raised her hand. "Stop there."

"You very perceptively noted the possible incorrect usage of tense, but I was, in fact, grammatically correct."

"There has been a change of plan," explained Harriet, "I've had Barrowclough on the line. Redhill is now out of the equation, so you need to call them straight away and cancel all your provisional arrangements."

"You're getting the red carpet treatment. There's an unmarked ambulance vehicle coming over, with a driver and security staff. Make sure that when the body is moved it is done as quickly and unobtrusively as possible. Use the back entrance, the same as with Mike.

They will have their own body bag. I bet it is a Scenesure 3-zip job. They will take you and the body to the Michael East Forensic Suite on Horseferry Road. When you get there, you will have two qualified assistants at your disposal, and fully secured premises."

"You mean the new state-of-the-art facility attached to the Westminster Public Mortuary?"

"Yes, that's it. Apparently, there is a bio-hazard post-mortem room, two more forensic analysis rooms, all the equipment you would wish, and an evidence store. All bells and whistles. A second vehicle will collect the bottles and glasses at around 1 pm and bring them to Horseferry Road. Everything can be done there."

"With all this, we want results very quickly. A preliminary report to me as soon as possible - just give me a call, interrupt whatever I'm doing, and complete the results of the PM as soon as you can. D.I. Scott and I will be here and contactable 24/7. You won't be getting any beauty sleep, and nor will we. Wake me up if necessary."

"Anything around seventy-five percent certainty is fine. Speed is of the essence here."

"Good postmorteming, or whatever you forensics specialists say to each other.

Speak later."

Harriet scurried off to her next appointment, joining Ian for a quick pre-11.30 am briefing for Collison, Van and Leila Zafiri. Harriet covered the police requirements succinctly, but briefly, agreeing on the speakers and their sequence and particularly making sure she had Collison's approval for the room searches.

17

Just after 11.30 am the last of the Doves had filed into the Conference Room and were seated in a single row of chairs arranged into a shallow, half-moon semi-circle facing the large table at the head of the room. Van was seated centrally behind the table, flanked by Harriet and Ian on one side, and Matthew Collison on the other.

A quiet, sombre atmosphere prevailed as Van rose to his feet with much shuffling taking place as several of the Doves tried to ease themselves into comfortable positions on their seats.

He cleared his throat, and addressed the group in a serious, businesslike tone.

"Good morning, Doves. Thank you all for being so prompt.

I will speak in English, for reasons which will become evident.

I hope you all travelled here safely yesterday and have settled into the hotel.

As you know from your Conference Agenda, I am scheduled to make the opening speech and introductions, then deliver my presentation on 20 years of the Doves. I know that several of you have been members for the whole of this time.

Unfortunately, I have some bad news. Due to a sudden and unexpected occurrence, I have to tell you that, sadly, none of this Conference or any of the associated visits, will now take place. Some of you may already be aware of the arrival and presence of the UK emergency services, both vehicles and personnel, and some of you may also have noticed that our Conference organizer Piet Kuppers is not with us.

I am very sorry to tell you that Piet was found dead in his room earlier this morning, and the death is, at this stage, regarded as unexplained. In these circumstances, UK law requires that the police investigate the death further.

This is why there is with me UK Detective Chief Inspector Graham and Detective Inspector Scott." Van indicated them with a hand gesture, and Harriet and Ian nodded in the direction of the assembled group. "Chief Inspector Graham will be in charge of the investigation, assisted by Detective Inspector Scott, and other officers.

Mr Matthew Collison, who some of you may have seen, is the Median Hotel Manager." The white-faced, smartly dressed youngish man adjusted his thick, black "Harry Palmer" glasses slightly and raised his right hand with a brief movement.

"Detective Chief Inspector Graham will tell you what will happen from now on, so I will hand it over to her, but in closing, I would just ask you to cooperate fully with the police in order that this matter is quickly resolved, and we can get back to the resumption of our normal lives."

Harriet stood up and spoke.

"Thank you, Mr Van Heemskerk, for that excellent summary."

As Mr Van Heemskerk said, we, the UK police, are bound by law to investigate this distressing incident. As you are aware, the Meeting was planned to finish on Friday, with you departing on Saturday morning. I am advised that none of you had booked any extended stay at this hotel beyond a Saturday morning departure.

This means we have very little time indeed available to us to conduct our investigations. As far as you are concerned, we will therefore proceed as follows.

Unfortunately, we will have to conduct a search of each of your rooms, and we have Mr Collison's permission to do this. This will commence immediately, and whilst that is being done you will all remain in this room.

The searches will be conducted by our Officers. We will endeavour to make this process as quick, and as considerate of your personal effects as possible, although any items may be removed if our officers consider it necessary.

It is unlikely, but possible that we may ask for your fingerprints to be taken, and we would appreciate your permission if this is deemed to be required.

Once your room search has been satisfactorily completed, you will be collected individually by one of our Sergeants, and then interviewed by an officer in your room.

You will appreciate that this exercise is purely for the purpose of collecting information as part of our initial enquiries.

Detective Inspector Scott, Mr Collison and I have to leave fairly shortly. However, when we leave there will be an officer stationed in this room until everyone has been called for interview.

Before your interview, please try to think of anything, however small, that may possibly assist in resolving Mr Kuppers' death, in his manner or circumstances whilst in Holland, any issues he may have confided in you, and so on. Your assistance will be much appreciated.

Assuming no problems arise from your interview, you will then be free to do whatever you wish, inside or outside the hotel, but you may be required in the future, and we may contact you at any time. If you take a mobile phone outside the hotel, you must leave that number with reception, unless you have already done so.

If outside, you must return to the hotel in the evening, and remain in the hotel until your planned check-out time of 12.00 am on Saturday morning. This is in order to allow time for forensic and other information, if needed, to be investigated and processed.

Again, assuming no difficulties, if you wish, you may meet for dinner in the evenings at your reserved table in the hotel restaurant, tonight, tomorrow and Friday.

So, please remain here until advised. Coffee, tea and sandwiches will be brought in shortly for you. After the searches have been satisfactorily completed this room will become the main operations room for the police. It will then be 'out of bounds' to you all.

A final point. On the table here are your conference name tags, intended for you to wear on the external visits. It would be of assistance to our team if you could wear these whilst in the hotel. Thank you."

Harriet looked at the group.

"Also, nothing is to be discussed with members of the public or media here in the UK, with family and friends in Holland and elsewhere, or appear on social media until you are advised."

"Any questions?" She asked.

There were no questions.

Ian called for the Detective Constable from the team, Steve Blishe. He arrived quickly, and Harriet, Ian and Collison left the room.

The Conference Room was to become the main operations room for the investigation until Saturday, but until the initial interviews were finalized Collison had provided them with a smaller, unused Conference facility, close to the Conference Room, and the entry key code.

Harriet buttonholed Van before he had left the Conference Room.

"Mr Van Heemskerk, I wonder if you have time now to assist me and DI Scott further, on a confidential basis?

He looked at them. "My appointment book has suddenly become free," he observed drily. "Yes, of course, I will assist you if I can."

"Good, if you could come with us, we can talk privately in our room." Harriet led the way down the corridor.

18

"Come in Mr Van Heemskerk, please sit down."

"I'd like you to tell us a little about the Doves, as a group, then as much as you can about some of the individuals. I guess you know, or knew, most of them well, and some very well, on a business and personal level.

We need to complete the investigation very quickly, but thoroughly, of course," she added.

"Therefore, we need to prioritize our time. After a few words from you about the group we would like to concentrate on three people. The dead man, Mr Kuppers, his companion Ms Durand, and Mr Willem Vonk. We will come back to any of the remaining Doves later if we think we need to.

Anything that comes to mind that you may think will help to explain the death of Mr Kuppers? Any personal jealousies or grudges within the group involving Kuppers or Vonk, for example, but don't feel restricted. Whatever you say to us now is purely of an informal investigatory nature and will not go outside of this room unless absolutely necessary."

Van nodded quickly, then cleared his throat.

"The Doves, yes."

"The Doves are a small group of motorcycle enthusiasts. Ten of them, now nine I suppose, are in attendance at the Conference. They all live within a reasonable distance of the town of Doventenar, which is located about 30 kilometres from Amsterdam. Hence the "Doves" name.

Most are engineers from various business organizations, either approaching retirement or retired completely. The age range is around fifty-five to seventy," he smiled. "So, I just qualify."

"I was a founder member, along with two others, both of whom have passed away. Piet Kuppers isn't included in that count," he added, wryly.

"We meet every month or so for lunch, and a presentation by a guest speaker, on technical engineering topics, or, say, performance cars, speedboats, that sort of thing. A couple of times a year we will arrange a tour on our bikes, usually for one or two days, to various European destinations."

Harriet nodded. "We get the idea, thanks. Were there any problems of which you are aware between any of the group members and Mr Kuppers?"

"No, not as far as I am aware. Piet counts as a fairly new member. He has been with us just over three years, and hasn't been to every meeting or event, but he was very keen to be involved in the group administration and has been organizing the guest speakers for us. Very successfully I must say. He has brought along several famous names."

"He is outwardly reasonably friendly, and generous with technical advice and help to the other Doves if they need it, but at the same time rather aloof. No deep friendships."

"I always had the feeling there was something beneath the surface. Something held back. More at home with ladies than gentlemen I would say. However, no enemies or arguments with people in the group, certainly that I know of."

"Have you known Mr Kuppers for a long time?"

"Let's say I have known of him and have been acquainted with him for a long time. Really known him? No, I think not. As I have indicated, I'm not sure anyone did."

Harriet took that comment in but remained silent, and Van continued.

"As I said, he hasn't been a member of the Doves for very long, but I knew him from work a long time ago. Let me go back, say..."

Van paused, raising his chin and head upwards as if trying to sharpen his recollection, and counting silently.

"Twenty-five... no, twenty-seven years, and give you some history."

"Piet Kuppers and I both had an aircraft engineering background, educationally and in practice. We were both career employees of Fokland, the major Dutch Aircraft Company, based in Amsterdam. I was in a more senior position than him, and some years older."

"I knew his name and was aware that he had been marked out as a top management prospect, apparently a very efficient worker and excellent engineer, confident and ambitious, too, but, at this point in time, there was limited personal contact between us, business or pleasure, and Fokland was a very large company."

"However, at a later stage when I was the Head of Engineering for Asia he worked closely for me on two assignments, firstly in Indonesia and secondly in Japan, so I suppose I do know, or rather knew, him better than the other Doves."

"As I recall, even then he had a reputation within the organization as a bit of ladies' man. Several of Fokland's young women considered him, how shall I say it in English, 'charming'. I suppose he was a good prospect. Only child, unmarried, no children, wealthy parents, intelligent, good looking."

"In early 1989 I was part of a small team of people negotiating and arranging the lease of 7 or 8 Fokland 150 aircraft to the expanding UK travel company Eurair, the headquarters of which were based near Gatwick Airport. I was there for about a month. The negotiations were satisfactory, and I returned to Amsterdam, and I was appointed to the post of Head of Asian engineering in January of 1990."

"As the Eurair engineering staff had little or no prior knowledge of the 150, several engineers were seconded to train and assist the Eurair people. They were effectively members of the Eurair staff and were absorbed into their organizational structure. Fokland Personnel Department sorted out the secondees, advising or consulting me where necessary."

"One of these engineers was Piet Kuppers. He came over to the UK in the autumn of 1989, to replace one of the secondees who had fallen ill."

Harriet thought this was all getting rather long-winded, but she had told Van to recount anything that came to mind connected with Kuppers, and he gave off the air of someone not used to being interrupted, so she had only herself to blame. She consoled herself with the thought that some comment or snippet of information would crop up eventually.

"Wait a second," said Van. "I have just remembered, another of the seconded engineers was Willem Vonk. He and Kuppers would have worked together for a short time. So Vonk will have known Kuppers during the Eurair period."

"For the next year, things went well. The holiday business boomed, the Fokland aircraft gained a very good reputation for airworthiness, reliability and comfort."

"Then, disaster."

"In late 1990, as you may remember, the UK economy unexpectedly entered recession. Eurair was already heavily in debt. As a private company, it was undercapitalized, with no financial flexibility, and ran out of cash."

Harriet looked at Ian. "When I do my OU degree in Accountancy and Economics I'll have a head start," she whispered.

Van took no notice and carried on.

"The business collapsed overnight, and all the Eurair workers lost their jobs. Fokland were affected also, and many workers were made redundant. Of the seconded engineers, only one lost their job. It was assumed that this would be Kuppers, as he was last in. However, when the announcement came it was Vonk who was made redundant."

"Rumour had it that Kuppers had pulled some strings behind the scenes with senior management, but that might just have been idle chatter in the aftermath. I didn't hear all this until some time afterwards, and have only just brought it back to mind. Apparently, Vonk took the whole thing very badly, had great difficulty finding another job, and his marriage collapsed almost as quickly as Eurair."

"However, Mr Vonk, as I shall tell you later, subsequently became a very successful businessman, and I have never heard the slightest mention of that matter within the Doves since I have been associated with them."

"No, not the slightest mention," he repeated himself, shaking his head slowly from side to side as he spoke, and he paused for a moment or two.

"I had completely forgotten all of this myself until my memory was stirred. Surprising what you can remember when you put your mind to it, isn't it?"

"As I mentioned, I had returned to Amsterdam in 1989, and was appointed to the position of Head of Asian operations in January of 1990. The business was expanding, and with it the need for more staff. I was in Indonesia at the time, based in Jakarta and Piet Kuppers was seconded to me on a year-long assignment."

"Workwise he was very efficient, assiduous, and knowledgeable. I could delegate to him with no problems, and he took charge when I had to visit other parts of Java or Sumatra."

"He looked after his body, and his mind. No problems with drink, as there often are with expats, and he always seemed in pretty good health."

"The almost entirely tropical Indonesian climate meant that we often started work very early, and finished in the early afternoon, leaving a block of spare, relaxation time."

"Over the year of the assignment, Piet took advantage of that pattern to invite a succession of girlfriends to visit. We were in a well-appointed compound, with separate accommodation, a swimming pool, an open-air cinema on the roof, servants, and all that. There were air hostesses from the USA, Dutch girls from Holland, there was a more mature, attractive lady from the UK, and occasionally Jakarta-based expats. Always one at a time, and he never let it interfere with his work. He made that very clear to them all. Whatever he said, went."

"When he didn't have the company of a lady he just kept himself to himself, going into Jakarta town sometimes, just staying in, or very occasionally going to the rooftop movie show."

"We very rarely went for a meal together, and then to discuss business. I never really got to know him personally as a friend, certainly not enough to explain his suspicious death."

"A similar pattern was repeated in Japan, although the daily working hours were longer, and his lady friends were fewer. One of the US air hostesses made a repeat visit, but I never saw any other the others twice."

"So, there we are, my complete knowledge of Piet Kuppers, but I would imagine nothing to help you in your investigation."

Harriet didn't respond. Just jotted down a few notes in a black, flat-top notebook, then closed it. If she had obtained any clues then she wasn't telling.

"Did you know if Mr Kuppers had any current financial problems, relationship problems, or health worries that he might have been willing to mention to you?"

"No, none I was aware of. He wouldn't have confided in me anyway, now, or in the past. He never discussed his personal affairs with me, if you pardon the wording, even when he was in a position to do so. He was a closed shop in that respect."

"What about the no longer current partner, lady friend, companion or whatever, Ms Angelique Durand? What do you make of her?"

"Strange though it may seem, I haven't actually met her, so I'm afraid I can't help you very much there."

"I think they have been together a relatively short time, two or three years maybe. I know their house, rather palatial actually, but have only visited it once, at Willem Vonk's invitation, and together with other Doves. The Doves are a male-only club, you understand, so one would only meet the wives and families outside of the Doves, which would be infrequent, if at all."

"I know that she is the owner of an art gallery, Dubreil et Cie, inherited from her father, and presumably wealthy in her own right. Mr Vonk has a large collection of paintings, and many are sourced by Angelique Durand's company."

"I believe Kuppers and Angelique never saw all that much of each other anyway. She was involved with her business, and he with his motorbike collection. In fact, she probably saw more of Mr Vonk, who I shall come on to next."

He paused. "Could I have a drink of water, please?" he asked, standing up from his chair to stretch his legs.

"Of course," said Harriet, going over to a table set against the far wall, where there was a jug of water and several glasses.

"D.I.Scott?" she queried, indicating the water jug. He shook his head, and Harriet brought just the one glass back to Van.

He resumed his sitting position and continued.

"Now for Mr Vonk."

"I have already explained his situation with Eurair, and whilst in Amsterdam I heard through the grapevine of his subsequent marital problems."

'Him and Marvin Gaye,' thought Harriet.

"Well, after that I had no knowledge of him for many years. As I said, I was appointed to run the Fokland Asia and Far East operation, and Vonk had left the company."

"He next came to my attention in 2000, as the owner-manager of MotoVonk, then a small, but expanding business based in Amsterdam. His name just caught my eye in 'Dutch Motorcycle Monthly' as the driving force behind its success. The business then went from strength to strength to its position today, as the leading distributor of motorcycles of all types throughout the Benelux countries. His personal wealth rose exponentially."

"He had never remarried but occupied a large property in the countryside outside of Doventenar, which included a purpose-built art gallery. This housed his private collection of Dutch seascapes, reputedly the best in the world, of lesser known, but excellent 17th century Dutch Masters such as Hendrick Van Minderhout, Johannes Peeters and Julius Porcellis."

"You may be aware of these artists?" he queried, looking in the general direction of Harriet and Ian.

They remained silent. Harriet didn't like to tell him that her favourite artist was Beryl Cook.

She muttered to Ian, "I prefer people in Plymouth pubs to sailing ships in stormy seas."

Ian looked lost in both the content of the conversation and alliteration, and Van droned on in his monotone fashion.

"I believe most of the works had been purchased through the Paris and Delft-based art dealership of Dubrueil & Cie. This company was owned by Auguste Durand, who also happened to be Angelique Durand's father. After he died Angelique inherited his shares in the company and had also taken over the business relationship with Vonk, sourcing and purchasing several of the paintings which were later additions to his gallery."

"I know all this because I did some research of my own after the tour, especially as I had always been interested in the 17th century Dutch 'golden age'."

"The tour?" queried Harriet.

"Oh, I'm sorry," replied Van. "I've gone a little out of sequence, but it doesn't matter."

"Vonk had joined the Doves, and although his extensive travel and business commitments meant he was unable to attend many meetings he was a popular, ebullient and extrovert member, but he never flaunted his wealth."

"You must understand us Dutch and money. We are different from some of the British and particularly different from most Americans in this respect. Wealth and modesty go together with we Dutch."

"He helped several members with repairs, spares and purchase of new motorcycles, and also paid for several of the monthly lunches. He is also bearing all the costs of this meeting. Hotel, travel, visits within the UK, meals, drinks, everything. That was just stated with typical Dutch directness. We met together and were discussing the arrangements. He simply said 'I will pay for all of this', and that was that."

"Also, about eighteen months ago he invited all the Doves on a tour of the house and gallery. Everyone was picked up by coach from, or near our homes, and brought to his property. After the tour the coach took us to the "Indrapurata" the best Indonesian restaurant in Amsterdam. Rijsttafel and as much of the finest matching Pinot Gris as you could drink. A hotel room had been reserved for each of us for the night, and the next day we were shipped back to our homes. All paid for by Willem. No big fuss. No ostentation."

"At the same time, he was inwardly very proud of the property and the art collection. There were more alarms, steel security doors, CCTV cameras and identity checks than in the White House. It took us as much time to get through security as it did touring the house and viewing the paintings."

"If there was any friction between Kuppers and Vonk, at the tour and meal, or subsequently, then I didn't notice it. They have interacted on the planning of this meeting, Kuppers doing all the organization, and Vonk all the paying, but they would have talked together at times during the past year from the start of the meeting process."

"Another blank, I'm afraid as far as any reason for Kuppers' untimely death is concerned."

"What about Mr Kuppers' partner, Ms Durand? Was there any friction between Kuppers and Vonk, as I believe Vonk and Ms Durand had worked very closely together for several years in relation to the acquisition of artworks for his gallery?"

Van Heemskerk replied immediately, without hesitation. "I believe this to be, and have been, a purely business relationship."

Harriet left that line of enquiry lie, and looked at her watch.

"Thank you, Mr Van Heemskerk. Very useful. That's all for now, you are free to do whatever you wish, but we would appreciate it if you could make yourself available at short notice if required."

Van left the room.

Harriet addressed Ian. "What do you think, then?"

Ian replied, "A few things."

"Firstly, I was wondering if a grudge could fester away in someone's mind for twenty-seven years. Secondly, that Mr Kuppers may not have been quite the charming person he seemed on the surface, and lastly, that the Doves, or at least Van, have no idea of Mr Vonk's recreational activities on the wild side of life."

"Very perceptive," said Harriet, without taking it further, and moved quickly on, speaking brusquely and decisively.

"The ongoing plan of action is this."

"Let's look at the CCTV before we interview anyone else, we will be in a position to match up the CCTV movements with the stories they tell us. MacAllister should have that ready by now."

"We then interview Leila Zafiri- I still wonder why she didn't tell us about the gift bottles of Genever earlier. Then the mysterious Angelique Durand, and Mr Vonk. Vonk is the priority for the Dutch, so I suggest we take him first, then Angelique Durand, but we'll see what the CCTV turns up before making a final decision on the order."

"We also need to find out as much as possible about Kuppers' movements since his arrival on Monday, and particularly yesterday."

"Whilst Van has been delivering his lecture there will have been a lot going on."

"As I said, the CCTV info should be ready. Sian and the body will be on their way to Horseferry Road. The sergeants will be progressing with their room searches. Coppell will be investigating the contents of Kuppers' room. She hasn't contacted me, so I guess there may well be something of interest for us there. The initial information from the Dutch police will either be on its way, or completed, and I expect Barrowclough will be up our backsides to find out why we haven't cleared the whole thing up in ten minutes."

"I'll contact Mac Allister now."

⸺⬦⬦⬦⸺

# 19

Sergeant Sandra Coppell had been given Harriet and Ian's own "ops room" and was sitting at a desk set against one wall when Harriet and Ian entered. She pulled the desk away from the wall, brought up a spare chair, and the three of them sat around the table.

Several items had all been neatly grouped and arranged on the desk, some in clear evidence bags with blue tamper-proof tops.

Coppell picked up several sheets of A4 paper.

"These are my notes," she said. "You can take them away with you if you need to, but I think it's best if I walk you through everything first."

"These are what the SOCO handed over to us," she said, indicating the effects on the desk. "He went over the main things with us, but in the meanwhile, we've taken a closer look."

"I looked at Kuppers' laptop, but it was password secured, so I've shipped it off to Digital Forensics for them to examine and report back."

"Apart from that, his clothes and all the rest, you may be interested in what else was in the room."

Coppell indicated firstly a small group of books. They were a Gideon Bible with its deep crimson cover and the words "Holy Bible" engraved into it in bold block gold lettering; a new-looking hard-covered slim volume entitled "Essential Concise Dutch/English Dictionary: Teach Yourself," and a facsimile first edition of "Walter, His

Secret Life," the one first printed in Amsterdam in 1888, with a cover of distinctive yellow.

"Only his fingerprints on them," Coppell said.

In a separate grouping were several A4 sheets of paper that had been screwed up before being unrolled by the sergeant, and a large, buff envelope, seemingly torn precisely into two almost equal halves, the tear dividing a white label on which appeared to have been printed a long name and an address. There was also a small light blue piece of thin cardboard, which had been similarly screwed up and discarded. The object had been smoothed and flattened as much as had been possible. It was about the size of a council car parking ticket, lined with a black edging, and inscribed with the words "Excess Luggage Co," below which was a 4-digit number, and below that printed "Paid £5.50".

Finally, standing by itself, a bulky briefcase with a wad of conference papers within.

Sandra Coppell continued.

"The screwed-up papers, envelope and ticket were out of the waste bin, Ma'am. Mostly connected with the meeting, I guess. I assume the envelope had some papers in it at one time."

"There was a glass, and a bottle of Dutch gin on the unit just inside the door. The glass had a small amount in the bottom of it, and the Genever bottle had about a third remaining. They've gone off to forensics, of course, but, funny thing, sir, the SOCO had made a note that neither of them had any fingerprints on them. Clean as a whistle."

While we're on the subject of the bottles, there's something that may or may not be important, that I've just remembered, not to do with Mr Kuppers. I'll come back to him in a minute.

As you know, after the meeting in the Main Conference Room, I was originally scheduled to search Mr Vonk's room, but that was then given to Sergeant Power. Well, Power did the search, and right at the end, at the back of his wardrobe, in addition to one on Mr Vonk's bedside table, were three more of those brown bottles, and one of them had been opened, or at least didn't have the white seal on it, but had the stopper in. I guess they were spares. Anyway, he added them to all the other ones from the other bikers' rooms that were going to the forensics lab at one o'clock.

He knew we were meeting up, so suggested I should know about it, and pass it on to you.

Ian made a quick note before Sergeant Coppell returned to the subject of the contents of Kuppers' room.

"Here's something that came out of Kuppers' wardrobe, ma'am," she said.

"He certainly didn't trust standard hotel security. The room safe in the wardrobe was unlocked, and completely empty, the security lock untouched, and no fingerprints. But there were these articles in the wardrobe, and there were fingerprints on those, all right, but again, only his."

She brought over a security bag, opened it, and removed a charcoal-coloured portable safe. Thin and elegant, but strong, it measured about eight inches by four inches. It looked as though Selby hadn't bothered with the intricacies of fathoming the combination lock but had simply sheared it off.

There was also a large, yellow, semi-transparent Perspex document wallet.

Coppell laid them out on the desk in front of them.

Ian put on a pair of thin, plastic gloves, opened the wallet and laid out the contents on the desk in front of him.

As Harriet was already aware, out of the portable safe had come a considerable quantity of cash, in notes of large denominations, two thousand euros, five hundred pounds sterling and five hundred US dollars, held together by a black metal spring clip. There was also an KLM Flying Blue Platinum Card and his passport.

In addition to that group of items -those you would expect from a standard traveller- were some more personal effects, a small, red notebook, about three inches square, with a plain cover, and a very small, unobtrusive, black mobile phone.

Out of the document wallet had come return airline tickets from Gatwick to Schiphol together with the associated documentation.

Oh, and there was this, sir," she said and handed Ian a small plastic bag. He shook it out onto the table. It was an unopened packet of condoms, featuring boldly drawn cartoon jungle animals in distinctive colours. The words "King Size" were in large black capitals on the front of the packet.

Ian looked at Sandra Coppell. "Very artistic. Spot the snake in the grass," he remarked drily.

"Just put the cash and the condoms to one side for the moment," said Coppell, "and I'll come back to the travel documentation shortly."

Coppell opened the notebook and passed it around. The first half contained about seven separate sections, in either black or blue ballpoint pen. On each line on the left-hand page was a website domain name, with each section ending in the same suffix, ".nl," ".jp," ".uk," ".us" and so on. On each line on the right-hand page was a single-word name followed by a telephone number. Everything was written in a meticulously neat hand.

After Harriet and Ian had looked at it Coppell thumbed through the remaining pages "All blank... apart from this," Coppell said, handing over the notebook to Harriet, who then passed it to Ian. There was a tiny, pencilled number inscribed on the inside of the back cover. The number was '1991'.

"Just remember that for the moment," said Coppell. "See if you can sit so both of you can see the same pages of the notebook at the same time." Harriet and Ian re-organised their positions.

"Go to the front of the notebook and focus on the page with the domain name suffixes of '.uk'," said Coppell.

"You'll see that all the domain names were the same- 'ww.maturework.co.uk'. There were five names and mobile telephone numbers. They looked down the list of names. Jacqueline, Gemma, Jaycee, Marianne, and finally, Michaela Gold. This looked like a new entry, written in a different colour than the others.

Coppell looked at them. "This is where my year in the vice squad comes in useful," she said, in a knowing tone.

"As you will probably know, these are sites which advertise the services of sex workers, with personal details, fees and contact telephone numbers and so on."

"When I came across all this, I asked myself a few questions. Had Kuppers visited any of them whilst in the UK on this visit, or in the past? Could any of them been involved in his death in some way? What about the most recent, Michaela Gold? Had Kuppers spoken to her, or seen her, over the last few days?"

Harriet looked through the little red book again and raised her eyebrows. "Our Mr K was quite a solicitor, wasn't he? And not as in the legal profession, either." She gave a thin smile. "It's certainly worth looking at. Perhaps someone else knew of the red book and was able to extort money from him to keep things quiet. Let's see what we've got."

"We have a schedule of his recent movements as far as it's possible to tell at this stage. Let's just go over that again," she said. Harriet went over to her desk and produced a couple of A4 sheets from a pile of papers and brought them over.

She picked up a pencil and began to speak, making rough notes as she did so.

"So," she said. "Monday 2.00 pm he checked in at reception, after arriving from Amsterdam. Monday 3.00 pm he met with Leila Zafiri, the Conference Manager for about an hour. He retired to his room to work on the Meeting arrangements, and at 7.15 pm he ordered a light dinner from Room Service. All this has been verified with Reception, Leila, Room Service and CCTV.

Tuesday morning, he was at Artemisia's Café, where his wallet went missing. Back to the hotel, then lunch at the Kamada along the road. Another meeting with Leila. Tells her he is not feeling very well and will have an early night. Returns to room. Not seen alive again."

"No time to contact or visit Michaela, then. So that theory's down the Swanee."

"That's what I thought, too," said Coppell, "until I investigated this."

She went to one of the bags and plucked out a very small, unobtrusive, black mobile and turned it in her fingers. It appeared to be a pay-as-you-go phone.

"I guessed we already had a request out to the Dutch police for his call records on his other mobile, and I could get this one out to them as soon as possible, and I reckoned that it would take a little while for them to get all the information back to us. So, I had the thought that his recent call history may be on this phone, unless it was locked, of course."

Coppell was enjoying her role and ratcheting up the suspense.

"I tried activating the small mobile," she said, "which was indeed locked. But then I thought 'It's a four-number code, right?' So, after a few tries I thought. Why don't I try '1991'?"

She looked at them both, somewhat triumphantly. "Bingo!" she exclaimed. "Would you Adam and Eve it! He wasn't so efficient after all, is he? I mean, was he? Fancy writing the unlock code in the red notebook. Especially one that could be remembered easily. It reads the same backwards and forwards."

"A palindromic number," remarked Harriet.

"I haven't any Dutch, but It was easy enough for me to find the menu selection for the recent call history. The most recent ones were all to UK 078 prefixed numbers, three to the same number, and two to another number, different from the first. Of the three calls, one was from Amsterdam, and two were from England, one at 9.15 am, and the other at 10.30 am on this Monday just gone."

"Hold on there a minute Mr Potter, just hold on there," said Ian, in his James Stewart voice. 'It's a Wonderful Life' had been his favourite film since his childhood.

His tone became more thoughtful.

"He checked into the hotel at 2.00 pm, straight off his flight from Amsterdam. Well, if he did, how did he make two mobile calls from the UK to a UK number in the morning, when he wasn't in the UK?"

"Good point," said Coppell. "That occurred to me as well. Then I remembered the yellow folder. That had his return air tickets in it, and a flight itinerary," Coppell located them and laid them in front of Harriet and Ian.

"Look at this," she said. "The itinerary says he was booked to fly over on the 8.15 KLM from Schiphol to Gatwick, return flight Saturday morning at 11.00 am. We can get the passenger list from the airline if we need to, but I'm certain he was on that flight."

"So, he arrives, and must do something with his luggage. Maybe leave it at Gatwick Airport, pick it up on his way back, and check into the hotel with it. Very clever. That then leaves him four or five hours to contact Michaela Gold, spend some time with her, and then return to the Median. I guessed she would be in London but watch this space."

Coppell then pulled her laptop in front of them. "Let's take a peek at the 'maturework' website, shall we?" she said, accessing the site.

"There aren't too many Michaela Gold's on there, are there?" she said. "Just one, in fact. And, look, there's her contact telephone number towards the bottom of the screen. A mobile number."

Coppell reached for the little red book and asked them to look at the telephone number written in it. She gave a broad smile. She was enjoying the "conjurer, hat and rabbit" moment, as Harriet and Ian noticed the exact match of the numbers. "Hey, presto," she said, emphasizing the metaphor.

They all looked at the computer screen. It was the profile of Michaela Gold. There was a long, rectangular image on the left-hand side of the page. It showed a lady with a somewhat bulbous nose set in a rather lined, craggy face, a wide mouth and tousled hair, a mixture of black and grey with crimson, dyed streaks. Even in the photograph, fifty appeared to be a considerable underestimate of her age.

She was wearing a long, ankle-length gold-coloured, evening dress. Her face had aged, but her body had not.

The tight dress hugged her shapely figure and legs. It sparkled as the artificial light of the photograph played on the very many tiny sequins sewn into the dress. Her pose, and dress, were similar to, and probably taken from, the striking publicity photograph of Rita Hayworth in the 1946 film noir "Gilda".

Harriet read the description alongside the photograph.

"Refined, mature, compliant lady, 50, invites mature, discerning business gentlemen to visit me in my cosy flat. I am conveniently located close to the Burtons Hill Rail Station, which is on the Victoria to Brighton line and stops at Gatwick Airport. There is also easy parking opposite my flat."

"Spend an hour or two relaxing with me, enjoy a glass of wine, and a blue film, and forget the stresses of your life as an experienced, submissive lady pampers you."

Ian clicked on the top banner menu of the website under the heading "Gallery". A group of nine or ten thumbnail photographs appeared. They showed Michaela in a variety of scanty lingerie, mainly diaphanous crimson and black, several featuring her wearing extremely high-heeled red shoes, or thigh-high black leather boots. There was also a "Private Gallery," which required online payment. A standalone very short, "free taster" video clip showed her naked, and in the process of engaging in sexual intercourse with a similarly unclothed, portly, older man, with a large pot belly. A "Private Video" button no doubt provided access to much more of the same, again for an online fee.

A column on the right-hand side, with a check box, advised the viewer of a range of her personal "likes" and "dislikes".

"She must be very well educated, with those 'A' levels and 'O' levels," observed Harriet, dryly.

Finally, there was a table of rates for the time spent with her, and below that, a mobile telephone number.

"Well, well, well," Harriet said slowly and deliberately.

"Mr K's idea of a BSA mounting plate wasn't a motorcycle part, then?" remarked Harriet. "The netherworld of human nature never ceases to surprise me."

She paused for a moment.

"Well done, Coppell," Harriet said. "Excellent detective work."

"I think we'll just keep this in our back pocket for the time being," she said and glanced at her phone to check the time.

She looked at Ian.

"It's five minutes before our discussion with Leila Zafiri - in her office," she said to Ian.

"Sergeant Coppell, I'd like you to stay here and double-check all the details you've discovered, and the conclusions drawn. Make sure it all fits together. Then complete your notes. We'll touch base later, OK?"

Coppell nodded, and Ian and Harriet made for the door and the short distance to Leila Zafiri's office.

20

"Come in Lelia," said Harriet, beckoning her to sit at the desk, opposite herself and Ian.

Harriet waited for her to lock the door of her room and settle, and then began. She noticed how calm and collected Leila appeared.

"Thank you for your help so far, Leila," Harriet said. "You don't object to D.I. Scott taking notes of this conversation, do you?" she queried.

"Not at all," replied Leila, without any hesitation.

"You have told us of your discovery of the body and your subsequent actions, and something of your impressions of Kuppers."

"We would now like you to tell us in as much detail as you can remember, of the genever bottles. From what we understand, these gifts were the idea of Mr Vonk, and no one had any inkling of them except yourself and Mr Vonk. It was Vonk's idea, and you were sworn to secrecy. Is that correct?"

"Yes, that is so," Leila responded. "Mr Vonk got in touch with me several weeks before the conference and explained all about the gifts. This is something I have come across before in the conference world, and have dealt with on a couple of occasions, so the nature of the gift arrangements, and the secrecy wasn't a surprise. He handled the purchase of the gifts, had them shipped here just before the event, and I organized the gift bags and tags."

"As you may know, we met in the conference room yesterday morning, prepared the gifts, and I then ensured they were placed in the rooms of the recipients."

"What was Mr Vonk's manner? Was there anything you might have considered out of the ordinary? Was he nervous, stressed, anxious?"

Leila paused momentarily.

"Yes, a little, I think. I know he was anxious to catch a train to London. He mentioned an important meeting with his bank manager. He seemed to be rushing around a bit, but this was the first time I had met Mr Vonk in the flesh, you will understand, so I didn't know of his normal behaviour, although he certainly didn't act in the assured and decisive way I might have expected from our telephone conversations."

"Oh yes, and he was very particular about the gift bottles. Although they were all the same, each had to be put into a particular room, and I had to mark them with their room number, in pencil. Thinking about it, he took particular trouble over Mr Kuppers bottle. I had to mark that one with a large asterisk on the back of the bag, and I had to make sure that it got into his room first, before anyone else's, and to make sure he wasn't around, which was quite difficult, and I only just managed it before all that kerfuffle happened when Mr Kuppers lost his wallet. Still. I got it done."

She paused as if to stop, and then continued.

"Umm, and another thing," Leila said, reflectively. "Counting the bottles. He was worse than our awful auditors. Counted them about four times. Seven bikers, himself, Mr Van Heemskerk, Kuppers, and two spares, making twelve in total."

Harriet interrupted her. "No, that can't be right Leila. My officers have told me that there were three spares in Mr Vonk's room that we have sent off for analysis, so thirteen bottles altogether."

Leila didn't even pause for thought.

"No. I'm correct. It's all coming back to me," she repeated her assertion and continued her explanation.

"Originally, we had thirteen bottles in total, which included two spares, so Mr Vonk took one of the spares off the order because thirteen would have been an unlucky number in the UK. He was very proud of knowing that and remarked on it. Trying to impress me? Maybe. I don't know, but I don't think so."

Leila continued.

"However, there was a late dropout from the Doves so we left the order at twelve, but that meant ten doves and two spares. No question about it."

"Thank you, Leila," said Harriet, in a seemingly matter-of-fact manner, that belied her true reaction to Leila's disclosure.

"That's all for now, but we will certainly need to talk to you again. Please make yourself available, and remember, anything said in this conversation is totally confidential- on either side."

"I quite understand," responded Leila, and she unlocked the door, and Harriet and Ian returned, at pace, to their room.

Harriet looked at Ian, immediately picking up her phone and pressing the dial button in one rapid movement. No verbal explanation was required as they exchanged glances.

"Sian?" she asked, "Are you still on the cadaver transport run?"

"Yes," came the reply. "Nearly there. Just crossing Battersea Bridge. We got through Checkpoint Charlie with no problems."

"Lucky we didn't get the Gehlen mob in on the act, then," said Harriet.

Her voice then became businesslike.

"I'm not phoning you only to pose a literary quiz question. Something much more serious has come up." Harriet went through her discussion with Leila, and the story of the spare bottles.

"So, there are three genever bottles from Mr Vonk's room, number 504, being shipped to you at the laboratory. A special courier set off with them about an hour after you left the hotel. So you should get them at about 2.20 pm."

"These bottles will be in a separate bag, possibly labelled 'Spares' in addition to the room number. I want them forensically analysed immediately. They are to be given priority over all the others. Got that. Absolute priority."

If you can't do it yourself, get an assistant to do it. Feed back the results to myself or D.S. Scott pronto, whatever the time of day or night. Eighty per cent certainty of the results of your analysis is fine 'seventy-five maybe'. Speed is essential. Interrupt me, if necessary, OK?"

Harriet rang off without waiting for any reply.

# 21

It was two o'clock in the afternoon when the man in the British Airways pilot uniform, complete with dark glasses and pilot briefcase, entered the Median Hotel reception area via the revolving doors and picked his way toward the Reception Desk through the crowded foyer.

He looked for the shortest queue and found one with only two people in front of him. He tapped the shoulder of the white-suited person directly in front of him in the queue.

The person turned to face the pilot. He turned out to be a small, thin man somewhere in his late thirties or early forties, with slicked back, greasy dark hair, a sallow complexion, and a thin pencil of a black moustache. To go with the white suit, there was a loud, wide multicoloured tie, and black and white elevator shoes. He looked as if he should have been selling nylons and Lucky Strike cigarettes in Oxford Street in the nineteen forties.

"I wonder if I could take your place in the queue?" asked the pilot of the white-suited man "I'm flying a load of passengers out to Larnaca shortly and any time I can save would be very helpful."

"No worries, guv," replied the man, his language conforming precisely to his stereotype. "Be my guest, as they say in a place like this," he replied, his grin revealing a mouthful of rather unhealthy-looking teeth.

"Thanks," said the pilot, "that's very helpful. Very crowded in here today, isn't it? Is there a special event?"

"In a manner of speakin' I suppose there is," responded Mr Whitesuit. "I've been stayin' on the second floor, room 212. I 'ad sum business early doors in Crawley, so 'ad breakfast at Sparrows, and off I went."

"I came back about half twelve, and when I went back to my room, there was a young copper sittin' outside in the corridor with red and white tape cordonin' off rooms 205 and 206. They are down the corridor from me, but a bit tucked away down a little passageway off the main corridor. So I went over to see what was goin' on."

"With the young lad was a plain clothes nark and he asks me what was my room number. I says '212', and he is then very interested, because apparently I was the nearest room to 205 with anyone staying. He asks me if I heard any noises in the night that might have been coming from … moanin' and groanin', or any other movin' about in the corridor, that sort of thing."

"Well, I couldn't help him there. I sleep like a baby me… when I'm by myself, that is."

The pilot expected him to smirk, and say "know what I mean, know what I mean", wink suggestively, and tap the side of his nose-but he didn't, well, didn't quite-he just left it at the smirk.

"I had a few drinks at the hotel bar, and was in bed by ten thirty. Woke up at about quarter past six in the morning, breakfast at seven, then off and out."

"Well, I asked him why he was askin' me all these questions, and what was happenin', and he said it was some foreign guy apparently. Food poisonin'. Brown bread e' was, if you get my drift."

The pilot showed no sign as to whether he got his drift or not, but Mr Whitesuit clarified it anyway.

"That's dead, to you, mate," he explained. "'ope he didn't eat the sea bass. I 'ad that last night for dinner," he added with another of his trademark smirks.

At that juncture, the lady in front of the pilot in the queue moved away, and the pilot moved up to the desk. He was confronted by a young man with glasses and carefully groomed fair hair, wearing a very new-looking outfit of a white shirt, and a somewhat ill-fitting blue blazer. The size of the queue behind had grown, and the young man looked increasingly harassed.

The pilot put a gloved hand into his jacket pocket and brought out a smallish manilla envelope. He exchanged a few brief words with the young man, and then handed him the envelope.

He gave a brief nod to Mr Whitesuit, then disappeared as quickly as he could, and before he was offered any cut-price perfume.

❖

## 22

Harriet had summoned Vonk to her and Ian's room, which was acting as an office, and in this case, an interview room. It was almost 2.00 pm.

The door had been left open. Vonk came into the room. Harriet hung one of the hotel's 'DO NOT DISTURB' notices around the outer handle of the door and shut it.

Ian Scott was already seated behind a rectangular wooden table of a light oak shade. On it was a manilla A4 file, notebooks and pencils ready for the interview, and a small, battered, tinplate ashtray in one corner.

What was not in view was a small tape recorder in a drawer in front of Harriet, although this had, deliberately, not yet been switched on.

There were three identical chairs around the table, two on one side and one on the other. They featured slightly splayed legs of black metal tubing, with thin, bright red fabric backrests and seats. They were conference chairs, but also, as Harriet had noted, doubled as good interview chairs, particularly regarding any suspect- not too spartan, but not too comfortable either.

Harriet took the chair alongside Ian, and Vonk levered his bulky frame into the chair facing them.

"Good afternoon, Mr Vonk," said Harriet. "You may recall from this morning's meeting that I am Chief Inspector Harriet Graham, and this is my colleague Detective Inspector Ian Scott, both from the Surrey and Sussex Police Force here in the United Kingdom."

"As you will also know, we are investigating the death - the suspicious death - of your colleague, Mr Piet Kuppers, and we believe you will be able to assist us in our enquiries."

Vonk made as to speak, but Harriet silenced him with an upraised hand.

"Please let me continue Mr Vonk-Willem. I will let you know when you can speak."

"You are in big trouble, Willem. Very big trouble indeed. So it will pay you to co-operate fully with us."

"I have in here," she said, picking up the manilla file from the desk and waving it in the air, "a European Arrest Warrant, signed and authorised by a judge in Amsterdam, requiring me to arrest you immediately pending your extradition to Holland to face charges of drug smuggling and money laundering."

"You see, Willem, the Dutch police have been following you for some time, and they, and now we, already know everything about your little, or not so little, sideline with the Schipol luggage handlers, and your money laundering activities both through your 'Motovonk' companies, and the purchases of artworks, arranged through Ms Angelique Durand's company. I can assure you the *politie* have an absolutely watertight case, confessions from others involved, and extensive evidence of your role."

"They knew you were here and, in any event, would have been waiting at Schipol to arrest you on Saturday. However, this matter has arisen in the UK, and needs to be attended to urgently before we return."

"You might also wish to know that the Dutch police have, a very short time ago, arrested and charged Messrs. Hans Hulshoff, Jan Mulders, Hans Van Kraay, and several other Dutch nationals, in connection with your drug smuggling and other illegal activities. I assume those I have named will be familiar to you."

"In addition, I believe that there are other arrests of Columbian and Swiss nationals currently taking place."

"Do you have anything to say?"

Vonk remained silent.

"We believe that the death of Mr Kuppers is not accidental, that he was deliberately poisoned, and that you are aware of the facts relating to it, and are involved in some way in it, together with Angelique Durand."

"You realise you will be going to prison for a long time for your drug and associated money laundering activities. A very long time. You can do yourself, myself, and the UK police a favour if you tell us what you know about the death of Mr Kuppers. In return, I will try to get the judge to take this into consideration when sentencing you, and we can try to see that you serve all of your sentence in Holland."

"This is an interview to obtain further information, and we are not charging you under caution at this point, so you can be quite open with us. Should you be cautioned later, you can then call your lawyer if you wish, but it may be easier for us all to get this UK situation over with easily and quickly."

"Also, any assistance you give will be taken into account by the UK police."

Harriet continued calmly, clearly and slowly, looking straight at Vonk.

"There is a very great deal we know, Willem. We know that you became aware that Kuppers was responsible for you losing your job at Eurair, all those years ago. We know of your relationship with Kuppers' partner, Angelique Durand. We know all the details of the gifts of the genever bottles, which presented you with the perfect opportunity to poison Kuppers. This was both to obtain your revenge over the Eurair affair, which you had been harbouring for some time, and also to enable you to pursue your relationship with Ms Durand without hindrance. We know this had been planned for some time and is not just an accidental event. You have nothing to lose, and something to gain, by providing a full confession. You will, of course, realise that we are interviewing Ms Durand similarly."

Vonk remained silent, unmoving, and staring ahead, whilst he took in, and processed the information Harriet had expounded. After a couple of minutes, he wriggled his posterior to move his chair back from its position close to the table to one about three feet from it. He then bent forward, his head lowered, supporting it on each side with a large hand just above his ears with an elbow resting on each knee. It was a posture similar to that of Rodin's statue of "The Thinker," and he certainly appeared to be doing a lot of thinking, his head rocking gently from side to side.

His face appeared to progressively lose its pallor, and his head movement seemed to become more pronounced.

The minutes passed. He was still saying nothing, staring down at the floor.

Harriet and Ian remained silent also.

This silence continued for several more minutes, then he suddenly gave a very loud, resigned, sigh.

It had been like watching Fred Dibnah's final demolition job - the Park Mill chimney in Oldham. Nothing happened for about twenty minutes, then the massive structure began to topple, and just seconds later it was all over.

Finally, Vonk slowly raised his head, moved his bulky frame into a more normal sitting position facing Harriet and Ian, and spoke.

His confidence seemed to have collapsed suddenly. His heavily accented, nasal delivery, with its near-perfect English, was clear enough, but spoken in a flat, unemotional monotone.

Willem Vonk shrugged resignedly.

"O.K.," he said. "I don't seem to have much option, do I?... But what I am going to tell you is only because I did not murder, or intend to murder, Piet Kuppers. His death is an accident. You must understand that. I am not going down on a murder rap."

Harriet stopped him. "I'm sorry Willem, would you mind repeating that, with this tape recorder switched on?" she asked, producing, and holding up, the small tape recording machine from the desk drawer.

"Makes no odds to me," he replied flatly, seemingly without any interest, or emotion, and he repeated his statement after Harriet had spoken a brief description of the event, time and place, into the tape recorder.

"Together with Angelique I intended to inconvenience, embarrass and discomfort him, sure, but to kill him, absolutely not."

"Also, I didn't want to run off with Angelique with him out of the way, whatever you think. Sure, we have slept together in the past, but our relationship was just one of convenience- and we didn't sleep together last night either."

At that moment Harriet's mobile phone on the desk rang and lit up. She picked it up and put it to her ear. It was Sian Parkinson.

"Excuse me," she said to Vonk, "I must take this call. I will leave the room, but only for a few minutes." She put the phone to her ear and went out of the room, and spoke into her mobile.

"Hello, Sian. No problem. I said interrupt me whatever I'm doing."

She listened intently for a few minutes, a short while, responding with a few "OKs", a "let me know the full detail later", a "thanks", and closed with a "speak soon".

She returned to the interview room, directed a "sorry" towards Vonk, and a "carry on".

He carried on.

"Where was I?"

"Ah yes, Angelique."

"She was a great asset in helping me assemble my collection of Dutch maritime paintings. You must have heard of them. They are famous in Holland. She was a world expert in that area, but I digress. I wanted occasional sex and intelligent company, and as far as I know, she wanted the same. But to live together? No way. She didn't want to live with me either. Ask her."

Harriet wanted to progress the question of the artworks, but opted to defer it for the present, and turned to the subject of the gifts.

"So, the plan was to put poison into the genever bottles, and the delayed reaction would let you both be far away from the scene when he became ill. Is that correct?" Harriet asked.

"Yes, that's right," Vonk replied. "But the poison was only to make him feel unwell, maybe a bit sick. I would then take over his job of running the conference."

"You overdid the dose of ricin, then? I suppose you got your underworld friends to provide it for you?"

"Ricin? Who said anything about ricin? What's ricin?" Vonk spoke in a staccato, puzzled series of questions, his brow furrowing as he did so.

"I was told it was tha..."

Suddenly his voice trailed away, then stopped, without finishing the word. He was silent for a few minutes, then he seemed to come alive, emotion returning to his voice. He almost spat out his thoughts.

"De dubbelkruisende teef"

Harriet's knowledge of Dutch consisted of two words at the most, but she didn't need the dictionary to translate that phrase.

Vonk repeated it, then continued.

"She set all that up. Gave me the liquid to put into the bottle for Kuppers. No one else's bottle would have been touched. I'm certain no one else will have been affected. She told me it was thallium, just a small amount, as I said, to make him feel ill and sick on Wednesday morning. I looked it up. It all seemed to make sense to me."

"Could you tell us more about the plan you concocted between you?"

"Alright. Makes no difference to me," Vonk shrugged.

"The Conference had been planned for a long while. Van was the big white chief, the *"grote chef,"* Kuppers was the organiser, and I bankrolled it. The presents of the genever were my idea, and they both thought it was a good one, and left that all to me.

Angelique and I were talking one day. She wanted out of the relationship with Kuppers, his womanising was getting too much, and she suspected his visits to, shall we say, 'ladies of the night', although there were probably quite a few during the day.

Also, her business was in trouble. Several of her larger clients had gone to the bigger dealers; Levin, Halpen and so on.

Unfortunately for her, they hadn't signed a cohabitation agreement, which she had been pushing him to do for some time."

He looked over the table at Harriet and explained.

"In Holland, this is an agreement that must be notarised, and would determine such matters as inheritance, division of assets, and so on.

This was very important to her, as Kuppers was an only child, no living parents, very wealthy, and, in the event of his death, without this document, she wouldn't inherit anything, which, as you would imagine, she was quite keen to avoid."

Vonk smiled, but paused to blow his nose, then seemed to be thinking for a couple of minutes, his head down in his hands again. He lifted it up to resume his upright sitting position and carried on.

He had now recovered much of his poise.

He shook his head.

"It is all becoming clear to me."

"*Stomme dwaas,*" he said, and then again in English, "Stupid fool."

"She has the cohabitation agreement alright, signed, sealed and delivered, and she has set me up. She has planned it all, right from the start.

I wanted revenge, of course I did, but thinking back it was her who first suggested the idea of using the genever gifts to make him ill, and she who said she knew of something that could be put into Kuppers' bottle. Something harmless at the end of the day, and she knew where she could obtain it. She told me it was called Thallium, which I had never heard of, but, as I said, I looked it up, and it seemed okay to me.

Once we had the plan it became quite exciting working it all out, and we had plenty of time to do it. I ordered the genever bottles-replicas of the old-fashioned clay ones, with the removable stopper, not the sealed tops. I ordered a few spares in addition to the Doves we knew were attending. They were delivered first of all to my house in Holland.

Angelique had given me the Thallium previously. It didn't seem very much to me. A couple of teaspoonfuls in a small glass bottle. That was all that was needed, she said. I poured some genever out of one of the bottles, topped it up with the Thallium, marked the base of it with a red dot, and had them shipped over the week before.

I worked closely with the Conference Manager. Lovely girl, and very efficient, Leila Zafiri. She ensured they were safely looked after in her room when they came.

We designed the bottleneck hangs, with the dove, the motorcycle, the greeting, and the attendees' names, and had them printed in Holland. Very professional looking, they were. I sent those to Leila to arrive the week before, but they were only to be put on the bottles on Tuesday morning, which I had arranged to do together with Leila so I could make sure that the marked bottle went into Kuppers' room."

Harriet had let Vonk speak for quite a while, but she now interposed.

"...and where does Angelique fit into all this after she provided you with the thallium, or ricin, or whatever the liquid was?"

"You probably know already. Angelique was never part of the Conference proper, but she was due to be coming to the UK for a few days in early May anyway, shopping and meeting a girlfriend in London, visiting Brighton and so on. It was that proposed visit that prompted the 'Kuppers Plan' if I can call it that.

So, she suggested to Piet that she be booked into the Median from Wednesday to Friday, and join the group for the closing dinner, on Friday evening. He asked me, so it all got fixed up. She was booked into the suite that was interconnected with Piet's room."

"Why go to all that trouble if all that would happen was that Kuppers would be ill for a day or so?" asked Harriet.

"Yes, it all seemed very complicated- unnecessarily complicated - to me, but she said that it was better to distance ourselves as much as possible from any involvement, so I didn't think a lot about it. I just went along with it."

Vonk paused. "I would like a toilet break, please?" he asked .

"OK," said Harriet, "this is a good point to take a time out, anyway," she said, switching off the tape recorder.

"D.I.Scott here will accompany you, and when you both return I would like you, Mr Vonk, to tell me your movements yesterday, in as much detail as you can."

They were back from the toilet promptly, Ian had entered them to keep an eye on Vonk, and to make sure he didn't go into a cubicle.

"Well, Willem, please carry on. Your movements yesterday, please?" asked Harriet, "in as much detail as possible."

Vonk seemed to have had recovered more of his poise. During the toilet break, Harriet had assembled some glasses and a large glass jug of water. She poured out three glassfuls. Vonk took one, followed by a couple of large gulps, then began.

"I arrived at the Median in the early hours of yesterday morning. The plane was late. Whoever put around the story of Swiss precision wasn't on my flight."

"So, I was in a bit of a hurry, and didn't really have time to organise myself as I would have liked, and it was really important to make sure Kuppers got the right bottle of genever, for reasons we have already talked about."

He allowed himself half a smile.

"As you probably know, I had scheduled a meeting at 7.30 am with Ms Zafiri in one of her training rooms. I tried to get there a little early to make sure everything was organised. I was early, but it didn't seem to work out. I guess I was a bit on edge.

I did manage to sort everything out with the bottles, though, to make sure the bottle that went into Piet's room was the one with the thallium. I'm sure about that.

I had also put a clean bottle of Genever into my briefcase from those on the table without Ms Zafiri noticing. That was a bit awkward, but I think I managed it okay.

I then left to catch a train from Gatwick to Victoria. I was in a bit of a rush but caught my planned train from Gatwick. I had a lunch meeting arranged at the Osier Graumann Bank Branch. They handle my Motovonk Business in the UK, as well as some of my personal portfolio outside of the Netherlands. The UK Motovonk sales are very small, and all imports, but I was hoping to expand it over here soon. My meeting was only concerning my personal investments, though.

When I arrived in Victoria, I had something to do first, though, before I went to the bank. I had to sort out the Kuppers business.

The arrangement with Angelique was that I would put the clean bottle of Genever into a safe place close to the National Gallery in London.

It was all very well thought out. No mobile phone contact or tracking. I had left my mobile back at the Hotel. I could always plead to be in a rush - which I was, anyway.

So, I had an orange plastic bag in my briefcase, like your supermarket bags, the thicker plastic ones, not those useless thin things. I had put the 'clean' genever bottle into the plastic bag when I was on the train.

I made sure the taxi dropped me outside the main entrance to the National Gallery, but then made my way to Short's Court, off Lime Street, just at the back of the

National Gallery. It's an ordinary cul-de-sac, well out of the way of any CCTV street cameras. Towards the dead end, there is a rubbish bin, with a lid, attached to a post." He gave a thin smile. "I am familiar with its use for drug drop purposes."

"Our plan, or rather Angelique's plan - it was far too, how do you English say? 'Cloak and dagger' for me - was for her to collect the clean genever bottle from the bin after her visit to the National Gallery. She would then bring it back to the Median and exchange it with the poisoned bottle which would be in Kuppers' room.

We had arranged to meet in my room to deal with the seascape painting purchase. She would bring the poisoned bottle along with her, and we would clean it out, and get rid of it at some point. I think we cleaned it out and just put it in the wardrobe in my room with the other spares. We were going to get rid of it later. We had to put that to one side with everything that was happening.

"So, there we are, Detective Chief Inspector. I've been played for a fool, taken for a ride, have I not – *'Belachelijk maken'*?" he said slowly.

"I'll have to look up the Dutch for 'rhetorical question'," thought Harriet.

"Hold on a minute," she said. "We need to go back to… where did you say… 'Short's Court'?"

"So, you put the bag with the bottle into the drop-box in Short's Court as planned?" asked Harriet.

"Yes. It all went exactly to plan," confirmed Vonk. "I put it in the bin, covered it up carefully with some waste paper that was already there, then went on to my meeting at the Bank." He would have continued, but Harriet interrupted.

"What time was all this?" she asked.

"Er, I guess about 11.30 am, 11.45 am something like that when I finished making the drop. It didn't take that long. Then I made my way to the Bank."

"I walked," he stated, proudly.

Once he had started Harriet couldn't stop him.

"It was, as I mentioned, the Banque Osier Graumann. Their London office is located near Aldermanbury Square.

They handle some of my private investments. It was a fairly recent business arrangement. My meeting was for lunchtime-12.25pm, with their Personal Investment Manager - Wietske Groskamp -you can call her to verify all that with her if you want. I've got her direct line number. Luckily the timings all went to plan, and I didn't need my mobile.

The walk was about 40 minutes, so it fitted perfectly, and a sunny day, too.

Two hours for lunch, then I travelled back to Gatwick. I didn't walk back to Victoria Station, I took a taxi ride this time. I was back at around 4.00 pm. Then I chilled out and met up with the boys later for pre-dinner drinks, and then the dinner. Then some work on the purchase of the painting, and finally the wait for Angelique."

"Yes, Ms Durand," said Harriet. "Was she your co-conspirator in your extra-curricular drug activities, as well as in the plot to inconvenience, or kill, Mr Kuppers?"

"Was she aware that she was indirectly, or directly, providing a significant conduit for your ill-gotten cash? Did she know that she was doing your dirty washing?" asked Harriet.

Vonk ignored, or failed to completely understand the inference, and just carried on.

"You mean the purchases of the paintings?" he questioned.

"I suppose I should say 'Yes', shouldn't I?" he continued, "and implicate her in retaliation for her landing me in *'de stront'*- the shit to you- but the correct answer is 'I don't know'.

Every art-related transaction between myself and Ms Durand's company was performed on a strictly correct basis. Properly invoiced, recorded and declared for tax purposes. There was no other agreement between us. I suppose, at least initially, she assumed that my money to buy the artworks came from my personal funds. From my business.

I first dealt with her father, Alphonse - the "old man" - until he died, then afterwards with Angelique. I am absolutely sure he had no idea of the source of the funds with which I acquired the paintings. I don't think she did either, at first. However, over the past year or so, her level of commissions began to increase considerably. I knew prices were rising in the art market, and, of course, I was making a great deal of money from the transactions anyway, but she might have guessed, or known.

In any event, any suggestion that things weren't completely legitimate was never discussed between us.

You might be surprised to know that not all criminals are violent, unintelligent, lying and disloyal psychopaths. Some are even a little cultured, with some moral values."

It was clear Vonk felt himself to be in that category.

He continued.

"If you look at my CV you will see that, after the Fokland fiasco in the UK, I had to start a career again, more or less from the bottom. My very first job was at Schipol, starting as a baggage handler supervisor, which is where I got my detailed knowledge of how everything worked in that area, and met the workers, some of whom I later recruited."

"Nearly all were Southeast Asians, some legal immigrants, some not. They were really exploited. Low wages, terrible living conditions. When I recruited them I made sure I gave each one of them a decent cut- and told them to save as much as they could for when it would, inevitably, come to an end. Even then, I knew what would happen eventually."

Ian glanced at Harriet. "He should have been working at Rotterdam Airport. He would have been the 'Robin Hood of Rotterdam' then. As it is he's just 'Saint Willem of Schiphol.'" She smiled.

Vonk went on. "Why did I become involved in drug smuggling, at all?" He asked, staring into space, and then was proceeding to answer his own question, but Ian cut him off.

"Because it provided you with the money to kick-start your Moto Vonk business?" queried Ian, "if that's the right way to express it."

"Yes," said Vonk. "I suppose that I should have given it up after Moto Vonk got off the ground. "I don't know why I didn't. I just wanted to get back at society, I suppose. I was going to give it up, and I did take more of a back seat. I became addicted myself. As big an addict as my customers, I guess."

"Funny, though," he said, "I've never touched legally prohibited drugs, soft or hard. I mean personally consumed them. Never ever. Money was the drug, I guess."

He gave a resigned look, then stopped. "I hope you will take all this into account. All of it is an honest recollection I can assure you."

"Thank you, Willem. I will see what I can do," Harriet remarked, less than convincingly, then spoke in an official tone.

"Mr Willem Vonk," she said, "As you were informed earlier I am arresting you, and taking you into custody under the terms of the European Arrest Warrant for the offences of Laundering the Proceeds of Crime and Illicit Trafficking in Narcotic drugs and Psychotropic substances."

"You have the right to be informed of the warrant, its contents, and the right to consent to surrender to the member state that issued the warrant."

"I assume, from what you have told us that you consent to such surrender."

Vonk paused for a few moments, then gave a brief "Yes".

With that, he departed with a Sergeant Brill who had come over from the Gatwick Station. He was then to collect some belongings and spend the night in the less comfortable cell of the Gatwick Police Station.

Harriet and Ian looked at each other.

"Well, well, well," Harriet said. "I didn't expect that."

"One thing before we decide how we are going to approach the interview with Ms Durand. Let's get the Met to check out the drop box. I have a contact there that could arrange things for me. His name is Jimmy Anthony. He's a Super now. I worked with him for a couple of years, and we've kept in touch."

Harriet picked up her phone, dialled a number, and waited for a reply.

"Hello, this is Detective Chief Inspector Harriet Graham of the Surrey and Sussex Force. Is Superintendent James Anthony available, please?" she asked.

"Ok I'll hold," said Harriet, and waited a minute or so. Someone answered.

"Hello, Jimmy. I'm fine, thanks. Could you scramble your phone, please? Thanks."

"Jimmy, I wonder if you could do a small favour for me. It won't take long. I'd like you to get one of your sergeants to pop down to Trafalgar Square for me. Immediately. This is off the record for the moment, completely off the record. I'll fill in all the details for you later, but nothing recorded for now. I wouldn't ask you this way normally but it's very urgent."

"Thanks, Jimmy. It's very simple. I want your officer to slip down to a little road near the National Gallery called Short's Court, off Lime Street. Near the end of the road is a rubbish bin attached to a post. The officer should look into the bin. Towards the bottom should be an orange plastic bag, of good quality, and inside the bag should be a brown, clay-coloured, bottle. If it is there, ask your sergeant to remove it carefully keep it, and wear gloves to handle it, and I will send someone round to pick it up from you. I can assure you one hundred percent it is absolutely safe to handle. It is not any kind of explosive or other hazardous device. If it isn't there, don't delay, get the sergeant to call you, and you can pass that news straight to me immediately."

"Thanks again, Jimmy. You know I wouldn't ask if it wasn't urgent. If it's there or if it isn't, call anyway."

Harriet rang off.

"What was that all about?" asked Ian.

"Just something in hand if we need it. I've got a feeling that Ms Durand is going to be a very slippery customer."

"Let's see what she has to say for herself, shall we, but before we do that I just want to take a quick look at Wikipedia."

Harriet opened up her laptop, typed a few short words on the keyboard, and beckoned Ian to look over her shoulder at the computer screen.

"Sian gave me a few details during Vonk's interview, but I need to quickly add a little to my knowledge - and yours, I think," she said to Ian.

He focused on the laptop.

The page reference was headed "RICIN," and they both read the content of the article.

Ricin is a highly potent toxin produced in the seeds of the castor oil plant 'Ricinus Communis'. A dose of purified ricin powder, the size of a few grains of table salt can kill an adult human.

Ricin can take several forms, a powder, mist or pellet, or be dissolved in liquid. Experts vary in the estimates of time to death but can be anything from 6 to 24 hours if not treated in the meanwhile.

The highest profile case to date was the 1978 murder of the Bulgarian dissident Georgi Markov. He was jabbed in the leg, in public, on Waterloo Bridge in the middle of London by a man using a weapon built into an umbrella. The weapon embedded a small pellet containing ricin into Markov's leg. Markov died four days later."

Ricin features in the TV show "Breaking Bad," in which the main character Walter White concocts the poison to kill a drug dealer.

"That's the answer then Ian," said Harriet. "We ask everyone if they watch "Breaking Bad," and the one who says they don't watch it is the murderer, but just in case that doesn't work, I'll read more on the subject when I have a spare moment, and you should do the same."

Ian kept his thoughts on the "spare moment" to himself.

23

Ian had just joined Harriet in their interview room.

"I'll go and collect Ms. Durand " she said to Ian." But before I do, have a quick read of this."

"It came through to me not long ago. It's from Barrowclough. Apparently, he made notes from a telephone discussion with the Dutch."

She handed Ian a single sheet of A4 with a couple of typed paragraphs on it.

"In case you were wondering, it's not the mysterious Kuppers page 2, but some sketchy info on Angelique Durand. Better than nothing before her interview, though."

Ian scanned the A4 sheet. It read as follows: -

'ANGELIQUE FLEUR DURAND

Age 46. Divorced. Only child. One 'Ex-stepchild'- a girl. That is to say, not her own child, but that of the father from a previous relationship before Angelique. Both ex-husband and daughter apparently now live in the wilds of the French speaking part of Canada. No record of any contact. Parents no longer alive. No known convictions in Holland or elsewhere '

Harriet paused for a short while to allow Ian to absorb the text, then carried on.

"As we know, she took over the running of the art dealership after the death of her father. She has retained her maiden name of Durand, both personally and in her business."

"So, surprise, surprise - I don't think. Clean as a whistle. Nothing incriminating, at least as far as the Dutch go, either in her personal or business activities. I'm sure the Dutch police would have given her a very thorough going over in the course of their Vonk investigations. Maybe they're just keeping schtum.

Anyway, that's it. Whatever paths she has trodden, she has trodden them very carefully - at least in public- and somehow has apparently avoided association with Mr. Vonk's off-piste enterprises."

"Now let's see what the lady herself has to say" said Harriet and headed out to retrieve Angelique Fleur Durand.

✳

A short time later, when Harriet entered the room with Angelique in tow, Ian Scott was already seated behind the rectangular wooden table.

The seating arrangements for the interview were identical to the set-up for that of Willem Vonk.

Harriet indicated the single chair. "Please sit down Ms Durand," she said.

"As you are aware, I am Detective Chief Inspector Harriet Graham of the Surrey and Sussex Police Force here in England, and this is my colleague Detective Inspector Scott."

"As you also will know, we are investigating the unexpected death of Mr Piet Kuppers, who we understand was your partner. I'm sorry if any of this will be distressing for you, but you will realise we have to progress things as quickly as possible."

Angelique looked at them across the desk.

"I may smoke," she said, eyeing the very low-quality battered ashtray disdainfully as she reached for it. It wasn't a question.

Harriet nodded, and Angelique took out a flip-top carton of her 'Abaira' cocktail cigarettes and her lighter from a bag and placed them on the table. She opened the carton lid, selected a cigarette, lit it, moved the ashtray to her right-hand side, and deliberately placed the open carton in front of her.

The cigarettes were of individual colours. Pink, light green, purple and yellow, with gold tips. The misty pink, blue and yellow shades on the box merged into a rainbow background, over which was inscribed a crest and gold lettering of the brand. The whole effect seemed to complement her appearance, which wasn't accidental.

'Attractive on the outside, which might mask something more harmful within,' thought Harriet, looking at the carton and its contents. 'Is this also the case with Ms Angelique Durand herself?' she mused, then got down to the nitty gritty of the interview.

"I understand that you were the first person to discover Mr Kuppers' body, and possibly also the last person to see him alive."

"The first statement is true, Detective Inspector, but the second may or may not be true."

Harriet looked at her quizzically.

She went on to explain more fully.

"As to the discovery of the body, myself and Ms Zafiri, the Hotel Conference Manager, went up to my room together at approximately 8.15 am. I went through the connecting door into Piet's room, and he was on the bed, not moving, or breathing, and with an awful white face. It appeared to me obvious that he was dead, but, of course, I am not as experienced in the discovery of dead bodies as an English Detective Inspector. "

"Detective Chief Inspector," corrected Harriet.

Angelique completely ignored that comment.

"As to the second statement, as you will know, or should know, that after arriving in England I spent the Tuesday afternoon and evening, as planned, in London, before coming to the Hotel. I had arranged for my luggage for these few days and a briefcase containing business correspondence, to be delivered to the hotel, and placed in my room ready for my arrival."

"I arrived quite late and had some very important business to conclude with Mr Willem Vonk before the Conference began. I took the briefcase and one of my suitcases with me, which included my nightwear and toiletries, and also, in a Chloe shopping bag, a lovely sweater I had bought in London which I wished to wear on Wednesday and did so. I have it on now." She looked at Ian. "You like?" she asked. It was another rhetorical question.

"The other suitcase I left in the room, together with a shopping bag. This bag had inside a dress I had also bought at the same shop in London, and a box of 200 Abaira cigarettes, the Cocktail ones, which I purchased earlier at Ivanoffs, an example of which you see before me now."

"It is one of the oldest cigarette brands in the world, you know. The original cigarettes were handmade in the Russian tradition. The Abaira Company was the supplier of the Austro-Hungarian Imperial Court and also, amongst others, the Court of the United Kingdom of Great Britain and Ireland. The packets feature the motif of the Austro-Hungarian Imperial Black Eagle, but of course, I forget, you already knew all of that."

Both Ian and Harriet ignored the heavy sarcasm and let her carry on.

"I am the buyer for his marvellous collection of Dutch seascapes. The Dutch painters of that period, the seventeenth century, were the very best in the world. The Dutch were the greatest maritime nation of the world at that time."

'Apart from Britain,' thought Ian. A thought he kept to himself, which was wise, because he was wrong, and Angelique was right.

Angelique continued. "Enough of the art history lesson. The urgency of the situation meant that I had to go directly to Mr Vonk's room to conclude all the paperwork for the transaction. I was buying two paintings, a Porcellis, and a Peeters from a dealer in California, which meant we were working to US Pacific daylight time. So, I just put my head around Piet's door. A cursory look, as you English might say. The lights in his bedroom were off, so his room was very dark. I couldn't make him out properly, but he appeared to be asleep, and I had a lot of work to do on our bid for the paintings, so I picked up the briefcase with the documentation, switched off my bedroom light, locked my door and went down the corridor to Willem's room."

"Don't you think it strange that practically the first thing you do after you arrive here is to go straight to another man's bedroom, with your toiletries and nightwear?" Ian queried.

Angelique looked for a second at the pink cigarette between her fingers with their silver and mauve-painted nails, then stubbed it out carefully and precisely.

"No, not at all," she said, straightforwardly and without hesitation. "My relationship with Willem is purely one of business and is of long standing. I - in actuality, my company - purchase paintings for Mr Vonk, some of which are for his famous collection of Dutch seascapes, and others, which my company sells on his behalf."

Harriet interrupted.

"Mr Vonk has told us that your artwork dealership acts as a 'washing machine' - a conduit for channelling and legitimising his illegal monetary gains from drug trafficking, and that you are well aware of that fact, and you took excessive commissions in order to shore up an otherwise failing business."

Angelique didn't bat either of her carefully made-up eyelashes. She looked straight back at Harriet.

"Pure fantasy," she replied unhesitatingly. "I employ highly qualified, and even more highly paid, Accountants, to audit and prepare my books. As even you, Inspector, would well be aware, the price of works of art has increased dramatically in recent years with the entry of Chinese, Russian and Middle Eastern buyers into the market."

I'm afraid Willem is letting his imagination run away with him. His little scheme to kill or injure Piet has backfired, and he is trying to deflect blame onto myself, as the easiest target. Total nonsense."

Angelique reached slowly and calmly for another cigarette, lit it, tilted her head upwards in a theatrical manner, exhaled smoke, and continued.

Harriet looked at Angelique.

"Carry on, Ms Durand," she said, with a half-smile. "I really don't mind that you are dictating the interview. Just tell me when you want me to answer any questions."

Angelique took no notice, ignoring the sarcasm.

"Now where was I?" she asked. "Oh yes. Piet," she said, continuing.

"In any event, Piet and I live separated lives, and I use that word deliberately. We simply have separate existences if that makes sense. He has his motorbikes, I have my art. He has his lady friends, and I can do what I want in that regard. Sometimes I do. Mostly I don't. It is a mutually acceptable arrangement. We understand each other."

"How long had you known Mr Kuppers?" asked Harriet.

"I think just about three years," replied Angelique.

"...and how did you meet?"

"It was at a post art exhibition dinner at the 'Bord d'Aux 'Restaurant in Amsterdam. Very inappropriate titling, don't you think?

It was the exhibition of Caravaggio and Rembrandt at the Van Gogh Museum. Willem was at the exhibition but couldn't go to the dinner, so he arranged for me to call Piet, to see if he would partner me for the dinner, which he did, and it all went from there."

Harriet had long realized that Angelique was an extremely cool and clever customer. She had pre-empted several of the questions she would have asked and provided facts that would support an alibi, steering them towards what she wanted them to know.

Harriet decided it was time she took the lead in the interview. It seemed clear that little was going to upset her about the death and the surrounding circumstances.

"We believe Mr Kuppers' death was the result of poisoning. Is there anyone you know who would wish to poison him? Any of his motorcycling acquaintances, for instance? Anyone holding a grudge against him?"

"Not as far as I am aware."

"Did you know that rumour has it that Mr Kuppers was instrumental in your friend, I mean business acquaintance, Mr Willem Vonk, losing his job with the Fokland Aircraft Company following the Eurair collapse?"

"Eurair?" she queried. "I have never heard of Eurair. I have a vague recollection that Willem mentioned that they worked together for Fokland for a short time. This Eurair collapse must have been a long time ago." She showed no signs of upset. No visible reaction at all. "Any rumour has passed me by, I'm afraid."

"I am led to believe Mr Kuppers was a wealthy man. Is that your understanding?"

"I believe that is so. I, too, as you will have deduced, am a wealthy woman in my own right."

Ian interposed, "Who will now inherit Kuppers' assets?" he asked, realising he had contributed little to the questioning so far.

"I assume it would be myself," replied Angelique in a matter-of-fact manner, stubbing out her cigarette.

"I know that Piet was an only child, and both his parents are no longer alive."

Ian switched tack. Harriet let him proceed. "Do you know of a very small, red notebook that was found amongst Mr Kuppers effects after his death?"

"A small, red notebook, you say. No, I know of no such article."

"I am sorry to bring this up, but were you aware that Mr Kuppers was in the habit of making the acquaintance of, shall we say, professional ladies, on an occasional basis? This red notebook provided contact details of such ladies."

Angelique didn't bat an eyelid. "No, I did not, but it does not surprise me. As I mentioned before, we have somewhat separate existences. I knew he had lady friends. Their nature or profession doesn't especially concern me. After the first months, our intimacy quickly passed."

"You are saying that such behaviour on his part, had you known of it, would not have angered you?"

"No, Detective Inspector, not unduly, and certainly not sufficiently for me to want to kill him, even if I had the opportunity, if that is the implication."

Ian ignored the comment, outwardly at least. Harriet then took over again as lead questioner.

She looked at Angelique. "One final thing, for the moment, Ms Durand. Could you tell me of your movements and whereabouts yesterday?"

"Certainly. I will start from my arrival in England until the end of the day."

Angelique began, "You will know some of this. Some, you will not. All timings are approximate, but close. Further investigation will allow you to become more precise."

"I landed at Heathrow Airport at 10.30 am, on the 10.15 am flight from Schiphol. There is the one hour time differential, of course. My purpose for the afternoon and evening yesterday was shopping, a visit to the National Gallery, and a dinner with an old girlfriend of mine, before coming to the Median hotel."

"After airport clearance, I took a taxi to central London and shopped firstly in Bond Street. I went to the clothing shop Chloe, where I bought the sweater, I have referred to and a dress, which I brought back with me and which is in my room, unopened. I also purchased a pair of Sermoneta leather gloves, the ones with the hand stitching, in dark cream. *'Tres jolie'*. I can show them to you if you wish. I have explained much of this already, as you know."

Harriet interrupted.

"What you haven't yet explained is why you were wearing those same cream Sermoneta leather gloves when you walked the short distance from your room to that of Mr Vonk at midnight last night, when you were not wearing them when you entered the hotel. *C'est tres inhabituel, n'est-ce pas?*"

Angelique didn't bat an eyelid. Didn't look surprised. Didn't deny it. Didn't ask Harriet how she knew.

*'Oui, c'est vrai,'* she replied, but then continued in English.

"I just wanted to wear them, I wished to have the luxury of the beautiful leather on my fingers, to wear them at midnight, and to show them off to Willem. I put them on in my room, looked at them in the mirror, and then left to attend to the business of the paintings."

Harriet, having obtained no reaction, of either surprise or guilt, let it go.

Angelique resumed the story of her day's movements.

"I then went to the National Gallery, to the Corot exhibition. His landscapes are incredible, particularly of Italy. A precursor of the French impressionists, you know- or perhaps you don't know."

"Is this too much detail?" queried Angelique.

"No, just carry on," said Harriet, "I'll tell you when my ignorance of art is matched by your lack of knowledge of police procedures."

Angelique produced a small smile, *"Touchè,"* she said appreciatively, and continued.

"Before viewing the wonderful Corots I had I had a bite of lunch in the National Gallery Café. I then proceeded to Harrods."

"What time was it when you left the National Gallery?" asked Harriet.

"About 4 pm, I would imagine," responded Angelique.

"I started walking, down past Trafalgar Square. I had gone as far as the Cenotaph, but decided it was too far to continue on foot, so I hailed a black cab for the remainder of the journey. I recall it was one of the newer ones, with dreadful technicolour advertising daubed all over it, like a late Jackson Pollock action painting with text overlay."

'...and that's coming from someone who is a walking advertisement for luxury fashion brand names,' thought Harriet. However, she kept those thoughts to herself.

Angelique continued, "I had only a quick look around Harrods. After that I went to the 'Luxury Nails Beauty Boutique' in Mayfair, where I had my nails freshly manicured and painted." She held her right hand up in front of her face, slightly away from her, fingers splayed apart, palms facing herself, the nails facing Ian. "Aren't they beautiful?" she said.

"Very distinctive," observed Ian, in a non-committal tone of voice.

"Oh, I forgot," she added, "just before I had my nails attended to, I called into Ivanoffs of London, in St James Street, for a fresh supply of my 'Abaira' cigarettes, which, again, I have mentioned to you earlier."

"I then went to Soho to meet my girlfriend. Her name is Sophie Bonnaire. Clermont hyphen Bonnaire actually, but she usually drops the Clermont, and therefore the hyphen also. She has a flat in Hampstead. We met at the famous 'Coach and Horses' pub for a few pre-dinner drinks, then down the road to Gaultier Soho, the French Restaurant, for dinner. Sophie had booked the table. We were seated at around 8.15 pm."

"At about 10.15 pm, we left the restaurant, and we travelled together by taxi to Victoria Station. I caught a train to Gatwick, arriving at 11.30-ish. I then checked in at the Hotel at 11.45 pm. The rest you know."

"Many of these activities were pre-arranged before I left Holland, and the bookings for them can be verified. I have Amex Centurion Gold Card receipts for the Corot, the sweater, the dress, gloves, cigarettes, and the nails. Sophie had booked the excellent Galtier, and she settled the bill."

"I often place the till receipts for my shopping expenditures into the bags themselves until I sort them later. I am sure you will find the till receipts for the items to which I refer, in the bags in my room. These will, of course, provide you with the exact date and time of these purchases."

"Sophie - you can check on her if you wish - paid with her card for the pre-dinner drinks and, as I mentioned, the meal. Oh, and she stood the taxi fare as well."

'I bet Sophie's card wasn't a Zampa 105 Classic Card for dodgy payers with a 50% APR,' thought Harriet.

Her thoughts were interrupted by the ringtone of her mobile.

"Yes," she said and listened.

"Thank you, Jimmy. Much appreciated," she said and rang off.

She picked up a pencil and wrote a few hurried words onto a scrap of paper, folded it in half and passed it to Ian. He unfolded it and looked down at the writing. "No orange bag, no bottle in bin" read the note.

"Sorry," said Harriet, "Carry on, Ms Durand."

Angelique continued.

"As I knew I would not be arriving at the hotel until late in the evening, and wished to travel around London with no baggage, I arranged for a small travelling case with some clothes and other items to be sent from Amsterdam to Ms Zafiri, who then arranged the placement of the case in my room prior to my arrival."

"I proceeded to Willem's room, and we prepared all the information we needed for our bids. We then participated in the auction for the Dutch seascapes at the Timothy Paul and DuPanne Gallery in Los Angeles."

"Unfortunately, we were unsuccessful. I believe they were purchased by the new monied collectors-either the Chinese or Saudis. I'm sure they will appreciate them as much we do."

"You can check the veracity of all this if you require it."

"Thank you, Ms Durand, that will be all for the moment."

"Oh, a few things I forgot to ask you," Harriet said, almost as an afterthought, then carried on.

"When you left the National Gallery, did you walk to Short's Court, off Lime Street, which is just a short distance, and collect an orange plastic bag containing a genever bottle from a waste bin located at the end of that road, and did you bring that genever bottle with you back to the Median hotel, and did you then take that, or another similar bottle to Mr Vonk's room when you had your late-night encounter to bid for your paintings?"

Angelique looked straight back at Harriet, "I have no idea what you are talking about," she replied, very calmly. "As I have told you, I walked down to the Cenotaph immediately I left the National Gallery, and caught a cab there."

"That's odd," said Harriet. "Because your account is at variance with what has been told to us only a short time ago by Mr Vonk. He told us that he had left a genever bottle inside the orange coloured bag in that waste bin in that location, and that an arrangement had been made between you for you to collect this bottle, and bring it back with you to the Median Hotel."

"I know of no such bottle, nor did I bring anything back with me from London other than my own purchases which I have already detailed to you. If I was not bringing any such bottle back with me from London, then I could hardly have taken anything to Mr Vonk's room, could I?"

Harriet didn't answer but continued.

"There are a few other things Mr Vonk has told us."

"He says you concocted a plan, at your suggestion, to cause Mr Kuppers to be ill, and then for him, Mr Vonk, to take over the lead role in the running of the event."

"This involved you acquiring a poison, thallium, which you did, which would cause Mr Kuppers to be ill. Not seriously ill, but sufficient for him to be incapacitated, and that the thallium was to be put into the bottle of genever specifically marked out for him."

"In fact, Mr Vonk says that you were, shall we say, the driving force in all this, and his actions were subordinate to your wishes. You duped him."

"What do you have to say to all that?"

"Well, Detective Inspector," Angelique said, deliberately choosing not to use Harriet's correct rank. Harriet similarly didn't bother to correct her this time.

"I would repeat the words, spoken in court in 1963, as I recall, of one of my favourite English ladies, 'He would, wouldn't he?'"

She then stood up and spoke.

"I have nothing more to say on the matter," and collected up her cigarettes and lighter.

"You will find I am more Rosalind than Lady Macbeth," she said, and then more decisively.

"I wish to leave now. If you think I did as he says, then prove it."

Harriet shrugged and turned off the tape recorder.

"I believe another room has been arranged for you," she informed Angelique. "You should speak to Ms Zafiri to find out the details."

"Please don't leave the hotel until notified by the police, and don't discuss anything with other of the Dutch attendees of the event."

"I will be in touch later."

With that, Angelique Durand left the room.

"There was no point in going further, anyway," said Harriet to Ian. "There are many questions to which we are very unlikely to find the answers from her, and even less the truth."

Harriet looked at Ian.

"Did she know about the red book, and did she really care? Was she really ignorant of the Eurair collapse, and Vonk losing his job because of Kuppers?"

"So, she had first met Kuppers at the suggestion of Vonk. How strange. Almost as if Vonk and Angelique had set that up between them. Were they conspiring even at that stage, and waiting for the three years citizenship qualification time to elapse?"

"Her story appeared to be carefully crafted, lacking any spontaneity. Her movements on the Tuesday had all the hallmarks of precise advance planning. There were no gaps. She had even arranged for the case of clothes to be sent to the hotel."

"As an alibi for those hours, it was undoubtedly rock solid. She had no doubt that everything would check out, otherwise, she wouldn't have taken the risk of mentioning her movements in such detail."

"I also think that she had cleverly anticipated things not going exactly to plan, and if that were the case, which did in fact happen, she would be squeaky clean. This is why all the arrangements seem so unnecessarily complex- and that was to distance herself totally from any involvement."

"She had, however, made a small slip-up. When she said she was walking from the National Gallery to Harrods and was at the Cenotaph when she caught the taxi, she would have been walking in the opposite direction to that in which she wished to go. This remark deflected the possibility she had visited Short's Court to pick up the Genever bottle.

She lost patience in the end, and was absolutely confident she could finish the interview peremptorily.

"During her visit to Harrods, did she go to the kitchen department to examine the Teflon non-stick pans?" Harriet wondered.

"They both did it, didn't they?" she mused, "But we can't prove anything of Angelique's involvement."

## 24

Harriet had called the team together for an "end of day" briefing in the "Ops Room".

Attached to one of the side walls of the room was a large whiteboard with a supply of marker pens and a schoolroom rubber on a narrow shelf beneath. The board and accessories would probably have been used for training meetings.

Harriet looked over at it, pointed to it, and then spoke to the team.

"If I were on T.V. in one of those police dramas, I would be standing in front of a whiteboard like this one. It would be covered with high-quality, identical large-scale photographs of the suspects, with their names beneath, neatly written and arranged, and the cat's cradle of crisscrossed lines of red, white, and blue wool linking the various photographs. All the suspects sitting around in a circle. Strictly for the birds."

"Well, I'm not going to break the pattern of an investigative career. No photographs, no wool, no suspects in the room. Just a plain old black marker pen and the whiteboard."

"Let's consider what we have," said Harriet, picking up a black marker pen.

Then, to the right of the centre, in a clear, decisive hand, also in capitals, she wrote 'MOTIVE, MEANS and OPPORTUNITY', each forming a column.

Then, beneath, a list of names, on separate lines, "Willem Vonk", followed by "Angelique Durand", "Dirk Van Heemskerk", "Leila Zafiri", and "Other Doves".

Harriet completed the chart. Of the names, only Vonk and Angelique Durand ticked all the boxes.

"So, we have the victim, Mr Kuppers, who has died of poisoning, almost certainly ricin poisoning by ingestion. We have Vonk and Angelique Durand as the main suspects, each with both separate and joint reasons to kill Kuppers, and the opportunity to do so, which increases considerably if we assume they were colluding."

Harriet nodded towards Coppell.

"We have to thank D.S. Coppell here for unearthing an additional motive for Ms Durand to possibly want to kill Mr Kuppers."

"We interview Vonk first. He breaks down and accuses Ms Durand of being in cahoots with him to poison Kuppers, but with Thallium and not Ricin. Ms Durand, we interview straight after Vonk. She is as cool as a cucumber, or whatever the French equivalent is. She denies absolutely everything, and confronted with Vonk's story, says he is delusional, and proceeds to deliver a rock solid, and carefully thought out alibi."

"So, all very messy. But that's not all. I'll just repeat our findings from this morning.

An envelope turns up, postmarked to Gatwick, and sent first class. Probably on Monday. The someone who sent it knows Kuppers' unusual full set of birth names, - 'Pieter Marius Franciscus Kuppers'- and that he was staying at the Median Hotel.

The envelope contained an English/Dutch dictionary with four pages missing, two from the English/Dutch section and two from the Dutch/English section. We have no idea who sent it, or why, but we may not need to know.

The final forensics findings may well give us definitive answers. I expect to hear from Sian Parkinson sometime in the night." Harriet grimaced.

"Go home, and I'll brief everyone tomorrow on any updates. See you all in the morning- probably around 9.00 am."

25

# Thursday, May 19th, 2016

At around two thirty in the morning Harriet had drifted into a light, shallow, "Wizard of Oz" restless, dreamlike sleep with Barrowclough, Vonk, Collison and Leila Zafiri morphed into gargantuan, misshapen, ghostly figures, whirling before her, and all pointing to and laughing at the dead body of Kuppers which was laid at her feet.

Towering above them all was a giant figure of Angelique, dressed as in the Tenniel sketch of Alice, in a blue dirndl skirt and white pinafore. She was holding a green, hexagonal Victorian glass poison bottle in her hand. A manilla luggage tag was tied to the neck of the bottle, and inscribed, as in the story, with the words "DRINK ME" in large capitals.

Her reverie was interrupted by the ringtone of her mobile on her bedside table, which she had deliberately switched up to its loudest possible volume. She stretched out and fumbled for the device. It was just after four am.

"Graham," she mumbled in a blurred, halting tone.

"It's Sian Parkinson," said the voice at the other end of the line. Her soft Welsh tones bore little of the sing-song inflexion of South Wales, or the nasal pronunciation of the North Walians, but a pleasant, understated, and understandable Mid Wales lilt.

She spoke calmly and precisely.

"I have the Kuppers postmortem results for you, DCI Graham."

Harriet was suddenly wide awake.

"Firstly," said Sian, "this is to confirm my earlier diagnosis of ricin poisoning as the cause of death. There is no doubt that this is the case. There was a large presence of ricin in the body, sufficient to cause death, not only to Mr Kuppers, but to all the other guests of the Median Hotel, and half the population of Crawley."

"This suggests to me that this poisoning was a deliberate act, perpetrated either by a professional who wanted death to be a certain outcome, or that of a complete amateur."

"Let me say that, be it a professional or amateur perpetrator, Mr Kuppers, once he had ingested the ricin, was destined for a highly unpleasant death, and pre-expiry symptoms."

"I'll give you the textbook list, most of which have been suffered by the late Mr K."

"Vomiting; diarrhoea that may become bloody; blood in the urine; severe dehydration; seizures; and just prior to death, failure of the kidneys, liver, and spleen."

Harriet's short time improving her knowledge of ricin had paid dividends, as she had no need to interrupt Sian's flow.

Sian continued.

"As to time, and to a lesser extent, place of death of death present no major difficulties. Let's take place first. He clearly died in his hotel room, and the body had not been moved after death. He was lying more or less face down on the bed, and my livor mortis tests support this."

"The ambient temperature of the hotel room was similarly unproblematic, and the body was also in the rigid state of rigor mortis."

"As to the time of death, we know that he went to his room shortly after 4.00 pm on Tuesday afternoon, and he was found dead just after 8.00 am on Wednesday morning."

"Ingested ricin would normally create initial symptoms after approximately six hours, and he was dead by 8 o'clock the next day. We assume ingested as there is no evidence of any injection, and there would have been no ricin in the atmosphere."

"None of the above is a precise science, but my best estimate of the time of death would have been somewhere between 11.30 pm on Tuesday night and 6.00 am on Wednesday morning."

"So he would have been dead when Ms Angelique Durand entered the room at approximately 11.30 pm yesterday?" asked Harriet.

"It is possible, but the balance of probabilities is somewhat against that scenario. However, he may have been in a coma and making no undue sound, or any movement, so Ms Durand may have assumed he was sleeping. In any event, there is nothing in my analysis that can provide a definitive answer to that question. So, unless you have any more questions at this point, I will move on, as I have one small observation and then there is some key information for you."

"The small point first. There were very small quantities of two other fluids, which need some further diagnosis, but the quantities are so minute that in no way will they affect the cause of death that I have already outlined to you."

Sian paused at this juncture, and Harriet took the opportunity to take a second pillow, prop it up behind her, and shift her body into a more comfortable, upright position.

Sian continued.

"Now for the lab results on the forensic analysis of the genever bottles and glasses from the Dove's rooms, I will leave Kuppers and Vonk to one side for the moment, so that leaves eight doves. You will recall that Ms Angelique Durand was not given a gift of the genever."

"Fingerprints. All eight bottles had fingerprints of varying quality - of the occupant of the room themselves, and of Mr Vonk and Ms Zafiri. On the glasses only their own fingerprints were evident."

"There were no traces of anything other than genever in the bottles or glasses."

"The results from the bottle and glass in the room of Mr Vonk were the same as the other Doves."

She stopped speaking for a short while.

"I hope you are still awake, because here are the unusual and interesting findings."

"Carry on. I'm all ears," responded Harriet, "just putting on my ruby slippers."

Sian ignored the latter comment completely and continued.

"Kuppers' bottle and glass had no discernable fingerprints. None at all. The bottle of genever was half full, and there was a tiny residual amount of liquid in the glass. There was no poison in the genever bottle, or in the liquid from the glass."

"All squeaky clean- and in my opinion, much too squeaky clean."

"Now, the final sweep of the search of Vonk's room revealed, in the bottom of his wardrobe, three additional genever bottles, two appearing unopened, and one opened, but empty, bottle. The sergeant guessed they were spares."

"The empty bottle contained a very minute trace of genever, but no poison. Of the two remaining bottles, both full, forensic analysis showed one bottle containing only genever, no contamination. The other full bottle contained genever, but that one was mixed with a significant quantity of poison."

Sian paused for a moment, either for unintentional or deliberate effect.

"Have you got all that?" she asked.

"Yes," said Harriet. "Understood - I think. So, the ricin was in that unopened bottle in Vonk's wardrobe, then?" she queried.

"Ah," said Sian. "Not quite. As Hamlet said, *'Therein lies the rub'.*"

"I'm sorry to tell you that this poison was not ricin. It was thallium, and of a dosage possibly likely to be lethal or life-threatening."

"Have you heard of, or are familiar with, Thallium?" Sian queried.

"Oddly enough, until earlier today I was totally ignorant of it, but I have subsequently heard the name of it. But that is the limit of my knowledge. Please enlighten me further."

Sian provided a few words of explanation.

"Thallium is known as the 'poisoner's poison', colourless, odourless and tasteless it is easy to slip into food or drink in liquid form, or spilt on skin. It produces severe stomach pain, nausea, vomiting, and diarrhoea, usually within 3-4 hours of exposure."

"As you might infer from that, thallium would have been a close fit for the scenario before us. Symptoms, timing, location, etcetera. There's only one small problem. It's the wrong poison. It's not the poison that killed Mr Kuppers."

Harriet interrupted, "Are you one hundred percent certain that ricin was the killer?"

"No," replied Sian. "One hundred and ten per cent, actually."

"'Genever and thallium everywhere, but of ricin not a drop', as Coleridge might have said," continued Sian. "Other than that which resided inside the stomach of Mr Kuppers, of course."

"Let me make a couple of observations."

"Firstly, about thallium. In several cases involving thallium poisoning the perpetrator poisoned the victim at intervals before death finally occurred."

"There was a case of this in Norway, in 1999 as I recall. A lady called Inger Bakken was admitted to hospital and diagnosed with thallium poisoning, and subsequently died. Her ex-husband was the poisoner. His intention was not killing, rather to stop her promiscuity by repeatedly poisoning her, the final time by adding the toxin to a bottle of cognac. He continuously pretended ignorance as to what had caused her excruciating condition."

"A similarity here? I just throw it out before we finish for tonight, or rather this morning."

"Secondly, do you know the name of the large, brown, furry bear in the old children's TV programme 'Rainbow'?" asked Sian.

"Never heard of it," replied Harriet.

"You're too young," said Sian. "I'll tell you, then. It's Bungle."

"You will have my written report first thing in the morning, but it will simply repeat most of what I have just told you, so don't await it before taking any further action."

"I'll leave you now to digest those findings if you'll pardon the pun. I'm off to get some sleep. Everything provided, including a comfortable bed, in this luxury Mortuary Hotel. If you have questions for me I will be here tomorrow, and maybe beyond, with the further forensics to be done, and body to be attended to."

"Pob lwc," she said, "That's good luck."

26

It was 6.00 am. Harriet called Ian.

He was neither fully awake nor particularly pleased, but he dressed hurriedly and came into Harriet's room.

She updated him on Sian's findings.

He thought for a little while.

"So, Sian's findings and conclusions put Vonk and Angelique Durand in the clear, then?" observed Ian.

"Well, only as far as poisoning Kuppers with ricin, but I would hardly say in the clear. They are guilty of conspiracy to cause grievous bodily harm, but we can only prove that in respect of Vonk. I guess that the devious and cunning Angelique can sail away and enjoy the Kuppers' legacy, a completely free and wealthy lady. I would say she has reached her personal goal six months earlier than she planned, and with less hassle in the end. Who says crime doesn't pay?"

"We will update Barrowclough and the Dutch police, and hand over Vonk completely to the latter. They can both sort out all the politics at the UK and Dutch ends, but I don't think Kuppers' death has anything to do with murky Dutch politics any longer, but we need to prove that by finding the real murderer, or murderers."

"As the song goes, there are more questions than answers, but I think the answer lies, not in the present, but in the past."

"Let's get some sleep. I'll arrange breakfast in our own little ops room, we'll brief Barrowclough. He can handle the Dutch police and Mister Vonk, and we'll push on with our investigation. See you there at around 7.30 am."

Ian gave a yawn, nodded, and left Harriet's bedroom.

## 27

7.30 am seemed to come along very quickly, too quickly, to Ian. He rubbed his eyes, splashed cold water on his face, took a quick shave, Ward Stradlater style, then made his way cautiously to meet Harriet.

He found her wide awake, and with a sheet of pencilled notes in front of her. She referred to them as she spoke.

"What we need to do now," said Harriet, "is to undertake a detailed investigation of Kuppers' movements on Tuesday, from as early as possible in the morning, to when he was last seen in the late afternoon, especially when he wasn't in the hotel.

We know he left the hotel at approximately 8.25 am and was at Artemisias Café in Crawley at around 9.15 am, which was the time at which he phoned Leila and told her about the missing wallet, and asked her to check quickly, in the unlikely event that it had been mislaid at the hotel.

I guess he would have been there, having breakfast, before then. He was picked up by a taxi sent from the hotel and returned to the hotel at 9.40 am. He sorted out his wallet business, the hotel reporting it to the police.

He was then lunching at the Kamada Japanese restaurant from 1.00 pm to 2.30 pm. He met again with Leila at 4 pm. After about twenty minutes or so he complained to Leila of feeling a little unwell and said he would retire to his room to run over some last-minute details. He collected his room key at 4.25 pm, entered his room shortly afterwards, and that was the last time he can be proved to be alive.

He was discovered by Angelique Durand, accompanied by Leila Zafiri, at approximately 8.30 am on Wednesday morning, and according to their report would have been dead by then. This was substantiated by the hotel doctor who was called urgently and arrived at 9.15 am.

We need to double-check the hotel CCTV to verify much of this, but I think the information I have just outlined will prove to be very accurate. So, if he absorbed the poison, or poisons, it might have been either at Artimisias or the Kamada.

If possible, I'll find out more from Leila Zafiri first thing, but in any event, I plan to start with a visit to the Kamada. Kuppers made that dining arrangement some time ago. Anyone knowing about that could have plenty of time to concoct and execute a plan to poison Kuppers, if you'll pardon the pun. A restaurant is an ideal place. I'll find out about his dining companions from the restaurant manager.

Artemisias was different. From what I can recall of what Leila Zafiri has told us, his visit to Artemisias Café was a relatively spur-of-the-moment, completely unplanned thing. No one is going to be sitting in the hotel with a fistful of ricin in their pockets waiting for him to call a cab, then tail the cab to the restaurant, sling the ricin in his drink, then vanishing into the ether."

That means the Kamada in the morning, and Artimesias in the afternoon. We can go together to both."

Ian nodded in agreement.

Harriet suddenly stopped.

"No, wait a minute," she said. "There's Monday morning to consider as well, isn't there?"

She paused for a minute or so, then continued.

"Yes, from our previous findings, it is very likely that on Monday morning he paid a visit to Burton's Hill to sample the sexual delights of Michaela Gold, our mature, but seductive, Sussex siren."

"We put it in our back pocket at the time, but I think it's now the time for it to come out. I think it would be a good idea for someone to contact her, or go to see her, but a phone call or a visit from a Detective Inspector would just cause her to clam up straight away. What is really required is a mature, successful business gentleman."

Harriet stopped there and gave Ian a fixed stare.

He looked back at her, then shook his head.

"Oh no, oh no..." he looked back at her, sighing audibly. "I'm not sure this is a good idea at all."

"Nonsense. You've got all the attributes. You just wanted to keep to the bright lights of Crawley, and not the *demi-monde* of Burtons Hill, didn't you?

Don't worry. A man of the world like yourself will soon acclimatise. If it's no dice from the word go if and when you see her, then just give me a call and get back here as quickly as you can, then you can come with me to Artimesias.

In the meantime, you can practise your mature business executive telephone voice. Then go to the airport. Use a public phone. Call her about 9.15 am for a meeting around 11.00 am. Give yourself time to drive down there. She says to call her anytime on her website. I would think her diary would be free at 11.00 am.

Get an appointment later today. She seems keen to take any punters at pretty well any time. It's like any physical game, isn't it? '...the older you get...'"

Harriet left the sentence there.

"Take a photograph of Kuppers, a copy of the one the Dutch police sent us will be fine.

"It's the best way. If you do get to see her, and Kuppers did pay her a visit, that will verify his movements, and she won't clam up, at least at first, and you can get some idea as to whether she is the poisoning type. Take a look around her place for any clues. Throw in Tuesday morning at some point. Ask her what she was doing then.

If you rule her out as a suspect, we move on. In any event, she might give you some useful insights into his character. If she didn't see him, get back here as quickly as you can.

I know it's snatching at straws, but at the moment this is the only lead we have.

If it is a goer, then phone me immediately you have got your clothes back on and got out of sight, and then get back here as quickly as your car will carry you."

Ian winced.

"You're enjoying this, aren't you?" he said tersely.

"A rather awkward silence prevailed for a few minutes, sustained on one side by veiled, slight amusement, and on the other by one of mild annoyance."

# 28

The silence was interrupted by a tap at the door. A stout, short middle-aged man with a crew cut appeared, answering the "come in" call from Harriet. He was wearing a white shirt with black trousers held up by red braces – the type of appearance that had vanished in the nineteen forties and fifties. He was holding a brown manilla A4 size envelope in a hand on which was a clear plastic glove.

"Sorry to disturb you, officer," he said directing his message towards Harriet.

"My name is Tom Eaves. I'm the mail room supervisor. This," he said, waving the envelope, "came in the first post this morning. We always have an early delivery here at the hotel.

It had this long, funny name on it. 'Mijnheer Pieter Marius Franciscus Kuppers'. I knew Kuppers was the surname of the dead man, and the address was' care of the Median Hotel.' It has a local postmark. Posting date yesterday.

I ran it through all the security checks in the mailroom, and our new X-ray mail scanner. Recommended by Mr MacAllister it was. Came through all clear, and no fingerprints at all. So, I thought you would like to see it straight away. I opened it at the top with a paper knife, and I was very careful." He held up the gloved hand.

"I only gave it a quick look. It seems to be a typed-out letter of some sort."

"Thank you, Mr Eaves," said Harriet. "Good thinking. We'll take a look now, and let you know if we need any further information from you."

Mr Eaves laid it carefully on the table, removed his glove, inserted both thumbs into his red braces level with his shoulder blades, hitched them up, and vanished into his world of stamps, franking and envelopes.

"If there's no fingerprints or anything, then we don't need to worry," said Harriet, removing a single A4 sheet from the envelope, and putting the envelope on the table.

She looked briefly, but carefully, at the sheet, then handed it to Ian, who looked at it quickly.

```
2/11/1991

P - You will no doubt realise the significance of the date.

Do you recall, all those years ago, our trip to Oslo to visit Lora
and Sally. We were only loosely acquainted then.

I remember it clearly. We had to leave so early in the morning. It
was lucky we were staying locally to Gatwick.

Wasn't the house wonderful, just outside the city, with those acres
of space. I don't know how you worked the oracle.

I've often fancied going back, to remind myself how beautiful it is,
but I've just been informed that my new assignment in the Far East
has been confirmed.

Have you noticed from the press that "The Pursuit of Love", your
favourite Nancy Mitford book, has just had a new edit? I admire the
style of her writing, but there's not enough "noir" in them for me,
so I tend to drift, and lose interest. As you know, I prefer
something more erotic.

The next time we meet, you are to be wearing the dress of red, and
for the night, the usual. If not, there will be consequences for
you. Things must go forwards and not backwards as it appears to me.
Is that understood?

Must Sign Off Now,

Vaarwell


PS The references you need to address the issue are here. Some
rearrangement will be necessary, and don't forget to get the right
order when concluding everything.

:612321 69623 641122 611425 572210 53626: 411437 4510311 33638
211144 111049:

:411361 421262 79553 29564 441065 35966 61357 86758 811259 8103510
2113611:

If you wish to purchase the book, Mrs Pears will additionally need
all to be able to really help you with the key below.

81L1-C9-4-P2-2D-1

PPS If still it is unclear, a ring will do.You will know the number.
It would be a grave error to forget the manner of it, or let it lie.

Even though all is a long,long time ago,it remains the present.
```

They looked at each other in mutual bewilderment.

"Well, we know what the sergeants will be doing today, don't we?" remarked Harriet. "We'll take three copies, and let them make of it what they can."

"I'll meet with them at 9 am. You can go to the airport a little before, after that we will know exactly where we are, and we can get moving."

"I'll let Barrowclough know... but maybe, accidentally on purpose leave out my plans for you until later."

# 29

Harriet held the team briefing. She updated them on the dramatic overnight forensic developments, the changed nature and direction of the investigation, away from the now absolved Vonk and Angelique as the prime suspects and the new intensive focus on Kuppers' movements, and the letter delivered to the mailroom a short time ago.

She advised them she had contacted Barrowclough, and he had given the go-ahead for the new investigative process, which involved the following short term steps: -

She (Harriet) would conduct interviews with the relevant personnel at the Kamada restaurant and Artimesias Café, in that order.

Secondly, Ian had been assigned to a "special investigation", on which she refused to elaborate for the moment. There were a few raised eyebrows and requests for more detail, but she passed quickly on without comment.

Finally, she would see them again, probably at lunchtime, or later in the day, to catch up on any progress they had made with the mysterious letter, which they should study individually first, then collaborate. She handed over the copies of the letter and left them to it.

## 30

Ian was back from the Airport at about 9.40 am, just after Harriet finished her team briefing.

"It's all arranged," he said without enthusiasm. "I'll drive down. We fixed a time, around eleven o'clock, but she told me to call her when I reached Burtons Hill, and then she'll give me the exact address. Standard practice, I assume.

Oh, by the way, I called myself Bryan...with a 'y'."

I'm also making sure I only use public phones" he said. "There's a payphone at Burton's Hill Station. I checked, and the station can't be far from her place, if her website can be relied on."

"That's fine. This all sounds like the voice of experience to me. You haven't done this before, have you, Bryan....with a 'y'? "questioned Harriet, with a smile.

"Ha Ha," said Ian, clearly less than amused. No reciprocal acknowledgement was provided.

"...and before you go", Harriet continued breezily, "don't forget to set things up with Artimesias, and make sure you have head and shoulders image of Kuppers."

"OK." responded Ian. "I've already got the Mr K image, but I'll call Artimesia's now."

He spent a few minutes on the phone to Artimesias, giving Harriet a "thumbs up" after he had finished.

"I'll keep you posted on Burton's Hill" was his parting shot, and he headed for his car with a gloomy face, and without a backward look.

# 31

Following Ian's departure to Burton's Hill Harriet was pondering on her prospective visit to the Kamada Japanese restaurant, where Kuppers had been scheduled to lunch on the previous day.

"...and now for the Kamada," she pronounced, speaking to herself and picking up her mobile from the desk.

The Kamada Hotel and restaurant was just a short walk from the Median, on the perimeter of Gatwick Airport. Formerly the Diademe Tower Hotel, it had been bought about ten years ago by the Japanese billionaire Aki Hokikara, of Hokikara Electronics, with the objective of combining fine, authentic Japanese cuisine, with top-class hotel facilities and service.

He had decided against competing in the Conference Market, leaving that to such establishments as the Median, and had converted the downstairs conference room into a top-class restaurant. It had rapidly become the "go-to" place, particularly for Japanese visitors and businesspeople, but also for all nationalities. It had become a particular favourite of the rich and famous. Bookings many months in advance were "de rigeur".

Harriet silently bemoaned her own lack of knowledge of Japan in general, and Japanese cuisine in particular. The latter was restricted to occasionally passing by the Sushi counter of her nearest Sainsbury's Superstore, with its row of severe looking, smartly uniformed ladies, assiduously assembling portions of maki, sashimi and temaki with production line efficiency.

However, her discussions with Van had enlightened her somewhat on Kuppers' love of Japan and things Japanese.

Kuppers had worked for several years in Tokyo, for Fokland, after their introduction of the KF55 aircraft, manufactured by Surato Industries, on the outskirts of the city.

He had become an expert on Japanese culture and cuisine. For many years, he had wanted to dine at the Kamada, and with the Conference taking place at the Median, the opportunity had arisen. He had made the booking considerably in advance once the Median was fixed as the location for the Doves.

Harriet dialled the number provided on the Hotel website that she had accessed on her laptop.

"Good morning. I am Detective Chief Inspector Graham of the Surrey and Sussex Police Force. Could I speak to the Manager of the Restaurant on a matter of urgency, please?"

There was a slight delay before any response.

"Good morning Chief Inspector Graham. My name is Haru Endomoto. I am the Manager of the restaurant. How may I help you?"

"I would like about an hour of your time Mr Endomoto, as soon as possible. Just a routine matter. I am only a short walk from your restaurant."

They agreed to meet in about half an hour, at the Kamada.

"Could you do something for me before I arrive? I am interested in a man, in his fifties, who had booked a table at 12.30 pm this Tuesday and leaving the restaurant at about 2 o'clock. He may have been dining alone, or with another person, I'm not sure about that. I would be interested in any information you have, from your booking sheet to receipts, address details provided and so on ."

"Oh, and by the way," said Harriet, "Do you have CCTV at the restaurant? And which areas of the restaurant do they cover?"

"Yes, we do," replied Mr Endomoto. "The cameras cover the foyer and entrance, dining room, stockroom, and kitchen."

"Thank you. I may need to access some footage" covering the period-day and times-that I have outlined. Please prepare for this."

❖

32

Octagon Road was a wide, straight, long, and unprepossessing road that ran parallel to the beginning of the Burtons Hill to Brighton stretch of the London to Brighton line. It was comprised of identical brick-built semi-detached, high, two-storey houses. Large windows on each floor faced the road. There were no front doors, pedestrian access being by side entrances down a narrow alleyway which separated each property. Surprisingly cramped front gardens, considering the width of the pavements, were demarcated by low brick walls or privet hedges.

It was refuse collection day. To go with the identical houses there were identical, tall, blue-topped refuse bins stationed outside each house, like a row of soldiers at a ceremonial parade. Pete Seeger would have related to the view. Many of the bins had large technicolour numbers affixed to their road-facing side, in clear view.

As Michaela's website entry had stated, parking was no problem. Council restrictions on parking hours had discouraged commuters, and at eleven o'clock in the morning, Ian had a choice of parking space. He looked for number 38 before he brought the car to a halt, spied it, and went about twenty yards past before stopping.

He walked back towards the house, which was one of those with a low brick front wall. Screwed into the wall was a rectangular metal notice which read "Private Property" on the top line and "No Entry" on the lower. Michaela had told him to look for the notice. He turned into the alleyway. Two plastic numbers placed high up on the right-hand wall advised you it was number 38. Ian noticed that they were more discreetly placed on the inner alleyway wall, and not on the front of the house, alongside the window, as with most of the houses.

Halfway down was a dark blue door, inset into the wall. At eye level was a silver-coloured intercom with two buttons to the side. Ian pressed the one marked "Flat 1". He waited a few moments and then there was a tinny, scraping sound, and a throaty female voice spoke.

"Hello, who is it?"

"It's Bryan," said Ian, "...with a 'y'." Ian used the phrase Michaela had requested.

"I'll let you in, Bryan, please close the door behind you after you've come through."

The door gave a dull click, and Ian let himself in, remembering to close the door.

A red door about halfway up the dark hallway opened a fraction. He came level with it. A craggy, lined face with tousled hair and a somewhat bulbous nose, recognizable from her website photographs, peered out from behind the opening.

"Come in Bryan, you are right on time, I like punctuality in a man."

Even in the dim light of the room Michaela Gold's face looked older. Her advertised age of 50 was receding further from reality all the time.

It wasn't the gold, shimmering "Gilda" dress that greeted him. Michaela was wearing a striking, bright blue, silk dressing gown, with Chinese motifs stitched into it. As she turned around to close and lock the door Ian could see the designs. Taking up a diagonal area from the right shoulder to her left side, level with the stomach was a light brown and fawn-mottled dragon with a yellowish frill around its neck. Extended legs, claws and tail all writhed across the blue silk. Beneath the dragon was an equally large bird, which looked like a mixture of a chicken and a peacock, with one wing visible and a profusion of tail feathers of green, white, and pink. Two roses, incorporating those same colours were on either side of the bird.

She was barefooted, which showed a delicate tattoo of a small butterfly on the top of her right foot. Her toenails were painted in a bright blue colour, matching her dressing gown.

Ian guessed that, beneath the dressing gown Michaela would be wearing one of the scanty outfits shown on her website page.

The room itself was almost in darkness, heavy crimson velveteen curtains covering the big front window. The carpet was of a deep tufted beige. To walk on it was like sinking into a bed of marshmallows, particularly with bare feet. A black leather two-seater settee with red, tasselled cushions was set along one wall. In front of the settee was a long, low table, and on it were wine glasses, an unopened bottle of St Emilion, a silver plated box, a green onyx table lighter, and a solid-looking glass ashtray, with several lipsticked cigarette stubs in it.

The only light in the room came from a grey Anglepoise lamp that was standing on a smallish octagonal ornate Indian table, which was on the right-hand side of the settee. The table was of dark rosewood, beautifully inlaid with circular ivory patterns of varying sizes on its top, down its legs and side supports. The lamp bulb was of low wattage and gave off an intentionally dull glow.

On the left of the settee, resting on the floor was a wide, low two-shelf bookcase, newly painted in a light grey colour. Both shelves were full of neatly stacked books. On the top of the bookcase was the black base unit of a landline phone, incorporating an answer machine, and an arrangement of indoor plants.

An assortment of house desert cacti, globular and columnar, in small white, ribbed pots were flanked by two medium-sized pots of dark blue. They contained almost identical attractive plants, with green leaves and bell-shaped light purple flowers with clusters of shiny, deep blackish purple berries at their base.

On the wall opposite the table was a small screen television set, with two large reproductions of Pre Raphaelite paintings, John Everett Millais' "Ophelia" and Evelyn de Morgan's "Medea", both in ornate gold frames, one on each side of the television.

In the far corner was a doorway, Ian assumed, leading to a bedroom. The door frame was occupied by a bold bamboo curtain depicting a sunset. A red sky with a fading yellow sun was atop a stacked pyramid of blue and purple mountains. Two dark grey silhouettes of palm trees completed the final effect.

Michaela turned back to face Ian. She saw him looking around

"There's a much bigger television behind the curtain. We can take a look in a few minutes if you like," she said, smiling, "and look at my specially chosen Klimt artwork over the bed. 'Portrait of Adele Bloch-Bauer' is its real title, but it's commonly known as the 'The Woman in Gold'.

"And you are Michaela Gold."

"Exactly."

"It's reproduction, of course. The Klimt, that is, not any other activities, hopefully." She smiled again.

She came over and sat next to Ian, on his right-hand side. In profile, he could see her puffy and bruised left eye, that heavy makeup couldn't disguise, and her swollen lower lip. She noticed his glance.

"Silly me," she said, "fell over in the kitchen yesterday after too many glasses of champagne, but it won't spoil anything, I promise. I've tried wearing dark glasses, but they're a bloody nuisance. Can't see a thing with them on."

She leant forward and flipped open the lid of the silver-plated box, with a blue-taloned finger, exposing the cigarettes within to view. "Smoke?" she said.

"No thanks," replied Ian, "I don't."

Michaela took one herself, and put it expertly between her lips, avoiding the swollen side, and lit the cigarette with the onyx lighter. She drew the smoke deep into her lungs, and exhaled a thick, blue funnel towards the ceiling.

"Glass of wine, then?" She gestured towards the bottle. "One of my gentleman friends from Paris gave me several cases quite a few years ago now. I wasn't in this place then, of course. I was with a few other girls in Mayfair. Never mind. It's OK here. I still have my regular clients, and nice-looking people like you, of course."

"By the way, did you know that a St Emilion can be laid down for up to 20 years, providing that it's done properly," she said, raising her eyebrows suggestively in Ian's direction.

Ian declined both the implicit offer in the raised eyebrows and that of the wine.

"I'll just have to drink it myself, then," Michaela didn't seem too upset by the outcome.

She stubbed out her cigarette, and seemed to adopt a more business-like attitude.

"So, let's get the money end out of the way, shall we? I think you know, but the hour will be one fifty, and if you want to stay longer, we can sort the extra out later, after the hour. Cash, of course, pounds sterling. In advance."

"Now, then Bryan, what did you say you did for a living?"

"I didn't," said Ian, reaching in his pocket for his warrant card. Actually, I'm a police officer, and my real name is Detective Inspector Ian Scott, I'm attached to the Surrey and Sussex force, and I'd like to ask you a few questions. You can tell me your real name in due course." He showed Michaela the card.

Michaela didn't bat an eyelid and gave the card only a brief glance. "The old bill, eh, what a pity," she said calmly. "Well, it's all legal here. I own the flat, all paid for. I'm the only one here, no other girls. Moved here from London after my last marriage went down the pan. I'm very discreet. There's no one in the top flat. Owned by an old lady, but she's been in hospital, or a home, for ages. I might buy it if it comes on the market. The people in the attached semi are both young, work in London as far as I know. They're out all day. Pay all my taxes. My adverts are all legal, too. Any payment from my gentleman friends is in consideration for my time, nothing else. Oh, my real name is Debbie. Deborah to be precise. Deborah Keeley." She smiled. My full name, if you really want to know, is Deborah Ann Titania Keeley. Mother was theatrical. Never knew who my father was, or at least I was never told."

"I'll continue to call you Michaela, if that's alright with you?"

"Sure, no problem, I've had quite a few different names in the past."

"What do you want to know, D.I.Scott?" she asked, lighting another cigarette. "Just excuse me a minute," she went out of the lounge briefly to what was probably the kitchen and brought back an opened bottle of red wine and poured herself a glass. "The good stuff can wait," she said, "but this isn't bad. Burtons Hill Waitrose." She demolished the glass with extreme rapidity and poured herself another. Ian was off the invitation list this time.

"OK, Michaela. We are trying to trace the most recent movements of a particular Dutch gentleman, and we can prove that he was here, in this flat, on Monday last, in the morning, somewhere between the hours of 10.30 and 12.30.

Stocky, bald, slightly overweight, 50's, white, smart appearance. Perfect grammatical English, but spoken with a Germanic accent. He may be known to you as Pete, or Peter." He fished in his pocket, and produced a head and shoulders print from a photograph of Kuppers. "Is this the man?"

"Why are you trying to find that out? What has he done?"

"I'm afraid there has been an accident, the Dutch gentleman is no longer alive."

"No longer alive? You mean he's dead? Don't you learn straight-talking at police college anymore?"

She looked at the photograph, then Ian, then the photograph again. She showed no reaction whatsoever. "I'm not sorry, I'm not sorry at all, and 'yes', he was here. No doubt at all. I recognise the forehead scar if nothing else. Gave his name as Paul, not Peter... fly away Peter, come back Paul, I suppose, but he fits the bill alright."

She stared into space.

"He was one of those," she continued. "You get them occasionally in my line of work. Absolutely charming before you meet, setting up the arrangements and everything, and with all the preliminaries. Then it comes to the sex, and they change. You can tell by the eyes. They glaze over. They become someone else.

You've seen my eye and my mouth. As they say, I know that you know that I know it wasn't an accident in the kitchen. Too much champagne indeed! That would be a fine thing. No, that's where he hit me right at the end, and

I was lucky to get away with that. As I said, I've met the occasional bad one, but he was probably one of the worst. Wanted me to wear exactly, to the last detail, one of the outfits in my website pictures, the black and red silk lacey one, with the nipple peepholes and crotch opening, and the very high-heeled red shoes.

He was cruel. He was participating in a sex act all of his own, nothing to do with me as a human being, mutual pleasure, or my pleasure. I was just the object he could exercise his fantasies on. He wanted sex all ways, many times. He was very large, you understand It really hurt me, even someone as experienced as me, but he wouldn't stop. You can see from my website that I like a strong, dominant man, and I'm not averse to a little touch of "rough," but nothing like that. Do you know, after he undressed, until he left, he never said a single word to me. Not one, even when I was being abused. Grunting, yes, plenty of that. Everything became more frightening, more menacing and, believe me, I was frightened. Very, very frightened.

Oh, yes and there were the socks. Very strange. When he undressed in the bedroom he folded all his clothes very precisely into a small, neat stack beside the bed, in the order he took them off. Last of all were his socks. He had on these yellow socks, sort of canary colour. Very bright. He smoothed them out and laid them on the top of the pile of clothes, very carefully, one across the other, making a kind of plus sign. Then he stopped and looked at them for about half a minute, I guess. It was like a religious ritual, or at least my idea of a religious ritual. I'm not into gods, of any faith, me. As I said, strange. Weird.

I was lucky that I think he had to leave. He just hit me, then stopped. He changed back, just like that his eyes, his breathing, his aggression. You remember the "Incredible Hulk" on TV? Well, it was just like that. Then he went to the loo, there's one in the bedroom, and spent ages getting himself dressed and smartened up. Never said a word. Came in through the lounge, knocked back the half glass of wine he had left on the table, and walked out. Just like that. He forgot one thing, though. He left a packet of condoms on the bedroom floor, the fancy ones from Condomerie, the Amsterdam condom shop. The ones with the multicoloured jungle animal design." She shrugged. "Very appropriate."

Ian pricked up his ears, but showed no emotion, and didn't interrupt Michaela.

"King size, they were. Brought them himself. Probably thought I would give him the clap, or something, although, thinking about it, it was more likely to be to impress me with the size. He had nothing to brag about, though. My mother told me that, back in the 1950s, she was closely acquainted, on a few occasions, with Porfirio Rubirosa, if you get my drift."

Ian had no problem with the suggestive inference, although the implication of the reference to Rubirosa meant nothing to him. He made a mental note to look it up, but said nothing, and let Michaela continue.

She paused and looked into his eyes for a few moments. "Sorry," she said. "I had to get it all out somehow. Thanks for listening. You haven't got very far with your questions, have you? I won't be long. Just going to the loo, then I'll grab another bottle of red and an empty glass from the kitchen, and I'll be with you." She got up from the settee, padded across the shagpile, and headed for the bedroom loo.

Ian had noticed it before. In side profile, it wasn't so evident, but in those moments in full face, his attention was drawn to her eyes. The pupils were exceptionally large and shiny. Huge, brilliant black discs. It was fascinating. Perhaps a family trait, he thought.

He took the opportunity to get up from his seat himself and stretch his legs before she returned. He looked down at the neatly arranged books on the shelves of the bookcase. Included amongst them were "The Complete Works of Shakespeare"; "The Greek Myths I and II by Robert Graves, the Folio Society edition in the tan slipcase"; "The set of three Simon Schama BBC Books 'A History of Britain'"; "The Complete Plays of Noel Coward"; "Woodland Plants and Fungi" and "Brewers Dictionary of Phrase and Fable (19th Edition)".

He picked a small book from the end of the shelf and studied it. Most of its black front cover was taken up by a full face, carefully crafted, sketch of a Pekinese in pale green, black and white. The dog's shiny black eyes stared straight at Scott. It was quite disconcerting.

Above the dog's face was the title in pale green capital letters - "The Labours Of Hercules". Beneath was the name of the author, in yellow - "Agatha Christie".

Michaela went straight from the loo to the kitchen and reappeared with a fresh bottle of red wine with the cork off and poured herself another large glassful. She came and stood alongside Ian.

"That's a UK first edition you have there," she said. "Crime Club, 1947".

"I'm just looking at your books," he remarked, with the Christie novel in his hand, which was an unnecessary statement of the obvious.

"Very interesting."

"Don't you mean surprising?" said Michaela.

"Yes, I suppose so."

"What should I have on my bookshelves then? 'Sexy Susan Sins Again', 'Girls Who Prefer Girls', or perhaps two years' copies of 'Atomage', in a nice binder with none missing?"

Ian didn't reply, and Michaela took a swig of red and continued.

"I used to be an actress, you know, and still am, I guess," she said, ruefully.

"I mentioned my mother. She was in theatre and rep. Quite well known on the circuit in the late 40's through to the early 60's. Enid Keeling. You'll find her somewhere on the net. Carted me all over the place, Birmingham, Guildford, Eastbourne, Taunton, Newcastle, and tons more. Even went to Germany when she was doing Shakespeare. What do they say, a peripatetic childhood, or is that word too long for the police force? No father, but plenty of nannies, and plenty of uncles, Uncle Fred, Uncle Arthur, Uncle Billy, no sisters or brothers, though.

I was on the stage from ever since I can remember. Became pregnant at sixteen. I miscarried almost straight away, and that was the end of children for me. Mother died when I was just eighteen. She was young, only in her early 40's. She managed to catch most of the swinging 60's though. I married my first husband a few months after that. Total disaster, so I turned more to acting. I became quite good. A lot of Shakespeare. As you can see from my books I love Noel Coward's plays. Have you ever heard of "The Vortex?" Ian shook his head. "Never mind. I started my acting career as Bunty Mainwaring and finished it as Florence Lancaster. A couple more marriages and then the drink," she said, taking another hefty helping of the red wine," and the rest is history.

"It was my last husband who got me on the game. Very lucrative it was- mainly for him. I did all the work, and he spent all the money, but after a while, I became smart enough to stow away some of the money. He knew nothing about that. As I said before, after that marriage went west, I came south, moved away from London, and bought this place, and here I am telling a policeman my life story, who would have believed that?"

She felt her lip a little gingerly, poured the last of the bottle of red wine into the glass, sat down on the settee and helped herself to another cigarette from the box. "I'm a tough old girl," she said to no one in particular. "Like good old Gloria, we will both survive."

"Well, Mister Detective Inspector, what would like to know? Fire away."

Ian continued to stand. "I'd like to know if, before the wall of silence came down, he mentioned what he was doing in the UK, where he was staying, was he seeing friends, things he liked and didn't like, any people he disliked, that sort of thing, and anything else that occurs to you."

Michaela thought for a moment. When she spoke the words were slightly slurred. "Let me see. I'd never met him, or even spoken to him before last week. I knew he was Dutch, he told me, and his first call came in from Amsterdam. Said he was in the UK the next week, and he'd like to pay me a visit on Monday morning. Didn't really expect to see him at all, in truth, but I kept the morning free in my diary, and gave him the usual. "Call me Monday morning when you arrive, then again when you get close to Burtons Hill, and then I'll give you the address." Didn't need to tell him all that, it was obvious he knew the ropes. I guessed he was an experienced punter. It all worked out, though. He called me at nine o'clock, then again after reaching Burtons Hill, and arrived here dead on time.

"When we were talking after he came into the house. He was charming, butter melting, and mouth and all that. I did ask him what he was doing in England, and why he called me. He said he was only here for a day. He was meeting someone in Brighton to buy a vintage motorbike.

Told me in great detail about it, but all over my head, I'm afraid, so can't remember any of that.

It was someone he hadn't met, got the details from a website, and he was hoping the bike was as good as its picture and description on the net. He was meeting this guy for lunch, then going back to London to fly home that night. He'd called me because I was near to Brighton, and he liked my website, and I looked a really sexy, mature lady… all the usual spiel. Anyway, he paid up, no problems at all, and the rest you know.

Wouldn't have been worth reporting things to the police, even if he were still alive, but now he's on his way to hell, or probably there already, it doesn't matter anymore."

Michaela didn't seem in the slightest bit perturbed. "I'm glad he won't be able to hurt any more women ever again," she said. "I hate him as much as he hated me."

"Thanks, Michaela," said Ian, who had been making notes in a small notebook. "I'll be off, now, but stick around. Don't go anywhere. I may need to contact you again."

"OK, Detective Inspector. I look forward to that. Just don't say you are a mature, discerning businessman this time." She smiled.

"Before you walk out of the door…," her words began to become even more indistinct as the Waitrose Cabernet Sauvignon bit in.

"Did you notice the Robert Graves in the bookshelf?" she queried, but continued without waiting for Ian to shake his head, which was a correct presumption. "Then you won't know about the Fates, and Atropos," she stated, equally correctly.

Ian looked blank.

"Never mind. You might need to do so someday."

This quizzical comment was left hanging in the air.

"Well, here's some paraphrased Shakespeare for you."

"Cheers," she said, and dispensing with any niceties, picked up the bottle, and drank what remained straight from it, but being aware enough to avoid the damaged lip.

She took up a theatrical pose and began: -

"I know a bank where the wild thyme blows

where violets and the belladonna grows

quite overcanopied with luscious woodbine

with sweet musk roses and with eglantine

There lives Titania, sometime of the night

Lulled by talion tales in dances of delight"

She performed a sweeping curtsey and threw both arms out to their full extent as if to receive applause from a packed theatre audience.

Ian walked towards the door to the hallway, As he was about to go through the door he paused, and turned halfway back, "Sorry, I forgot to ask. Could I have the condoms that were left in the bedroom?"

"Of course," replied Michaela, "No use to me now."

She weaved an uncertain route to the bedroom, and quickly, and equally uncertainly found her way back, holding the technicolour pack of king-size condoms in one hand. She handed it over to Ian.

"Thanks," he said, "goodbye for now," then turned back as he was about to go.

"Sorry, I almost forgot. Could you tell me where you were on Tuesday morning?"

"That's a long time ago, Mr Detective, but I can just about remember."

Ian ignored the thin layer of sarcasm, as Michaela continued.

"About 10.30 I had my nails done. At Jaeger's, on Nimrod Road, just around the corner, Charlene always does them for me. After that- it took about an hour and a bit- I went down to Brighton Marina to have a few glasses of wine and lunch with a girlfriend of mine. We went to one of the cafés there, in front of the boardwalk, looking out to the boats. Not under it, but in front of it. She's in the same line of business as me. We swap stories and all that. Then back mid-afternoon."

"I'll give you her telephone number if you want, I'm sure she'd be pleased to see you."

"No thanks," said Ian. "That won't be necessary."

Leaving the flat he proceeded down the corridor, shut the entrance door behind him, and walked back down the alleyway into Octagon Road. He hadn't the faintest idea what all that verse at the end meant, if anything. "What the hell was 'paraphrased Shakespeare?'" he thought, "and who was Robert Graves and Atropos?"

As he crossed the road he tried to commit as much of it to memory as he was able. He opened his car door, sat in the driving seat, took out his notebook and wrote down as much of Michaela's parting shots as he could recall, and her description of her Tuesday morning whereabouts.

⊷⊶◄◊►⊷⊶

# 33

Harriet took the walk from the Median.

Mr Endomoto was waiting in the lobby to greet her.

A shortish, squat, wide man, his build similar to Oddjob in the James Bond film "Goldfinger". He was smartly dressed in a grey suit, white shirt and grey tie. His hair was black, cut short, and he sported a trim, equally black "Hercule Poirot" moustache, or whatever the Japanese equivalent of the fictional detective was, Harriet mused. She gave the customary Japanese 30-degree bow when meeting a stranger, to which Mr Endomoto reciprocated.

He led the way down a flight of red-carpeted stairs. "Have you seen our restaurant before, Chief Inspector," he asked. "No," replied Harriet, truthfully. "Well, here we are," said Mr Endomoto, proudly. "Isn't it magnificent?" His English was perfect.

Interesting, is probably more the word, thought Harriet, but just nodded. It was certainly different.

At the bottom of the stairs, the room opened out into a cavernous space, with a very high ceiling, painted black. The plastering had been removed from the far wall, leaving the brick faces exposed, some level, some slightly raised, some slightly sunken. This produced an attractive, stippled effect, rather like a huge computer screen, with the pixels delineated. Onto this brickwork had been painted an enormous mural, taking up two-thirds of the wall space, and dominating the room.

It depicted two Japanese ladies, in the two-dimensional flat relief of much Japanese art, in side view from the waist upwards, facing each other and leaning towards each other slightly. They were dressed in brown kimonos. Their hair was dark and full, each tied in a bun, with carefully positioned, cherry blossoms pinned in them. They were each holding chopsticks in one visible hand, the hands and arms carefully placed for artistic effect. Behind them was a huge red sun, with thick, red rays extending outwards on a pale yellow background. The heads of the ladies were precisely framed in the circle of the sun. It was altogether a stunning design effect.

Underneath the mural was a series of open boxes, in three rows, in the style of a "cabinet of curiosities" (known by the German loan word of Kunstkammer). Inside the smaller boxes were a series of wooden Japanese artefacts-circular chests in light wood, logs, jars and ornaments. On the left-hand side were larger storage areas, filled with rows of bottles, of wine and beers.

Plain wooden dining tables were placed along the side walls of the room, with uncomfortable-looking upright wooden chairs with wicker backs, painted all over in a light blue colour.

There were plenty of diners consuming breakfasts, and delicious smells of steamed rice, grilled fish and egg permeated the restaurant as they walked through to the back office.

Harriet had performed a rapid "google" before the meeting with Mr Endomoto and the spartan nature of the furniture was certainly not repeated in the quality of the food – or the prices, and their five-star reviews.

On the pretext of a shortage of time, Harriet graciously declined the offer of a green tea, and they went through to Mr Endomoto's office at the back of the restaurant. The decor was all gleaming chromium and light wood, in complete contrast to the restaurant interior, and pristine in its organisation.

Endomoto politely indicated a chair for Harriet and took his own seat behind a large, light oak desk. There were a few sheets of paper, neatly stacked, in front of him on the desk.

As she went to sit down, she realised that she hadn't mentioned Kuppers' name, more forgetfully than deliberately, but any attempt to rectify this omission was interrupted when Endomoto spoke, referring to the papers before him.

He looked at Harriet. "Your questions as to the diner Detective Chief Inspector."

"Yes, here they are." He raised one of the sheets of paper a little and read from it.

"We had only one single diner who had a table at that time. Booked a long time ago, and confirmed again on Tuesday 10th May, and that was Mr Agnew, a Mr David Agnew."

"I have some further information also," he said.

Harriet assumed he, or whoever had provided him with the information, had confused the names.

"That isn't the name of the person I'm looking for. Let's view the CCTV footage before we go any further. We'll come back to the other information later."

Endomoto nodded.

"Come this way," he said, leading the way up a flight of stairs.

The Kamada CCTV room and equipment weren't a patch on MacAllister's set-up. Harriet could imagine MacAllister swelling further with pride had he been present. However, the Kamada did have their own Simon- a young techie whom Mr Endomoto introduced as Neville.

Neville quickly produced the CCTV footage from Tuesday. Harriet looked closely. She watched as the chunky, smartly dressed, middle-aged man was shown to his table. He was alone. Even with the somewhat fuzzy images from the poor-quality CCTV picture, there was no doubt. It was the same man she had already seen on the Median CCTV earlier. It was Piet Kuppers.

"You say that was a Mr David Agnew?" she queried Endomoto.

"Yes. That was the name he confirmed to our staff member at the door who checked the booking."

Harriet said nothing further, and they continued to scan the film.

The CCTV included him only intermittently, and not particularly clearly, but he appeared to eat and drink alone, concentrating only on the meal, and his expert use of chopsticks. He didn't appear to make any phone calls, or even have a mobile with him. He then left after about an hour and a quarter and turned back towards the Median as he left.

"Thank you, Neville," said Harriet, "I would now like to see some footage of the kitchen, a little before and a little after the times that Mr Agnew was present in the restaurant."

"Is that necessary?" questioned Endomoto, "I'm not sure any kitchen footage is available."

"Yes, it is," piped up Neville. "I logged it myself."

Endomoto didn't look at all pleased, either with the answer or with Neville. "I don't know why you wish to see this," he said, "first class restaurants such as ourselves like to keep the secrets of their cuisine."

"I hardly think that an hour's footage shown to me – and it won't be that long – will result in the bankruptcy of your restaurant under a deluge of imitators."

"No, I suppose not," said Endomoto, resignedly. "Carry on Neville," he instructed his overzealous underling through gritted teeth.

Neville fast-forwarded through the film, Harriet stopping him a few times, and asking him to slow the film down on those occasions, whilst she made notes.

"OK," she said finally. "Can we now return to your office Mr Endomoto, as I have a couple more questions for you."

Back in the office, she faced Endomoto across his desk.

"Firstly, I would like to know what he had to eat and drink."

Endomoto had a till receipt.

"He ate the Bara Chirashi lunch. A good choice, I must say. It has many ingredients, but our own includes Albacore Tuna, salmon, Turbot, Prawn, Egg Omelette, and some seaweed and cucumber.

He drank, with the meal, one glass of Plum Wine, with ice, and after the food, a small bottle of Mori beer, which you would know as a type of pale ale."

"Thank you, Mr Endomoto. Very helpful," said Harriet. "...and do you have details of any credit card he might have used to pay for this delicious lunch?"

"He paid in cash," said Mr Endomoto, responding rather too quickly for Harriet's liking, but she left it there.

"...and the address and contact details he provided when he booked and later confirmed on May 10th?"

Endomoto gave her a folded piece of paper.

"They are written here," he said.

"Nearly finished," said Harriet, "Just one last thing."

"There wasn't much footage of him, but I seemed to notice that his food was brought to him by a chef, with a distinctive apron, whilst the other diners were served by waiting staff. Was there any reason for that?"

Mr Endomoto hesitated for a moment, then said curtly, "A special customer, an important person."

Harriet nodded but said no more. So important, she thought, that he didn't even use his own name.

"Thank you for your time," she said. "If we need to contact you further, myself, or one of my officers will give you a call. If there is anything more you feel you may need to tell us, we can be found, for the next few days, at the Median."

She got up from the table, and bowed to Mr Endomoto, who was remaining in the office. He returned a somewhat stiff, unsmiling, and formal bow, and Harriet departed.

❖

# 34

Harriet had already decided her next steps as she made her way back to the Median. Sitting in her and Ian's office she looked at the contact details that Endomoto had handed to her. They were sparse, and not at all helpful.

There was a Hotmail address of david.p.agnew.505 and a Netherlands telephone number. No home or other address. So he might well have been known as Mr David Agnew to the restaurant.

But before progressing anything on that front, she made reference to her notes from the Kamada CCTV footage and called Van.

"Hello Mr Van Heemskerk, could you spare me about half an hour, in my office here at the Median?" she asked.

Van concurred, and in a couple of minutes they were sitting together.

"Mr Van Heemskerk, from our previous conversation I know that you spent several years in Japan, during some of which you worked closely with Mr Kuppers." She didn't wait for a response.

"You said he became an expert in Japanese cuisine and loved Japanese food. I assume you are also very familiar with Japanese dishes?"

"Yes, that is so," he responded, which was the answer that Harriet was very keen to hear.

"In that case, you might be able to help me. I will give you a description of the appearance and preparation of a particular Japanese dish, which I have viewed on CCTV, and hopefully, you can provide me with more facts and details of it. I'll explain more fully later."

Van appeared somewhat mystified but let Harriet carry on.

"The CCTV was not always complete or clear, but I think adequate.

The dish in which I am interested is a fish. This fish would be about a foot in length, mottled dark brown and white in appearance, quite fleshy, but, curiously, it seemed to have no scales.

As to its preparation, the chef – a Japanese gentleman – seemed to have taken it live from a smallish tank behind him, but I can't be sure of that. He then appeared to pull the skin off, and gut it with a vicious-looking knife, then cut the head off.

There wasn't any more useable CCTV until the serving at his table, where there was a good close-up. It was the same chef performing the preparation that brought the meal to the table.

The dish was on a large blue and white round plate, with very thin, almost transparent, white slices. The slices were arranged in a circle, rather like a flower, and with what looked like sprouts and other fancy items. Very clever.

What do you think?" Harriet looked at Van.

Van smiled. "A very good description if I might say so. I know exactly what the dish is, and quite a lot about it."

Harriet settled back in her chair, making herself comfortable.

"You learn something every day in this job. When you've finished, I'll add Japanese cooking to my CV."

Van didn't smile but launched into serious, university lecturer mode.

"The dish which you have described, Detective Chief Inspector, is called '*fugu sashimi*', and is one of the most celebrated, and expensive, dishes in Japan. It is prepared from the flesh of the fugu fish, and the arrangement on the plate, as you correctly identified, is that of a flower, actually resembling a chrysanthemum. As you are in the business, Detective Chief Inspector, you may like to know that in Japan the chrysanthemum is known as the flower of death."

'Very apt,' thought Harriet.

Van continued.

"The slices are eaten raw.

And now for the really interesting facts," he said, pompously.

"The fugu fish is a pufferfish- fish that swell up to avoid their enemies. Fugu can be lethal to humans due to its tetrodotoxin, a highly toxic poisonous compound that the fish contains, meaning it must be carefully prepared to remove toxic parts and to avoid contaminating the meat.

Only chefs who have qualified after years of rigorous training are allowed to prepare the fish. I understand that the best fugu chefs can fillet the fish in such a way that a very small, safe amount of the poison remains to create an additional euphoric feeling.

The restaurant preparation of fugu is strictly controlled by law in Japan and several other countries, and in fact is banned in the EU, which includes the UK," he added meaningfully.

"However, I have heard that in the UK there is a Fugu Supper Club, where fugu is served to private diners, in conditions of utmost secrecy. This gets around the EU regulations. I may be mistaken, but I thought I heard that from Piet Kuppers, who I assume is your reason for asking me all these fugu questions."

Harriet didn't reply.

"I hope that is informative, Detective Chief Inspector," he concluded, as if swelling up with self-satisfaction in a similar fashion to the puffer fish he described.

"Very helpful, thank you, Mr Van Heemskerk," Harriet acknowledged, and he left the room.

'Well, Mr Endomoto is off the hook, so to speak,' she thought. 'At least on the murder count. I didn't notice anyone shovelling any ricin into the food as they went along. But I'm going to pay him a little visit.'

## 35

She called Endomoto, and said there were a couple of things from their conversation that she wanted to clear up urgently, and asked if she could come along to the Kamada. They wouldn't take too long, she said, and she would be over very shortly. Endomoto agreed.

They went through the formal introductory motions once again, but this time with little mutual enthusiasm.

Harriet didn't waste any time with further niceties. She sat opposite Endomoto and looked him straight in the eye.

"Now Mr Endomoto, in our last conversation, as the English would say you were "using terminological inexactitudes". According to Wikipedia, the Japanese would say "kyomu". Personally, I would say, disguised untruths. But not disguised enough, Mr Endomoto."

Endomoto started to interrupt, but Harriet raised a hand to stop him.

"The person that we were viewing on the video, and who dined in your premises from 1.00 pm until 2.30 pm, was not a Mr David Agnew, and you may or may not have known that. He was, in fact, a Mr Piet Kuppers, a Dutch national, visiting the UK. He was found dead in suspicious circumstances in his hotel room at the Median Hotel early yesterday morning. He had been poisoned, and I am the police officer in charge of the associated murder investigation."

Harriet again raised her hand as Endomoto tried to speak.

"When you read out to me that delightful selection of menu items that Mr Kuppers purportedly consumed, you, unfortunately, omitted one dish, which must have, quite inadvertently, slipped your mind for a few minutes."

"Now, Mr Edomoto," Harriet spoke deliberately, and in a somewhat threatening tone.

"I know all about the fugu fish and fugu sashimi. I know all about the lethal poison the fish contains. I know all about the Fugu Club in London, and I know it is illegal to prepare and serve fugu in UK restaurants, and since we last spoke, I have received some forensic data in relation to the crime."

That wasn't quite true, since Harriet had only acquired her knowledge of fugu from her conversation with Van less than half an hour ago, and neither had she received any new forensic information in the time period to which she was referring, but Mr Endomoto was clearly very shaken.

"It is all an accident," he blurted out rapidly and incoherently, staring into space. "A complete accident. Mr Kitade is a fully qualified fugu chef of many years…"

Harriet cut him off.

"Calm down, Mr Endomoto," said Harriet.

The time has come to tell the truth, the whole truth and nothing but the truth. Start from the beginning. The whole story. The true story.

Endomoto took a deep breath, paused, then shrugged resignedly.

"All right." He said, gradually regaining his composure.

"This all started a few months ago when I received a telephone call from Mr Kuppers. As you know, he called himself David Agnew, and told me he was a UK citizen, working in Holland, but he was organizing a short conference in the UK, which meant he would spend a few days here. This I believed.

He also said that he had worked in Japan and had a love of Japanese food. He spent some time demonstrating his knowledge in this area, and remarked on his favourite Japanese dish, fugu sashimi.

He said he had become a member of the Fugu Dining Club in the UK, in anticipation of his UK visit, but there had been some changes to the Club meeting dates and they didn't fit into his UK schedule any longer, so would it be possible for him to eat fugu sashimi at the Kamada. He was aware it would be illegal to do so, but he knew an excellent chef at the Fugu Club who would be prepared to travel up to the Kamada and prepare and serve fugu sashimi from the Kamada kitchen. He, Kuppers, would organize the chef, arrange his travel and accommodation, and pay him handsomely. No one would know. He would reward me, and my kitchen staff similarly. There was no risk. Two hours. One meal. All over.

He was very persuasive and sounded charming on the telephone."

Harriet winced.

Endomoto went on.

"I knew of the Fugu Club, and the reputation of their chefs. I am afraid I succumbed to his wishes.

He then made a further telephone call from Holland to confirm the arrangements, and that everything was set up with the fugu chef, a Mr Takuya Kitade.

Then, on the Tuesday of last week, the 10th May, he called in personally, here, introduced himself and paid me a considerable amount of money, in cash for myself and my staff.

After that, Detective Chief Inspector, you know the story as well as I."

Endomoto took another few very deep breaths.

"What are you going to do now?" he questioned.

His composure was beginning to rapidly fragment once again.

"I am not a murderer of any description, and nor is Mr Kitade. It is all an accident, a terrible accident."

He put his head in his hands.

"I will be ruined. Everything will be lost. Everything."

Harriet let him suffer for a little while longer, then spoke.

"I don't think you were listening closely enough Mr Endomoto.

I said Kuppers was poisoned, but at no stage in our conversation did I say the name of the poison that caused his death, but I do know for certain that it wasn't tetrodotoxin.

No. Neither you nor Mr Kitade are guilty of murder, or manslaughter. You are off the hook."

Endomoto looked baffled. His perfect English being proven to be only almost perfect, understanding neither the idiom nor the allusion.

"What I am going to do," she emphasized the 'am', "is to pass a report to the Food and Hygiene authority here in the UK who will liaise with the European Union authorities, and you will hear from them as to the consequences."

"I will mention your eventual cooperation in the matter, and trust that, should the restaurant continue to remain open, you will not ever break the law again. In the meanwhile, I wouldn't spend any of the money that Kuppers gave you, there's a good boy."

With that, Harriet left a bewildered Mr Endomoto grappling with his new reality.

## 36

"...**a**s Endomoto's confession unravelled. I knew it wasn't going to lead us to Kuppers' murderer, unless someone at the Fugu Club wanted to bump him off, a theory I rapidly dismissed, but I thought I'd put the frighteners on him anyway."

These were Harriet's closing words to Ian, as she summarised the results of her dip into Japanese culinary waters.

They had met for a quick lunch of prawn sandwiches and coffee in the Ops Room after each had completed their latest morning investigations.

Ian had a different cultural experience to recount but kept it brief. His conclusion was similar to that of Harriet.

"Michaela was very unlikely to have killed Kuppers. Despite her experience with him, she was aware such clients were out there. She had given me an alibi with details that could be checked, and she certainly appeared to have no idea that he was staying at the Median, only going on to Brighton, which wasn't true anyway."

Ian thought back to Michaela's words "I'm a tough old girl", she had told him. And she was. He had pondered on his visit whilst driving back to the Median. He wasn't going to admit it and be open to a lack of impartiality in the investigation, but he rather admired her, her resilience, her ability to face the world head on. 'A pity. She might have been a famous actress' he thought.

He snapped himself out of that train of thinking as Harriet concluded their morning's work.

"So", she said "Who knows who did murder Kuppers? We don't."

"Yet" said Ian.

"A for optimism "responded Harriet, "or should that be O?"

"So, now on to Artemisias. I assume you know the layout and everything", queried Harriet. "More or less," replied Ian, with a perfunctory nod, "if it hasn't changed too much."

"Just one thing that occurs to me. Did they have CCTV at Artimesias when you were on the Crawley beat?" asked Harriet.

Ian thought for a minute. "Not as far as I can remember," he said. "But it's quite possible it's changed now. We mustn't forget to ask."

"O.K.," said Harriet.

Before he went to Burton's Hill Harriet had instructed Ian to arrange with the owner, manager or whoever was in charge, for Harriet, or both of them to talk to the staff who were on duty on Tuesday morning, between about 8.30 am and 9.30 am. He was to disclose no more than it was concerning the missing wallet, but to stress it was very urgent. He was to fix up a time for them to be at Artimisias around 2.30 pm. And to get it done before he headed for the airport."

Ian had called the café. He was able to speak to Francesco Cascarino, Stefano's grandson, who was the current operational manager. He was in the Restaurant Office. He briefly explained that the police were keen to retrace the movements of an important foreign national, whose name he was not permitted to release, but who had visited the café on Tuesday morning, between roughly 8.30 and 9.30. During that time he was believed to have lost his wallet, and due to that fact, and as it was only a couple of days ago, the duty staff might remember him well.

Francesco was very willing to help. He told Ian there were two staff on duty that Tuesday morning, as springtime morning business was generally steady, but required only a table waiter, and someone behind the bar, preparing sandwiches, breakfasts and coffee, tea, and other drinks. Luigi was the table waiter that day, and Mario was the person behind the bar. They would both be there today, and he would arrange for them to meet with him.

Francesco told him that he had been away for a few days, as it was a quiet time for business, and he had arrived in the Office that morning a short time ago, and had, in fact, just accessed a brief email from one of the duty staff, about the lost wallet, and the circumstances, which indicated that there was nothing much to be bothered about.

An appointment was made for 2.30 pm, and Francesco also offered to be there to stand in, if necessary, for whichever person from his staff was being interviewed in turn.

## 37

Artimesias was somewhat of a Crawley institution. A traditional, fourth-generation, Italian family-owned café and restaurant business, it currently occupied a solid building on the corner of High Street, in the old town. The frontage and café faced the large pavement area at the beginning of High Street, where the outside tables were located, and the restaurant area at the back of the café extended into Smith Street, the turning to which immediately adjoined the High Street.

On moving to its present location, almost 60 years ago, Stefano Cascarino, the then owner/manager, had continued his grandfather's favourite colour scheme, and arranged for the walls to be painted their distinctive Naples Yellow, which had been carefully and deliberately faded. That signature colour had been retained unchanged, from that date to the present. When outdoor tables had been introduced, the table awnings were of the same yellow shade, as was the long awning across the restaurant frontage. At the same time, Virginia Creeper had been planted to cover some of the higher levels of the outside walls, and pots and planters containing red geraniums were liberally set around the premises. The "Artimesias" name, again taken from Stefano's grandfather's original business, was picked out in bold, black, uppercase Lucida Sans script. Although somewhat different from the row of preserved, half-timbered Tudor buildings which made up the rest of that side of the High Street, it had added its own touch of character, beloved of the locals.

As Ian walked, with Harriet, from the far end of the High Street, past the Tudor buildings, and Artimesias gradually came into view, he saw exactly the same comforting schema with which he was familiar from his earlier time in the Crawley force.

It was a pleasant morning, similar to Tuesday's weather, with the sun starting to warm the atmosphere. A few customers were dotted around the tables on the frontage.

They spied a short, rotund, balding man, with what hair he had remaining slicked back with a touch of brylcreem, standing in the doorway of the café. He was immaculately dressed, in the Artimesias "uniform" of white shirt, purple waistcoat, dark trousers, and gleaming black patent leather shoes with the obligatory, slightly pointed, toes.

The man moved forward as Harriet and Ian approached.

"You will be Detective Graham, yes?" he said, extending his hand. "Yes, that's right," said Harriet, not wishing to correct him with respect to the title, "and this is my colleague, Detective Inspector Scott."

"You are Mr Francesco Cascarino, I presume," said Harriet, as if she had just discovered a long-lost explorer on the shores of Lake Tanganyika.

"That's also right," said Francesco, and clasped Harriet's hand for several seconds in an overly firm grip. When it was his turn for the introductions Ian withdrew his hand swiftly to avoid the same fate, and just nodded.

Francesco indicated a vacant chair, directly in front of the doorway, but some yards back from it on the wide pavement. "Would that be ok for your discussions, or would you wish for an office?" Francesco asked.

"No, it's fine here. I'd like to recreate things as close as possible to the way they were on Tuesday morning. Oh, there's something to ask you at the outset. Do you have CCTV cameras, and if you do, where are they located?"

"Yes, we do. Recently we have installed them, so I know this. We keep up with the times here," he said with a hint of pride. "They are in the main dining room, in the kitchen, the office, and to cover the doorway here, which is the only entrance and exit."

"What about this front pavement area here?" asked Harriet. "Any CCTV coverage for that?"

"No, there is no CCTV coverage in that part. It was not in my opinion needed during the day, and at night the Council have a camera on that large pole over there." He indicated a tall, grey, metal structure halfway down the High Street. "We have never had any trouble here, and the Council system does a sweep of the frontage every so often in its usual operations."

Harriet spoke to Ian. "That won't help much," she said. "When Kuppers reported the wallet missing he said he was outside nearly all the time, and only went in for a wee, and to order more coffee whilst he was there."

"Any footage will probably only show him going into and out of the café entrance and coming out again, and possibly back in after he discovered his wallet was missing. It won't show if anybody came up to talk to him, or approached the table when he wasn't there, or anyone hanging around the café."

"I'll have to get all that info from the duty staff."

A young waiter appeared from the café carrying a cup of coffee on a small, circular, black plastic tray. Francesco halted his progress.

"Who is that for?" he asked the waiter. "The lady on table twelve," the waiter replied. "I'll take it over to her," said Francesco. "You see, I have dressed especially for the job." He had changed into a waiter outfit, several of which were kept in the office. He looked down the front of the outfit, towards his shoes, with a pleased expression on his face. He looked up, and said, "This is how I started, you know," addressing no one in particular.

He turned to the young waiter. "Luigi," he said, "these people are from the police. I mentioned to you that they were coming to talk to you and Mario this afternoon, about the gentleman whose wallet went missing on Tuesday. Not that you took it," he smiled. "I pay you too much."

Francesco headed over in the direction of table twelve, leaving Harriet and Ian with the waiter. "Let's sit at that table over there," said Harriet, moving to the table and chairs indicated by Francesco.

The young man was probably in his early twenties, tall and rather gangly, with a dark complexion, and a head of thick, dark hair, brushed back smartly. He was dressed in precisely the same style as Francesco, the Artimesias 'uniform'. A rectangular name badge was pinned to his waistcoat, which proclaimed him as "Luigi" in large white letters on a black background.

"Well, Luigi," said Harriet. "I believe that you were the table waiter on Tuesday when the wallet went missing."

"Yes, I was, but there's no need to call me Luigi. My real name is Hywel Thomas. I expect that you, being a policewoman –" "Detective Chief Inspector," interrupted Harriet.

"Well," said the young man, jocularly, "I expect even a Detective Chief Inspector would deduce eventually that I'm Welsh, which I am, by blood. Welsh parents, but born in Crawley, so no clue in my accent there.

I graduated last summer from Birmingham, with a degree in modern languages, so my Italian is really good.

The customers like it, so I lay it on thick, and if any of them are Italian anyway I'm quids in. I'm doing a year's work before I go travelling around the world for a year. When it's winter here, Australia here I come. It'll be all sunshine for me," he exclaimed joyously.

"This is only my fourth stint on daytime duties. I normally do nights. When I'm not in the café I do home schooling in either French or Italian. I can usually pick those times, so it's a perfect fit.

My father got me this job. Funnily enough, he used to be in the police force, in Aberystwyth, but he moved to Crawley to take a job in Gatwick security. He's just retired from a senior management position at the airport. He knows Francesco. He met him somewhere called the CWBC, which I think stands for Crawley and Weald Businessmen's Club. It's a load of mainly old, retired business guys. They meet once a month for lunch at the Hawley Theatre, just outside town, and do loads of other social activities.

It's not what you know, but who you know, they say, but in my case, I know as well."

He paused. "I bet it's only old, long gone Giuseppi, who started up the whole shooting match just before 1900, and me, who really knows why the place is called Artimisias. It'll be named after the 17th century female painter, Artimisia Gentileschi. Painted beautifully, like Caravaggio, same style, but pretty well ignored up till recently. If you want to see where the yellow theme of the café and restaurant comes from, and you're ever in Detroit, call into the Detroit Institute of Arts, and look at her painting entitled 'Judith and her Maidservant'. A very cultured guy, that Guiseppe."

'There goes a very self-confident young man,' thought Harriet, 'but he is obviously pretty sharp, so his observations will be worthwhile.'

"Enough of all that rambling," said Hywel, "what exactly do you want to know?" he asked.

Harriet was just about to ask him exactly what she wanted to know when her mobile rang. She held up her free hand to Hywel in a gesture of apology and listened carefully, then spoke.

"I'll look at it with you when I get back," she said, ending the call.

She turned to Hywel. "Sorry about that. A policewoman's lot is not a happy one, you know. Now where was I?"

"With Gilbert?" Hywel questioned.

Harriet let that pass and began.

"Just tell me what you saw, heard, and noticed, from the moment he arrived at the café, to the time he left in the taxi after his wallet went missing. As exact timings as you can recall would help."

"I'd like to know exactly where he was sitting, what food and drink he ordered and consumed, and what he didn't eat or drink, if anything. What happened around the time his wallet went missing."

"I'd like to know about his manner. Did he look agitated, nervous? Keep looking around? Did he get up from the table? Any phone calls he made whilst at the table or near it. Any notes he made. Did he have a briefcase or file? Did anyone sit with him, or come up to him, or approach him?

Were there any people around looking suspicious, or paying attention to him, either sitting at other tables, or on the paved area, or walking past? Or anything else you can think of."

"Oh, not much, then," said Hywel. "I suppose you're asking me all this because there's no CCTV out front at this time of day."

"Good thinking," said Harriet, "I would have asked you anyway, but you are right, and that certainly does make your observations a lot more important."

"OK," said Hywel, "I'll give it my best shot. It was a quiet morning before he arrived, one or two tables occupied, but no one really near him. There was a young girl with a baby, over there," said Hywel pointing to a table on the far side," and two middle-aged ladies on table twelve, the one that Francesco went over to." Harriet noted that the table was also on the far side of the café frontage.

"He came along at round about half eight in the morning, and chose a table positioned pretty well where we are now. I think a taxi dropped him off, but I wouldn't be certain of that. He was by himself, no briefcase. Smartly dressed. Cream jacket, khaki-coloured trousers and brown shoes. Sat with his back to the café entrance, where I was standing, so he was facing the paved area and the road.

I took the order. Coffee, croissants, orange juice, fruit. A continental breakfast, really. He seemed pleasant. He remarked on how nice a day it was, and how he had been here yonks ago, and how it all seemed to be the same, which was good. I could tell he was foreign but spoke English very well. Certainly, it wasn't Italian or French. I worked that out. Clever, eh? Birmingham Uni would be very pleased with me. My call would be German, maybe Dutch.

I brought him the order, which was pretty quick and easy for Mario to prepare, and I seem to remember him writing in a small black journalists flap fold notebook, the sort that goes in your inside pocket. He stopped writing and put it away in his jacket pocket when I put the breakfast on the table.

Nothing much else was happening. I collected two more teas for the ladies. It was definitely warming up, and by the time I got back to my station, he had taken his jacket off and hung it over the back of the spare chair facing him. He was tucking into his breakfast. He seemed quite relaxed, not looking round, quite unconcerned, I would say.

After about ten minutes or so the young lady with the baby asked for another tea, and some hot water, so I went back inside to Mario to get that fixed up when Mr...what did you say his name was? What with everything going on I don't remember any name."

"I didn't," said Harriet, "let's just leave that for the moment. Just call him Mr X. Carry on, this is very useful. I appreciate the detail. You have quite exceptional recall."

"Thanks. Well, Mr X then, came into the café. He asked for directions to the toilet, and at the same time ordered more coffee. He said again, this time to Mario, that he had been here nearly 30 years ago, at least I think he said thirty years, and how good it was that the café was still here. He was staying about a week, at some conference or other, and then he toddled off to the loo. After a few minutes, he came back and said he shouldn't have needed to ask directions to the loo, because they were in the same place. All this had put me off a bit, because I had forgotten about the cup of tea and hot water for the lady, so I got that moving, and got Mr K's coffee order from Mario, which I took out to him.

The food and orange juice had gone, but he was just finishing off his first cup of coffee. He handed me the empty cup, I cleared everything up that needed clearing up, taking care to avoid his mobile, which was on the table, and went back inside to Mario to get rid of the cup. I waited a couple of minutes for the young lady's order and took it to her. I gave her my big Italian – or Welsh – smile, big apologies, and that worked a treat.

On my way back from delivering the young lady's order I passed him. He seemed to have finished his breakfast and was standing up, and taking his jacket from the back of the chair. He asked me for the bill, and I went into the café and asked Mario to print it out.

He was just in the process of doing that, when in walks Mr X, rather casually, I thought, and asked us if we had seen a wallet, slim, black leather, with monogrammed, gold initials 'P.K' in one corner. Had anyone handed it in? He asked if he could look in the toilet. He thought he had it with him, in his jacket pocket, but couldn't be sure. He looked in the toilet and the restaurant area, then came back. No joy apparently. I asked Mario if anyone had handed it to him, but he gave the thumbs down as well.

He had his mobile phone in his hand and said he would call the hotel for them to check there, and to arrange a taxi to collect him, which he did.

Whilst he made the calls nothing much else was going on. When he had finished, he noticed the bill in Mario's hand. He ferreted around and came up with a new £20 sterling note from his back trouser pocket, which was more than enough to pay the bill, but he just told us to keep the change. I certainly remembered that bit.

Didn't seem too worried, in my opinion. No rush, no panic about the wallet. He seemed more anxious to get back to the Hotel for some meeting or other. He said, anyway, it was more an emergency 'travelling light' wallet, just containing some notes, a credit card and a couple of business cards. He said he didn't think it had been stolen, because neither the phone nor notebook was missing – particularly the phone, so he didn't think it necessary to take it any further as far as the café was concerned. He thought he had probably mislaid it somewhere in the hotel.

I had noticed about the phone and had come to much the same conclusion. I suggested he might have left it in the taxi that had brought him. He thanked me and said he would check.

I had to attend to a customer outside, and whilst I was there, his taxi came along. As he was about to get into the taxi, he remembered something. He took his reporter notebook and a pen from his pocket, wrote something down quickly, tore off a piece of paper, handed it to me, and then zoomed off, and that was the last I saw of him. Once I could decipher the note all it said was, 'If the wallet is found please contact Leila Zafiri, Conference Manager, Median Hotel Gatwick. She will have a contact telephone number and address for me. Thank you.' No name. He seemed in a big hurry at the end. I left the note on Francesco's desk in the office."

"Very good, Hywel, nearly through, one last point that I mentioned at the start - did you notice anyone acting strangely, either customers or people in the vicinity of the café before, during or after his time with you? Anyone hanging about?"

Hywel thought for a moment. "Not really. As I said, it was very quiet. The customers I have mentioned. Mother and baby, middle-aged ladies. Nothing at all out of the ordinary there.

As far as people in the area, I can only remember a handful, and I can only remember a few of those well. There was a couple. Middle aged I would say. A man and a younger woman. She was smartly dressed. Attractive. He had a beard. Dark blazer, I think. Academic looking. Could have been a Birmingham Uni lecturer. She had a dark blue suit, blue shoes, blue handbag. I think she may have liked blue." He delivered his words with a straight face, but he smiled inwardly at both his witticisms.

"They came up from Smith Street and stopped on the corner, to my right. Mr X was facing the High Street, so with his back to them. Don't think they, or Mr X, even saw each other. Looked like they were deciding whether to sit down or not and have a drink. Sort of 'umming and aahing' if you know what I mean. Then the woman looked at her watch. I assume it was her watch, then they moved off. They went their separate ways. The woman back down Smith Street and the man went across the road to look in a shop window. Just after they split up Mr X went inside for a wee."

"Oh, yes, of course. I nearly forgot. There were the cabin crew girls. At about the same time as the middle-aged couple, but over the other side of the paved area. About 3 or 4 of them, oh, and a pilot, usual pilot gear, dark suit, white shirt, tie, double-breasted jacket, all rings and badges on the jacket, sunglasses, pilot case. Don't know whether he was with them or not. Seemed as if he was. I think they were talking together. The girls were Flynnair, chattering and laughing. Quite loud. Wonder what the collective noun is for a group like that? A chattering of cabin crew? a chirrup of cabin crew?" Hywel smiled, then continued. "Stopped outside for a few minutes. I know all the aircrew uniforms, especially the girls. Flynnair was dark blue, with golden yellow scarves, pocket trims and vents. Very stylish. Their blue was like the colour the lady I mentioned earlier was wearing. Perhaps she was Flynnair herself. Could have been. Don't stand out so much in Crawley, aircrew. I guess they were all around about ten to fifteen minutes after Mr X arrived.

When I came back outside, they had all gone. The only others I can remember were just about the time that Mr X's taxi came. Two young people, a man in a sharp, Italian suit and a woman, blonde, grey business suit, attractive. Both had clipboards. Chatted for a short while and got into a flash car. Estate Agents would be my guess."

Hywel stopped. "That's it, Detectives," he said, as if from an American TV police spoof show. "That's absolutely all that's in my memory bank. I hope it's helped."

Ian, who had been making notes, put his notepad away in a slim, zipped notecase. "That's very helpful, Hywel," said Harriet. "We'll say goodbye later. Could you ask Mario to come out, please? I assume you can operate the till?" "Yes, no problem," said Hywel, and made his way towards the café entrance.

Mario, whose real name actually was Mario - Mario Bianchi - could add little or nothing to Hywel's excellent observations. He was a cousin, or someone in the Cascarino family. His recollections were nowhere near as sharp as Hywel's but dovetailed broadly with them. Harriet sent him back to relieve Francesco and asked Francesco to come over to him.

"Thank you, Mr Cascarino," she said, "your people, and especially Luigi, have been very helpful, and you are obviously still a brilliant table waiter. If we need to come back to you, we will, and if the wallet turns up here, please let me know as soon as possible, as well as Leila Zafiri at the Median Hotel."

"A pleasure. There's just one more thing." He spoke in a rather jocular tone. "If you need to involve Luigi any further, I must tell you his real name isn't Luigi, it's Hywel, Hywel Thomas, and he's the son of a friend of mine. It's not too important, but in the business a few little secrets we like to keep, you understand."

Harriet stopped him. "That, I already know, Mr Cascarino. It won't be discussed any more than is necessary."

For reasons of personal digital safety, both refrained from a farewell handshake. They gathered their effects together and walked towards their car. As he crossed the seating area Hywel came along, carrying a tray.

"Goodbye, Luigi," said Harriet, with a smile, "good luck in whatever you do, you will be a great success in life."

"Thanks," replied Hywel. "Good luck to you, too, but there's something puzzling me."

"What is it?" asked Harriet.

"It's why you send, not a local P.C. Plod, and not one, but two super duper high-ranking detectives hotfoot over here, under the pretext of a lost wallet, which the guy doesn't seem to give a toss about, when he was only here for an hour at the most, and where no one is hurt, and nothing is damaged.

Then you ask me a shedload of detailed questions, and you are so interested in my very detailed account that, apart from telling me you are D.I.'s, you don't even interrupt me, and at the end of all that, you won't tell me his name.

It stinks. There's much more to all this than you are making out. I'll watch this space."

Harriet gave Hywel a stare, with a knowing twinkle in her eye, but said nothing, turned, and with Ian in tow, they went on their way.

◆

# 38

The handover of Vonk to the Dutch police was one thing that went without a hitch. Immediately Harriet had relayed the Vonk situation to him, following the final forensics Barrowclough had organised the liaison with the Dutch and all the paperwork.

Arrangements had been made for an officer from Scotland Yard to accompany Vonk and the Dutch officers as far as Gatwick Airport, and then to ensure the three Dutch Nationals caught the requisite Amsterdam flight.

All that would be required from Harriet was a couple of quick signatures.

The Scotland Yard officer, a youngish, smartly dressed individual in his thirties, arrived at the hotel just before 4 pm, followed by the Dutch policemen a quarter of an hour later.

The senior Dutch policeman was an Inspecteur Van Rijn, and his colleague, a Hoofdagent Haan.

Van Rijn was a thickset powerful man, well over six feet, who could have partnered Vonk in the back row of a rugby team. Harriet placed him in his fifties. Haan was almost as tall, but a much thinner, and younger man, with floppy fair hair.

Both featured designer stubble, check shirts, faded blue jeans and trainers. Blue and white for Van Rijn. Orange and black for Haan.

Who were criminals, and who were police officers would have been impossible for the ordinary person in the street to distinguish.

It was all over quickly. The Scotland Yard Officer produced a sheaf of official-looking papers and sorted those required for Harriet to sign. He thanked her, and the three of them moved off to the Gatwick Station cells to collect Vonk.

As the Dutch officers left, Harriet whispered to Ian.

"Van Rijn over there should have been doing the night watch, not us."

Ian looked blank.

"Never mind," Harriet said. "It's another one I'll explain later. I'll just call Barrowclough to update him. At least that's something out of the way."

# 39

Harriet and Ian were taking a coffee break and mulling over Ian's notes from their visit to "Artimesias" when there was a knock at the door. It was one of the Sergeants, Dermot Power. He was wearing thin cotton, scene-of-crime gloves, and holding a medium-sized manilla envelope in one hand.

Harriet gestured for him to come in. He remained standing and handed her the envelope.

"Kuppers' wallet has turned up," he said. "It's in the envelope. No doubt it's his. Expensive black leather with the gold monogrammed initials 'K.P.' on it."

Power shook the envelope gently and the black wallet came out onto the desk.

"The hotel manager, Collison, brought it to me. I've been very careful with it, but I would guess there will be no particularly useful fingerprints on it. He got it from a lad called Derek Breach, on the Reception Desk. The wallet was handed to Breach on Wednesday afternoon sometime. Breach is a new hire, in his first week, and was also very busy. He didn't really know the procedure, so he didn't bother with the wallet too much, just put it aside, in a 'lost property' drawer. I guess he should have logged it, but that wasn't done. Also, it was a plain envelope, no name or address on it.

Anyway, he didn't remember about it until a couple of hours ago, when he opened the envelope and saw the wallet inside, and probably panicked a bit. He saw Collison passing the desk, so Breach handed the wallet to him, and Collison took it from there, finding out as much as he could from Breach, and then bringing the wallet – and the story – to me.

I've come along to see you as quickly as I could.

Apparently, Breach was handed the envelope containing the wallet by an airline pilot. The pilot said that he found it in one of the North Terminal toilets, took a quick look inside it and discovered one of those cardboard, pre-printed, credit card size Median Hotel Cards with the address, telephone number and so on.

Inside there was a wad of money, actually two hundred pounds sterling and a hundred US dollars, an Amex Gold Card, a Median Hotel address card, and a couple of business cards, which I have removed and bagged. So, this pilot popped along to the Median Desk and handed it over to Reception.

He said he wasn't a guest of the Median himself. He was a B.A. pilot and was just about to fly his plane to Larnaca. I think that was the location Breach said. Anyway, the pilot said he had to rush. He left without giving Breach his name, or any details.

I didn't find a Median Hotel Card in it, but I don't think that's important."

"Thanks, Sergeant. Anything else in the wallet that might be of interest?"

"Different, yes, ma'am, but of interest to you, I'm not sure.

You know that, in a wallet, there is often a zipped compartment inside, but towards the back. I don't think Breach either noticed it or took any notice of it. I unzipped it and inside were these."

He felt into the envelope and produced two pieces of paper that had been folded precisely into two-inch squares.

Power unfolded them slowly, flattened them carefully, and laid them out on the desk in front of Harriet and Ian.

"What are they, Seamus?" asked Ian, who knew him from the Guildford Station, so using his forename.

"They are pages that seem to have been cut from an English/Dutch dictionary. A new one I would say."

He turned over one of the shiny sheets, then turned it back again.

"There are dictionary entries, printed front and back, two pages to one sheet. They are pages 18 and 19 from the English to Dutch section, and 24 and 25 from the Dutch to English part.

Don't know what to make of it myself." Power said. "No fingerprints on these sheets at all, so you can handle them without gloves."

"Thanks for bringing it along," said Ian. "We'll look at it and see if we can come up with anything. If there's anything else we want you to do we'll let you know."

Power turned and left the room.

Both Harriet and Ian were silent for a few minutes, examining the sheets. Then Harriet spoke.

"What happened to the exhibits from Kuppers' room that didn't need to go to forensics?"

"Bagged and labelled and locked in the filing cabinet over there," said Ian, pointing to a tall, grey metal locker on the other side of the room. "Key is in my drawer."

"Let's unlock it, then," said Harriet, "I have an idea."

Ian did the unlocking. First his drawer, then the cabinet.

Harriet went over to the drawer, rummaged around, and brought out the evidence bag holding the Dutch/English dictionary, and that containing the torn envelope. She brought the evidence bags over to the desk and took out the dictionary and the two halves of the manilla-coloured, padded envelope, which was just over the size of an A5 sheet of paper.

She married the two parts of the torn envelope together, then placed one of the dictionary sheets on top of the envelope. It was a perfect fit, allowing a small space around the sheet.

"There we are," she said, "the envelope contained the dictionary."

They looked at the envelope. It had a white label stuck onto its front. A name and address had been typed on the label in a bold, black Ariel 14-point computer font.

It read: -

"Mijnheer Pieter Marius Franciscus Kuppers

c/o The Median Hotel

Gatwick RH6 0ZZ

It was postmarked "Gatwick" and with the date of Saturday 14th May.

Harriet put that to one side for the moment and picked up the dictionary. She riffled through the pages quickly, stopping at page 17 in the first section of the book. She looked up.

"The sheet with pages 18 and 19 has been removed," she said, and held it so Ian could see.

"Look how precisely it has been removed. Not torn, but cut neatly with one of those small, very sharp artist's crafting knives, I would say. You could hardly tell anything was missing, which is presumably why no one picked it up at the time."

She proceeded to the Dutch/English section, and page 23, with the same result. Pages 24 and 25 had been removed in the same manner.

"Let's take a close look at these missing pages, to see if they might mean anything. Why those particular dictionary entries have been removed."

"I've got some admin to tidy up, so you take a look for fifteen minutes, and I'll do the same. Then we'll compare notes.

Ian examined the dictionary sheets for fifteen minutes.

"OK. Time up," said Harriet, looking at her watch. "Don't say a word."

Ian stopped and made a brief pencil note on a scrap of paper.

Harriet picked up the sheets. After about five minutes she spoke.

"What have you got, then, Ian?"

"Finished already?" he remarked. "This is the best that I can do."

"There is only one word, and its translation, that appears on both the English/Dutch and Dutch/English pages, and that is 'coercion' in English, and 'dwang' in Dutch."

"Snap," said Harriet. "I agree... and the fastest contestant was Harriet Graham, in three hundred seconds."

Harriet stood up and paced around the desk.

"What do you deduce from all this, Ian?" she asked." Off the top of your head is fine."

'She probably has more idea than me,' thought Ian. 'I know she's just testing but let me think'.

He pondered for a couple of minutes.

"There is no reason at all why he should have a Dutch/ English dictionary in his possession. Not only himself, but all the Dutch, speak English far better than ninety-five percent of the English-speaking population of the globe. So, I conclude he didn't bring it with him."

"Therefore, it was sent to him. Sent to him by someone who knew his full name, and his whereabouts, and sent on, or before, Saturday, 14th. That would probably have arrived on Monday 16th."

"The pages would probably have been cut out before mailing. It makes no logical sense to think that he cut the pages out himself in his hotel room, and kept them, put them in his wallet and trekked off to Crawley with them."

"The "coercion" bit means nothing to me. I have no idea at all on that score."

"Then there's this business of the discovery of the wallet and the pilot."

"Found in the North Terminal toilets? An unlikely story if ever I heard one. If you recall, there was a couple of hundred pounds and a hundred dollars inside it, in cash and untouched, and exactly the amounts Kuppers said he took with him. That's not the Crawley I know and love..."

"...and the pilot. Why mention Larnaca? That was really of no relevance. Why not leave his name? Did he look in the zipped pocket?"

"I think BA should be called immediately and asked for the names of the aircrew on the outward-bound afternoon Larnaca flight, then friend MacAllister, or Simon, asked for some CCTV footage of the pilot handing over the wallet at Reception, and finally someone should go and see the new hire, Derek Breach."

"Very good, Ian," she said, "Give me your thoughts quickly, then call Power and get him started on the BA angle as a matter of urgency."

Ian carried on.

"Nothing in this case makes sense as a whole. It's all a load of disparate disconnections. We still have no idea who the real murderer is. We are no nearer solving the case than when we started. In fact, the more we find out the more confusing it becomes."

"Anyway, I'll make those calls before you tell me your own conclusions."

Ian made the call, and when he had finished Harriet spoke.

"How about this scenario, then," she said.

"What if the dictionary was sent to him, and he removed the pages, and took them to Artemisias, as a coded handover message for a contact, with the key words being "coercion" and "dwang," and it all relates to the death of de Boer and the shady Dutch politics?"

"His plan was scuppered by the loss of the wallet, and he was poisoned on Tuesday afternoon by the 'Dutch connection', maybe at the Kamada, and the perpetrator or perpetrators have already hightailed it back to the Dutch flatlands?"

"In which case we are completely sunk."

"Think about the contents of the wallet. Apart from the dictionary pages hidden in that zipped compartment, there was only money, no bank cards or anything personal and the hotel address card. Now that's a "going to Crawley for a cup of coffee" special-purpose wallet, isn't it?"

"Very creative," observed Ian. "Remotely, but possibly, plausible. But you've been reading too many spy stories. It's all conjecture, and there's not a shred of provable evidence to support it."

"Besides, according to Leila Zafiri, he didn't seem at all concerned about the loss of the wallet-as you say, his "morning coffee in Crawley wallet"- and he seemed to go about his normal, planned business once he was back at the hotel. That seems hardly like the actions of a man who has just lost some vital information, as a consequence of which he would find himself on a mortuary slab in the not-too-distant future."

Harriet appeared to "freeze" a little. She put her right hand to her lips and stroked them slowly, once or twice, pensively. "Pilot," she said quietly, to herself, then "Mmm, pilot," she repeated.

"Let's have another look at your 'Artimesias' notes, Ian," she said.

"Here we are," she said, looking down at the notes.

"I was talking to this *faux* Italian waiter, Luigi, and asking him if there were any people hanging around the café around the time of the Kuppers wallet incident. "

"He said, and I quote from your notes. 'There was a pilot and a group of cabin crew girls.' You have noted that down word for word."

"Remember, he wasn't sure if they were together or not. So, this might have been our wallet pilot. If so, it places him at the scene on Tuesday morning. Could he have stolen the wallet? Could he be the murderer? Perhaps, perhaps not. There was also an oldish, middle-aged couple Luigi mentioned as being there at the same time, and other breakfasters in the café itself, but ...."

At that juncture, the ringtone of Harriet's phone interrupted her flow. She listened for a couple of minutes.

"Thank you, D.S.Power. Very helpful." Said Harriet and continued speaking to him.

"Can you do a couple of things for me? Check with reception if Derek Breach is around. If so, ask him to remember as much as he can about the pilot who handed him the wallet, physical description, accent, appearance, mannerisms, and all the usual stuff. Then pop along to MacAllister to discover what CCTV footage there is of the pilot handing in the wallet. Thanks."

She then turned to Ian.

"As you probably heard, that was Sergeant Power. He's just spoken to B.A...... and the plot thickens."

"B.A. told Power that, in September 2015, they altered or cancelled a whole raft of flights for the 2016 Spring and Summer season. The last Gatwick to Larnaca flight took off last week, and that service isn't scheduled to recommence until September."

"So, either the pilot wasn't a pilot, or he wanted to keep himself as anonymous as possible. If he wasn't a pilot why didn't he keep the money, and why bother to hand it in?"

"...and there's another thing," said Ian "when did the pilot, or the not a pilot, actually hand in the wallet? Wednesday afternoon."

"Now, Mrs Parkinson tells us Kuppers died probably late on Tuesday. On Wednesday he was very dead. If this was carefully planned- and it probably was- as the lack of evidence at the crime scene seems to show, the murderer would very likely have established that Kuppers was dead on Wednesday. Job done.

Assuming for the moment the pilot was the murderer, why appear in person a day later, at the place of the crime, in pilot gear, knowing there was CCTV, and hand over what might be incriminating evidence?

After all this, we have absolutely no idea who he is, or even may be.

This case is all questions and no answers. Nothing makes sense.

"Good point. Well made, Ian," and we've not yet mentioned the odd events at the Kamada."

"Let's take a coffee break, and a half hour rest, then regroup"

They were just finishing their coffee when there was a knock at the door, and Detective Sergeant Power came in.

"No real luck with the CCTV or Breach, ma'am."

"The CCTV did pick up a pilot person going to Reception and handing over an article around the time you mention. Couldn't see whether it was a wallet or not. Probably was. Unfortunately, it's a back view, and he was only there for a very short time. He was in front of a character in a white suit, and they seemed to exchange a few words, but very briefly. His leaving movements were blocked by other people milling about. Close-up didn't help. No facial shot, I'm afraid."

"Breach hadn't got a great recollection, but he did confirm that the pilot said he was flying to Larnaca on a BA flight, Breach remembered because of the unusual destination name."

"He described the pilot as average height. Seemed to think he had a well-spoken English voice. Dark glasses, dark blue uniform, and cap, black attaché case. Couldn't remember if he had a BA name badge, or wings on his jacket."

"See one pilot and you've seen them all sort of scenario, ma'am."

"Thanks anyway, Sergeant. Well done. Go and get something to eat. We'll call you if we need you."

# 40

Harriet had summoned her small team to the Ops Room at 6 pm.

It had been a busy day.

The morning visits of Ian to Michaela, Harriet's own to the Kamada and their joint afternoon trip to Artimesias had been completed. The sergeants had continued to wrestle with the missing pages of the dictionary and the letter that had arrived earlier, and finally, the wallet had turned up.

Harriet addressed the team.

"As you know, D.I. Scott and I have completed several interviews this morning. I have visited the Kamada Restaurant next door and Artimesias café in Crawley. This morning D.I. Scott undertook a special investigation under my orders and relating to the Kuppers situation."

Harriet went on to describe Ian's assignment, his visit to Burton's Hill, and its outcome, and a summary of the investigations at the Kamada and Artimesias.

She continued.

"Unfortunately, none of these visits has produced either the murderer or any real clues that would lead to the murderer, or murderers, and a consequent arrest."

"As to yourselves, you already had the dictionary and its missing pages. You now have a further letter, written in some kind of code, that you have started to try and decipher. Now we also have the re-appearance of the missing wallet and its contents."

"Right," said Harriet. "It's election day - Thursday."

"Hands up those who think that the sender of the dictionary, the cryptic letter and the mysterious wallet returner are the same person, who is also Kuppers' murderer?" asked Harriet.

Everyone raised their hands.

"Hands up those who have any idea who that person may be?....and with reasons," she added.

No hands went up.

"Let's go through the possibilities, then," said Harriet.

"Willem Vonk was at Gatwick on Monday, so he could have posted the first letter then. He could also have posted the cryptic letter on Tuesday before he went to London. Even if  Kuppers was totally mistaken about losing the wallet at Artimesias it is highly unlikely Vonk could have stolen it, inserted the missing dictionary pages and left the wallet in the airport lavatories."

"In addition, the poison that killed Kuppers was ricin, and Vonk's story about Thallium is substantiated by the results of the forensic analysis received this morning. I am sure that he knew nothing of ricin. So, we have ruled Vonk out already."

"Anyway, he is in the custody of the Dutch police, and is being shipped off to Holland to stand trial for separate offences committed over there. Better for us not to be involved."

"Angelique Durand was in Holland on Monday and only arrived at Gatwick on Tuesday night and was definitely in London all afternoon until late on. She would, therefore, have missed the Gatwick postal collection."

"She might have colluded with Vonk, but we can't prove that. There is nothing that suggests she was involved in any way with the wallet. She is free to go. Not because she is not guilty in some way, but because nothing at all can be proven against her that would stand up in a court of law. She is a very devious and cunning lady. Rule her out, too."

"Michaela Gold. She didn't know him from Adam until his Monday morning visit, and even then, didn't know his real name, certainly not his full name. Not worth further consideration in this particular scenario."

"The staff at Artimesias. Nobody in the café knew Kuppers would visit it on Tuesday morning, so the staff are all clear, plus the fact none of them knew him. But he might have met someone there-maybe a someone who slipped some ricin in his coffee?"

"The Kamada. Same thing. The Manager, Mr Endomoto, knew he was coming, and had prior communications with him, but wouldn't have known his real name. Kuppers called himself David Agnew in every contact with the Kamada. He ate alone, and no other diners or visitors approached him throughout the meal. CCTV is conclusive. Endomoto would have no obvious reason to kill him, anyway, as Kuppers was paying himself and the restaurant staff handsomely for the illegal fugu meal."

"No crosses on your ballot papers, then, which leads us to the conclusion we are looking for some other person, or persons, unknown."

"We are looking for someone who knew him very well, or certainly knows all about him, knew he was coming to the Median and when. Someone who had planned and pre-prepared the letters, dictionary, and letter."

"Whoever may be the originator, or originators, of these items is playing with us. Having succeeded in their objective of murdering Kuppers they could have high-tailed it for the hills, not sent further clues."

"But why bother with letters, wallets, dictionaries, and the rest, even poison? Why do all that? Why not just trail him and bump him off in a dark car park, or pay someone to do it?" asked Harriet.

"A professional gangland hit man, or woman, would be drinking champagne in Monte Carlo, and reading and re-reading their bank balance by now, not hanging around near the scene of the crime."

"No, this is someone who wants to show us how clever they are, and how stupid the police are - the "Father Brown" rule - whoever is immediately arrested, charged by the police and put in a cell goes straight into the "completely innocent" column."

Ian chipped in. "The letters and the rest are all diversionary tactics. Not identical, but similar to Hitchcock's 'MacGuffins'." he said.

"I know of Hitchcock, but what's a MacGuffin?" asked Harriet.

Ian provided the explanation. "Hitchcock described the "MacGuffin" as a meaningless, unimportant detail that solely existed to serve as a reason for the story to exist. A MacGuffin is something that a story is built around and yet has no real relevance." he said.

"Quite right," said Harriet. "They are diversionary tactics, giving no real clue, but designed to waste our time, and from someone who knew a great deal about Kuppers."

"They will have known him well at some time, and, for instance, have known or been aware of his full names, and to use them quite deliberately."

"I think they will be in the UK, and most likely local to the Gatwick area. The letters are postmarked Gatwick, and recently posted. "

"They knew the conference was taking place, its time and location, and that Kuppers was due to attend."

"They know we, the UK police, are investigating the case. They may or may not have knowledge of poisons, but enough to prepare a dose sufficient to kill Kuppers."

"... and they clearly hated Kuppers enough to murder him."

"I am convinced this murderer is lurking nearby somewhere. We now need to dig deeper into the info we have on Kuppers, and his distant past. Somebody will know something, somewhere."

"Let's try to get as much as we can out of the letters, Kuppers' effects, and any other information. I will speak again with Van. His knowledge is of key importance. Let's go over everything we have in detail, and then in more detail. We will exchange the letters, dictionary, and other information so that each of us has looked at each element at least twice. Don't regard anything as trivial."

"I will try to placate Barrowclough."

"Let's stop there for tonight. Go home and we will meet, as usual, at 9 am tomorrow."

"We need a lucky break, and I'm sure something will turn up...but from where I have no idea." said Harriet to Ian, quietly.

## 41

It was a couple of hours or so later. Harriet and Ian were in their room, still trying to work out the puzzle of the letter. Neither was having much success, and just about to give up and eat at the hotel restaurant after their long day, when there was a knock on the door.

"Come in," said Harriet.

It was the fair-haired lady from the Reception Desk.

"Detective Chief Inspector Graham?" she asked.

"Yes," replied Harriet "that's me."

"I'm Sally Bideforde, from Reception," said Sally, "am I disturbing you?"

"No, carry on Sally."

"Well," said Sally. "Matthew Collison, the Hotel Manager asked me and the reception staff to go through the names of all the guests, apart from the Dutch motorcycle people, who had checked in, or out, since Monday, and let him know if there was anyone who might be connected with Mr Kuppers, or who might possibly be suspicious. Anything at all that might occur to me."

"Clutching at straws I thought, but I have been on Reception all day this week, so I got going on it, anyway." He asked me to report anything back to him."

"There was a little something that came up, and I have just been to see him, but he was really busy, so asked me to come along to see you, as he would pass it on to you in any event. So here I am. Sorry to waste your time, but I thought I should tell someone."

"Don't worry Sally," said Harriet. "Speak out"

"Thank you," said Sally "Now where was I?"

"Oh yes, going through the guest check-ins."

"Well, I was ploughing through the names when I came across a Mr and Mrs Masson, from Antwerp. That's 'M.A. double S. O.N'. - Masson." Sally paused between each of the letters of the names, pronouncing them carefully and deliberately.

"Now that name in itself didn't mean anything relating to Mr Kuppers, but it jogged my memory."

"We have a couple of regular guests with a very similar name. A Mr and Mrs Mason, and oddly enough the initials of their first names were exactly the same. Mr R and Mrs P. - Masson and Mason"

"I've been here for ten years now, and I know Mr and Mrs Mason quite well to talk to, particularly Mrs Mason. They come to us four or five times a year, on cruises and other foreign holidays, returning or going. They live quite locally but like to stay if they are travelling early or back late. They are both retired now."

"Not this week but last week, last Tuesday I think, they were checking out as usual. I was seeing to Mrs Mason at the desk, and Mr Mason was standing, waiting in the lobby with their case, straight across from me and not far away. I could see him quite clearly."

"On that day Mr Kuppers was here by himself. I had checked him in earlier. Mrs Mason was sorting out some papers and looking down at them, and I was looking over towards Mr Mason."

"Then along comes Mr Kuppers. As he approached Mr Mason he halted, and they sort of stared at each other. For about a minute I would think. They looked as though they were going to speak, but didn't, and Mr Kuppers walked on."

"A few minutes later the check-out was all finished, and Mr Mason came over to the Reception Desk. He tells Mrs Mason to go to the car, because he wanted to speak to me for a couple of minutes and then would follow on."

"Off she goes, and Mr Mason says to me that he thinks he might know the gentleman he had just seen from years ago but wasn't sure. Was his name Kuppers, and was he staying in the hotel for very long, as he might want to contact him to meet up?"

"I told him that the gentleman was indeed a Mr Kuppers, and he was leaving that day, but he would be back next week for three or four days as there was a conference he was helping to organise. He thanked me, picked up the case, and left, and that was that."

"I deal with people all the time, you know, and have a sense of their behaviour. It was just the way they looked at each other, and the length of time they took, just that bit longer than usual."

"Sorry, I meant to say something earlier, but what with all the goings on I must have put it to the back of my mind."

Sally took out a piece of paper from her pocket and handed it to Harriet.

"Just in case it's useful, I have noted down their names, addresses and telephone numbers for you. The ones we have on our records, that is."

"Thank you very much, Sally," said Harriet. "Both for the information and the details on your piece of paper. Very interesting. Not a waste of time at all. "

"You say you had talked to Mrs Mason on a few occasions over the years?"

"Yes, that's right." Replied Sally

"Did Mr or Mrs Mason mention where they worked in their pre-retirement days?"

"Not in much detail. I think both worked locally. From what I remember of the forms they sign here at the Hotel Mr Mason was an industrial chemist. Funny though, he has big labels on his suitcases with "Dr R. Mason" written on them. It is right, of course, because he is an academic doctor, and he is a nice man, but it is almost as if he wants people to think he is a surgeon or a GP or something."

"Paula-Mrs Mason- was in the airline business for many years. She puts down 'retired Executive Personal Assistant-Airlines' on her forms if I remember correctly. I can check the exact details for both of them if you like."

"No, don't worry about that Sally, but as far as you can recall, did Mrs Mason, or Mr Mason for that matter, ever mention Mr Kuppers, or a company called Eurair in conversation?"

"Not that I am aware of. It's possible, but before last week I don't think they had mentioned either to me. If I see them again, I will ask them."

"Thanks, Sally, you can return to your duties now. I will get in touch with Mr Collison to tell him you have seen us."

Harriet looked at Ian.

"But before that, I need a few words with Van," she said.

Her phone was answered quite quickly.

"Hello, Van," she said. "Sorry to trouble you, can I speak? "

"Go ahead" replied Van.

"Another memory test," said Harriet. "Cast your mind back a short time, only 29 years or so, to when you were at Gatwick on the Eurair project."

Van didn't acknowledge the little jest but continued listening.

"I know you weren't there very long, but you just might remember something. Anything. Even the smallest thing."

"Does the name Robin Mason mean anything to you? He would have been around forty at the time. Solid businessman type. Average everything, pretty well. Height, dress, manner. Maybe a beard."

Van thought for a moment

"No, not that I can recall."

"Or perhaps a Paula Mason? Probably a little younger. Mid-thirties, possibly. Attractive, dark hair and complexion, bubbly personality."

Again, there was a silence, but this time a much longer pause before replying.

"Ah, Paula. Paula Mason. Yes, now you mention it I do recall a Paula Mason. I was in the Gatwick office for about a week, I think around September 1989, finalizing, and signing off the agreement for the leasing of the Fokland 100 aircraft. She was the PA to the MD, Brian Wheeler at the time. She was very attractive, with an outgoing personality. Very efficient, too."

"However, soon after I left, there was a big row at the top management level at Eurair. Wheeler was fired, and another MD from outside came in, with his own team. I think I heard Paula was found a job as PA to the Head of Engineering."

"When would that have been, Van?" Harriet asked.

"Sometime in October 1989, I guess. I was in Southeast Asia by then."

"Engineering? Kuppers was an engineer, wasn't he?"

"Yes, he was - and a good one, too."

"And when did Kuppers start his assignment with Eurair?"

"Somewhere around late November 1989, I guess."

"And that would have lasted until the Eurair collapse in March of 1991?"

"Yes, that would be correct."

"Thank you, Van," said Harriet.

## 42

"I think a few words with Mr and Mrs Mason would be in order, don't you?" observed Harriet.

"It's 8 pm. I could try to arrange to see them tomorrow, but I'm not going to call them now, and give them a chance to talk together overnight and first thing tomorrow. I think we'll take a chance. Let's pay them a surprise visit tomorrow morning. They're both retired, officially at least. It's a Friday morning, and it's not far for us to travel. If they're not in their house, then I'll telephone them later and set something up a.s.a.p."

43

# Friday, May 20th, 2016

Harriet and Ian had given themselves plenty of time on Friday morning to make the journey from the Median to the Mason's house to achieve their planned time of arrival at 10.30.

Harriet had brought forward the daily team meeting to 8.00 am, to brief them as to their surprise call on the Masons and to task them with finding out as much information about the Masons as possible as quickly as possible.

Just before they were due to set off for Slinfold, Dermot Power called Harriet and Ian over to his desk, where he was looking at his computer. He addressed Harriet and Ian.

"About the Masons, ma'am. It's all here, but I'll summarise."

"Generally, pretty straightforward. Long marriage. No children. Comfortable home. No criminal records for either, clean as a whistle on that front, but there are a few facts you may find interesting. Mrs Mason you already know, was at Eurair. Mr Mason retired a short while ago but guess what his career was?"

"No idea," said Harriet, "surprise me. "

"It might. He's a career toxicologist. Related qualifications coming out of his ears. For the last 20 years before retirement, he worked for PharmaGat Laboratories, based in Crawley, finishing up as a senior Board Member.

Mrs M also worked there, on the secretarial side, just for a couple of years. She retired at more or less the same time as he did. She had several airline-related jobs before that, at Gatwick, but I can confirm where she worked from 1986 to 1991." D.S.Power didn't wait for any suggestions.

"Yes, that's right," he said "Eurair."

44

Harriet was encouraged by the typically rapid changeability of the British weather. It was a good day for umbrella salesmen. The shroud of thick drizzle which had fallen persistently from the leaden sky for the whole of their journey had developed into a steady downpour. Just the kind of weather to keep people inside their houses.

The continual, rhythmic noise of the windscreen wipers had diverted her thoughts from the investigation and the Masons, and her mind recalled some of the lyrics of one of her favourite country songs, "Me and Bobby McGee." She had known the song word for word at one time." Bobby McGee," she thought. Very appropriate.

Just past Slinfold Golf Club Ian Scott turned off the A29, the old stereotypical, unerringly straight Roman Road, and into a smart estate comprised of relatively modern detached houses, with the modern property developer's template for increasing their profits. Large houses, but not too large, and as small gardens as they feel they could get away with.

A notice in XL size Pseudo-Roman capital letters at the entrance to the estate advised us we were entering the 'Tiber Park Estate'.

All the roads had been named after Roman Emperors. They encountered Vespasian Villas, Octavian Way and Claudius Cottages before they reached their destination -Nero Close.

"I wouldn't like to see their Home Fire Insurance premium," remarked Harriet, as Ian slowed the car to a crawl. He parked up, and they disembarked. Ian had erected a very small, black-and-white striped umbrella, which was insufficient to keep them both dry. Ian was the one who got wet as they scurried over to number 26-the Mason's residence.

The house was exactly what he had expected to see. The small front garden was meticulously tidy, gravelled with small grey shingles and several neatly arranged terracotta and Positano Green pots. A series of circular flagstones of various pastel colours led towards the front door. A ' Peeblers' weathered stone figure of a small feline dragon sitting atop a globe was carefully placed to one side of the final flagstone. The door was painted in faux Farset and Ball blue, with a "No Hawkers" sign marked out in clear black script underneath a white bell push. A white, oval bespoke cast iron house sign, outlined in black, informed callers that they were at "The Nest". Above was "No 26," and below a small, red-breasted robin.

Harriet had no doubt they would find Robin Mason to be a fastidious, organised, but somewhat dull individual - and she was right.

She rang the bell and waited. They didn't have to wait long. The door was opened by a portly, thickset man with a beard and thinning grey-black hair, which was looking a little wet. He was dressed as though he had just come in from his garden -which he probably had. His outfit consisted of a heavy, cable stitch navy blue pullover, brown corduroy trousers, and completed by solid brown, lace-up shoes.

"Mr Mason. Mr Robin Mason?" queried Harriet, showing her warrant card. "I am Detective Chief Inspector Graham. This is my colleague, Detective Inspector Scott. Ian showed Robin Mason his warrant card.

"We are sorry to disturb you unexpectedly. We are investigating an unexplained death which occurred at the Median Hotel, Gatwick on Tuesday, May 17th. The death was that of a Dutch gentleman, a Mr Piet Kuppers. We are led to understand that you, and your wife, were acquainted with Mr Kuppers in the past, and therefore might be able to help us. We were in the area conducting other enquiries close by and thought we might call on you on the off chance. I'm sure it won't involve much of your time. Is your wife with you in the house?"

He paused. Stared closely at the warrant cards, gave them a prolonged, bewildered look, and then spoke. "Alright," he said, revealing a row of stumpy, yellowish teeth each one set a little apart from the other. "Come in," he said, removing his gardening shoes, and replacing them with a pair of tartan fabric slippers, which were placed neatly by the door for such a purpose. He showed Harriet and Ian into the lounge. They hadn't removed their shoes.

The room was comfortably furnished, in a style reminiscent of the 1940's or 1950's. Yellow ochre wallpaper with very large, entwined white flowers decorated the walls along with several assorted strategically placed mirrors. A small, rectangular fawn rug sat on top of a plain rust-brown carpet of a thick pile. A standard lamp with a very large circular shade in a beige colour was on the floor standing alongside a large light green sofa.

Sitting on the sofa was a woman. Harriet guessed she was in her sixties, which he knew was about the same age as her husband. However, she presented quite a contrast, both to Mason and the décor. Of a petite and slim build, she looked much younger than her years, with dark hair framing an attractive open face of an olive complexion, which hinted at a Mediterranean strain at some stage of her ancestry. It was a face that needed only a very light touch of make-up.

She was wearing a floral print dress of a small white and green pattern, with short sleeves and a square neck style, and cushion walk moccasins in light green. A simple gold oval double-link chain necklace was around her neck.

"This is Paula, my wife," said Robin Mason, gesturing in her direction., "This is Detective Chief Inspector Graham, dear," he said to her. "And this is Detective Inspector Scott. They tell me they are conducting some enquiries with which we may be able to help." Harriet noted that he was one of the very few people to get her own and Ian's correct names and ranks immediately.

"They are police officers investigating the death of…….. who did you say?" He looked at Harriet. "A Mr Piet Kuppers. At the Median Hotel, Gatwick Airport," she replied.

Paula seemed to shift a little uncomfortably, but said nothing, just giving a brief nod. Robin Mason brought two chairs from the other side of the room for Harriet and Ian, set them facing Paula, and then sat down on the settee beside his wife.

Harriet spoke. "As I understand it, Mr Kuppers was known to you both some years ago, and you were also in the Hotel on Tuesday 10th May, at the same time as Mr Kuppers."

"I wonder if you could help us, particularly if you can recall any unusual behaviour or incidents involving Mr Kuppers either at the time - he was in the UK many years ago- or at the Median Hotel last week. Any information, however irrelevant it may seem, could be very useful."

Robin Mason didn't stop to ask the obvious question as to how Graham had come to be in possession of that information. He paused for a short while, as if in recollection, then spoke.

"Well, Detective Chief Inspector, I am not sure we can help you very much at all. Paula, as you seem to know, worked for the holiday company Eurair, in the 1980s until they became bankrupt in early 1991. She was a high-level

PA, latterly to the Engineering Director. Mr Kuppers was an engineer on assignment from Fokland. I believe she saw very little of Mr Kuppers, as it was a large organization, and a big department within it."

"I believe I met him only twice, or only twice I can remember. These were at a couple of Eurair company lunches, where both Paula and I were seated next to him at the same table, and other people were there also. I have no impression one way or the other. He seemed pleasant enough, and was accompanied by a lady from Holland, a different lady, on each occasion."

Oh, by the way, neither of us was aware that Mr Kuppers was in the Median Hotel on 10th May. We were staying overnight on our way back from the Middle East, and even if he were there, on my own part, I would have been very unlikely to recognize him after all this time."

He stopped there, and Harriet kept her thoughts on that matter to herself.

"Thank you, Mr Mason," said Harriet, "Can I ask Mrs Mason for any observations she may have, as she clearly knew Mr Kuppers far better than yourself?" He looked across at her. "Mrs Mason?" she queried.

Paula, who had taken no part in the conversation so far, spoke up.

"It was as Robin said. Mr Kuppers came to work in Eurair engineering in, I think, 1989, from Holland. I saw very little of him but found him pleasant and efficient. From what I recall the girls in the Office found him charming, and quite fancied him. He was good-looking." She paused. "... and single." She smiled her engaging smile. "Even if I was interested, which, as a married woman, I wasn't, I was too old, and he had several girlfriends in Holland, who used to come over to the UK at weekends, to the big house he had near Gatwick, or he would go back home to his flat in Amsterdam.

I wasn't aware of any problems with him within the company, or outside office hours, and, of course, when Eurair collapsed in March of 1991 he returned to Holland immediately, and I never saw him, or heard of him again, until now."

Robin Mason took over. "So, Detective Chief Inspector, I'm sorry we can't really be of any help. If there is anything that occurs to either of us, we will be in touch if you leave your contact details. If you will excuse me, I have some gardening to complete and some paperwork to attend to."

"Just a couple of things before we go Mr Mason."

"Am I correct in the fact that you, Mr Mason have what I might call an arrangement with PharmaGat Laboratories, in Crawley, your former employers, whereby you can come to their premises on an occasional basis at their request to assist with any issues in your area of expertise?" Harriet asked.

Robin Mason nodded.

"...and you, Mrs Mason, are completely retired?"

"Yes," said Paula Mason without further elaboration.

Harriet stood up.

"Thank you both for your time" she said and gave Robin Mason the telephone number of the Gatwick Police Station, and her name and that of Scott.

"If there is anything else that occurs to you, just ask for either of us, and someone will put you in touch."

45

I an took a wrong turn into Augustus Avenue in trying to extract themselves from the estate. "I'm on 'Mastermind' next week. Special subject, Roman bleeding Emperors," he said, paraphrasing Basil Fawlty.

They eventually came to the main road junction and turned back onto the A29. Ian drove in silence for several minutes, before Harriet spoke.

"I think that's enough time, Ian. I know you've been reflecting on our visit. Your conclusions and observations?" she asked.

"I'm suspicious," he replied. "They were telling us only what they thought they wanted us to hear. It all seemed too orchestrated. No hesitation. No real signs of surprise. Their replies dovetailed too perfectly.

They didn't bat an eyelid when you asked them about his arrangement with PharmaGat, which hinted at us knowing about a 'ricin connection', in an area in which he was a world expert.

Also, neither of them asked us how he died, why the police were involved, or expressed any sorrow. Their comments all seemed very defensive, right from the off. Bit like watching Arsenal under Geoff Graham in the late 1980s.

Robin Mason was controlling the conversation. He was protecting her, or himself, by emphasising how little they knew Kuppers, and how little they had to do with him. Why would he deny the fact that he had seen Mr K outside reception on 10th May? He had clearly recognized him and spoken to Sally about his coming whereabouts. It is quite possible that Paula might not have seen Mr K, as she was busy at the Reception Desk, but he knew Kuppers alright.

Now for Paula. How do you work for two or more years probably on the same floor of the same Office, and barely know anyone, particularly as a PA to the Engineering Director, and Kuppers was an Engineer?

If she knew so little of Mr K, how did she know of his big house in Gatwick, of his various Dutch girlfriends' visits, and his flat in Amsterdam?

Why did she remark on herself being too old, of not being interested in him, or not fancying him?

It all smacks to me of someone who was very interested indeed in Mr K, and not in his professional life, either."

"Very perceptive, Ian," said Harriet "The lady and gentleman doth indeed protest too much, methinks."

Ian ignored the Shakespearean reference and continued. "Do either, or both of them, seem like murderers? On the face of it, that would appear unlikely, but Harold Shipman appeared to be your respected, ordinary family doctor, so appearances can often be deceptive."

"Let's surmise a little. The attractive Paula and the charming Mr K get to know each other well - very well - during his time at Eurair, but their relationship is suddenly brought to an end by the Eurair collapse. Maybe the very ordinary, but worthy and intelligent Mr Mason gets to find out, either before or after that event. It's the quiet ones that often have the most extreme reactions. He harbours his jealousy for years, but never forgets it. Then one day, completely out of the blue, Mr K appears in the foyer of the Median. Mr Mason makes inquiries, as Sally told us, as to Mr K's movements, and discovers he is coming back to the Median the next week. This gives him just enough time to plan, and execute the plan, so to speak. Obtain, or steal, the ricin, in regard of which he has both the detailed knowledge, and relatively easy access, send the letters, and to somehow administer the poison. His revenge is complete."

"That would be Mr M by himself. Perhaps Mrs M also had a reason to hate Mr K. I think it is unlikely that she would have acted alone, but not totally beyond the realms of possibility. Maybe she did or didn't see Kuppers in the Median foyer. Maybe Robin Mason told her about the fact that Kuppers was returning the next week, as she had no obvious means of knowing otherwise. As I just mentioned, he could have obtained ricin from the PharmaGat company."

"Collusion in the poisoning? I would say quite likely. As a long-married couple, they would know each other very well. They could have sat down and repaired their marriage after Eurair, both hating Mr K but possibly for different reasons. They would also know each other's behaviour and movements, particularly both being retired. Altogether it would make it a little easier to operate in tandem, rather than separately."

"To sum up. Singly or together, they tick a lot of the boxes. All the classic requirements are there. Motive, Means, and Opportunity. They are the only real suspects we have right now. Our only hope."

"So, there we are. In my opinion, Mr and Mrs M aren't going anywhere. I notice you had no problem when he ended the conversation quite abruptly."

"We have given them no real indication we suspect them, so we have some time to progress things more fully. What we have is conjecture. No proof. There are likely to be a lot of things we don't know that we may be able to uncover. We need to delve much more into the past, of both the Masons, and Kuppers."

"I don't think this is the last we have seen of the Masons. I think we will be taking the trip down Stane Street again, and it will be for a very different kind of interview. At the end of it all they may not be the free Masons they are now."

"Very funny," said Harriet, shaking her head.

"Just one thing you haven't mentioned," said Harriet. "The pilot who handed in the wallet. We don't have much from CCTV, but does Mr Mason appear to you to be someone who would dress up, and act like a pilot? "

"It would have to be Mr M, either that, or there's someone else involved, which is very unlikely, but maybe it's the quiet ones, eh?"

# 46

Harriet picked up her phone and dialled Van. He responded rapidly.

"Hello Van." she said, "I wonder if you can help us further with a couple of things?"

"We're looking back to when Kuppers was in the UK, on the Eurair project, both inside and outside of his working hours, and whether he might have had any problems during that time or had any adversarial relationships or situations."

"I calculate he was there for roughly eighteen months. Plenty of time for him to make enemies-male or female. Or even to become better acquainted with the Masons, both the dull and worthy Mr Mason, or the lively and attractive Mrs Mason."

"Did any such feedback filter back to you after you had left the UK, say on the Fokland company grapevine? "

Van understood the innuendo in the observation but ignored it.

"Nothing you don't already know, Detective Chief Inspector. You are already aware of the situation within Fokland, where it was rumoured that Kuppers would lose his job after the Eurair crash, but at the last minute he was reprieved, and Vonk was made redundant instead. There were, allegedly, some underhand manoeuvres that made that possible, but they were never substantiated, and nothing came to light."

"Kuppers was also rumoured to have several, shall we say, lady friends. I believe the ladies found him charming, but I heard no more of that after my Eurair assignment was finished, and I had finished the set-up work before Kuppers and the other engineers came on the scene."

"Thank you, Van. We were wondering where he stayed on his assignment, where he might have gone at the weekends, and so on. Where did you stay, when you were in the UK, assigned to Eurair? A nearby hotel, or travel from London each day?"

"No Detective Chief Inspector. At that time in the UK many multinationals, or companies with international businesses, rented houses locally. In the Middle East, Asia or Africa there would be gated compounds where assigned staff would be based, but not the UK."

"I wasn't there long, but I got the VIP treatment for my last visit. I stayed in a large house in Maidencroft, close to the Airport, near Three Bridges. I understood Eurair had rented several properties in that general area for their seconded personnel.

"On my visit, everything was organised on that front for us by Eurair. We just collected the keys, and off we went. They even had a housekeeper from an agency come in three or four days a week to hoover, wash and dry clothes, tidy up, and make the beds. A car would have been provided if the assignment was long enough. Pretty good, eh? Just like your own UK Police Force, I expect."

She imagined him treating himself to a rare smile on the other end of the phone.

"I don't know exactly where Kuppers may have stayed. Vonk might or might not know. I understand they weren't exactly best friends, and I think Vonk was only in the UK for the month before the Eurair collapse. Anyway, he's probably now back in Holland. There is no point in trying to ask him at this stage, anyway. Angelique or the other Doves didn't know Kuppers at that time."

"Thanks, Van, that's very helpful." Harriet paused before speaking, at a slow, measured pace.

"I have a feeling about this, Van," she said. "It is our first decent lead, and you are now a key figure in this investigation. I know that you, as the rest of the Doves, were booked into the hotel, and paid for until tomorrow morning. I would really appreciate it if you could stay on for a few days. I'm sure that could be organised with the hotel. I will let you know as soon as possible when we no longer require your advice and evidence. I think we have started to move forward, and I need you to be readily available. What do you say?"

Van barely hesitated. "My pleasure," he said. "Good luck with the investigation. I'll stay around. Call me if and when you need me."

"Thank you, Van." said Harriet.

❖

47

"Well, as Eurair went bottoms up, there won't be any joy with them," said Harriet to Ian. "Let's think. Eurair would probably have used a letting agency for the houses, but it's all such a long time ago, and we've ruled out an approach to Vonk."

They thought for a while, and then Ian spoke up. "Let's have the sergeants look at local Letting Agencies, or Estate Agents that were around in the 1980s and are still going, or have been taken over, and who might have some records, and the same thing for Employment Agencies. "

About forty-five minutes later the sergeants reported back. Dermot Power did the talking.

"We have a couple of things on the house, ma'am. Very thin on the ground, but it's all we've got. There is only one Letting Agency that's been around since that period. They've been established in Crawley for 40 years, and that's the "Blueway" Letting agency. We spoke to the current Manager, a Mrs Margaret Bolton. She thinks they were very likely to have organised the lettings for Eurair, but haven't retained the records from that far back, so a blank there."

"Now, as far as the Employment Agencies go, there is one company that has been around a long, long time, well before, and within the period we are talking about. It's not strictly an employment agency but might fit the bill. It's called AJC Cleaning Services, on the Royal Business Park. They're a family firm. Started in a very small way, then as Crawley developed, and Gatwick expanded, so did they. They picked up cleaning contracts from the Airport itself,

Offices and Hotels, and also for companies like Eurair, who were providing houses for staff and people on assignment. They moved out to larger premises on the Business Park in 1980."

"We spoke to a Mrs Miriam Jacobs, granddaughter of the founder- Albert John Cohen –AJC, see? She runs the business now. Her mother, Beatrice Meyer, used to do that job, but she's retired now, at least in theory. She comes in occasionally to help out. She would have been there at the time we are talking about, 1989 through to 1991. We briefly explained the purpose of the visit. One of her workdays is today, and she will be in later this afternoon. It may be worth calling in to speak to her. Shall I get back to Miriam Jacobs, and arrange an appointment?"

"Good work," said Harriet. "Yes, set something up for, say, 3 pm if that's convenient. You go along, Ian, and see if anything turns up. Unlikely, but you never know there might be a little something."

Just after 3 pm, Ian was sat in Beatrice Meyer's smallish, very tidy, office in the AJC building, sandwiched between "C Squared Light Aircraft Training Services" and "Burling Kitson: Pan-Asian Airfreight" on the Major Royal Estate, between Crawley and Gatwick. He looked round at the rows of grey filing cabinets, carefully and clearly labelled in bold initials on white cards slotted into their fronts and arranged in alphabetical order.

He was seated in front of a large desk, of deep mahogany, with a green leather, rectangular covering, with several filing trays parked in appropriate spots upon it. Behind the desk sat the equally smallish and tidy, birdlike figure of Beatrice Meyer. In her early 70's she was wearing a smart grey and blue flecked, woollen suit. Her grey hair was in tight curls, and she wore small gold-rimmed glasses. Ian noticed that both hands featured an array of gold rings, some with large stones that glittered in the artificial lights set into the ceiling.

There was a knock on the door, and a young girl, wearing a white top, black leggings and bright orange trainers came in, carrying two cups of tea on a tray.

"Thank you, Alice," said Mrs Meyer, "could you see to it that I'm not disturbed for about an hour or so." Alice nodded in agreement, and left the room, closing the door.

They sipped the teas, raising their cups to their lips in perfect unison, akin to a pair of Olympic synchronised swimmers, and then Ian began.

"I think we gave your daughter some idea of why we wanted to see you, and I'll just go over that quickly. We are trying to discover more about the movements of a Mr Piet Kuppers between the years 1989 to 1991. He was a Dutch citizen, employed by the Fokland Aircraft Company, but working for Eurair, the holiday company based at Gatwick. We believe he may have occupied a property, rented by Fokland, in Maidencroft in that period. It is a possibility that your company would have had the contract for the housekeeping of those premises. I assume any contractual arrangements would have been made between Eurair and yourselves. Of course, these all came to a halt when Eurair collapsed in 1991."

"It is all a long time ago, but I wonder if the name Kuppers means anything to you, and if you might have known the property he occupied, and, if so, whether you can recall of any problems with him. Any disputes with yourselves, or with neighbours, that sort of thing. If not, perhaps there is something in your records, that you could locate?"

He looked around the room, then at her.

"From what I can see here of your record keeping I should think that is a distinct possibility."

Beatrice allowed herself a few moments to preen, then replied.

"I remember the Eurair collapse very well. It was a big blow to us at the time, as we had a good deal of business with them, but we survived and progressed. I don't recall any problems with the properties at that time, from our point of view, but I'm afraid that name itself means nothing to me. I won't be able to provide anything immediately, because of the length of time that has passed, and any records will be in storage, but I'll get someone to research them, and I'll give you a call if anything is found."

Then she paused. "Wait a minute," she said. She pondered for a short while, then spoke. 'Her pondering time would have been precisely a minute, thought Ian.'

"Maidencroft.... Maidencroft, you say, that was Julie, of course," Mrs Meyer paused, then suddenly exclaimed "Ah ha. Yes, I remember," and she pointed a bejewelled forefinger into the air "the terrible twins". She almost shouted the words.

She composed herself and continued. "There were two young girls, Julie Jones, and Mary Watts, both local, probably about 16 or 17, schoolfriends and pals, a little bit odd, in a way. Mary was very East End, very cockney, their family moved to work in the Airport when she was about 8. Julie was more, shall we say, Sussex. But they just hit it off, inseparable, they were. With the Eurair business growing, we were cleaning about 6 or 8 rented properties in Maidencroft for them at that time, so we decided to allocate people specifically to Maidencroft and advertised for cleaners. Not a great rate of pay, I must say, but Julie and Mary applied together. They had done one or two odd jobs for a while, so this would have been their first real job. They were nice girls. They took the jobs together, and came through the trial period with no problems Good workers, and very reliable. We always called them the terrible twins, although they weren't related."

"Mary left after Eurair went bust, and got another job, at the airport I think, and I lost touch after that, but Julie I still know very well. I found her another job with us, and she worked for the company for about 20 years, before and after marriage and children."

"She still lives locally, in the same house as she did when she left us. We bump into each other occasionally in town. She works from home now, making those colourful panelled crochet blankets, cushions and so forth. Sells them on the "Crawleybuylocal" site. I bought a couple of them myself, straight from her though. They look very nice."

"Now I won't have anything for Mary, but I have a telephone number for Julie. I often still call her Julie Jones, although her married name is Jenkins. "J.J" before, and "J.J" after, eh" Mrs Meyer smiled. She picked up her mobile from the desk and glanced at it. "Not there," she said and put it down again. "I haven't kept it on my mobile, but it will be in the files, as she left us a relatively short time ago." She went over to the filing cabinet labelled "I to K" and fished around before removing a couple of documents and bringing them back to the desk.

"Here we are," she said, reading out the number, "that's the landline, but it should be okay. Why don't I try it whilst you are here, she may be in the house, then you can talk to her yourself, which will save time. If it works out, I'll speak to her, and then hand you over."

"Thank you, Mrs Meyer, this is very helpful."

Mrs Meyer this time dialled from a green-coloured company phone on her desk. A very faint ringing tone could be heard from the other end, and then someone answered.

Mrs Meyer covered the receiver with a bony hand. "Looks like we're in luck," she said to Ian, before withdrawing the hand.

"Hello, Julie. This is Beatrice speaking. How are you? Good. Me too, Julie. I'm in the Office, and I'm with a Detective Inspector Scott from the police. Nothing whatsoever to concern yourself about. Inspector Scott wants to ask you a few simple questions about the time you worked for us around 1990 to 1991 on the Maidencroft houses, when you were with Mary. Can you spare a few minutes?"

"Yes, of course." Beatrice handed over the telephone to Ian.

"Hello, Julie. Thank you for your time. I will be as quick as possible."

"In relation to the Maidencroft housekeeping work, does the name Piet Kuppers mean anything to you?"

Julie thought for a few moments. "Kuppers...no, that wasn't one of mine. There were about eight houses altogether. We split them four and four, and always stuck to the same ones, even if one of us was sick or on holiday. Beatrice would slot a replacement in, but I don't remember that happening very often. So Kuppers might have been one of Mary's." There was a short pause. "Wait a moment," she said "was he a Dutch gentleman? Pete, did you say?" She pronounced the forename very much the English way.

"Yes, that's right," Ian replied.

"Then I do remember. It would have been the first house that Mary ever did, and the last, I reckon. Royall Close, I think, probably number 2. Big house, as a lot of them were. I started with number 5, quite close. Pete, yes. Charming guy, Mary said. Lots of girlfriends. Mary fancied him herself, I think, but he was too old anyway. Early thirties at the time. Early thirties, too old, how about that," she exclaimed, "...and she had a boyfriend. You'd be surprised at some of the things we came across in the houses, but we were very discreet. Part of the job.

We've kept in touch over the years, we used to see each other quite a lot when the kids were young and meet occasionally now. She has two girls, grown up now, same as me, two girls, grown up. Terrible twins all the way, eh? We send cards every Christmas and birthdays.

Beatrice will probably remember, but Mary got a job at the airport after the airline folded. That one didn't last, and she went to live in Pheasant's Green, down towards Worthing. Lived there quite a while, but she's only just moved again. Back to Haywards Heath this time.

Anyway, I think you need to speak to her if you want more info. She's Mary Wilson now. I'm a 'JJ' before and after marriage, Mary's an 'MW' before and after marriage. Strange world, isn't it?"

"Do you have Mary's new Haywards Heath address?" Ian interrupted gently, before any more similarities came out.

"Actually, I think I can help you with that." She stressed the 'can'. "She sent me a change of address card, and telephone number on it. I'll just go and get it, won't be a couple of minutes, just hold on." After a minute or so she returned, and she read out the address and telephone number, and Ian wrote them down carefully.

"Thank you very much, Julie," Ian said. "You've been extremely helpful. We'll try to get to see Mary tomorrow. We may come back to you if we need to." He handed the phone back to Beatrice Meyer, and she said her goodbyes, and replaced it on its rocker.

Ian showed the address and telephone number to Mrs Meyer. "Oh yes, she said 'Gracelands'-but not that one." She smiled at Ian. "Your Satnav will get you there, it's off New England Street, just before you get to America

Way, but a little tip for you. Parking is difficult, but there's a small Church Hall up to the left. Use their Car Park. "Not many people use it on a Saturday"

"Thanks for that tip, Mrs Meyer, and thank you for all your time and your help, it's been extremely valuable."

Beatrice Meyer allowed herself another little preen and said "I'll have a look through our storeroom records and see if I have any information there, and I'll get in touch with you straight away if anything comes up. Is there anything else I can help you with?"

Ian smiled to himself. He thought that Beatrice Meyer rather liked being part of a police investigation. "No thank you, Mrs Meyer. I'm just going back to base to discuss things with my boss. I'm sure we will be in touch in the near future."

Mrs Meyer led the way down the stairs, and Ian stepped out into the Major Royal air.

## 48

B ack at base, Harriet greeted Ian. "You can debrief me on your visit to AJC. How did things go this afternoon?"

Ian recounted the discussions with Mrs Meyer and said, "I think it would be a good idea to give Mary a call, and try to meet with her as soon as we can."

"Agreed." said Harriet. "Let's call her now, to arrange something for tomorrow, if that's possible." Ian made the call. Mary was at home. He gave a "thumbs up "to Harriet. He talked to Mary for a few minutes. "OK, thank you, Mrs Wilson, I appreciate that, we'll see you at 10.30 am tomorrow."

He replaced the receiver and turned towards Harriet. "Right. She works either mornings or afternoons at 'Ewans'. You know, the small supermarket chain. There's a branch at the start of America Way, not far from her house. Used to be a pub there, apparently.

Well, tomorrow is her 'mornings' slot, but she has kindly agreed to arrange to swap that for the afternoon. She will phone one of the other 'half-day' girls and is certain that will be no problem.

Mrs Meyer gave me some handy insider information about parking near Mary's house. Next time anyone wants to show that the CID is inclusive, they should consider hiring a mature lady in her 70s, intelligent, hardworking, inquisitive, and who would just love to be a detective."

# 49

It was 8 pm on Friday. To celebrate the unexpected progress in the case Harriet and Ian had decided to eat dinner in the Hotel restaurant. After her customary daily update sessions with the team and Barrowclough, he had given them the go-ahead to push the boat out a little.

The menu choices were Steak and Chips followed by Sticky Toffee Pudding with a pint of Harveld Lager for Ian; Zucchini and Quinoa Baked Fritters and Vegan Chocolate Banana Ice Cream with a glass of local Bolneye Pinot Gris for Harriet.

They were at a further "clinking glasses together" stage and awaiting coffee when a message came through on Harriet's mobile. It was from Sian. "Call me when you have a moment. Nothing desperately urgent."

Harriet replaced her glass on the table and called Sian.

"You messaged me?" questioned Harriet.

"Oh, yes" replied Sian." You remember that earlier I said there were a couple of other trace elements in Kuppers' body that needed additional analysis, although they were highly unlikely to affect anything already established in relation to the cause of death. Well, the results of that analysis have just come through, so, for completeness, I will pass those findings on to you."

"Thanks" said Harriet "They will no doubt complete our dinner nicely."

"Sorry," said Sian "I didn't realise you were eating."

"No problem, we're at the coffee stage. "We're nearly done. Our coffees are coming now. I'll call you back in about fifteen minutes from our own ops room, so we will be away from any other diners with 20/20 hearing, or whatever the correct description may be."

In any event they had restricted their conversation to "off case" topics and had selected a table tucked into a smallish alcove at the far end of the dining room, with only one other table close to them.

That table had been vacant for most of their meal, but from their sweet course and coffees onwards it was occupied by two younger men, most probably English. Almost identically dressed in large-collared open necked white shirts and extremely narrow navy-blue slimline trousers, their highly polished tan shoes progressed to points sharper than Agincourt archers' arrows.

Their conversation was conducted in earnest tones and featured prominent use of acronyms. LIBOR, GSV's, GMV's and IRR were bandied around liberally. Their menu choices seemed low on the agenda.

Harriet and Ian finished their coffees and thankfully left the dining room. When settled in their ops room Harriet dialled Sian and got straight through.

"I'm putting you on speaker, Sian, so Ian can listen in as well." she said.

"O.K.," said Sian. "Well, there were two substances present in the body, and, as I said, in very small quantities. Those substances are Tetrodoxin and Belladonna."

"Have you heard of Tetrodoxin? "asked Sian, clearly expecting 'no' for an answer, and preparing to launch into a detailed technical explanation, but Harriet cut her off.

"Actually, I am quite well versed on that particular substance" Harriet replied. "Thanks to our good friend Van."

"I believe it is lethally poisonous to humans, and present in the Fugu Pufferfish, which is served as a delicacy in Japan."

She didn't pursue her discussions with Endomoto.

"Do you wish me to go on? "Harriet asked, with a small, but noticeable, hint of superiority in her voice.

"No, there is no need "replied Sian, noncommittally. "How is your knowledge of Belladonna?"

"Not good" replied Harriet. "I only know it is contained in the plant deadly nightshade. And that's it."

This was Sian's opportunity, and she wasn't going to miss it.

"Quite right," she said, "but that's not all there is to it."

"I didn't think it would be," said Harriet.

Sian ignored the remark and continued.

*"Atropa belladonna"* has a long history of use as a medicine, cosmetic, and poison and was named after Atropos, one of the Fates in Greek mythology, who, it is said, cuts the person's thread of life, and Belladonna, 'beautiful woman' in Italian, in reference to the cosmetic use of the plant during the Renaissance, when women used the juice of the berries in eyedrops intended to dilate the pupils and make the eyes appear more seductive."

"The use of deadly nightshades as a poison was known in ancient Rome, Roman empress Livia Drusilla used the juice of Atropa belladonna berries to murder her husband, the emperor Augustus."

"I could give you more information if you are interested." Sian questioned.

"No, no thanks, Sian," said Harriet, we have some more work to do before we go to sleep, so there's no need to call me in the early hours this time."

They ended the call together and finished their drinks.

"Here endeth the lecture," said Ian, spoken out loud, followed by, "not another bloody Roman Emperor," but this latter remark was muttered under his breath.

Apart from that, there were no more comments. If either of them had any further observations, then they weren't telling.

# 50

# **Saturday, May 21st, 2016**

Mrs M had been right about the car parking. Harriet turned off America Way, and into Gracelands. To the left was the wall of the Church Hall, and to the right a long, low, terraced block of red-bricked houses fronted by a long stretch of grass. "It's number 17," said Harriet, "The red door. About halfway down."

Harriet carried on for about twenty yards, then turned left, and found a tight parking space just past a narrow passageway that led down to the entrance door of the Church Hall. Harriet and Harriet walked towards the terraced block, and down the concrete pathway that led across the grass to number 17.

Mary was clearly expecting them, as the door was opened just before they reached it. "Mrs Wilson?" asked Harriet. "I am Detective Chief Inspector Graham, and that's Detective Inspector Scott."

"Come in, I've been expectin' you," said Mary Wilson, which was rather a statement of the obvious. Mary Wilson was a very thin woman, slightly above average height, in her late forties. It was obvious that Weightwatchers wouldn't be getting any of her custom. She had shortish, dyed blonde hair, and smartly dressed in a floral print dress, red cardigan and flat-heeled, black shoes. She led the way into a rather cluttered, but comfortable lounge, decorated in a variety of colours. A large dark brown, leather sofa took up a great deal of one side of the room, and a cinema-size television screen took up a great deal of the opposite wall, to which it was attached. Harriet and Ian sank into the sofa, and Mary fetched a dining chair from one of the other rooms, and sat opposite them.

"Would you like a cuppa?" she asked. "Freddie, my 'usband, he's gorn to work, and my girls 'ave both left 'ome now, so we won't be disturbed," she added, by way of explanation.

That was another thing Mrs M was right about. Mary's cockney upbringing and with it, the accent.

"No, we won't have a tea, thank you," said Harriet, "but you help yourself, if you would like."

"Nah. I'm fine. You said you wanted to talk to me abaht when me and Julie was 'ouskeepin' in Maidencroft. Well, I've bin pretty busy, we've just moved 'ouse, 'wiv all the paperwork and that so I didn't 'ave much chance yesterday to think abaht it, and it's all a long time ago, but I'll do my best."

By the way she spoke, and her demeanour, it was clear that Freddie took a back seat when it came to the organisation of household matters, and probably the finances as well.

"We wonder, in particular, if you can remember anything about a Mr Kuppers? Piet Kuppers. A Dutch gentleman. Julie thought that he might have been the occupant of Royall Close. Number Two, and that was one of your properties."

"Kuppers, you say, Pete. Oh, yes, nah you mention it, I do. 'ouse number two."

"Just to confirm. Was that number two, Royall Close?" interjected Harriet.

"Yes, Royall Close. It was my first one I did the 'ousekeepin' for. My first proper job- and the very last one in Maidencroft, I reckon, when everything went arse uppards later on."

"Yes. Pete. He was the one wiv all the ladies."

"By the way," said Harriet, "was he occupying that particular house for all of the time from late 1989, all through 1990, and then for the first couple of months of 1991, until, as you said, everything went 'arse uppards'?"

"Yeah, don't remember the dates exactly, but if you say so. Yeah. For sure, 'e woz there all the time."

"Thanks," said Harriet, "just tell us what you thought about him, about anything you might have noticed, or any problems you had with him, anything odd in general about the house, that sort of thing. Nothing is too small."

"Well, I didn't see that much of 'im when he was was aht at work in the week, but he was sometimes around when he weren't in the office, when it was one of my cleanin days. We worked some Saturday mornin's so saw him then, sometimes."

"'e was pleasant enough to me, no trouble, charmin', good lookin', seemed well off, bit of a ladies' man. There were a few girls who stayed at the 'ouse from time to time, some from 'olland, or the States, 'uvvers from England, sometimes one after anuvver. I fancied 'im a bit, I must say, but I 'ad Freddie at the time."

"Flash company car, 'e ad, too. Red BMW sports job, soft top roof and all the trimmings. Went abaht too 'undred miles an hour. Till 'e rote it off that was. Made the local rag and everything. Got a replacement straight away, but only a VW. That didn't please 'im much."

"Oh, and of course..." she hesitated for a minute, "...it's surprisin' wot you remember when you fink abaht fings, it's all comin' back to me...there woz this older woman. Very funny business."

" She used to come to the 'ouse occasionally at first, usually durin' the evenin's as far as I knew. Then she sort of moved in for the whole week, but went 'ome, or wherever, at weekends. She said her husband was doin' big alterations to their 'ouse, and she was stayin' with Pete, as a friend, until the 'ouse was fixed. I fink she lived quite close, but I never knew where. Then she started stayin' for the weekend as well, so she was 'ere the 'ole time. She 'ad a separate bedroom, but that was all pretend for my benefit. She used to mess up the bed as if it 'ad bin slept in. As if that would fool me! I knew for sure they woz sleepin' together."

"Then there was the ring. Very expensive, I would say. There was a little, sort of joolery box, very small, that was tucked away in one of the drawers under all the knickers and that. I shouldn't have bin lookin' in her drawers, or in the box, but there, you can't always keep those sorts of secrets from another girl, you know, particularly a Crawley girl. I never nicked nuffin, mind. Wouldn't dream of it, but I was curious. Well, sometimes the ring was there in the box, sometimes it wasn't. She didn't hide the sexy lingerie, though. Folded up carefully. Some black, some red. A few sets. Didn't leave much to the imagination. Very Angela Summers. She was attractive, mind you, looked after 'erself."

"I fink she was around about nine mumfs altogevver. Didn't get to talk to 'er much- at least not on a girl to girl basis. I woz usually cleanin' when she was workin'. She kept 'er self, to 'er self and er secrets to 'erself as well. Quite pleasant though, never nasty or up 'erself wiv me.

All ended suddenly though. Never really knew why. I got anuvver job straight away. That was no problem in those days."

"A couple of questions, Mary," said Harriet. "Do you remember her name?" she asked" and how old would you say they both were? just an estimate is ok."

"Hmm...ages. Let me fink" pondered Mary, answering the second question first. "I wud say that e-Mr K- woz mid firties, and she wud look abaht the same. 'Ard to tell, but when you got close up, she woz a bit older, but, like I said before, in very good nick."

"Don't know her second name," she continued. "Can't remember if I ever did. Her first name, let me think. It was a 'P' …. Patricia…Pauline…no, I got it." Mary smiled delightedly. "It was Paula That's it - Paula."

"How did they get on together? Do you recall any arguments, or physical disagreements between them? As far as you know, was she happy?" asked Ian.

"Oh, physical disagreements," responded Mary, in a somewhat sarcastic tone. "You mean did 'e 'it 'er?"

"Yes, that's what I mean," responded Ian.

"Not as far as I knew, well- almost- right at the end, just before Eurair crashed- so to speak," said Mary.

"It was one of my Saturday mornin's and I let myself in the front door. Pete was there, in the lounge, sort of pacin' up and down. I just got the 'oover out, when in comes Paula. Pete suddenly goes spare, and starts shoutin at 'er, in a real rage. They'd 'ad a few ding dongs of late. I'd sort of noticed that fings seemed to be gettin' worse between them, particularly after she moved in full-time, but it woz the first I'd seen of sumfink so bad.They carried on just as if I wasn't there. She'd turned up late to meet 'im, or summat like that. Anyway, I went up the stairs to the landin' to get away from it, but I cud still 'ear 'im shoutin. Oo do you'effin fink you are, and a load more swearin'."

"Then 'e said 'You will do wot I say, is that understood? or else….somefink wud 'appen.' Some long word I didn't catch or can't remember. Sounded sort of menacin', like in the old black and white gangster films."

"Was it 'consequences'?" asked Harriet.

"Might have bin. Might not. Dunno. Anyway, after I finished the bedrooms, and came dahnstairs, it all seemed to 'ave calmed dahn, although she was cryin' and that, but after I finished my cleanin' that mornin' that woz the last I saw of them both, to this very day."

Mary stopped speaking at this point, and looked reflectively into the distance, at nothing in particular. Harriet and Ian exchanged 'end of conversation' glances, and Harriet spoke.

"Thank you, Mary, thank you very much. We might need to ask you to sign a statement, which will record what you have told us, but we will let you know in advance about that. Is that alright with you?"

"Yeah, OK wiv me. Glad to 'elp. Funny business altogevver. Surprised 'ow much I cud remember. Still, ain't nuffin so strange as folk, they say."

"I thought she was going to ask me if I wanted to go up the 'Apples and Pears' for a 'Jimmy Riddle' and hand me a copy of "The Definitive Dictionary of Cockney Rhyming Slang" with several pages missing as we left." said Ian as they made their way to the Gracelands Church Hall, and their car.

# 51

Harriet and Ian had returned to the Median from their morning visit to Mary Wilson in Haywards Heath. They had fed back their findings to the team, who had spent their own mornings diligently researching Eurair, Kuppers, and the Masons.

Harriet had arranged a further meeting with the Masons, on the same pretext as their earlier visit , that several hotel guests around at the time were being asked if they could help, and the police were going to call on another couple close to the Mason's house who weren't available when they had called on the Masons yesterday. She was trying to keep it as low-key as possible.

The information the team had unearthed had been given to Harriet and Ian, who were all set to commence the drive down to the Slinfold outpost of the Roman Empire, when D.S Power scurried over to them.

He was carrying an orange shopping bag of solid plastic and he put it on their desk.

"I'll open that in a minute" he said, in a conspiratorial tone, then continued.

"I've only just managed to get this information together", said Power, gesturing towards the opposite wall. A smallish pine bookshelf, with room for three rows of books was affixed to the wall.

"You see that bookcase" He stated. "We haven't paid any attention to it, have we? I guess the books are for the delegates and conference attendees if they want some reading during their stay. I took a look at it when I was taking a breather and a cup of tea, not too long ago.

The books are all aviation related, and neatly arranged shelf by shelf. On the top shelf, 'Aviators and Aviatrixes', if I have my grammar correct. Biographies of Amy Johnson, of course; and Amelia Earhart, Shelia Scott, Charles Lindbergh and so on. On the second shelf, 'General Aviation' Concorde, Histories of Gatwick and Heathrow Airports, Aviation-A History', and several more."

"And now we come to the bottom shelf".

"Thank goodness", said Harriet. "I hope it's quick. We need to be in Slinfold before sunset- or sundown, as Barrowclough would say.

Power took little notice but ploughed on.

"On the bottom shelf are books on histories of airlines-British Caledonian, British Airways, and several more. Then, finally, there was a book entitled "Flying with Friends. The Story of Eurair" by Graham Simpkins.

"You won't see that on the shelf." said Power dramatically," because here it is", and he delved into the orange bag to produce, and display a slim hard back volume with a picture of a Eurair aircraft with its distinctive orange, black and white livery, and the book title in bold, thick black script beneath.

"This was published in 1995" said Power "but it seems to be completely untouched".

'Unread and left on the shelf for years' thought Ian. 'Rather like the copy of "Finnegan's Wake"' in Crawley Library,' but he kept that thought to himself, since he knew that observation would apply to practically every other library in the U.K.

Inside the front of the book was a bookplate on which had been written-

'To all my good friends at the Median-Happy Days Gone By'.

from Graham. October 1995

Below this was a typewritten line- "12 of 50"

There was a small, square, yellow sticker marking one of the pages. Power used the sticker to locate the page, and opened the book, laying it out with both recto and verso pages visible, side by side.

Ian and Harriet adjusted the position of the books so they could both see clearly. The whole book was of very high print quality, with a glossy finish and sharp, clearly legible photographs and text.

A bold heading across the top of the left hand page proclaimed, "Gatwick Office Staff: November/December 1989" and beneath that, on the right hand page, was the sub-heading "Finance", and directly beneath that a colour print of a group of smartly dressed people, men and women, mainly young, stationed by their desks, smiling at the camera and wearing name badges that were visible if one looked closely. That took up about half of the page.

The other half of the left hand page was taken up by a similar grouping but entitled "Personnel".

Then, on the right hand page was, again, a similar grouping. This group was described as "Engineering".

There were three people at the front of this photograph, lined up ahead of the other staff. The first was a slightly older man, with a suit and Eurair tie. His name badge told us that he was "Robert Reed" and his position was "Director of Engineering".

Next to him was a dark haired, very attractive, petite lady. She looked as if she were in her early thirties, very smartly dressed in a sea-green linen suit, and white, flat heeled shoes. Her name badge told us that she was "Paula Mason. PA to Director of Engineering".

The third person was a man, in his thirties. Stocky and balding, he was dressed casually but smartly in a plain white shirt, grey slacks, and shiny black shoes. He appeared to be standing very close to Paula and was smiling broadly.

Paula's desk was located outside Reed's office, and standing on it was her desk name badge, of smartly designed thick plastic in the distinctive Eurair colours, about six inches long, and two inches high, with her name picked out in bold, but tasteful black 'sans serif' capital letters.

Another desk sat across the other side of the office, opposite to Paula's, the occupant of which, on a normal business day, would be directly facing her across the central walkway that ran though the office. On that desk was a miniature orange flag, with a small circular base, allowing it to be stood upright, and a similarly designed desk name badge.

"Guess the name on the desk with the orange flag? "Asked Power, and he continued speaking quickly before any response could be given. "That's right "he said." Our charming Flying Dutchman."

"Fancy that. Right under our noses from the moment we walked into the Median. Although there was no way we could have known. Isn't life strange?"

"Thanks," said Harriet. "Really good job. I'll pop the book into my effects, but I think I'll leave mention of it unless the interview with the Masons isn't producing anything. I think we have enough here, she said, patting the top of her large briefcase, but it just might be the final piece of the jigsaw, so I'll take it in with me, in case."

With that, Harriet and Ian gathered their effects together, and headed for the car.

They were joined by Detective Sergeant Brinda Tulsi. A tall woman, of Indian origin, based in Guildford, she had been almost four years with the force. Today's job for her on this assignment was to perform a search of the

Masons' house, to look for any evidence or link to poisons, or any bottle or container that might look suspicious, and secondly, to take away any computers and associated equipment for further analysis.

She had come equipped with a large, black canvas bag, which itself contained a variety of sizes of plastic "see through" evidence bags. Each could be sealed with a tamper-resistant strip and a "write on" panel for sample description and identification.

A few random thoughts crossed Harriet's mind as the journey progressed.

'The Masons lived locally, so they could have been in Gatwick or Crawley on Tuesday morning. What had Hywel said about two older people in the vicinity at the time? They could have sent the dictionary, and the wallet, with it's dictionary extracts. What dark secrets were lurking in the background? Could the poisoning have been done by Robin Mason himself, or Paula Mason alone, or both in collusion? Or were they just innocent bystanders in the whole thing, and she and Ian were back to square one in the investigation?

Scott was almost at the turnoff to the Mason's estate.

"Only a few miles from here, unless I lose my bearings on the Appian Way" he said.

Harriet turned around to speak to Tulsi, who was in the back seat.

"I've had a thought", she said.

"Whilst you're doing your search, just take a good look inside each of their bedroom wardrobes and let me know if you see any pilot gear that looks like a British Airways outfit, hanging up or lying around. Hat, jacket and tie, badges, dark glasses and so on. Look closely at Mr Mason's effects but give Mrs Mason's wardrobe a once-over as well."

Tulsi gave a half smile. "Well, that's a first", she remarked. "Do you want me to hum "The Flower Duet" from Lakme to indicate when I've found the B.A. stuff, but don't want them to know?"

"Steady on, Tulsi," said Ian. "We make the clever classical references."

They all enjoyed the repartee, but then the atmosphere became more serious.

"They should be in the house together, with no visitors" Harriet said, mainly to herself as Ian weaved his way, accurately this time, through the tight, interlocking streets of the estate.

Ian parked the car a short way away from the house. The sky was the colour of an HB pencil lead and, although threatening, there was no rain on this occasion. They all hurried to the front gate of "The Nest" and grouped themselves under the cover of the small porch roof. Harriet rang the bell. After a short interval, the door was opened by Robin Mason, this time looking a little tidier in a red and white checked shirt, a red "V" necked sweater, and black casual trousers and shoes.

"Good afternoon, Mr Mason. You will, of course, remember myself and Detective Inspector Scott from our previous visit. This is Detective Sergeant Tulsi who will be assisting us. They all showed their warrant cards. Mrs Mason is in the house, I presume?" Harriet asked.

"Yes, she is."

"That's good, and is there anyone else with you, or expected this afternoon?"

"No, but if it's about this Kuppers business, as I said quite clearly before, I- we- are unable to help you. We have already provided you with all the information we know."

"Yes, I understand that," replied Harriet. "However, as I indicated on the phone, a few more matters have arisen that we think you may be able to assist us with. These can be explained more fully inside the house. Is it possible for us to come in?"

"All right. Please go through into the lounge," Robin Mason spoke in a flat, somewhat dull tone, with little or no inflexion. It was hard to discern any emotional reaction from his responses.

The officers went into the lounge, and Robin Mason arranged the seating.

"Just a moment," he said, "I will summon my wife." Harriet was rather amused by the stiff, formal, Victorian nature of his language. It sounded like a royal proclamation.

He went to the bottom of the stairs and called up. "Could you come down, dear? Those police people are here again," and he returned to the lounge.

By the time Harriet and Ian had organized their papers, Paula Mason had come downstairs and into the lounge. Harriet was again struck by the contrast with her husband. Her black hair was cut tidily, to just below the ears, and she wore little make-up or jewellery. She was wearing a long, patterned, midi tea dress in a floaty material with full sleeves. Pink and white flowers were imprinted on a black background, and flat black shoes with heels in patent leather completed the outfit.

'And that's on a dull ordinary Saturday in the early afternoon,' thought Harriet.

Harriet reprised the introductions and Robin his "inability to help" line, both for Paula Mason's benefit.

Harriet got down to business, with Ian taking notes.

"Now, Mr Mason," she said, referring to her own notebook, "when you saw us previously, you said the following. I have the full text here, but I quote summarized and slightly amended versions of the key phrases, which give a clear picture of your comments and knowledge of Mr Kuppers.

You said - 'Mr Kuppers was an engineer on assignment from Fokland to Eurair. I believe she, Paula, saw very little of him, as it was a large organization, and engineering was a big department within it.

I believe I met him only twice, or only twice I can remember. These were at a couple of Eurair company lunches.'

This was corroborated by yourself, Mrs Mason and you said, I also quote,

'Mr Kuppers came to work in Eurair engineering in, I think, 1989, from Holland. I saw very little of him but found him pleasant and efficient.'

Do you disagree with any of that, and is it still your understanding of the limits of your knowledge of, and interaction with, Mr Kuppers?"

"Yes, that is correct," said Robin Mason, "isn't that right, dear?" Paula Mason nodded.

"Well, Mr Mason, and Mrs Mason, I'm afraid you have both been, as they say, economical with the truth. Very economical with the truth."

Harriet looked straight at Paula Mason and began.

"Do you recall, Mrs Mason what you were doing on Saturday, 12th May 1990, and particularly in the early evening of that day?"

Paula showed no emotion and said nothing.

"You must be aware of the significance of that date," said Harriet.

"No, why should I?" she asked.

"Because it is your birthday, Mrs Mason. The twelfth of May."

"Oh, I'm sorry, I thought you said the tenth."

"My birthday. All that time ago," she replied, seemingly thoughtfully.

"I suppose we ate a birthday meal at home. That would be right, wouldn't it, Robin?" She looked across at Robin Mason.

"Yes, dear," he replied, "A quiet celebration at home. Yes, that would have been the case."

Harriet didn't respond but delved into her briefcase and pulled out a couple of A4 sheets.

"That's very interesting Mrs Mason. Because I have here a photocopy of a news report from the front page of the 'Crawley Courier' which is dated Monday, May 14th, 1990. You might care to look at them, which may improve your memory."

Harriet was probably not going to continue much further, but Paula cut her off anyway, without looking at the proffered sheets.

"You can put that back in your briefcase, Detective Chief Inspector. I am completely aware of the contents of that press cutting." Paula spoke softly but clearly.

Harriet paused, then reached down towards her briefcase, but one of the A4 sheets she was holding slipped from her grasp and fell to the floor beside her chair, face upwards. She looked down and ran her eyes quickly over the photocopied newspaper page which she had been given the previous evening.

Beneath its 'Crawley Courier' title and date was a large block advertisement telling you that there was £500 to be won at Bingo. Below that, a banner headline proclaimed, in bold black capitals.

***"MIRACLE ESCAPE FOR FIVE IN CRAWLEY TRAFFIC ACCIDENT"***

And advised it was brought to us "*by our Travel Correspondent- Bernice Jarvis.*"

'Bernice was probably,' thought Harriet, 'also the Fashion Correspondent, the TV and Radio Correspondent and the Sports Correspondent.'

The headline was followed, in more muted text, by details of the accident, vehicles and the relatively unscathed occupants. There was a young van driver, an elderly couple, and another driver and their passenger in a red BMW Sports Saloon.

The article told us of these people in the Red BMW as follows.

"......this was driven by Mr Piet Kuppers, age 33, a Dutch national working for the Fokland Aircraft Company on a project involving the holiday travel airline Eurair, at Gatwick Airport. His passenger was a Mrs Paula Mason, aged 37, from Horley."

Harriet snapped out of her brief reverie.

"We may come back to that again Mrs Mason, but I have more to add."

"Are you aware of the address of number 2, Royall Close, in Maidencroft, Crawley?"

The Masons didn't reply but kept very quiet, each staring at the ground rather than Harriet.

"I'm surprised," Harriet continued, "because since our previous visit, we have both evidence, and witnesses, to the facts that this property was rented and paid for, between September 1989 and March 1991 by the Fokland Aircraft Company, and the occupant of those premises was listed in the records of the letting agency as a Mr Piet Kuppers. In addition, at various times in that period, and particularly from June 1990 to October 1990 and living there on a full-time basis, was another occupant..."

Harriet paused.

"... and that occupant was a Mrs Paula Mason."

"In addition, we can also prove that Mrs Mason spent three weeks in the month of July 1991 in Indonesia, without you, Mr Mason, in the company of Mr Kuppers, where they were both staying at his premises in the Fokland Company compound near Jakarta."

She looked hard at both in turn.

"Do either of you deny the accuracy of these facts?"

They both looked blank, but neither of them challenged her, or said anything at all.

"This clearly changes the nature of the investigation, and I must tell you now that this is a murder inquiry. I have to advise you also that you are now both suspected persons in this case. You are not under caution or arrest at present, but this is how I wish to progress matters."

"You will now need to be interviewed separately. I will interview you, Mrs Mason, and Detective Inspector Scott will interview Mr Mason. Detective Sergeant Tulsi will be with me for the moment."

"Could you please find a separate room for Mr Mason and Detective Inspector Scott? I will remain here with Mrs Mason."

"Concurrently, Detective Sergeant Tulsi will search the premises, and may remove items such as computers and associated equipment. This will all be done with the greatest of care, and will be signed for by yourselves, and returned at the earliest possible time afterwards."

"Is all this entirely necessary, Detective Chief Inspector?" asked Robin Mason.

"I'm afraid it is Mr Mason. We are dealing with a very serious case here. A death of a foreign national on English soil, in suspicious circumstances and I would like your permission to proceed in this way."

Robin Mason spoke quietly. "I suppose you must, but you will find we have nothing to do directly with the death of Mr Kuppers."

"'Directly', so why did he say 'directly'?" thought Harriet, as they all sorted themselves out.

Robin Mason hummed and hawed, but directed a "follow me" towards Ian and disappeared down the corridor, closing the door of the lounge behind him.

Harriet took paper, pencil, pens and a small recording machine out of her briefcase and put them down on the floor beside her. She placed her seat so as to face directly towards Paula Mason, but spoke firstly to D.S. Tulsi.

"Carry on, Tulsi. I'd start with the computers and equipment first, then the other part of your brief, and don't forget the other matter that I mentioned in the car," she said, not wishing to mention "poison" whilst within earshot of Mrs Mason. Tulsi put on her gloves, picked up her bag and went to speak with Robin Mason about the location of the computers.

⸺◈⸺

# 52

Harriet was then alone with Paula Mason.

"It might be a good idea to start with the truth this time, Paula. I hope you don't mind if I call you Paula."

It was a statement rather than a question.

"If you were not instrumental in the death of Mr Kuppers, then you have nothing to hold back."

Paula shrugged.

"All right then, but does everything I tell you have to get back to Robin?"

"As you know, this conversation is being recorded, as is that of DI Scott with Mr Mason. I can't guarantee that nothing will get back to Mr Mason, and much will depend upon the progress of the investigation, but I will try to respect your request."

"Thank you," said Paula, and commenced speaking.

"Why didn't I tell the truth? Why didn't Robin tell the truth? Probably for the same reason. We are both trying to protect each other, trying not to hurt each other. It was all so long ago. Another world. Forgotten. Then this all comes up out of the blue. I didn't even see him myself at the hotel, Robin told me he had seen him. But let's start at the beginning."

"He came to Eurair, as you know, in late 1989. Things weren't right at home with Robin-we were living in Horley then. You can see that he is a good man, worthy but serious, unexciting. Unfortunately for me, sexless as well. Not gay, but no interest in sex. Of course, I saw a lot of Piet. He was charming."

'If I hear that word again...' Harriet grimaced inwardly.

Paula continued, "Yes, charming, travelled, well off, sort of single. He had plenty of other women, in both senses. Younger than me, too. We got along well, and one thing led to another, as they do. In 1990 Robin was having extensive building work done in our house in Horley, and so I went to stay with- live with- Piet in Maidencroft. Robin thought he was only a work colleague, with a Dutch girlfriend, so it seemed an acceptable arrangement to him."

"So, our affair went up a notch. He bought me a very expensive ring that I wore when we went out in public together. He gave it to me during a weekend we spent together at Lyegrave Manor. You probably know of it, it's not that far from Gatwick. Built around 1600, set in 1,000 acres of countryside. Very flash. Even then, I thought it was too soon in our relationship, but 'heigh-ho'. We were very careful, mind you. I don't know where it is now, but he told me, very nastily, to keep it, when we finally broke up. At the time I intended to leave Robin for him, and travel the world, no money worries, and, of course, he was very good in bed."

"We were happy to begin with- living together, but he soon began to control my life, Did it become an abusive relationship? Yes. Was it physically abusive? No. At least not in the sense that most people would understand it. Why did I put up with it? I don't know. I was lost at the time, and more subservient than I am now. I didn't seem to have any alternative. I was vulnerable. My life became a mess."

"I thought it was all over with Piet when Eurair went bust in March 1991, and he was reassigned to Indonesia, but he contacted me, and I did go there to see him in July of that year. I had lost my job, and I was technically still with Robin, but things hadn't improved much. I needed a break, and yes, I knew that sex would come with it, but perhaps

Piet would have changed after a little while apart. No such luck. It was a disaster."

"When I came back, I took stock, and Robin and I sat down and decided to try to repair our marriage, so I broke it off with Piet, and here we are, Robin and I, a quarter of a century on further on and still married."

"It will seem strange, but Robin wasn't aware of the full extent of my relationship with Piet at the time, how often we saw each other, the ring and all that. Even now he doesn't know it all, and I don't want him to know. It was only after I came back from Indonesia that I told him, but I played down what really happened."

"...and the abortion?" Harriet probed gently. "Did Robin know about the abortion after you returned from Indonesia?"

Paula's face drained of colour. She took some time to reply.

"No, I don't think he did, or does now," she replied, resignedly. "Nothing in life is secret, is it?" Paula said bitterly, to no one in particular.

"Did you hate Piet Kuppers at the end of it all?"

Paula stared out of the lounge window.

"Yes, I did, and yes, I still do, which is probably what you want to hear. He didn't want to know about a baby. Just told me I was a stupid cow for getting the pill wrong. He always wanted me on the pill. I think the pill is the Dutch way."

"I wasn't keen on a baby anyway, and I was also approaching 40. He told me to keep the ring, and we never saw, or heard from each other again, not even at the hotel. I told Robin the operation was a 'woman thing' and I paid for the procedure, and for it to be as confidential as possible, and he just left it at that. Robin is a very good man."

"Did I hate Piet enough to murder him? At the time of the abortion? Yes, probably. After the passage of time? No. Am I sorry he's dead? No. Did I have anything at all to do with his death? No."

"Sorry, I've rambled on. Have you any more questions? Strangely enough, it feels like I've got a lot off my chest."

"Just a few random things," said Harriet.

"Would you have ever bought an English/Dutch dictionary?"

"What an odd question. No, I have never bought one myself, but Kuppers bought a dictionary for me at one time, together with several 'Learn Dutch' books. The Dutch insist on people speaking Dutch when living in Holland. He wouldn't let me live with him there until I had learnt enough Dutch."

"What happened to the books?" Harriet asked.

"I don't really remember properly. They used to be on view in my room upstairs, but I took them to a charity shop so as not to upset Robin once we had got ourselves together, but now I think about it, the dictionary wasn't there on my shelves when I got rid of them, just the language books. Don't know. I just forgot about all that stuff and tried to move on. As Robin said to me, 'We'll have no more of that Dutch nonsense, then, shall we?'"

"As I said before, a very nice, forgiving man is Robin. You see, I settled for a steady life with someone easy to live with, who wouldn't give me any hassle. We are reasonably well off, we have two or three cruises each year, and other short breaks. I have several long-time girlfriends that I meet up with a lot, go to the Hawth for jazz, the Arnaud for plays, the Pallant, and the Towner. I have a lot to be grateful for. We get by."

"You probably won't understand, but at the same time, I need more than that. I need love, and I need physical love. Sex if you like. My Italian blood, I suppose. I have been a good girl really. Up to now, I have only had one other dalliance, shall we call it, in all that time after Piet. I am pretty sure Robin wasn't aware of anything of that affair. Sex sometimes doesn't always need two people, you know."

She stopped suddenly and composed herself.

"You only realise a lot of things on reflection, don't you?" she said, looking into space.

"So," said Harriet. "If you weren't involved in Kuppers' death, do you know of anyone who might have been? Any pillow talks? Colleagues, work conflicts, arguments. You implied he had a string of relationships in the past. Jealous husbands or jealous boyfriends in the wings?"

"Not that I can recall immediately. I'm sorry, but I don't think so."

"Did Robin hate him?"

"Enough to kill him, you mean?" Paula didn't wait for a reply. "I really have no idea. He's not very demonstrative. We never talked about it much afterwards. As I said, I only told him as much as I thought I could get away with. As far as I know, or thought, he just wanted to forget it. I don't know for sure what he knew and what he didn't. He might have known more than I think he did. If he was planning anything, he didn't and hasn't told me."

"Thank you, Paula. I appreciate your candour. However, there are just a couple more things."

"Could you tell me your whereabouts and movements last Tuesday, 17th May?"

"Tuesday, did you say? That's not difficult. We have our little 'Tuesday Routine', that we have kept to for quite a while now. We are out of the house quite early. We drive to either Guildford, Tunbridge Wells, Horsham or Crawley, and have a cup of coffee, usually between half eight and half nine. I go shopping, either by myself or with one of my girlfriends, and Robin goes off to a garden centre or D.I.Y superstore. He's into D.I.Y. Don't see the attraction of looking at a load of nuts and bolts, wood, screws, paint, tools and all that myself, but I guess ladies' clothes shops don't appeal much to him either."

"We lunch separately, then Robin comes back and picks me up at a pre-arranged place and time."

"Last Tuesday was our Tunbridge Wells Day. We drove over to the Pantiles for a coffee in our usual place, "The Pantiles Cafe and Bar.""

"What time did you arrive there?"

"About 9 am."

"I don't know where Robin went. I looked around the shops, walked up to Fenwick's first, then back down past the station to High Street. Saw a nice bottle green number in Jacques Vert. Went into a few of the clothes shops there, then lunch. Normally, I would lunch at the Ivy, but it was a nice day, so I bought a sandwich and a tin of ready mixed Gin and Tonic and sat in the gardens of 'The Grove' and watched the world go by. That would have been between about 12.30 and 1.15 pm."

"A gentle stroll back to the Pantiles, and Robin came to pick me up at about 1.30, then off home for the rest of the day. I suppose we arrived home at about 2.00 pm."

"Were you with any of your girlfriends?"

"No, by myself this time."

"Did you buy any clothes?"

"No, as I said, I loved the Jacques Vert dress, but decided against buying it this time."

"Did you use your credit card for anything?"

"No, Robin always gives me his Credit Card each Tuesday morning, for my personal purchases of clothes, shoes, cosmetics, underwear and so forth." She stressed the 'his'. "It's part of our Tuesday routine. I buy my own lunch. Robin always buys the coffee."

"Do you go to the same cafe for your morning coffee at each place?"

"Yes, that's what Robin wants to do."

"...and when you go to Crawley, which cafe do you use?"

"Oh, the Italian one in the Old Town, 'Artimesias'."

Harriet feigned disinterest, referred to her notes, and, moved on.

"Finally, Paula, are you aware of the word 'ricin'?"

Paula looked back directly at Harriet, and responded in a changed, business-like tone, quite different from the emotional vulnerability she had shown earlier.

"As I know you are aware, for the last two years before my retirement I worked at the PharmaGat Laboratories as a Secretary, and some of the correspondence I dealt with was on the subject of ricin, so I would say I know more than the average person about that substance. You are also aware that Robin is one of the foremost experts on ricin in Europe. Jointly with the medical profession, he has been involved for many years in research into the development of beneficial uses of ricin for the treatment of cancer."

"Thank you, Mrs Mason, no more questions for now, but please don't go anywhere for the next few weeks without checking with us first."

"Oh, wait a minute. There is one more thing.

You knew Mr Kuppers pretty well, didn't you?

Did you ever come across a small, red pocket size diary in his effects at any time?"

Paula seemed to give a short, shallow swallow before answering.

"No" she said. "I have no recollection of such an article."

There was a knock on the lounge door. Scott poked his head around the corner.

"Are you finished, ma'am?"

"I have completed the interview with Mr Mason a little while ago, and he has gone to his study upstairs, and Tulsi has finished her job, and everything she has collected is in our car.

I reviewed Tulsi's list and approved it, and Mr Mason has signed the form for those items on behalf of both of them. I have advised Mr Mason that they are both to remain on call from us."

"Thanks, both. Good job," Harriet said, exiting the lounge, Paula Mason following almost immediately.

"We will say our 'goodbyes' for now," said Harriet, "thank you both for your cooperation. We will be in touch."

Robin Mason, who had come down from his study, opened the front door and they stepped out. The grey sky had now begun to produce a steady drizzle. Harriet unlocked the doors, and they got inside the car as quickly as possible.

"We need to get the computer equipment and accessories over to the digital forensic expert a.s.a.p. So, we will need to drive to Guildford first for Tulsi to liaise with digital forensics and hand over the evidence bags."

"Scott," Harriet didn't want to call him Ian whilst Tulsi was present, "let's just ponder on our own interview by ourselves for the journey time, then we'll exchange and compare notes back at the ranch."

"What Paula told me, and what Robin told you. Sounds like the title for a book."

Harriet provided the final comment before silence descended as they absorbed themselves in their own thoughts.

"Well, they ought to get their house sign fixed. Swap the robin for a cuckoo."

## 53

Back at the ops room Harriet and Ian swopped recordings, returning to their own desks, and both made brief notes as they went along. After about twenty-five minutes, Ian came over and sat at Harriet's desk.

"Well, she said, where do you think we are with the Masons, Ian?"

"They're singing the same basic tune from the same hymn sheet," said Ian. Not much change from the first interview in principle, but with a good deal more truth included, but not all, of course."

"Both were asked pretty much the same questions in the same order, Paula provided a lot of information on her relationship with Mr K, and her marriage. All of that I thought was very honest."

"Robin Mason was much less open, although not directly contradicting Paula. His responses were terse, and sparse, with no visible indications of emotion. He said the first encounter on the previous Monday with Kuppers, and his inquiry at the reception desk was just curiosity."

"As to the affair, he said little of substance. I didn't mention the abortion, and he didn't raise or refer to it at all. It is possible he didn't know, but he didn't directly contradict anything in Paula's story."

"He didn't allude to the car accident and newspaper headline either and dismissed my reference to the Dutch Dictionary as "not meaning anything to me, one way or the other.""

"He just said that any feelings towards Kuppers had faded, or disappeared over time, and anyway were of sadness at the affair, rather than dislike or hatred of Kuppers himself."

"I'm not sure all of that was true. I believe he is a man capable of controlling his emotions in a logical way, presenting a dispassionate exterior, but who knows what lurks beneath?"

"His knowledge of ricin, he said, was entirely focused on research into its benefits in treating cancer and related diseases."

"It is when we get to her and his movements on the Tuesday that their stories, although they dovetail, become less believable."

"The structure of the "Tuesday routine" I'm sure is real. Just what I would imagine Mr M would do, precise and unchanging-the petty pace creeping on from day to day. Mrs M just goes along with it," getting by" as she said. However, she didn't go to Tunbridge Wells, I'm sure, and nor did Mr M go to the Wickes Superstore outside Tunbridge Wells," as he had told me.

"Wasn't it odd that, according to their accounts, neither of them bought anything, and everything was paid for in cash, so no traceable evidence of any purchases, both of their timings fitted perfectly, but they could recite them by heart?"

"It all makes it much more difficult to prove or disprove their accounts."

"One thing. Neither of them asked how Kuppers died, or what was the cause of death. They wouldn't have known from the papers, because what little information we gave out just stated that the person was a foreign national, and the exact cause of death was subject to further investigation and subject to contact being made with the next of kin."

⊷⟨⟩⊶

## 54

At about 7.30 pm Harriet's phone rang.

"Good evening, ma'am. This is Colin Crane. I'm the Digital Forensic Officer at Guildford. I've been going through the computers and all the other bumf that you delivered to me from the Masons' house in Slinfold, you know, the Kuppers case."

"Hello Colin, good evening, thanks for being so quick."

"Nothing much to report on any of the laptops. All very ordinary stuff. Passwords very easy to crack. Nothing suspicious as far as I can tell, but there is something that's a bit unusual. I thought you might like to look at it in person."

"Better bring it over here, then Colin," she said "I'd like you to come yourself, as soon as possible. Sorry for the lateness of the hour, but we'd like to take a look."

"No worries, ma'am. I was told it was urgent. About half an hour then. I'll be as quick as I can."

Harriet carried on with her paperwork, then broke off to talk to Ian.

"Ian, Colin Crane from Digital Forensics is coming over. He'll be here in about twenty minutes to half an hour. He's got something from the items Tulsi impounded earlier that he thinks we ought to see. I'll give you a shout when he arrives."

Sergeant Colin Crane was a tall, bespectacled, serious-looking young man, roll neck sweater, blue jeans, and loafers. More or less everything you'd expect from a Digital Forensic computer buff.

Harriet and Ian sat together on one side of her desk. Crane sat himself opposite them. He delved into a large briefcase that he had carried with him and brought out what appeared to be a handful of white tissue paper. He set it on the table in front of them, and unwrapped it, casting the tissue paper to one side.

They looked at it as if it were the final prize at the end of a children's "Pass the Parcel" game, or a Christmas present. It was a small, sturdy, shiny black box, made of thick, high-quality cardboard. It was about two inches square. The tightly fitting lid sat securely on top, coming about halfway down the sides of the box, and featured a faintly embossed pattern of transparent white, writhing leaves.

"All fingerprinted and photographed. You can handle it," said Crane. "Came out of the evidence bag marked 'Paula Mason- Computer Drawer. Odds and Ends'. There were lots of other things. Wires, socket plugs, earphones, batteries, old but untouched CD and RW disks still in their wrappers and so on, all gathering dust, but the box caught my eye."

Harriet took the lid off the box. Inside were two objects. She fished out the first, a standard computer memory stick and placed it in front of her.

"Have you looked at the data on this?" she asked Crane, holding up the memory stick.

"Yes," he replied, "but as I said, I only gave it a quick look. Just a collection of personal emails didn't mean anything to me. Lots of 'Word' folders. Most marked up with titles like "Holidays", "Household Expenses", "Family", Food Shopping Items", and so forth Nothing suspicious, or incriminating, in my assessment, and before you ask, it's been virus-checked. You can give it a more detailed examination."

"It's the other item that's the strange one to be in someone's odds and sods computer drawer that I reckon hasn't been looked at for yonks."

Harriet put the memory stick to one side and turned the box upside down and shook it. A cheap, spectacle case, made of wafer-thin black cotton, with drawstrings tightly tied, fell out onto the desk. Harriet unfolded it and smoothed it out. The words "EYELEVEL READERS" in bold white capital letters were inscribed on the side of the case." Van der Valk might be more interested in this than me," she mused.

"What's special about an old glasses case?" she asked Crane.

"Keep going, ma'am," he prompted.

Harriet undid the drawstrings and felt inside and withdrew an object between finger and thumb. Arms outstretched, she held it up to a level just above her eyes and tilted her head slightly upwards. The ring glistened in the artificial light. Harriet let out a low whistle. It was a white gold diamond eternity ring. A narrow-channelled band was divided into equal segments. Into each segment was inserted a baguette-cut diamond. It appeared simple and understated, as very elegant and very expensive jewellery often does.

"I took a look in the case to see if it was anything computer-related and then tied the drawstrings back, so it was just as it was," advised Crane.

"Well, that didn't come out of a Christmas cracker," said Harriet.

Harriet turned to Colin Crane.

"Thanks for your awareness and promptness Sergeant Crane. You can return to Guildford now."

Crane bid his farewell, and Harriet spoke to Ian.

"We'll take a look at the contents of the memory stick one at a time, then compare notes. I'll go first." She inserted it into an appropriate USB slot in her laptop and bent her head towards the screen. Ian Scott returned to his desk, and to completing his log.

After about three quarters of a an hour Harriet suddenly left the room,re-appearing about a further twenty minutes later. She came over to Ian.

"Have you heard of Nicholas Franklin?" she queried.

"No. Should I have done?" Ian responded.

"Not necessarily, but you're going to meet him tomorrow afternoon. I've set up an appointment for us both at his house at 2.30 pm."

"Have a read of the contents of the memory stick first."

## 55

# Sunday, May 22nd, 2016

"It's coming up," said Harriet, "next house on the right." Scott slowed the car, and drew up outside a medium-sized property, set back from the country road. A carefully crafted black wrought iron gate had the words "Westmacott Cottage" cleverly woven seamlessly into it in two semi-circular shapes, one word above the other, in stylish copperplate script. These words were painted a dark green.

They advanced up the winding path of circular concrete slabs, and towards the front door. The front garden around them was small. But beautifully designed and kept. A profusion of alliums, delphiniums, bluebells, roses, phlox, peonies and geraniums greeted them. "Real picture postcard stuff," muttered Scott.

They rang the modern doorbell, which emitted a few dull chimes from within. After a brief interval, the door to Westmacott Cottage opened. Harriet and Ian were faced with a smallish, broad-shouldered man. Clean-shaven, he had an open, friendly face, still handsome, despite the advancing years, with a full head of curly, grey hair. Graham noticed his blue eyes, and steely look behind the friendly persona. Stocky, but muscular, his figure hinted at his many earlier years of playing sport. He was smartly dressed, in a brown and black checked open-necked shirt, lightweight fawn trousers and dark brown loafers.

"Mr Nicholas Franklin?" queried Harriet. "I called you last evening. We're sorry to disturb you, sir."

Showing her ID, she said, "My name is Detective Chief Inspector Graham, and this is my colleague, Detective Inspector Scott.

As I explained briefly to you on the phone, we are investigating the death of a Dutch citizen, Mr Piet Kuppers, at the Median Hotel in Gatwick on or around last Tuesday 17th and Wednesday 18th May.

What I did not tell you is that information that has recently come into our hands indicates that you, to coin a well-worn phrase, may be able to assist us further in our enquiries. Is it possible for us to come in to discuss the matter?"

"Yes, of course," replied Nicholas Franklin.

"Do come in," he said, and led the way into the cottage.

He showed them into a large room, to the right of the hallway, and motioned towards a brown leather two-seater settee, with a low coffee table in front of it. On one of the sofa seats was a heavyweight volume with its title displayed on the cover. The ornate medieval script read 'The Complete Canterbury Tales. Illustrated by Edward Burne-Jones and William Morris'.

"Sit down, please," said Nicholas Franklin, only then seeming to notice the book on the seat. Harriet sat down, whilst Scott shuffled uncertainly, looking down at the book on the seat whilst setting down his large briefcase on the floor to one side of the sofa.

"Tea or coffee?" asked Franklin, not 'would you like a drink?' It was a choice, not a question.

"Two coffees, please. One black, one milk, both no sugar," answered Harriet.

"Make yourself comfortable, I'll get the percolator going, I won't be long. Fortnum and Mason Connoisseur would be alright for you?" said Franklin, without waiting for any answer, and left the room.

"I wasn't going to ask for instant coffee, anyway," said Harriet, turning her head towards Ian with a slight trace of a smile."

Almost immediately Franklin popped his head back around the door and looked at Harriet.

"I'm sorry, I wonder if you could kindly replace the 'Canterbury Tales' for me. It goes there," he said, pointing to a large gap at the end of one of the lower bookcase shelves, then withdrew his head rapidly, like a tortoise sensing danger, and closed the kitchen door.

They looked around the room. No English country garden here. It was in bright, modern colours and styles. Good taste wherever your gaze took you. An Axminster of thick pile carpeted the floor. Around three sides of the room were sunken bookshelves, full of books. The bookshelves were built around and over the modern, tiled fireplace, and similarly styled to incorporate a long, low, sideboard.

Harriet got up from the settee and took a closer look. The bookshelves were divided into three main sections - a huge collection of quiz and general knowledge books, and similarly large collections of works of Agatha Christie, and those of Len Deighton. Half of the remaining wall featured a large window, and beneath it, a sizeable Jehs and Laub Lane desk and Ray Eames chair, and an array of up-to-date computer equipment and accessories, all very neatly organised.

The other half of that wall was floor-to-ceiling purpose-built shelving, holding CDs, Vinyl LPs, old 78s, 45s, and 33.1/3 rpm records, and a stack of sheet music, next to what appeared to be an old record player. An acoustic/ electric guitar fitted neatly into one compartment.

She slotted 'The Complete Canterbury Tales' into its designated position, then stopped to look at several framed items that stood on the sideboard, and as she did, she turned towards Scott.

"Is there anything a little odd, you've noticed so far, Ian?" she asked.

"Yes, I have," said Scott. "He didn't ask who Kuppers was, or refer to him in any way, or ask any more questions."

"He just said, 'Do come in,' as if you were his favourite aunt calling for afternoon tea."

"Right on, Ian, right on. It's almost as if he has already determined what questions we would ask, and what his replies would be - even before we had gone into any detail at all."

She turned back to the photographs and read the descriptions that had been carefully typed and affixed to the bottom of each, underneath the glass.

On the left-hand side, there was a colour photograph of two men in golf attire standing in front of a clubhouse and smiling. Both were in plus-fours, black and white Footjoy golf shoes and Pringle golf sweaters. One of them was Franklin, with a restrained sweater of a light blue shade. The sweater of the other featured the garish design of a multi-coloured umbrella filling the whole of the front of the sweater. Franklin's companion was a short, fat man, with sparse, gingery hair, a less sparse, bushy ginger moustache, and splayed, protruding teeth. He appeared to Harriet to be the spitting image of Hugo Drax, the villain in Ian Fleming's Bond novel 'Moonraker'. Beneath the photograph was the text 'Golf with Sinner-Sunningdale: 7 September 2007'.

In the front, given pride of place, was a picture of Franklin holding a cheque for £500,000. On the right-hand side, arranged in a semi-circle were pictures of him taken at "Greenways," the former residence of Agatha Christie, one at Checkpoint Charlie, and a group of competitors, with a smiling Sandra Tolleson, in a "20 against 1" Quiz programme.

Behind all of these was a photograph of a gathering of members of the "Masterbrain" Club at one of their social activities. The description at the base of the photograph read "Harrogate 2014 – Masterbrain Club Fancy Dress Ball". In the front row of four, by looking closely, Harriet could make out beneath their disguises, the faces of three well-known TV Quizzing personalities. There was Ken Ashfield, Julia Kingston, Padraig Gilbey - and Nicholas Franklin. She took a second close look at that photograph but said nothing.

Before she had returned to her seat Franklin came back into the room, carrying a large, silver tray, with three mugs of coffee, and a large glass of water.

"Sorry for the delay, the percolator was playing up," He said to no one in particular, and went to fetch a comfortable-looking armchair, also in leather tan, which he set behind the low table, opposite Harriet and Ian.

He looked at Harriet, smiled, and said, in an amused tone "I see you've been having a look at my library."

The coffees came in large mugs with literary titles imprinted on them in black Gill Sans typeface. Between them, they had "The Mysterious Affair at Styles," "Funeral In Berlin" and "The Little Book of Knowledge".

He swept his arm in a wide arc "There's every Agatha Christie work that she produced, including the American ones. The same books but many with different titles. There are many first editions. Then there's the Len Deighton's. An incredibly talented individual, Len. A raft of spy novels, of course, but also an excellent writer on military history and cookery, and an illustrator of considerable talent. "

"My own quizzing credentials I think you will know about."

⊷⊷⊰◆⊱⊶⊶

## 56

"So," he said finally. "How can I help you?"

Harriet delved into the large attaché case on the floor, and brought out a black folder, took out several sheets of A4 paper, and laid them out on the table between himself and Harriet.

Harriet looked across at Franklin.

"Well, Mr Franklin, we believe that in the past, you were acquainted with a Mrs Paula Mason."

"Yes, that is correct," replied Franklin.

Harriet went on. "And there was a relationship between you."

"Yes, that is also correct," said Franklin.

"You became aware that Mrs Mason had also had a previous, long-term relationship, with the now-deceased Mr Kuppers."

Franklin nodded, "and that relationship was of considerable concern, and distress, to you."

"Go on," said Franklin.

Graham picked up the papers. "We have here a transcript of some of that email correspondence, which, although written some time ago, appears to relate directly to events surrounding the recent death of Mr Kuppers."

"Would you like me to explain further?"

"No, that isn't necessary. I am well aware of the emails that you refer to and have in front of you," said Franklin.

"I have read them many, many times over the years. I know them by heart and can recite them word for word. They are burned into my memory."

"I expected that you might come across Paula's connection with Kuppers at some stage, and then mine with Paula if you were prescient enough, and I had no doubt of those facts following your phone call. I congratulate you, Detective Chief Inspector."

His blue eyes were fixed on Harriet Graham all the time. Scott might as well have been on Mars as far as he was concerned.

"Have you heard of retroactive jealousy, or coercion and control?" he queried.

Harriet gave no immediate response. She looked back at him. "Just tell me, in your own words, and in your own time," she said softly and slowly.

Franklin paused, sat forward in his chair, breathed deeply, and spoke, in a calm, measured way that Graham could sense was just a front for the inner turmoil. "I'll come on to all that shortly, but let's take things in order."

"Paula and I met at Gatwick Airport; I believe in early 2002. I was working on a consultancy basis in Expo House, the large red brick building on the left as you come into the South Terminal. It has another name nowadays. She was working for Safetrans, an Airline Baggage handling company, based in the South Terminal, in quite a high-level Administration post."

"We were both heading to South Terminal one lunchtime, and walked along together, began talking, and it went from there. She was bright, bubbly, very attractive, smart in both thought and appearance, and that was the start of a passionate and loving affair."

"As lovers do, we talked about our current situations - and past relationships."

"You wouldn't have called without prior research, so you are aware, of course, of my own brief marriage. The famous 1960s model Jennifer Aysgill, beautiful then, and still stunning today. Jenny and I, who would have thought it?"

"There was no acrimony when we split up. It was all very amicable. We were both too young, and even then, we knew it wouldn't work." Franklin gave a little smile, "and, as you can read in the gossip magazines, three further husbands later, Jenny still has some difficulties in this area."

"I have remained unmarried for the rest of my life to date. A few brief relationships - I call them my 'daytime dalliances' - but nothing to compare in any way to Paula. No one else had wanted me so much, said such lovely things to me, made me feel so wanted..." his voice trailed away, and he looked away into the distance for a while, before turning back to Harriet.

"Am I digressing too much?" he asked.

"No, not at all, please continue," said Harriet. Scott had taken out a pencil and paper and was making notes.

"Paula told me of her own situation, of her long-lived marriage to Robin, a rather dull, but solid, worthy man, childless, which was of her own choice, and sexless, which wasn't of her own choice. The first time we met and talked over Cappuccinos in the South Terminal Café she told me that, ten years before, she had a two-year relationship, with a man called Piet. I only learnt his surname, Kuppers, at a later stage."

"She thought I wouldn't be other than mildly curious, or it wouldn't affect me at all. Unfortunately, that became very far from the way things worked out. I believe it was her way of showing me that she wasn't an easy touch, that once she was involved, it was for the long term, that she was reliable. At first, I did read it that way, and didn't take an undue amount of notice, other than to think it was a little unusual."

"As we became more involved, that relationship gradually became more important to me. Very strange, really, as no others bothered me. Her marriage didn't concern me, nor any other lovers. As I learnt more from her, little by little, drop by drop, the significance of that particular affair grew, until it took over my whole being for days on end. Fading sometimes, but always recurring, and never disappearing, and that situation has continued to this day."

"For a long time, I didn't realise, or recognise, that I was jealous, and obsessively so. She knew immediately it was jealousy. Women are always more intuitively aware of underlying feelings, nuances, small facial expressions and gestures, phraseology, and behaviour, where human interaction is concerned. I had no reference point in my life to cope with it."

"Those emails you have read, and have with you, were Paula's attempt to help me, and take away my jealousy, thinking that the more I knew of the events and circumstances, the more I would be re-assured. Unfortunately, in many ways, it made things worse for me."

"The extracts give you some idea of Kuppers and Paula's relationship - how they met, her home situation, how things developed, the sex, the living together in Maidencroft, the ring, the Eurair collapse, the Indonesian "holiday" and how that was cut short, the pregnancy-yes, she told me of that, which must have been painful for her, and the end of the affair."

"I always felt her e-mails downplayed the relationship, to assuage my feelings. It's like completing a thousand-piece jigsaw puzzle, with two hundred of the pieces missing. The missing pieces are as important, or more important than the pieces you have, but you can't find the pieces, what they show, or how they fit in. You don't really understand the picture until it is completed."

"I didn't know the name of it then but what had overtaken me is sometimes called 'retroactive jealousy'. I would learn much more about it in the years that followed. People suffering from retroactive jealousy get caught in a loop of obsessive thoughts and depressive emotions. Jealousy is something most people recognise. However, this kind of jealousy is quite different. A person sometimes has flashbacks to events they didn't see that they were never part of, and that is what happened to me."

"Her past suddenly became my present. Time had no meaning. I imagined them making love in Maidencroft. I wanted to know the house they shared there. I imagined them in Indonesia, dancing, kissing and making love. Did she take the ring to wear there? Did she wear it on the long plane journey? The relationship with Kuppers was ever-present in my thoughts, in varying degrees."

"As Princess Diana famously said in her 1995 'Panorama' interview with Martin Bashir, 'there were three of us in this marriage, so it was a bit crowded'. That is how it was to me, with our relationship. Paula, myself and Kuppers."

"Only the third person was a ghost, someone I had never corresponded with, never talked to, had seen only a small, out-of-focus photograph of him as he was at the time of the relationship with Paula. To the best of my knowledge, I had never met anyone who knew him, and never met him in the flesh, although I had studied very carefully the many recent pictures on the Doves website that had included him."

Harriet held up her hand to stop him, and spoke quietly in measured, clear tones, fixing her eyes on his.

"But you did see him in the flesh for the first time last Tuesday, didn't you?"

There was a long silence, as if Franklin was pondering on something. Then he finally spoke.

"Yes, that is so," agreed Franklin. "Indeed, that is correct."

Harriet turned to Ian Scott, who had been making notes, "Make sure you have that, D.I. Scott."

"I have everything, don't worry."

Harriet turned back to Franklin.

"Please carry on Mr Franklin."

Franklin didn't pursue the Tuesday reference, and Harriet decided to remain silent on that matter for the moment.

## 57

There was a pause in proceedings for a short time. Nobody spoke or moved until Franklin got up from his chair, picked up a clear plastic document wallet and opened it. He took two sheets of paper from it, one of a pale pink colour and one of a pale green. He handed both to Harriet and then walked over to his bookshelves. He plucked out a paperback book. Protruding from the top of the leaves of the book in several places were pink, sticky page markers. He held the book in one hand and raised it to eye level.

"This book is entitled 'My Prince Charming- the Man Behind the Mask' by a lady called Amy Harrington-Ellis and published in 2014.

I came across it quite by chance, in early 2015, as some of the events in the book took place in a local hospital, within reasonable distance of my house here.

Have you heard of it?" Franklin questioned.

Both shook their heads.

"The popular press gave the court case that preceded the book quite prominent coverage," he added.

"It is the story of an intelligent, well-rounded woman, in her thirties, who entered a relationship with a professional man of roughly the same age. It covers the relationship from its beginnings, its progression into an increasingly coercive and controlling one, and her narrow escape from being strangled by this same man some years after she had ended it."

Franklin looked towards them.

"This book, and the characteristics of the relationship described in it, referred to events that occurred in 2011 and 2012, which is some twenty years after Paula's relationship with Kuppers."

"I'll repeat that. Twenty years."

"Yet the descriptions that Ms Harrington-Ellis provides are uncannily similar, even identical to those in the transcript of the emails you have in front of you."

"Take any slip," said Franklin, holding out the book with its protruding pink slips in front of Harriet like a conjurer with a pack of cards.

She took one. The thin slip had "p123" written on it at the top. Below was an asterisk followed by the number "3".

"What page number is on the slip?" asked Franklin.

"I assume the small 'p' is page, so it is one hundred and twenty-three," she replied.

Franklin looked down at the book.

"Here it is," he said, "bottom of page hundred and twenty-three." And he read from it.

"'... if he didn't get his own way, he would become sulky and petulant, and I often ended up going along with what he wanted, just to make my life easier. He wanted to own my life.'

Now look at the pink page I gave to you," said Franklin.

Harriet looked down at it. It had an asterisk at its head, with a numbered series of short, typewritten paragraphs below.

"You will, of course, recognise this," said Franklin. "It is an abbreviated version of the transcript of the emails between Paula and me that you have acquired. Oh, by the way, could I ask how you discovered the information? I do not, of course, doubt its veracity in any way, or deny that I am one of the people involved."

Harriet shrugged, "OK. It was found on a memory stick, which was in a box with a ring."

Franklin winced, but composed himself, and returned to the pink slips and pink sheet.

"What is written besides number three on that sheet?" he asked.

Harriet read out item number three.

"He seemed to change once we were living together - almost as if he wanted to own me. He didn't like it at all if he didn't get his way and I avoided any arguments. I felt I was in a 'subservient' role, and I didn't want to rock the boat."

"So, there you are, Chief Inspector. An almost identical match of the situation of two women, both in coercive and controlling relationships but twenty years apart."

He put the book down on the floor to one side of him. "I could replay this procedure many times, but I am not a variety entertainer, and I'm sure you get the picture."

"One after another," he continued, "the pink slips of similarity built up – the initial charm changing as the relationship progresses, the isolation from family and friends, the demands for over-frequent sex, the manipulation, the belittling.

Quite remarkable of all, to me, were the rings. Both remark on having rings 'forced' upon them far too early in the relationship, and both said they felt physically sick when they were presented with them. It is a characteristic of controlling partners that they try to move things along very quickly, and presumptuously. The ring, of course, for the controlling person, is the sign of ownership- 'you belong to me'."

"The discovery, fact by fact, as I trawled through Amy's book, that her situation was an exact replica of Paula's was my epiphany moment, or epiphany time," said

Franklin. "It seemed positively surreal, as amazement and understanding descended on me in equal measure."

"From that moment I researched the internet thoroughly and obsessively. I am now highly expert on coercion and control, but I have never been asked a quiz question on the subject."

"Why do women stay? I asked myself many times why Paula remained in the relationship for as long as she did, and why she went to Indonesia when Kuppers had left the UK."

"I think the answer is a mixture of reasons. There are good times in most of these situations, particularly at the beginning, and there may be a misapprehension that these will return."

"Also, the woman may be left with little alternative. In Paula's case her marriage was in serious trouble, her home was being significantly renovated, and the offer from Kuppers to live with him in a large, comfortable house was a good option, but with no easy way back."

"As to the Indonesian visit, although Kuppers had left the UK, she was still emotionally involved with him, and Kuppers was extremely persuasive, and manipulative, and she was subservient to his demands."

Franklin went on, "It was shortly after my 'epiphany moments' and my thinking about, and discovering the truth about the relationship, that I found out from the Doves website that they were holding their Anniversary Conference at the Gatwick Median, in May of the following year, and Kuppers' attendance and involvement. It was then I made up my mind."

"Made up your mind." interjected Harriet. She spoke slowly and clearly, looking first at Scott and then at Franklin. "You mean you made up your mind to kill Mr Kuppers, didn't you, Mr Franklin?"

She left the question hanging in the air.

Franklin gazed back, and said calmly and deliberately, pausing for a short time between each word of Kuppers' name, which seemed to lend to it an air of menace.

"Yes. To kill Minjheer Pieter Marius Franciscus Kuppers." He resumed his more normal pace and emphasis on delivery. "He deserved to die, for what he did to Paula, and to me, he deserved to die."

58

Franklin paused for a little while, as did Harriet, as she realised, and had suspected early in the interview, that she was about to hear a confession.

The interview was unlike anything she had encountered before. Scott sat on one side, listening, and making notes, but otherwise was not involved at all. It was a dialogue only between Franklin and Harriet, his eyes fixedly on her the whole time.

It became an eerie experience. It was as if the two of them were enclosed in an invisible Confession Box, and at the end of it all she would close the invisible door and they would all return home to their everyday lives, their souls cleansed.

Her reverie was interrupted.

Franklin began speaking again.

"Tell me, Detective Chief Inspector, in your lexicon of police procedures and UK law, are you acquainted with section 76 of the Serious Crime Act, which received Royal Assent in March of 2015, and became law in December of that year?"

"I believe that section covers the offence of control and coercion in an intimate relationship."

"I am very impressed," Franklin remarked.

"...and section 77?"

"I believe it provides a list of controlling behaviours which would constitute an actionable offence under the provisions of that Act. However, I can't quote chapter and verse offhand."

"You are really on the ball, Detective Chief Inspector," Franklin said, admiringly, and went on.

"You have probably been wondering why I haven't yet mentioned the green sheet I gave you earlier. I will do so now. The green sheet you have is taken from the Guidance Notes issued with the Act that list the controlling behaviours referred to above. As you can see, I have numbered each of them in order and inserted a hashtag symbol at the head of the page.

The relevant hashtag symbol and numbers on the pink slip directly link Amy's book to Paula's email to the Act.

This conclusively demonstrates that had that Act been in force earlier, both Amy's assailant and Mijnheer Kuppers would have been guilty of a criminal offence, and jailed.

However, that would not have been the end of it, even if Kuppers had gone to jail, it would only have been for a relatively short time.

Amy would have died. Her death was only averted because two young, male neighbours who had lost their water supply called unexpectedly at her flat to ascertain if her water had also been cut off. They were able to rescue her and report the matter to the police.

You see, Detective Chief Inspector, those people never change. Kuppers was quite capable of revenge for her ending the relationship, and with the conference in Gatwick would have had the ideal opportunity to attempt to track her down, harm her, or even worse, and I had checked that she still lived in Sussex, and within easy reach of Gatwick.

Yes, I knew Paula would never be safe until Kuppers was completely gone from her life.

After a few moments of silence, he became more animated.

"Would you care for more coffee?" he asked as if hosting the Bolscombe Village Ladies Afternoon Tea Club, and not confessing to a murder.

"No thank you," replied Harriet, without consulting Ian. "I would prefer to continue if that is alright with you," she said.

"Of course," said Franklin in his polite, measured manner. His only departure from this mode of delivery was the slight trace of venom whenever he had pronounced the complete Dutch name.

❈

## 59

Her intuition had told her, very early into the interview, to let Franklin proceed on his own terms If she listened and interjected only to clarify or repeat some key points, or to gently guide the conversation, he was going to complete the whole story, unburdening himself of years of his scrambled feelings of love, jealousy, depression, and repressed hatred.

"So, you had been planning this murder for some time, Mr Franklin," Harriet prompted.

"Would you like to tell me more about the whole thing? Just carry on, in your own words, we have all the time in the world."

Franklin looked up, stared to one side, and said, to no one in particular, "Composed by John Barry, sung by Louis Armstrong, and a secondary musical theme in the 1969 Bond film 'On Her Majesty's Secret Service.'" He then looked back at Harriet.

"Thank you, Detective Chief Inspector, of course, you need to know all the facts, don't you?"

Well, ever since meeting Paula I had become ever more curious about her relationship with Kuppers. Some of that I have already described and provided you with the information you have seen. Obviously, there was much more I knew, from the discussions and correspondence between Paula and myself, but there were many gaps in my own knowledge, which I wasn't ever going to discover.

Paula and I just drifted apart at the end of our affair, after about 18 months. No dramatic break-up or bad feeling on either side. We exchanged brief 'happy birthday' messages for a couple of years, and since then have had no contact. She presumably went back to a satisfactory enough married life with Robin.

I threw myself into my book collection, research, and quizzing activities, but, as I mentioned, I never forgot Paula and Kuppers' affair. Dorothy Parker once said 'Elephants, and women, never forget', but that can apply to men as well, Detective Chief Inspector.

I tried to discover more about Kuppers through the internet, but the trail went cold. I guess he was on several overseas assignments, probably still with Fokland. I didn't bother with him for several years.

Then, as I have described, I came across the Amy Harrington-Ellis book, and my 'epiphany' moments. For a few nights, I slept very little, if at all, turning things over in my mind.

That prompted me to look up Kuppers on the internet again, and, after a few false starts, 'hallelujah!', there he was. I had little idea of his actual appearance after all those years, but there was absolutely no doubt that he was the person I was looking for. He was featured in an article in the online edition of a local paper with some others of the Doves, alongside their motorbikes, with their names captioned beneath.

I guessed he had retired, moved back to Holland, and was a member of the Doves. The article and pictures were about the Club, their history, and their 20th Anniversary celebration being planned for the next year. The main picture featured Kuppers, Willem Vonk and Dirk Van Heemskerk. Everything I needed to know was mentioned, dates, location, an outline of the programme and events, reference to Kuppers as the organiser. The venue was just a short distance from here, but far enough. I couldn't believe my luck. I knew it was fate. I was the instrument of revenge.

I set to planning immediately. I had time. I was going to be careful, methodical, and work everything out. The perfect murder. I wanted a method which wouldn't involve me face-to-face with Kuppers. No shooting, stabbing or that sort of thing. Something where I could be distanced. That didn't take much thought."

He paused and looked around the room. "Agatha helped me, of course. Her knowledge of poisons was exceptional. In the First World War, she volunteered as a nurse in a local Torquay Hospital, and later passed the Apothecaries Hall examinations to qualify as a dispenser, and she also had extensive practical experience in chemistry and pharmacy.

Do you remember one of my special subjects in 'Masterbrain'? It was 'The Tommy and Tuppence novels of Agatha Christie'.

Her book 'Partners in Crime' is up there," he said, looking over his shoulder and pointing towards its approximate location on the bookshelves. "The book is a series of short stories featuring sleuths Tommy and Tuppence Beresford. The story 'The House of Lurking Death' tells of four members of the same household dying from poisoning by..."

He paused. "Guess what? Yes, that's right," he said, replying to his own question, then looked around for effect.

"Ricin," he said.

"Ricin was perfect. I made it myself. I bought some castor beans online, under a false name and had it delivered to a 'dropbox'. Quite untraceable.

You can make it in your own kitchen, with coffee filters, jars, and everyday solvents. To purify it is more technical, but I researched it carefully, and made my own homemade product as toxic as possible, and therefore deadly enough for my purposes."

Harriet spoke, "So then you had some time to think about exactly how you were going to commit the murder?"

"Yes, plenty of time. I just had to be patient, to wait until May 2016. Fortunately, I was working a great deal on my upcoming book 'Quizzing and Winning'. You must read a copy when it comes out.

I worked out my plan, and kept my eye on the situation in Doventenar, via the internet.

Another highly significant factor in my favour was that he had never seen me, unless he followed UK quizzes, and even then, he couldn't have made any connection. His affair with Paula was over long before I appeared on the scene so it is highly likely there would have been no contact between them. So, if I was careful, I could get as close to him as I am to you without arousing any suspicion, and also get away easily.

Where and when? The hotel seemed perfect, with plenty of people milling around. I wouldn't be able to get into his room unless I could steal the room key, and, anyway, I wouldn't need to do that, for reasons I will explain.

A meal, coffee break, or after-dinner drinks would be times that would offer the best opportunities. I could dine, or have a coffee, or drink on the Hotel premises without having to check-in. All I would need to do would be to slip the ricin into a drink, make myself scarce, and there we are- the perfect crime. The ricin would take a few hours to take effect, by which time I would be long gone.

I gave some thought to my appearance, what dress would be inconspicuous, so there would be the least possible chance of anyone recognising me? There was just a chance, of course, that some local people might recognise me from the television quizzes. I had been famous for fifteen minutes shortly after both 'Masterbrain' and 'Quiz for a Million', but without regular appearances on television, your face is soon forgotten. However, I had to be as cautious as possible. So, what could I do?

Then, another flash of inspiration, excuse me saying it myself," Franklin said, looking towards her.

"What appearance could, on the face of it, be conspicuous in some settings but not others?"

Harriet stopped him and looked straight back into his eyes.

"So you decided to become an airline pilot, didn't you Mr Franklin," she stated, staring straight into his eyes.

"Congratulations, Detective Chief Inspector Graham. An excellent piece of deductive reasoning.

Of course, you noticed my little vanity in placing the photograph where you would come across it. You also probably guessed that my longish absence from the room in preparing coffee was quite deliberate, to allow you an examination of my lounge. Nonetheless, your conclusion is worthy of Poirot. Agatha would have been proud of you.

Yes, an airline pilot. Lots of aircrew in and around all the Gatwick Hotels. Hat, pilots' case, a uniform similar to many others, and particularly the dark glasses for extra anonymity. An airline pilot, a clever disguise, and, as you can see, I already had the outfit from the 'Masterbrain' Club outing. Perfect.

And so to the puzzle pieces, the diversionary 'clues'. Did you like those? Did you think them ingenious?

The first one, the English/Dutch dictionary, with the carefully chosen pages removed. That was one of my earlier ideas, and I had already bought the dictionary a little while ago, from a charity shop. And then the letter. I hope you had a late night trying to decipher that one?"

"We did," affirmed Harriet, "and it is not yet deciphered in its entirety."

"But the wallet wasn't planned, was it?" Harriet said.

"No, it wasn't. Quite right.

The wallet was pure happenstance. There I was, sitting in the foyer of the Median that Tuesday morning. I arrived early; I was in the Hotel at about 8.00 am. I thought that's when my best chance would be. Still plenty of people around in an airport hotel at that time, and I knew the Doves would be arriving during the day."

I was wearing my airline pilot gear, fiddling in my pocket with the very small, clear glass phial which contained the ricin, looking for my opportunity to deposit the tiny, deadly droplets into one of Kuppers' drinks, and turning that over in my mind, when I looked up, and there was Kuppers, large as life. The spitting image of his internet photograph. I recognised him immediately

He was talking to this lady from the hotel staff. Lovely looking, dark-skinned girl, very smartly dressed. She had the name 'Leila Zafiri' imprinted on a tasteful gold badge in the lapel of her blue jacket. They were almost on top of me. I heard every word.

Kuppers told her that he was going to breakfast in Crawley at the Italian restaurant just off King Street- 'Artemisia's'. As it was a pleasant day he was going to sit outside. Get some fresh air. He would take a taxi from outside the hotel. He said he would see her for their later meeting, and double-checked the time with her. Leila wished him a good morning, and walked back towards the Conference Room.

I sat where I was, and waited whilst Kuppers left the hotel, for about 10 minutes, I guess. Then I went outside, collected my car, drove to King Street, parked, and walked towards 'Artemisia's'.

There was a scattering of black, metal matching chairs and tables on the patio outside the cafe. A couple of people were sitting there, and there was Kuppers, eating a croissant and drinking coffee. He had taken his jacket off and hung it over the back of his chair. I took a seat behind and away from him but keeping him in view. As I did so, the couple of people moved off. I thought about ordering a coffee, then Kuppers left his seat and walked towards 'Artemisia's' entrance and went inside. He was either going to the toilet or ordering some more breakfast.

I moved quickly. I glanced around. No one was looking my way. I took the ricin phial from my pocket, unscrewed the top, and carefully let several large droplets fall into his coffee cup, which was about a quarter full. I glanced down at his jacket. I could see his phone and wallet bulking up the inside pocket.

I left the phone, but, on impulse, I took the wallet, and walked briskly away. I was sure no one had seen me. I went back to my car, took off my hat, dark glasses, and pilot's jacket and drove home. So now, I just had to wait and see, wait and see if he had drunk the coffee, and if the ricin would do its job."

"And it did, Mr Franklin, and it did."

"Yes, Detective Chief Inspector. It did."

## 60

Franklin paused for a second, then continued, "When I returned home, I looked through his wallet. I could see there was a significant amount of notes of various denominations inside, a credit card- an Amex Gold Card I think- and a couple of business cards, one with the Doves insignia with Kuppers' name inscribed on it, and one with 'Motovonk', with bearing the picture of a motorcycle and 'Willem Vonk. Chief Executive' in copperplate writing.

I wasn't interested in the money, or the credit card, and I thought it was a little odd, having only one credit card, and no driving licence, but on reflection, if he was only spending the morning in Crawley, it might make sense to strip down his wallet.

However, I was lying in bed late that night, awake, staring at the ceiling, when the idea came to me. I would put the pages from the dictionary into the wallet and use it as an additional diversionary clue. "That would put the cat amongst the pigeons, wouldn't it?

'Agatha again,' I thought and settled down to sleep.

I woke up very early on Wednesday morning, trying to temper my excitement in wanting to see if my poisoning plan had worked, with more cool and logical thinking.

In any event, I had the wallet tactic in mind, and I needed to get that together on Wednesday morning.

I ensured that the task was all finished before making myself a late breakfast - scrambled egg, as I remember- at about 11.30 am. I then donned my pilot outfit, almost forgetting my dark glasses and gloves in my heightened anticipatory mood. I waited until about 1.30 pm. I made sure the brown manilla envelope was in my pocket, with the wallet safely inside. I wasn't too worried about fingerprints, but I wore my pilot's gloves anyway. I deliberately didn't address the envelope to anyone, not even Mijnheer Kuppers, then drove to the airport car park, parked the car, and walked towards the hotel. It was around 2.00 pm by then.

There were crowds milling around the entrance and in the reception area. I suspect you may know the rest; the wallet, and the pretence of the Larnaca flight. I deliberately chose Larnaca. I knew that BA had recently stopped flying there and I checked in the morning. If I hadn't wanted you to discover my little deception, I would have chosen New York or Sydney, somewhere like that.

I didn't think you would find everything out quite as soon as you did, however, but once you telephoned to make this appointment, I knew that you knew, as they say, and I am quite prepared."

Franklin stopped at that point, leaving any further conversation in the air.

'What does he mean by that?' thought Harriet, but before she could question him further, he got up from his chair.

## 61

"Would you mind if I played a little music at this juncture?" he asked.

Harriet didn't know quite how best to respond.

"OK, if you wish," she said, finally.

Scott had closed his notebook, sat back on the settee and looked at Graham with a look that was somewhere between resigned and quizzical.

"It's something I compiled especially. A few extracts from some of my favourite songs, the music and lyrics are just a perfect fit, as I think you will find." He went over to his faux music player, extracted a CD from the tall CD shelf alongside it, and inserted it into the appropriate slot. He turned the volume button down a touch.

Everything was quiet as the mellow tones of Frank Sinatra began to intone the song "One For My Baby".

Despite the comfort of the lounge and surroundings, the atmosphere seemed strangely spectral. Unnatural.

No one spoke as the music continued.

Franklin broke the silence for a moment, "Best torch song ever. Best male torch song singer. Listen to the way he delivers the lyrics. Draws out the words in all the right places. Isn't that great."

It wasn't a question.

A snippet of Andy Fairweather Low's "Wide-eyed and Legless" was up next, followed by Solomon King - his deep, resonant voice delivering "She Wears My Ring".

Then the grainy tones of Marc Bolan.

Franklin went over and turned the sound down on the CD player, stood by it, and began to sing along, quietly, but tunefully.

The music, and Franklin, stopped. An eerie silence persisted. He walked over to the table and stood facing Graham and Scott. He looked at them with a glazed look in his steely blue eyes.

"Thank you for listening to me, Detective Chief Inspector Graham." He seemed to ignore Scott's presence completely.

He stared up at the ceiling.

"You see, I never could work out the answer. Arveragus or Aurelius."

"But it doesn't matter."

"Nothing matters."

His voice trailed away, and he spoke very softly, almost in a whisper.

"... Life's A Gas."

He reached into his right-hand trouser pocket, took out what looked like a small white tablet, opened his mouth, and put the tablet under his tongue. He picked up his half-full glass of water, and raised it to his lips, took a mouthful of water, and swallowed the tablet.

62

# Thursday, 10th November, 2016

Ian Scott stood in the foyer of the Gatwick Median Hotel staring at "Jason," still suspended from the ceiling at its precariously low elevation. It was 2.30 in the afternoon, and he was awaiting the arrival of Harriet Graham.

It had been almost six months since the suicide of Nicholas Franklin, and the conclusion, at the English end, of the messy "Kuppers Affair".

All the police administration had been sorted out, in as low-key a way as possible. Coroner and post-mortem reports, liaison with the Dutch Police, where the "political" theories attached to the early investigation had been discounted. Barrowclough was fading into contented retirement, his copybook unscathed.

The Masons- Robin and Paula, had been totally exonerated. Willem Vonk was awaiting trial in Holland on multiple counts of drug and money laundering offences. After some further deliberation, and possibly in exchange for some further information on the activities of Willem Vonk, it had been decided not to press charges against Angelique Durand.

Since then, Scott and Graham's pathways had almost immediately diverged. Pressures of police caseloads meant they had spoken little and seen even less of each other. However, they were both on upward trajectories in their career paths, each eyeing up their next advancement- Scott to Detective Chief Inspector and Graham to Superintendent.

It was to help his career progress that was the reason for Scott's presence in the Median Hotel on that day. He was attending a three-day seminar as part of the National Detective Programme organised by the College of Policing but using the conference facilities of the Gatwick Median. The second afternoon of the course allowed for a break of about two hours, and it was in this time slot that he and Graham were getting together.

Graham had phoned him, about two weeks before. She had said that she was having a very rare two days off, and was going to stay with her sister, who had just moved to Brighton, and could break her journey at Gatwick to meet for an hour or so. She knew he was attending the course, and its scheduling, so the arrangement was made.

He looked across to the Reception Desk and gave a little wave to Sally, who had just come on duty for the first time since his course had started. He had already met with Leila, who was involved, albeit in a minor role, with the organisation of the course and Matthew Collison, the Hotel Manager, both of whom had vivid memories of the earlier events in the Hotel.

As he smiled at Sally, Harriet Graham came through the revolving door. She was smartly dressed, in a lightweight, blue tailored jacket, black trousers, and blue, flat-heeled shoes. Her short hair was brushed back, and her only concession to her visit to Brighton was a pair of large, brightly coloured blue and red speckled glasses in place of her small, gold-rimmed "business" pair.

They exchanged pleasantries.

"Hello Ian, how's the course going?" Harriet queried.

"Very well, thanks," Ian responded, "How strange of it to be taking place here?"

Harriet nodded in agreement.

"You must be pleased to have a little time off, for a change, and to see your sister," he said.

"Yes, Brighton is a great place. Lots of variety, lively, and by the sea too. She's in Kemp Town. I expect we will walk along the seafront down to the Victoria Monument in Hove, and back, a few times. Shall we move into the Coffee Lounge, and find a quiet corner?" she said, bringing the polite, superficial conversation to an end.

They moved through, past Reception, with another wave to Sally, who was busy with a guest, and settled in the Coffee Lounge. The place was very quiet, and they selected a table for two, in the far corner. Harriet fetched two coffees from one of the machines, and brought them over.

"Well, Ian," said Harriet, "a little water has flowed under the bridge since we were last here. I expect you've had time to think over the 'Kuppers case'. I'd be interested in your thoughts and conclusions."

Ian immediately sensed that he was being tested. It was Harriet who had suggested the meeting, Harriet who knew his schedule, Harriet who had arranged everything about the meeting, he thought. Was she really going to see her sister in Brighton? He decided to choose his words carefully, whilst giving his honest opinions.

# 63

I an took a sip of coffee and began.

"Some of what I say will have been in our post-investigation debrief, so apologies for any undue repetition, but a great deal of it is my own thinking."

"That's what I'm interested in," Harriet said, "please go ahead."

"Are you sitting comfortably?" asked Ian, "Then I'll begin," he pronounced, like the fifties "Listen With Mother" introduction.

"Franklin said he had planned the perfect crime. If you completely forget about the dictionaries, wallets, letters and all that, the moment that Kuppers had swallowed the coffee containing the ricin at the 'Artemisias' Café, he had indeed committed the perfect crime.

But I'm getting ahead of myself, and I'll come back in due course to the perfect crime scenario. Let's step back a little.

I divide the case into two distinct parts. What I call the 'Dutch Connection', and the other the 'Franklin Affair'. I think I'll write detective fiction when I retire from the force." Scott and Graham exchanged thin smiles.

"So, the 'Dutch Connection'. If you look at the textbook, there are three factors in any murder investigation-motive, means and opportunity, there were, on the face of it, all there in abundance for many of the people from Holland, but it didn't take much thought or investigation to eliminate most of them.

The prime suspects were Willem Vonk and Angelique Durand. In the end, Vonk bungled their joint plot by mixing up the Genever bottles, and, like the criminals they were, they fell out, and blamed each other. However, they didn't intend to murder Kuppers – at least at that point in time -and forensic evidence proved that they didn't in fact do so.

But how did we discover proof that they didn't murder Kuppers by ricin poisoning? It was because Leila Zafiri was smart enough to realise that the bottle count didn't add up, which led us in turn to discover the unopened thallium bottle.

After this, we were at a dead end, completely lost. A very dead, ricin and mildly fugu-poisoned body, but no idea whatever of who might have been responsible. Do you remember the conversation? I do.

At the end of it, you said, 'As the song goes, there are more questions than answers, but I think the answer lies, not in the present, but in the past'.

So, we started delving into the time that Kuppers spent in England, all those years ago, and that set us on the right path.

But where to start? Again, the real breakthrough didn't come from us. It was Sally. She remembered to tell us of the short encounter - I won't say 'brief encounter' - between Kuppers and the Masons, when they were checking out in the week before the Doves Meeting. That put us on to the Masons, and finally to Franklin, and the conclusion of events here in England.

I'll return now to the 'perfect crime' scenario.

As I said, once Kuppers had downed the ricin-infused coffee at 'Artemisias' Franklin had committed the perfect crime. He should have just walked away. He couldn't be associated in any way with Kuppers except through the

Masons, and then probably only through Paula. The exact time between poisoning and death couldn't be estimated with any certainty. The fugu tetrodotoxin muddied the waters further.

Even if Paula's e-mails to him had been found, and he had been interviewed following this discovery, he could have denied everything. He hadn't met, seen or communicated with Paula for more than fifteen years. He couldn't be clearly identified in the Hotel, or at the café.

He had also meticulously organised his alibi. Before, and after returning from the café he had telephoned his agent about his 'Quizzing and Winning' publication and had done so again in the afternoon. He had been careful not to take his mobile with him to the Hotel and café.

As events moved much more quickly than he had imagined, he had time to walk down to the local pub in the village 'The Full Moon', where he had lunched, as he had done many times, with the Chairman of the Bolscombe Preservation Society, Peregrine St John Sinclair –known widely in the village as 'Sinner' Sinclair.

Do you remember Sinclair? He was Franklin's fellow golfer in one of the framed photographs on the sideboard. You mentioned afterwards to me that he was a dead ringer for Hugo Drax. Wealthy. Family money. Also made a mint by selling a field attached to his property for new housing. Bought another big pile in the village with the proceeds but made sure it was well away from the new housing. Has a half share in the 'Full Moon', or a full share in the 'Half Moon', can't remember which. Referred to as 'The Moon' by the locals. Its usage defined you as a villager if you did, as an outsider if you didn't.

Typical upper middle-class Sussex village for you."

He smiled at Harriet. "You live in an upper-middle-class Kent village, don't you?" She smiled back, and he continued.

"Sinclair was there most days at lunchtime, so no prearrangement would have been needed. I checked this all out personally when the entry in Franklin's diary 'walked pub, lunch Sinner' was examined. If ever you needed to prove your alibi, then lunch with a Peregrine St John Sinclair is most certainly the name of the person you would have wanted to be dining with.

So, only a very small window of time would have been available to him, and that assumed the ricin was administered at the café at around 8.45 to 9.15 am. As you know from examining his desk diary afterwards, all these events had been noted there.

There would have been no subsequent 'clues' to link him with the Paula emails. The emails were the key to unlocking the whole affair-making sense of every one of the clues and their sequence and providing the motive. Only someone with an intimate and detailed knowledge of all the emails, and all the events they represented, could have been the murderer, and that someone was Nicholas Franklin.

However, up until the final clue it was still possible, as we thought, that Robin Mason could have been the guilty party. We could rule out collusion with Paula, and indeed Paula herself. She wanted to forget the whole affair; she had wished it had never happened. She wouldn't have wanted to draw attention to herself, so would have no reason to send the 'clues'. I think that after her affair with Franklin was over, she just stowed away the ring, and the memory stick in that little box, and put them to one side along with the affair with Kuppers, all of them buried together under that tangled mass of cabling, DVD's, plugs, hard disks, loose memory sticks and camera chips, the old satnav screen, and all the rest, in the deep drawer of the keyhole chest of drawers on which the computer sat.

So, once the memory stick and the emails had come into our possession, we could have deduced that Franklin was the murderer, but could we have proved it in a Court of Law? No, we could not have done so. Franklin was highly intelligent, so he would have known this. So why did he confess?

My theory is that the perfect murder to Franklin was not only to escape justice. As I said earlier, he could have just walked away at 'Artemisias'. It was to escape justice together with the carefully laid 'clues' unsolved... like setting a series of Quiz questions where no one succeeds in getting the final answer right."

'The Dutch-English dictionary with the missing pages placed in the wallet, and the letter full of cryptic clues were his personal 'signature' items woven into the crime. They are similar to those left by serial killers- a personal stamp, specific fantasy-driven rituals based on needs or compulsions. Graffiti tags fall under that heading in less macabre ways. He knew that, once he had committed the crime, they might confuse any investigation. As I said at the time, he was playing with us, challenging us to solve the puzzles he had set.

It didn't matter in the end that we couldn't solve the methodology of the coded letter. As a matter of interest, did you know it went to the newly formed Police Digital Service to play around with as a prelude to more serious matters... and they have only just totally unscrambled it a couple of days ago?"

That wasn't really a question in anticipation of an answer, and Ian carried on without waiting for any further comment, or response.

"I think he had it all worked out. Once he knew we had the emails in our possession, he had failed, although that discovery was just a chance act, and he was not to know that Paula had kept them on the memory stick. His 'death wish' then came into play.

Once you telephoned to set up the meeting, he realised we were in possession of some information linking him with Kuppers, but not what or how much, but when you produced the emails, his response was pre-orchestrated. The whole affair had festered in his mind for a long, long time, re-activated by the UK law on coercion and control. At some point, probably more than once in the past, he had contemplated suicide, hence the ready availability of the suicide pill."

"What about the reference to Arveragus or Aurelius, just before he swallowed the pill?" Harriet questioned, interrupting Ian's flow.

"Oh yes, thanks for reminding me," replied Ian, and continued.

"Arveragus and Aurelius are characters in the Canterbury Tales, in 'The Franklin's Tale' in fact. How about that! A final, clever charade, or conceited gesture. Take your pick.

I looked it up straight away on the net. Unfortunately, my Late Middle English, despite the London inflexion, was just a bit rusty at the time.

The meanings behind the 'Franklin's Tale' can be interpreted in several different ways, Franklin obviously related it to his own situation.

The placing of the book, the gap on the bookshelf, the time he took with the coffee, the timing of that literary reference just before swallowing the poison pill. All those actions were pre-determined.

The man who knew so much, who could answer so many questions, could never solve the puzzle of his own complex relationship problems."

⊰⊱

# 64

I an paused for a moment, reflecting on his observations, then continued.

"He was a clinical depressive, capable of occasional deeply depressive periods, but he was aware enough to hide the worst of them to the outside world, as some people can. Unfortunately, Paula's affair with Kuppers was a trigger point, and any reminder, totally innocent to most people, could set off the depression. A simple example might be looking at a map of Indonesia, which would remind Franklin of the time they-Kuppers and Paula-had spent together there, travelling around, eating meals, having sex, just being together. Ridiculous to us, but not to him.

This associated combination of clinical depression and retroactive jealousy meant he was mentally unbalanced. Not in the manner that madness is often thought of, with wild rages and uncontrolled and violent actions, but reflected in calculating and logical thought processes. Within his soul was the deep-seated hatred of Kuppers, and his burning desire for ultimate revenge.

We noticed that during the whole of his confession, he paid minimal attention to me, everything was directed to you, and it was you he was talking to, and looking at, all the while. I thought that curious at the time, but I reflected on it, and am pretty sure I know why.

He wanted to unburden himself, and I believe he had done so for a long time, and he wanted to unburden himself to a woman, who he considered would have more empathy for his feelings. Not necessarily approval but understanding. You just listened, and quite deliberately didn't hector him, question him, harass him, and little by little, it all came out, like water, not dripping, but running very slowly, but evenly, from a tap. He wanted to confess, but at the same time couldn't resist showing off his cleverness, just as male birds show off their beauty to attract females. In his mind, his beauty was his intellect."

# 65

"Well, Harriet, there's just one important - very important - point left, and a final observation from me."

"Do you remember the phrase Franklin used? 'He deserved to die, for what he did to Paula, and for what he did to me.'

I totally disagree. However reprehensible and obnoxious a person he was in his conduct in his relationships with women, as with Paula Mason, and conduct that would later have warranted criminal prosecution, and potentially a jail sentence, he didn't deserve to die, that was the judgement of Franklin's mind, warped by depression, hatred, and jealousy.

In fact, Kuppers did nothing to Franklin. Franklin's retroactive jealousy was entirely self-inflicted, reflecting his own lack of self-confidence and self-worth in his own relationship with Paula.

Kuppers was wealthy, self-confident, and sexually proficient. Franklin felt he had to prove himself better than Kuppers, and depressed that he never could."

Ian continued.

"Isn't human psychology strange? Franklin was an intelligent, good-looking man, an excellent sportsman and quizzer, confident enough to demonstrate his abilities on television programmes watched by millions of people yet felt sufficiently inadequate in a personal relationship to become judge, juror and executioner- a murderer himself.

Now my final observation.

At each stage of this investigation, we were only able to make a significant move forward because of a common factor, and that common factor, you will be pleased to hear, was feminine intuition. It's something that can't be precisely defined, nor does it appear on the curriculum of the Police College.

It was Leila Zafiri's sharp thinking and memory that picked up the incorrect Genever bottle count that led us to eliminate Willem Vonk and Angelique Durand as responsible for the murder.

It was Sally Bideforde that led us to the Masons. Her feeling that there was something that didn't feel 'quite right' about Kuppers and Robin Mason's encounter in the week before the Conference, and it was your quite deliberately careful handling of Franklin that led to his confession, the truth, and the resolution of the case. You just let it all come out naturally, guiding him gently at times."

Ian stood up, stretched, and flexed his leg and stretched out his arm muscles, then sat back in his chair.

He looked at Harriet and said quietly.

"There was nothing more we could have done to prevent Franklin's suicide. Nothing at all."

## 66

"Thanks Ian," said Harriet. "That was an excellent analysis, and thanks for the compliments, but everyone involved was instrumental in some way in solving the case. Your conclusions show that investigation isn't all of the 'elementary my dear Watson' kind, dust from Afghanistan on the guilty party's shoe, or assiduously ploughing through textbook tick lists. All may have their part, but it is also psychology, and as you so rightly pointed out, intuition. It's dealing with human beings, and feelings and senses. You are going a long way in the force, as I hope I am, but never forget your own conclusions in this case.

There's only one thing I would add. The processes of the law are often very slow in bringing proper justice into the statute books, but more often than not they do so eventually, as it was in this instance. Paula was unfortunate that the law didn't come along early enough for her. But the answer isn't to exact revenge as Franklin did. The only way for a civilised society to operate is within the framework of laws that are as fair as they possibly can be to law-abiding citizens, protect them and bring them justice." She paused. "... and we are the guardians of those laws."

With that Harriet looked at her watch and stood up. "Goodbye, Ian," she said, in a rather business-like tone, "I must be going now, I have a train to catch in 10 minutes." She headed for the lounge exit, walked briskly across the foyer concourse, glanced up at "Jason" and went through the revolving doors of the Median Hotel, and out into the open air.

## 67

In the Coffee lounge there was a rather battered bookcase, featuring a selection of out-of-date books that guests could read, borrow, or sometimes steal. Ian had gathered his effects and was preparing to go back to the Seminar room. On a table beside him, a book had been left by one of the guests or visitors. He picked it up. It was an aged Penguin paperback, dog-eared, with a bent spine, and pages faded to a nicotine brown shade, darker at the edges. The cover featured a dark grey fuzzy figure looking in the general direction of an equally fuzzy grey column, with the shapes of large orange-coloured rose petals in the foreground. The orange banding across the top of the cover featured the Penguin symbol and the original price - three shillings and sixpence. The bottom line, in white text, was the name of the author, Graham Greene. Between them, in the centre was the title of the book, in black, Gill Sans lettering. It read 'The End of the Affair'.

"Yes, the end of the affair," Ian, spoke softly and quietly to himself, then let his thoughts continue. 'The last page turned. The book closed. Replaced on the shelf. Consigned to history.'

'But real-life affairs, particularly extra-marital ones, aren't like that at all. Messy. Untidy. Regrets. Misunderstandings. Unfinished loose ends.'

## 68

To the relief of the police forces on both sides of the Channel, Franklin's detailed confession and subsequent suicide had provided all the information necessary to enable the case to be closed quickly. Officially at least, there were no unfinished loose ends. The coroner and other regulatory authorities were properly involved in the wind-up.

Barrowclough was particularly pleased with the official "clean sheet" accorded to his final investigation. His considerable pension was safe. He had eased into 'imminent retirement' mode. His most pressing immediate operational worry being deciding the best cruise ship route between Miami, the Panama Canal, the Bahamas, and Mexico.

Ian, in contrast, since that rather hurried and frantic process in May, had subsequently reflected further on the case, and the Graham Greene paperback had jogged his memory further.

The forensic, and other aspects of the investigation had intrigued him, and he had spent some of his rare spare time improving his knowledge of poisons, and ricin in particular. He, and Harriet had readily accepted that once Franklin had seen Kuppers swallow the coffee that he had committed the perfect crime, and although that was in itself true, his research had led him to consider a further element - luck.

Depending on whose perspective you view it from, perpetrator or victim, Franklin was either lucky, or unlucky with his poisoning of Kuppers with ricin. Franklin had told them that he poured the ricin into Kuppers partially drunk cup of coffee, then exited at speed.

Well, the coffee in Kuppers cup..the 'Kuppers Cup. Now there's a thought', Ian mused, then returned to his original line of thinking.

Yes, the coffee in his cup. This would have had to be cool or colder, because a normal freshly poured cup of coffee could have a drinking temperature of up to 80 degrees centigrade, and at that temperature, the toxicity of the ricin would have been nullified, so Mr K would have walked away unpoisoned and unharmed.

Ian thought on towards his conclusion. Franklin was either lucky, or was it a perfectly researched event combined with exquisite medium range judgement of the temperature of a partially drunk cup of coffee?

So, was Franklin really as smart as he, and we, liked to think?

"He also thought again of Selby's photographs of Kupper's body, etc of the slightly strange angle of Kuppers' head and neck as he lay on the bed in his yellow socks, and the time of death that didn't quite fit with the customary slow-acting effect of the ricin.

'And what of those yellow socks? No one questioned at either Artemisias or the Kamada had mentioned yellow socks, which surely would have been a distinctive and noticeable feature of his appearance. Yet he was wearing them the previous day on his assignation with Michaela.

Was it a token that he wore on his visits to the ladies of a certain profession? Who might have known about those visits, and have taken his shoes and socks off as he lay dead on the bed, hurriedly replacing the socks with a yellow pair from the clothes drawer in his room as their own personal token of revenge, then attempting to put his brown suede shoes back on, but abandoning the idea under time pressure?

Could the gradual procession to Kuppers' untimely death have been given a couple of helping hands?

Could that have been someone with newly painted silver and mauve fingernails who had unaccountably decided to don a pair of dark cream luxury leather lady's gloves during a brief late-night visit?

Or could it have been a lady whose ambition was to look, and act, like a forties film noir femme fatale, with shiny, black, bulbous eyes and a book on her shelf containing information on the deadly plant belladonna?

Or both, in their own ways?'

Ian stared for a considerable time with glazed eyes at the ceiling, then replaced the book on the table and turned his thoughts towards his Seminar.

# ACKNOWLEDGEMENTS

To L, A and P for any "good bits" that can be found.

To my Mother and Father who I didn't thank enough in their lifetimes.

A big "Thank You" to Vrinda, Amy and the team from "White Magic" who coped patiently and admirably with the many mistakes in content and process of a novice author, and with the special conditions surrounding the publication of the novel. Any errors in the text of the book are those of the author alone.

# MEET THE AUTHOR

Now in her 82nd year, this is long time Sussex resident Naomi Fenstra's debut novel.

Conceived late in the 2020 Pandemic and confronted with a very busy family and social life, Naomi subsequently wrote everything secretly in her very limited spare time, scribbling hurried notes on pieces of paper, waking in the night to jot down ideas, and writing the scripts in early mornings, late nights, and any other available moments.

Until publication and distribution, the existence of this project was known only to Naomi herself and the publication team.

Completion of the book included her design of the cover, in collaboration with the White Magic team.

Altogether, we believe this is a significant achievement.